SURRENDER

"I can hear each beat of your heart, Sophie," Alpine said against her temple, his voice deep and seductive. "I can hear the blood rushing in your veins. I can smell your desire," he whispered and lightly nipped her earlobe. I can taste it upon your lips." He teased her lips with fleeting kisses.

"And I can feel your desire, Alpin." She nipped at his bottom lip and smiled faintly when he growled low in his throat. "It feeds my own." The way his narrowed eyes glowed, his nostrils flared, and his features tightened into a predatory expression should have frightened her, but Sophie only felt her passion soar. She suspected she might look nearly as feral as he did as she ran her tongue between his lips and said, "So taste it, Alpin. Drink deep . . ."

Books by Hannah Howell

ONLY FOR YOU * MY VALIANT KNIGHT
UNCONQUERED * WILD ROSES
A TASTE OF FIRE * HIGHLAND DESTINY
HIGHLAND HONOR * HIGHLAND PROMISE
A STOCKINGFUL OF JOY * HIGHLAND VOW
HIGHLAND KNIGHT * HIGHLAND HEARTS
HIGHLAND BRIDE * HIGHLAND ANGEL
HIGHLAND GROOM * HIGHLAND WARRIOR
RECKLESS * HIGHLAND CONQUEROR
HIGHLAND CHAMPION * HIGHLAND LOVER
HIGHLAND VAMPIRE * CONQUEROR'S KISS
HIGHLAND BARBARIAN * BEAUTY AND THE BEAST
HIGHLAND SAVAGE * HIGHLAND THIRST
HIGHLAND WEDDING * HIGHLAND WOLF
SILVER FLAME * HIGHLAND FIRE

Books by Jackie Kessler

HELL'S BELLES * THE ROAD TO HELL *
HOTTER THAN HELL

Books by Richelle Mead

SUCCUBUS BLUES * SUCCUBUS ON TOP *
SUCCUBUS DREAMS

Published by Kensington Publishing Corporation

ETERNAL LOVER

HANNAH HOWELL
JACKIE KESSLER
RICHELLE MEAD
LYNSAY SANDS

KENSINGTON BOOKS
http://www.kensingtonbooks.com

CONTENTS

THE YEARNING

Hannah Howell

Prologue

Scotland, A.D. 1000

"Nay!"

Morvyn Galt woke shaking and sweating with fear. The scent of magic was thick in the air. She scrambled out of her bed and yanked on her clothes. She could feel her sister's anger, feel how Rona's broken heart was twisting within her chest, changing into a hard, ugly thing that pumped hate throughout her body instead of the love it once held. Morvyn knew she would not be in time to stop the evil her sister stirred up, but she had to try. She grabbed her small bag and raced toward Rona's cottage, praying as hard as she could despite her fear that her prayers would go unheeded.

When she reached Rona's tiny home, she tried to open the door only to find it bolted against her. The smoke coming from the house was so heavy with the scent of herbs and sorcery that her eyes stung. She banged against the door, pleading with Rona as she heard her sister begin her incantation.

"Nay, Rona!" she screamed. "Cease! You will damn us all!"

"I damn but one," replied Rona, "and well does he deserve it."

Placing her hand over her womb, Rona stared into the fire and saw the face of her lover, her seducer, her betrayer. He was marrying another in the morning, forsaking love for land and coin. She would make him suffer for that, as she now suffered.

"Rage for rage, pain for pain, blood for blood, life for life." Rona swayed slightly as she spoke, stroking her belly as she tossed a few more painstakingly mixed herbs into the fire.

"Rona, please! Do not do this!"

"As mine shall walk alone, so shall yours," Rona continued, ignoring her sister's pleas. "As mine shall be shunned, so shall yours."

Morvyn scrambled to find something to write with. She needed to record this. As she sprawled on the ground to take advantage of the sliver of light seeping out from beneath the door, she realized she had no ink. From beneath the door she could see the smoke curling around her sister and saw Rona toss another handful of herbs upon the fire. Morvyn cut her palm with her dagger, wet her quill with her own blood, and began to write.

"Your firstborn son shall know only shadows," intoned Rona, "as shall his son, as shall his son's son, and thus it shall be until the seed of the MacCordy shall wither from hate and fade into the mists."

Morvyn scattered her blessing and healing stones in front of the door, praying they might ease the force of the spell.

"From sunset of the first day The MacCordy becomes a man, darkness will take him as a lover, blood will be his wine, fury will steal his soul, yearning will devour his heart, and he will become a creature of nightmares." Rona felt her child kick forcefully as if in protest, but continued.

"He will know no beauty; he will know no love; he will know no peace.

"The name of the MacCordys will become a foul oath, their tale one used to frighten all the Godly.

"Thus it shall be, thus it shall remain, until one steps from the shadows of pride, land, and wealth and does as his heart commands.

"Until all that should have been finally is."

Morvyn sat back on her heels and stared at the door. She could not believe her sister had acted so recklessly, so vindictively. Rona knew the dangers of flinging a curse out in anger, knew how the curse could fall back upon them threefold, yet, in her pain, she had ignored all the dangers. Morvyn placed her hand over her heart, certain she could feel the pain and misery of countless future generations, those of their blood as well as those of the MacCordys.

The cottage door opened and Morvyn looked up at her sister. In the light of the torch Rona held, Morvyn could see the glow of hate and triumph in Rona's blue-green eyes. Rona thought she had won some great victory. Morvyn knew otherwise and was not surprised to feel the sting of tears upon her cheeks.

"Rona, how could you? How could you have done this?" she asked.

"How could *I*? How could he?" Rona snapped, then frowned when she saw the blood upon Morvyn's palm. "What have you done to yourself, you foolish child?"

Morvyn began to pick up her things and return them to her bag. "I had no ink to mark down the words."

"So you wrote in blood?"

" 'Tis fitting. The Galts and the MacCordys shall be bleeding for ages after what you have done this night." She felt the heat in her stones as she put them away and hoped the power they had expended had done some good.

"You cannot keep such a writing about. Not only is it considered a sin for you to write at all, but those words could condemn me, condemn us all."

"You have condemned us, Rona. You knew the dangers."

"Unproven. *That* is proof of sorcery, however," she said, pointing to Morvyn's writing.

"I shall write the tale upon a scroll and hide it. Mayhap one of our blood will find it one day, one with the wit and strength to banish the evil you have stirred up this night."

"He had to pay for what he has done!"

"He was wrong, but so were you. The poison you have spit out tonight will infect us all, the venom seeping into our bloodline as well as his. To do such magic on this night, at the birth of a new century, only ensures the power of the evil you have wrought." Morvyn stood up and looked down at what she had written. "I fear you have stolen all hope of happiness for us, but I will not allow this to endanger your life. It will be well hidden. And every night for the rest of my life I shall pray that, when it is found, it will be by one of our blood, one who can free us all from the torment you have unleashed this dark night."

Chapter One

Scotland, 1435

Sophie Hay stumbled slightly as another fierce sneeze shook her small frame. A linen rag was shoved into her hand, and she blew her nose, then wiped her streaming eyes with her sleeves. She smiled at her maid, Nella, who watched her with concern. Considering how long she had been scrambling through this ancient part of her Aunt Claire's house, Sophie suspected she looked worthy of Nella's concern.

"I dinnae ken what ye think ye will find here," Nella said. "Old Steven said her ladyship ne'er came in here; thought it haunted, and he thinks it may not be safe now."

"'Tis sturdy, Nella." Sophie patted the stones framing the fireplace. "Verra sturdy. The rest of the house will fall ere this part does. The fact that that stone was loose," she pointed to the one she had pried away from the wall, releasing the cloud of dust that had started her sneezing, "was what told me that something might be hidden here."

"And ye dinnae think this place be haunted?"

Sophie inwardly grimaced, knowing she would have to

answer with some very carefully chosen words or Nella would start running and probably not stop until she reached Berwick. "Nay. I sense no spirits in this room." She would not tell Nella about all the others wandering in the house. "All I sense is unhappiness. Grief and a little fear. It was strong here by the fireplace, which is why I was searching here."

"Fear?" Nella's dark eyes grew wide as she watched Sophie reach toward the hole in the wall. "I dinnae think ye ought to do that. Fear and grief arenae good. God kens what ye might find in there."

"I am certainly nay sticking my hand in there with any eagerness, Nella, but," she sighed, "I also feel I must." She ignored Nella's muttered prayers, took a deep breath to steady herself, and reached in. "Ah, there *is* something hidden here."

Sophie grasped a cold metal handle on the end of what felt like a small chest. She tugged and felt it inch toward her a little. Whoever had put it into this hole had had to work very hard, for it was a tight fit. Inch by inch it came, until Sophie braced herself against the wall and yanked with all her might. The little chest came out so quickly, she stumbled backward and was only saved from falling by Nella's quick, bracing catch.

As she set the chest on a small table, Sophie noticed her maid edge closer, her curiosity obviously stronger than her fear. Sophie unfolded the thick oiled leather wrapped around the bulk of the chest, then used a corner of her apron to brush aside the dust and stone grit. It was a beautiful chest of heavy wood, ornately carved with runes and a few Latin words. The hinges, handles, and clasp were of hammered gold, but there was no lock. She rubbed her hands together as she prepared herself to open it.

"What are all those marks upon it?" asked Nella.

"Runes. Let me think. Ah, they are signs for protection, for hope, for forgiveness, for love. All good things. The words say: *Within lies the truth, and, if it pleases God, the salvation of two peoples.* How odd." She stroked the top of the chest. "This is verra old. It must have just missed being discovered when the fireplace was added to the house. I wouldnae be surprised if this belonged to the matriarch of our line or one of her kinswomen."

"The witch?" Nella took a small step back. "A curse?"

"I doubt it when such markings cover the chest." She slowly opened the lid and frowned slightly. "More oiled leather for wrapping. Whoever hid this wanted it to last a verra long time." She took out the longest of the items and carefully unwrapped it. "A scroll." She gently unrolled the parchment and found another small one tucked inside. When she touched the erratic writing upon the smaller parchment, she shivered. "Blood. 'Tis written in blood."

"Oh, my lady, put it back. Quickly!" When Sophie simply pressed her hand upon the smaller parchment and closed her eyes, Nella edged nearer again. "What do ye see?"

"Morvyn. That is the name of the one who wrote this. Morvyn, sister to Rona."

"The witch."

"Aye. No ink," she muttered. "That is why this is written in blood. Morvyn had naught else to write with and she was desperate to record this exactly as it was said." Sophie opened herself up to the wealth of feeling and knowledge trapped within the parchment. "She tried to stop it. So desperate, so afraid for us all. She prays," Sophie whispered. "She prays and prays and prays, every night until she dies, sad and so verra alone." She quickly removed her hand and took several deep breaths to steady herself.

"Oh, m'lady, this is no treasure, is it?"

"It may be. Beneath that despair was hope. That would explain the words carved upon the chest."

"Can ye read the writings?"

"Aye, though I dinnae want to."

"Then dinnae."

"I must. That chest carries the words 'truth' and 'salvation,' Nella. Mayhap the truth as to why all the women of my line die as poor Morvyn died—sad and so verra alone. I willnae read it aloud." Sophie's eyes widened and she felt chilled as she read the words. "I cannae believe Morvyn wrote this. She feared these words." Sophie turned her attention to the larger scroll. "Oh, dear."

"What is it?"

"I fear Rona deserves her ill fame. She loved Ciar Mac-Cordy, The MacCordy of Nochdaidh. They were lovers, but he left her to marry another, a woman with land and wealth. He also left her with child."

"As too oft happens, the rutting bastards," muttered Nella.

"True. Rona was hurt and her pain twisted into a vindictive fury. One night she cursed The MacCordy and all the future MacCordy lairds. Morvyn tried to stop it, but failed. Her fear was that the Galts would pay dearly alongside The MacCordy, if in a different way. She writes out the curse again and, trust me, Nella, 'tis a bad one. She expresses the hope that some descendant will find this and have the courage and skill to undo what Rona did. Ah, me, poor Morvyn tried her whole life to do just that, with prayer and with healing spells. She wrote once right after the curse was made, and again when she was verra old. She leaves her book of cures and spells as well as her stones. The use of the stones is explained in the book.

"Morvyn says she thinks she has discovered the sting in the tail of Rona's curse. A Galt woman of their line will know love only to lose it, to watch it die or slip through her grasp. She will gain land and wealth, but such things will ne'er heal her heart or warm her in the night and she will face her death still unloved, still alone." Sophie wiped tears from her cheeks with the corner of her apron. "And she was right, Nella. She was so verra right."

"Nay, nay. Your ancestors just chose wrong, 'tis all."

"For over four hundred years? This is dated. It was written in the year 1000. The verra first day." Sophie muttered a curse. "That fool Rona sent out a curse on the eve of a new year, a new century. It was probably a night made to strengthen any magic brewed and she stirred up an evil, vindictive sort."

Nella wrung her hands together. "There isnae any of that evil in this house, is there?"

Sophie smiled at her maid. "Nay. I sense that magic has been stirred in here, but nay the black sort."

"Then from where comes the fear and sadness?"

"Heartache, Nella. Lost love. Loneliness." Sophie cautiously picked up the two small bags inside the chest and gasped. "Oh my, oh my."

"M'lady, what is it?"

"Morvyn's stones." She gently placed one bag back inside the chest on top of what she now knew was Morvyn's book of cures and spells. "Those are her healing stones. These," she clasped the small bag she held between her hands, "are her blessing stones."

Nella stepped closer and shyly touched the bag. "Ye can feel that, can ye?"

"Morvyn had magic, Nella, good, loving, gentle magic." She put everything back inside the chest. "How verra sad that such a woman suffered heartache and died unloved because of her own sister's actions." She closed the chest and started out of the room.

"Where are ye taking it?" asked Nella as she hurried to follow Sophie.

"To my room where, after a nice hot bath and a hearty meal, I mean to read Morvyn's wee book." She ignored Nella's mutterings, which seemed to consist of warnings about leaving certain things buried in walls, not stirring up trouble, and several references to the devil and his minions. "I but seek the truth, Nella. The truth and salvation."

It was late before Sophie had an opportunity to more

closely examine her find. The house, lands, and fortune her Aunt Claire had bequeathed her were welcome, but carried a lot of responsibility. Aunt Claire had been ill during her last years, mostly in spirit and mind, and there was a lot that had been neglected. Although wearied by all the demands for her attention during the day, Sophie finally sat on a thick sheepskin rug before the fire, sipped at a tankard of hot, spiced cider, and looked over what her ancestor had left behind.

A brief examination of the book revealed many useful things, from intricate cures to simple balms. Sophie only briefly glimpsed the spells, few and benign, before turning to the explanation of the stones. She considered them a wondrous gift, having long believed in the power of stones, which were as old as the world itself. Sentinels and possessors of the secrets and events of the past, Sophie was sure all manner of wonders and truths could be uncovered if one understood the magic and use of them.

Still sipping at her drink, Sophie next turned her attention to the scrolls. She read both Morvyn's letter and the curse several times before replacing them in the box. The truth was certainly there, but Sophie was not sure she could see the salvation promised. Nothing in Morvyn's writings or the words of Rona's curse seemed to indicate a way in which to end the despair suffered by so many Galt women.

Staring into the fire, she grimaced, for she could feel the spirits of those who had gone before, including poor old Aunt Claire. Generation after generation of Galt women, who briefly savored the sweet taste of love only to have it all go sour, had returned to this house to die or spent their whole sad lives here. Each one had spent far too many years wondering why love had eluded them, why they had held it for so short a time only to see it trickle out of their grasp like fine sand. Although she had only been at Werstane for a fortnight, several times she had felt the despair of all who had gone before, felt it weigh so heavily upon her that she had come close to weeping. If Aunt Claire had felt it too, had spent her whole life feeling it, it was no wonder she had become a little odd.

And now that she understood the curse Rona had set upon the MacCordys, understood the "sting in its tail," as Morvyn called it, Sophie knew her fate was to be the same as Aunt Claire's, as that of all the lonely, heartbroken spirits still trapped within Werstane. Her own mother had suffered the sting of their ancestor's malice, but had let that despair conquer her, hurling herself into the sea rather than spend one more day in suffering. As Sophie faced her twentieth birthday, she was surprised she had not yet suffered the same fate, but love had not yet touched her. Most people considered her a spinster, an object of pity, but she was beginning to think she was very lucky indeed.

Sophie finished her drink, stood up, and set the tankard on the mantel. She would not join the long line of heartbroken Galt women. If it took her the rest of her life, she would end the torment her vindictive ancestor had inflicted upon so many innocent people. If it was God's wish that the Galt women should suffer for Rona's crime, surely four hundred and thirty-five years of misery was penance enough. Perhaps He wanted a Galt woman to put right what a Galt woman had made so wrong. It was her duty to try. And, she mused, as she crawled into bed, there was only one proper place to start—Nochdaidh.

"Nella isnae going to like this plan," she murmured and almost smiled.

"I dinnae like this, m'lady. Not at all."

Sophie glanced at her maid riding the stout pony at her side. Nella had not ceased bemoaning the plans Sophie had made in the entire sennight since she had made them. It had been expected, but Sophie was weary of it. Nella's fears fed her own. What she needed was confidence and support. Nella was loyal, but Sophie wished she was also brave, perhaps even a little encouraging.

"Nella, do ye wish me to die alone, sad, and heartbroken?" Sophie asked.

"Och, nay."

"Then hush. Unless Rona's curse is broken, I will suffer the fate of all the Galt women of her bloodline. I will become just another one of the sorrowful, despairing spirits roaming the halls of Werstane."

Nella gasped, then gave Sophie a brief look of accusation. "Ye said there werenae any spirits at Werstane."

"Actually, I said there werenae any spirits in the room we were in when ye asked about them." She grinned when Nella snorted softly in disgust, but quickly grew serious again. "'Twill be all right, Nella."

"Oh? The woman in the village said the laird is a monster, a beast who drinks blood and devours bairns."

"If he devours bairns, he obviously has a verra small appetite, for the village was swarming with them. And that village looked far too prosperous for one said to be ruled by some beast." She looked around her, noticing how stark the land had grown, then frowned at the looming castle of dark stone before her. "That place does look a wee bit chilling, however. The boundary between light and dark is astonishingly clear."

"Do ye feel anything, m'lady? Evil or danger?" Nella asked in an unsteady whisper.

"I feel despair," Sophie replied in an equally quiet voice. " 'Tis so thick, 'tis nearly smothering."

"Oh, dear. That isnae good for ye, m'lady. Nay good at all."

Sophie dismounted but yards from the huge, ominous gates of Nochdaidh and placed her hand upon the cold, rocky ground. "Rona's venom has sunk deep into this land."

"The verra ground is cursed? Will it nay reach out to infect us as weel?"

"Not ye, Nella. And what poison is here is for The MacCordy, nay ye and nay me."

Nella dismounted, moved to stand at Sophie's side, and clasped her hand. "Let us leave this cursed place, m'lady. Ye feel too much. What lurks here, in the verra air and the earth, could hurt ye."

"I am hurt already, Nella, and I face e'en more hurt. Long, lonely years of pain, the sort of pain that drove my mother to court hell's fires by taking her own life. The MacCordys also suffer. The pain should have been Rona's alone, and, mayhap, her lover's. Yet she inflicted it upon countless innocents. Aunt Claire did no wrong. My mother did no wrong. The mon behind those shadowed walls did no wrong. One woman's anger has tainted all of us. How can I ignore that? How can I but walk away? I am of Rona's blood and I must do all I can to undo this wrong. If nay for myself, then for the MacCordys, for my own child if I am blessed with one."

"So, if ye can break this curse, ye will love and be loved and have bairns?"

"Aye, that is how I understand it."

Nella took a deep breath, threw back her thin shoulders, and nodded firmly. "Then we must go on. Ye have a right to such happiness. And I can find it within me to be brave. I have protection."

Thinking of all the talismans, rune stones, and other such things Nella was weighted down with, Sophie suspected her maid was the most protected woman in all of Scotland. "Loyal Nella, I welcome your companionship. I shall be in sore need of it, I think." Sophie took the reins of her pony in her hand and started to walk toward the gates of Nochdaidh.

"'Tis as if the verra sun fears to shine upon such a cursed place," Nella whispered.

"Aye. Let us pray that God in His mercy will show me the way to dispel those shadows."

Chapter Two

"A visitor, Alpin."

Alpin MacCordy looked up from the letter he had been
reading. His right-hand man Eric stood across from him at
the head table in the great hall. There was no hint of amusement upon the man's rough features, yet he had to be joking.
Visitors did not come to Nochdaidh. Anyone traveling over
his lands was quickly and thoroughly warned to stay away.
The dark laird of Nochdaidh was not a man anyone came
calling on.

"Has the weather turned so ill that it would force someone to seek shelter e'en in this place?" he asked.

"Nay. She has asked to speak to you."

"She?"

"Aye." Eric shook his head. "Two wee lasses. The one
who calls herself Lady Sophie Hay says she *must* speak to
you." He suddenly turned and scowled at the doors. "Curse
it, woman, I told ye to wait."

"My lady is cold," said the thinner of the two women entering the great hall, even as she pushed the other woman toward the fireplace.

"I am fine, Nella," protested the other woman.

That soft, husky voice drew Alpin's attention from Eric, who was bickering with the woman called Nella. He felt a slight tightening in his belly as the lady by the fireplace pulled off the hood of her cloak, revealing a delicate profile and thick, honey-gold hair. At the moment she was distracted by her maid's efforts to get her cloak off and the argument between Eric and Nella. Alpin took quick advantage of that, looking his fill.

Her beautiful hair hung in a long, thick braid to her tiny waist. The dark blue woolen gown she wore clung to her slim, shapely hips and nicely formed, if somewhat small, breasts. Her face was a delicate oval, her nose small and straight, and her mouth full and inviting. She was tiny but perfect. Her maid was also small, dark haired, somewhat plain, bone thin, and plainly not at all intimidated by the burly Eric's harsh visage or curt voice.

Alpin rose and moved closer to his uninvited guests. When the lady looked at him, he needed all his willpower not to openly react to the beauty of her eyes. She had eyes the color of the sea, an intriguing mix of blue and green, and just as mysterious. Her eyes were wide, her lashes long, thick, and several shades darker than her hair, and her equally dark brows arced delicately over those huge pools of innocent curiosity.

For a moment he thought this beautiful young woman had somehow made it to his gates without hearing about him, then he looked at the woman she called Nella. That woman's dark eyes were filled with fear and horror. She clutched one thin hand tightly around what looked to be a weighty collection of amulets draped around her neck. The women had obviously been thoroughly warned, so why were they here, he mused, and looked back at Lady Sophie. That woman shocked him by smiling sweetly and holding out her small hand.

"Ye are the laird of Nochdaidh, I assume," she said. "I am Lady Sophie Hay and this is my maid, Nella."

"Aye, I am the laird. Sir Alpin MacCordy at your service, m'lady."

When he bowed, then took her hand in his and brushed a kiss over her knuckles, Sophie had to swiftly suppress a shiver. Heat flowed through her body from the spot where his warm lips had briefly touched her skin. She started to scold herself for being so susceptible to the beauty of the man, then decided she should have expected such a thing. They already shared a bond in many ways. They were caught in the same trap set by the vindictive Rona so long ago.

And he was beautiful, she thought with an inner sigh. He was a tall man, a foot or more taller than her own meager five feet. He was lean and muscular, his every move graceful. His hair was long and thick, gleaming black waves hanging past his broad shoulders. Even his face was lean, his cheekbones high and well defined, his jawline strong, and his nose long and straight. He had eyes of a rich golden brown, thickly lashed, and nicely spaced beneath straight brows. His mouth was well shaped with a hint of fullness she found tempting. If this was how Rona's lover had looked, Sophie could understand the pain and anger of losing him to another, even if she could never forgive the woman for how she had reacted to those feelings.

"Why have ye come to Nochdaidh, m'lady?" Alpin asked as he reluctantly released her hand.

"Weel, m'laird, I have come to try to break the curse the witch Rona put upon the MacCordys."

The disappointment Alpin felt was sharp. She was just another charlatan come to try and fill him with false hope. As too many others had over the years, she would ply her trickery, fill her purse with his coin, and walk away. She but hoped to slip her lovely hand into his purse using lies and fanciful spells or cures.

"The tale of Rona the witch and her curse is just that—a tale. Lies made up to explain things that cannae be understood."

"Oh, nay! 'Tisnae just some tale, m'laird. I have papers to prove 'tis all true."

"Really? And just how would ye have come to hold such proof?"

"It was left to me by my aunt. Ye see, Rona was my ancestor. I am one of a direct line of Galt women—"

She squeaked when he suddenly pulled his sword and aimed at her, the point but inches from her heart. The fury visible upon his face was chilling. Sophie was just thinking that it was a little odd to still find him so beautiful while he looked so ready, even eager, to kill her, when Nella thrust her thin body between Sophie and the point of Alpin's sword.

"Nay!" Nella cried in a voice made high and sharp by fear. "I cannae allow ye to hurt my lady."

"Now, Nella," Sophie said in her most soothing voice as she tried and failed to nudge her maid aside, "I am sure the laird wasnae intending to do me any harm." A sword through the heart was probably a fairly quick death, she mused.

"Are ye? Weel, ye would be wrong," Alpin drawled, but sheathed his sword, the surprising act of courage by the trembling maid cutting through the tight grip rage had gained on him. "There would undoubtedly be some satisfaction in spilling the blood of one of that witch's kinswomen."

"Mayhap, but that wouldnae solve the problem."

"How can ye be so sure?"

"Why dinnae we all sit down to discuss this?" said Eric, pausing to instruct a curious maid to bring food and drink before grabbing Nella by the arm and dragging her toward the head table. "Always better to sit, break bread together, and talk calmly."

"Fine. We will eat, drink, and talk calmly," Alpin said in a cold, hard voice, "and then they can leave."

This was not proceeding well, Sophie mused as she watched Alpin stride back to the table. It was not going to be easy to help someone who, at first, wanted to strike you dead, then wanted you to leave. She should have suspected such a reaction. She had not sensed one good feeling since entering the shadows encircling Nochdaidh. Despair, fear, and a bone-deep resignation to the dark whims of fate were everywhere.

The laird was filled with the same feelings and much darker ones. When he had touched her hand it was not only attraction Sophie had felt, his and her own. There was anger in the man. It was there even before he had discovered exactly who she was. She had also felt dark, shadowy emotions, ones she had only felt on the rare times she had somehow touched the spirit of a predator, such as a hawk or a wolf. Alpin Mac-Cordy was fighting that part of him, the part born of her ancestor's curse. As she collected the chest with Morvyn's things and started toward the table, Sophie hoped she could convince Sir Alpin that she could be an ally in that battle.

"What's that?" demanded Alpin as Sophie took the seat to his left and set the small chest covered in runes on the table.

"The truth about the curse," Sophie replied, opening the chest to take out the scrolls. "Rona's sister Morvyn wrote it all down and, just before she died, she hid it. I found it whilst cleaning the cottage left to me by my aunt."

"So, to help me ye thought it wise to bring more sorcery into my keep?"

Sophie was prevented from responding to that by the arrival of the food and drink. When Sir Alpin asked if her men needed anything and she told him no men traveled with her, the look he gave her made her want to hit him. She was pleased, however, when he cleared the great hall of all but the four of them as soon as the food and drink were set out.

"Ye traveled here alone? Just ye and your maid?" he demanded the moment they were alone.

"I have no men-at-arms to drag about with me," she replied. That was close to the truth, she mused, for the men guarding Werstane were not yet her men, not in their hearts. This scowling laird did not need to know that she had slipped away unseen to avoid having to take any Werstane men with her. "I have a cottage, sir, and nay a castle like this." It was another half-truth for, although she was determined to stick to her plan to hide her wealth, she found she did not really want to lie to this man.

"But your maid calls ye her lady."

"Good blood and a title dinnae always make for a fat purse. I am a healing woman." She unrolled the scrolls. "Now, about the writings Morvyn left—" She tensed when he touched the smaller one.

"This was written in blood." Alpin studied the hastily scrawled writing. "Rage for rage," he murmured then scowled. "Curse it, my Latin isnae so good."

"Allow me, m'laird." She saw how the other three at the table all tensed. "Without the herbs and all, they are but words." She began to read. "Rage for rage, pain for pain, blood for blood, life for life. As mine shall walk alone, so shall yours. As mine shall be shunned, so shall yours. Your firstborn son shall know only shadows, as shall his son, as shall his son's son, and thus it shall be until the seed of The MacCordy shall wither from hate and fade into the mists.

"From sunset of the first day The MacCordy becomes a mon, darkness will take him as a lover, blood will be his wine, fury will steal his soul, yearning will devour his heart, and he will become a creature of nightmares. He will know no beauty; he will know no love; he will know no peace. The name of the MacCordys will become a foul oath, their tale one used to frighten all the Godly.

"Thus it shall be, and thus it shall remain, until one steps from the shadows of pride, land, and wealth and does as his heart commands. Until all that should have been finally is."

Sophie nodded her agreement with the action when both Eric and Nella crossed themselves. The laird stared at the scrolls, saying nothing, but she could feel his anger. She knew he wanted to deny the curse, but that a part of him believed in it.

"Why write such filth down?" he finally asked. "Why not let the words die with the bitch who spoke them?"

"Because Morvyn needed to ken exactly what was said if the curse was e'er to be broken," Sophie replied. "Morvyn spent her whole life trying to undo the evil her sister had created. She failed, but hoped someone who came after might succeed."

"And ye think ye are the one, do ye?"

His sarcasm stung. "Why not? And what can it hurt to at least let me try?"

"What can it hurt? I believe your ancestor Rona showed what harm can be done by letting a Galt woman practice magic. Ye must excuse me, but I cannae help but view any offer of aid from a Galt woman with mistrust."

"Then view my offer as utterly self-serving. Curses carry a price for the one who makes them, m'laird. When Rona cursed your family, she cursed her own. 'Tis said that a curse will come back threefold upon the one who casts it. As every MacCordy of Ciar's blood has suffered, so has every daughter of Rona Galt's blood."

"Ye look fine to me." Too fine, he mused, but tried to ignore her beauty.

"Rona cursed your soul, your heart. In doing so, she robbed all women of her line of any happiness. The moment a Galt woman finds love, tastes the sweetness of having her love returned, 'tis stolen away from her. No Galt woman of Rona's blood can hold on to her heart's desire. She grasps it just long enough to ken the pleasure of it, to gain a need for it, and then it dies."

"It sounds like a tale spun to explain poor choices in a mate."

Sophie inwardly cursed. "Do ye really think every woman born in Rona's line for four hundred and thirty-five years chose wrongly, gave her heart foolishly? *Every* woman, m'laird, ended her days gripped tightly by despair. The heart's ache was deep and everlasting. 'Twas worse for the ones who actually married the men they loved, for they were bound forever to a mon they loved, one who had once loved them, but would ne'er do so again. Many lived to a great age burdened by that loss. Others couldnae bear it, and, despite the threat of suffering in hell's fires for such a sin, took their own lives. My mother hurled herself into the sea, unable to bear the pain another day, a pain e'en the love of her children couldnae ease."

It was Eric who finally broke the heavy silence. "Ye believe we are cursed then? That the ill fate which has befallen the MacCordys for so verra long is born of the curse of this one angry woman?"

"Are ye nay shunned?" Sophie asked softly. "Do ye nay walk alone? Do ye nay live in the shadows? Although the sun shines o'er the village, this place sits in the shadow. Do ye think that natural?"

"If this Morvyn couldnae end this curse, what makes ye think ye can?" asked Alpin.

"Weel, Morvyn ne'er came here," Sophie replied. "I doubt any Galt woman has e'er come here. That could make the difference. I have the strongest feeling that I will be the only one to e'en try since Morvyn hid this chest. Ye may not believe in curses, m'laird, but I do, and I wish to try and end this one. I wish no more Galt women to hurl themselves into the sea out of despair," she added softly.

Those last words killed Alpin's refusal on his tongue. He could deny *himself* hope, but not her. Hope was a paltry thing to cling to; bitter, fruitless, and painful, but she needed to discover that hard truth for herself.

"Stay then, and play your games, but ye best not trouble me with such nonsense."

Before she could protest that, he had called in two maids to take her and Nella to a room. Sophie decided she had pushed him hard enough for now. She had succeeded in getting permission to stay and try to find a way to end the curse. There was a chance she would not need his complete cooperation, but, if she did, there was now time and opportunity to sway him. As she and Nella went with the maids, Sophie prayed the hope that had stirred to life inside of her was not doomed to be crushed.

Alpin glared at the door Lady Sophie and her maid had disappeared through. He took a deep drink of the wine mixed especially for him, a thick mixture of sheep's blood and wine. It fed the need which grew stronger every year and he doubted some wide-eyed lass could effect a cure. He wanted to feel pleased that the women descended from Rona Galt had suffered as his family had suffered, but could not. None of them had deserved the misery visited upon them. He also wanted to hold fast to his previous scorn concerning the possibility of a curse, but found himself wavering, and that angered him.

"Mayhap she can help," said Eric, watching Alpin closely.

"So ye believe me cursed?" drawled Alpin. "Ye think our troubles caused by some woman long dead who danced about a fire one night, uttering those fanciful words as she sprinkled some herbs upon the flames?"

Eric grimaced and dragged his hand through his roughly cut dark hair. "Why do ye resist the idea of a curse? What besets ye and has beset every MacCordy laird before ye for hundreds of years isnae, weel, normal."

"Not every disease affects so many people it becomes common. Just because an affliction is rare doesnae make it the result of some curse or sorcery."

"Then, if ye truly believe 'tis nay more than bad blood, why have ye let the lass stay?"

Alpin grimaced. "A moment of weakness, or insanity. It was her wish to nay see any more Galt women hurl themselves into the sea out of despair. I have no hope left, but I couldnae bring myself to kill hers. 'Twill die soon enough."

"I sometimes think that is some of our trouble. We have lost hope."

"Only a fool clings to it for four hundred years," Alpin drawled.

"Mayhap." Eric stared out the window, seeing only another of the many shades of darkness he had spent his whole life in. "I often wonder if that loss of hope brought on this never-ending shadow we live under."

"Ye grow fanciful. And, if it is born of the death of hope, then we best be prepared for it to grow e'en darker."

"Why?"

"Because our little golden-haired Galt witch will all too soon be burying hers."

Chapter Three

"Eric, wait!" Sophie ran the last few feet toward the man she had been hunting down and grabbed him by the arm. "If I didnae ken better, I would think ye are trying to avoid me." She did not need Eric's glance behind her to know Nella had caught up to her; she had heard the rattle of her maid's many amulets. "I just wish to ask ye a few things, Sir Eric."

"M'lady, ye have been here but a sennight and have spoken to near everyone within the keep, outside the keep, and probably for near a dozen miles around," Eric said. "I cannae think that I can tell ye anything that ye dinnae already ken."

"If I am to break the curse, I need all the knowledge about the MacCordy laird that I can gather. I am certain the grip of this curse can be broken if I can just find the right key. Morvyn failed, but she ne'er came to see exactly what the curse had done. That might be why she failed. So, I am gathering all the truth I can and recording it. The answer is in there, I am certain of it. I can feel it within my reach."

Eric leaned against the side of the stables he had been trying to escape into when she had caught sight of him. "The lairds of the MacCordys grow to monhood watching their fathers change into some creature from a nightmare. They then become men and begin to change themselves."

Sophie crossed her arms beneath her breasts. "That isnae verra helpful. How do they change? A lot of what I have been told is difficult to believe. I do ken that the laird cannae abide the sun."

"Nay. The light of the sun fair blinds him. Alpin finds it increasingly painful as he ages. Three years ago he spent but an hour in the sun and it was as if he had been dropped into boiling water. If not for the heavy clothing he wore, I think he would have died. He hasnae ventured beyond the shadows since that day, except at night, or, if heavily cloaked, on sunless days."

"And he needs blood."

"Aye," Eric snapped, then sighed and dragged a hand through his hair. "That need grew slowly. He now eats naught but nearly raw meat, seared just enough to warm it, to make the juices flow. His usual drink is now an even mix of wine and blood."

"Do ye ken if he felt the change immediately, or if it was a slow awareness?"

"Since this affliction has been visited upon every laird, 'twas expected, so I cannae say. The first hint comes when the heir becomes a mon and when next he becomes angry. The eyes change to those of a wolf and the teeth become sharper. After so many years we have learned to watch for the change, to guard against that first attack of anger. There were some tragedies in the early days ere we learned what to expect. Alpin was little trouble, for he, too, had studied the matter and was prepared." Eric shook his head. "He has great strength, m'lady, and fights to control this affliction, but the change cannae be stopped."

"What if one ceased to feed the need for blood?" she asked.

"Och, nay, ye dinnae wish to do that. 'Twas tried and the need grows to a near madness, endangering all who draw too near."

"Restraint willnae work?"

"Nay, not e'en if one finds the means to hold him in a way he cannae break free of. The strength of these men can be terrifying to behold. So can their ability to persuade, to beguile, be beyond compare. E'en if ye find chains strong enough to bind them, they can eventually get some poor fool to set them free."

Sophie stared down at her foot as she tapped it slowly against the hard-packed dirt of the bailey, her hands clasped behind her back. Most of what Eric told her matched what she had learned from others. He told her the truth without any gruesome elaborations or tales of the devil, however. The truth was not good. No normal restraints or cures had worked. It had been foolish to think the MacCordys had left any stone unturned in the course of over four hundred years. Rona's curse refused to be denied its victims.

"None of the lairds lives to a great age, aye?" she asked, looking back at Eric.

"Sadly true. A few have killed themselves, a few died in battle, some are murdered by their own people."

"But nay until they have bred an heir."

"Aye, and after the son is born, the change often happens more quickly. The old laird, through sheer strength of will, held back the worst of the affliction for thirteen years, but I believe seeing the curse appear in Alpin broke his spirit. The verra next battle he fought, he died, and I think he planned to do so. In battle, the beast within the lairds bursts free in many ways. Their strength is that of many men, their ferocity unmatched, and their skill at laying waste to the enemy a source of legends. 'Tis why we are so often sought out by men who wish us to fight their battles for them."

"Has there been a laird or two who was seduced by such power, began to welcome it?"

"Oh, aye, a few. But nay Alpin," Eric said firmly, "if that is what ye think. Alpin has more strength of will than any mon I have e'er kenned or heard of. If any mon could beat this, he could, but there isnae any sign that he is winning that battle. Nay, at best he but slows the tightening of the grip of this affliction."

"Then he doesnae grow worse as quickly as his father or grandfather?"

"Nay, but his father was married by now and had bred the heir. His grandfather, weel," Eric shrugged. "He was verra bad from all that I hear. I dinnae ken if he was weak or one of those who reveled in the fear he could stir. He was killed by the villagers after he killed his wife. Tore her to pieces, 'tis said. Her and the lover he found her with."

Sophie ignored Nella's muttered prayers and nodded. "The rage. Catching one's wife with another mon would certainly stir it up." She suddenly smiled at Eric and rubbed her hands together. "I think I have a plan." She briefly scowled at Nella, who groaned, then looked back at Eric, pretending she did not see the smile he quickly hid. "I shall immediately start doing all I can to help Sir Alpin fight this curse. I ken all manner of things to shield him, protect him, strengthen him. Rowan branches, rune stones, herbs," she muttered, trying to recall all she had and to think of what more she might need.

"Er, m'lady—" Eric began.

Caught up in her thoughts, Sophie started toward the keep. "I dinnae suppose the laird would wear an amulet or two. Nay, he is being most uncooperative. He avoids me as if I am some toad-sucking demon waving a dead mon's hand at him," she mumbled to herself.

"Arenae ye going with her?" Eric asked Nella, who just stood there frowning after Sophie.

"She is muttering," replied Nella. " 'Tis sometimes best nay to hear what she is saying when she mutters. She only mutters when she is angry, and though she be a sweet, big-hearted lass, when she is angry she can have a verra wicked tongue."

"She willnae give up, will she?"

"Nay. She is a stubborn woman, and I think she is weighted with shame o'er what her ancestor did. Aye, and she was sorely grieved by what happened to her mother. M'lady will keep at this 'til she joins the angels."

"Nella?" called Sophie, suddenly realizing she was alone.

"Coming, m'lady." Nella hurried to Sophie's side.

"Good. We must change and go to collect some rowan branches."

"For what?"

"I intend to place as many as I can around this keep to try to weaken the power of the curse," Sophie replied as she entered the keep and hurried up the stairs.

"The laird isnae going to like this," Nella said quietly as she followed Sophie.

"Then we shallnae tell him."

Alpin knew he should not go to the great hall even as he found himself walking toward it. Sophie would be there with her smiles, her undampened hope, and that innocent beauty that made him ache. Avoiding her did not work, for he found himself trying to catch glimpses of her like some besotted youth. She also had a true skill for appearing around every corner. It was time to stop hiding in his own keep, he mused, as he strode into the great hall and straight into something hard.

Cursing softly, Alpin was just wondering what fool had placed a stool upon a chair right inside the doorway when something soft landed on him. His body immediately recognized Sophie, and he quickly wrapped his arms around her to stop her fall. Despite his best efforts, however, he lost his balance. Knowing he could not stop his own fall, he turned so that he took the worst of it, sprawling on his back with the sweet-smelling, viciously cursing Sophie sprawled on top of him.

He quickly became almost painfully aware of how good she felt in his arms, her gentle curves fitting perfectly against him. The scent of her filled his head, a stirring mixture of woman, clean skin, and a hint of lavender. When she shifted slightly on top of him, he tightened his grasp, unwilling to let her go. He could hear her pulse quicken, sense a building heat within her, and was sharply disappointed to find that she, too, feared him. Then he took another deep breath and realized it was not fear but desire that was stirring within her. Alpin beat down the strong urge to toss her over his shoulder and run to his bedchamber. He met her wide-eyed gaze with a hard-won calm, idly noting that desire made her eyes appear more green than blue.

"Might I ask what ye were doing?" He glanced at the stool and the chair, then looked back at her.

"I was hanging a few rowan branches o'er the door," she replied.

"Ye could find no one to help?"

"I didnae ask. I was trying to do it secretly. If I got someone to help me, then it wouldnae have remained a secret, would it?"

Alpin looked at the branches nailed over the door to the great hall, and sighed as he returned his gaze to her face. "Why?"

"For protection. Ye are fighting the curse," she hurried on before he could protest, "and I decided to do what I can to help. I plan to surround ye with protection, shields against evil, and things to help strengthen your will to fight, or, at least, keep it strong." She sighed. "I ken ye dinnae like such things so I thought to do it secretly."

"So ye planned to lie to me."

"Nay! I planned on telling ye nothing at all. Ye need such things to help ye hold firm whilst I search for a cure, but since I kenned ye would deny that or argue against my plans,

I decided 'twas simplest to just boldly grasp the reins and charge ahead."

"And ride right o'er me."

"Weel," she grimaced, then smiled at him, "more like ride *beside* ye."

It was all nonsense, of course, Alpin mused. Rowan branches, magical stones, special herbs, and all such trickery could not save him. The earnest hope in her lovely eyes both attracted and annoyed him. He wanted to savor the sweetness of it and crush it with the cold, heartless truth. She was going to drive him mad long before his affliction accomplished the deed.

Then he found himself asking when had anyone at Nochdaidh last felt any hope at all? When had anyone worked so hard to try to help him? Never in his memory was the answer. Alpin did not share her hope, but her desire to help touched some deep need within him. He put his hand on the back of her head, tangling his fingers in her long, soft hair, and pulled her mouth down to his. The feel of her slender body, the scent of her, and even her foolish plots to help him shattered his resistance. He had to kiss her, had to steal a taste of her sweet innocence, of her precious if fruitless hopes, and of her desire.

Sophie tensed as he brushed his lips over hers. Heat flooded her body and she gasped. Alpin's kiss grew fierce and demanding as he invaded her mouth with his tongue. Such a sudden assault should have frightened or angered her, but it did neither. It inflamed her. Each stroke of his tongue coaxed forth a deep, searing need. She did not need to feel the telltale hardening of his lean body to know he desired her. She could feel it in his kiss, could taste it upon his tongue. That desire fed her own. The passion flaring to life within her was so heady, so sweet, she had no will to fight it.

"'Tis a strange place ye have chosen for some wooing," drawled a deep voice, "and nay verra private, either."

The kiss ended so abruptly, Sophie felt lost and unsteady.

Alpin gracefully stood up with her in his arms, and set her on her feet. She swayed a little, then, realizing Eric stood there, nervously tried to tidy her appearance. Not only was she severely disappointed that the kiss was over, but she suddenly wished she were alone. After experiencing something so stirring, so shattering to her peace of mind, she would like a little privacy to sort out her feelings and thoughts. It would be easy enough to leave, but she did not want anyone to think she was fleeing out of embarrassment or shame.

"Sophie fell and I caught her," Alpin said, giving Eric a hard look that dared the man to argue.

Eric met that gaze for a moment, then shrugged and moved to pick up the stool and chair. "What are these doing here?"

"The stool was upon the chair and Lady Sophie was upon the stool. I walked into them."

"Why would ye do something like that, m'lady?" Eric asked, only to have Alpin silently reply by pointing to a spot above the doors. "Oh, I see. Rowan branches."

"Aye," replied Sophie. " 'Tis said they protect against witches."

" 'Tis about four hundred and thirty years too late for that," murmured Alpin, and met Sophie's cross look with one raised brow. "Do ye plan to do a lot of this?"

"In every place I can. I have a few other ideas as weel. I dinnae suppose I can convince ye to wear an amulet or two, can I?"

"So I might rattle about the place like Nella? Nay, I think not." He looked up at the rowan tree branches. "I must resign myself to the constant sight of dying greenery, must I? I think this might count as sorcery."

"I consider it healing." Seeing the look of amused disbelief in his eyes, Sophie decided it was time to retreat. "I shall just go and clean up," she murmured as she hurried out the door.

Alpin was surprised when Nella glared at him before following Sophie. He shook his head and looked at Eric, only to find that man eyeing him with an uncomfortable intensity. Kissing Sophie had been an error in judgment. He had succumbed to a weakness, and, he mused, being caught at it was probably a just punishment.

"What ye saw was a moment of utter madness," Alpin said before Eric could speak.

"Are ye certain that was all it was?" asked Eric.

"Aye, and that is all it ever can be. A woman like Lady Sophie Hay can ne'er be for me. She is all hope, sweetness, and smiles."

"With a hearty serving of tartness, stubbornness, and passion."

"Aye. A perfect mixture," Alpin murmured and shook his head. "Sophie needs laughter, sun, and love. She cannae find any of that with me. Although I am drawn to her, the first woman to show no fear, to offer help, I must turn from her. When she realizes nothing she does will help, she will lose that innocent faith that is so alluring. If I try to hold her, she will see me become the creature my forefathers did. 'Tis cowardly, mayhap, but I find I cannae stomach the thought of watching her begin to fear me, revile me, to watch me become more beast than mon."

"But she might be able to help you," protested Eric.

"Nay, I doubt that verra much," said Alpin as he picked up the chair and took it back to the table. "I dinnae doubt for one moment, however, that *I* will destroy her. If I try to hold her, I will simply smother all that sweet light with my own darkness. I am not yet beast enough to commit that sin."

"Nella, I need some time alone," Sophie said, halting her maid when the woman tried to follow her into the bedchamber they shared.

"But, m'lady," Nella began to protest.

"I need to think, Nella. Just give me a wee while alone, then come help me ready myself to dine in the great hall."

"Because the laird hurled ye to the floor and tried to ravish ye?"

"Actually, Nella, I fell, knocked him to the ground, and he kissed me. That is all. Now, go. Please. I will be fine."

The moment Nella left, Sophie hurled herself facedown on the bed. She knew she had been attracted to the laird from the first moment she had set eyes on the man. Now, with one kiss, he had shown her that what she felt was far more than an interest in a mysterious, troubled, handsome man. She loved him. She loved a man who could not abide the sun, drank blood, ate raw meat, and could tear his enemies apart with his bare hands. Sophie doubted she could have hand-picked a man more certain to ensure that she continued to walk the sad path trod by far too many Galt women before her.

Chapter Four

The curses were bellowed so loudly Sophie was surprised they did not shake loose a few of the stones in the thick walls of Nochdaidh. She was strongly tempted to ignore Alpin when he shouted her name. After all, he had ignored *her* very thoroughly for the last week. If not for the times she and he had crossed paths and she had caught a look in his eyes that could only be described as passionate, she could easily think he hated her. The only other times he had taken note of her existence was to flay her with his temper. She was only trying to help the ungrateful fool. It was hardly her fault he kept stumbling upon her shields and protections in ways that tended to cause him some minor injury. Did the man never sleep? she thought crossly.

"Sophie Hay!"

It was a little astonishing how that deep voice could penetrate such thick walls, she mused, as she rose from the pallet she slept on. Although it was not the most comfortable of beds, she far preferred it to the one she had been given. That bed had been the site of far too many trysts. Sensitive to such things, she had felt the ghostly remnants of passion, lust, pain, and even fear; had been unable to shield herself completely from all the lingering memories of so many strong feelings. Nella now slept in the bed. Fortunately, Nella was so accustomed to Sophie's ways, she had not questioned the why of such an unusual arrangement. Sophie could not tell her very protective maid that those memories of lovemaking had caused her to have some very shocking and sensual dreams concerning herself and Sir Alpin.

As she hurried out of the room in response to a snarled demand that she best be quick or be prepared to suffer dark, but unspecified, consequences, Sophie was a little surprised to see that Nella still slept soundly. The sight that met her eyes as she turned toward Alpin's bedchamber had her feeling both aroused and a little amused. Sir Alpin, the much-feared laird of Nochdaidh, was wearing only his hose and a loose shirt that revealed a great deal of his broad, smooth chest. He was also sitting on the floor grimacing and rubbing one of his bare feet.

When he looked at her, she understood why he inspired such fear in people, even though she felt only a brief flicker of unease. His eyes resembled those of a wolf, the golden brown having become more yellow in color. The lines of his face had changed slightly, giving him a distinctly feral look. She could feel his anger, feel the wildness of it. Then he ran his gaze over her and she felt his emotions shift from anger to need. Her body quickly responded to that look, but he seemed unaware of that. His control was admirable, even somewhat astonishing, but she was beginning to heartily dislike it.

"Ye roared, m'laird?" she asked, crossing her arms and inwardly grimacing when she realized she wore only her thin linen nightshift.

"What are these?" he demanded, pointing to the stones lined up outside his bedchamber door.

"Rune stones," she replied. "Since ye had retired for the night, I set them there to shield ye as ye slept. I had planned to collect them ere ye woke. I hadnae realized ye were in the habit of slinking about in the dark of night."

"Nay? Perhaps I felt the need to feast upon some innocent bairn?" He noticed she had begun to tap her small, bare foot against the floor. "I am, after all, a creature of shadows, comfortable beneath the cloak of night, which so many others fear."

"Ye dinnae help matters by saying such foolish things." She gasped in surprise when he suddenly grabbed her by the arm and pulled her down until she was sprawled in his lap. "My laird, this is undignified and improper."

Sophie had wanted to sound imperious, but even she could hear the breathlessness in her voice. It should not surprise her that she was so weak-willed around this man. She had spent the last week dreaming of that first kiss, aching for another, and for so much more. Falling in love with this man had to be one of the most idiotic things she had ever done, but her heart refused to be swayed by good sense. Instead of learning how to fight his allure, she found herself hurt and angered over how easily he could fight the attraction between them.

He gave her a faint smile that barely parted his lips, then nuzzled her throat. Sophie trembled and wrapped her arms around him. When she felt the light touch of his teeth at the pulse point in her throat, she supposed she ought to be a little concerned. Instead, she curled her fingers into his thick hair and held him closer as she tilted her head back. The feel of his tongue upon that spot where her blood pounded in her veins, the damp heat of his mouth as he lightly suckled her skin fed her nearly desperate need for him to place those soft lips against her own. When he kissed the underside of her chin, then her cheek, she turned her face a little, trying to press her mouth to his.

"I can hear each beat of your heart, Sophie," he said against her temple, his voice deep and seductive. "I can hear the blood rushing in your veins. I can smell your desire," he whispered and lightly nipped her earlobe. "I can taste it upon your lips." He teased her lips with fleeting kisses.

"And I can feel your desire, Alpin." She nipped at his bottom lip and smiled faintly when he growled low in his throat. "It feeds my own." The way his narrowed eyes glowed, his nostrils flared, and his features tightened into a predatory expression should have frightened her, but Sophie only felt her passion soar. She suspected she might look nearly as feral as he did as she ran her tongue between his lips and said, "So taste it, Alpin. Drink deep."

Alpin did, holding her tightly as he kissed her. She met his growing ferocity with her own. It was astonishing to him that this delicate woman did not flee his raw desire, but welcomed it, equaled it. A flicker of sanity pierced the madness seizing him. It would be easy to simply revel in what she offered, but he had to resist. Instinct told him that Sophie would not give herself lightly, and he could offer her no more than a bedding.

He ended the kiss, pulling back from her until his head hit the wall. He closed his eyes against the sight of her flushed face, her passion-warmed eyes, and the rapid rise and fall of her breasts. When he felt his control return, he looked at her again only to catch her staring at his bared chest with a look so heated he almost lost control again.

"Cease staring at my chest, Sophie," he drawled, pleased at how calm he sounded, no hint of the need tearing at his insides to be detected in his voice.

For a moment Sophie did not grasp the almost cold tone behind his words, then she felt the sting of the abrupt ending of their passionate interlude. She felt anger push aside her desire and glared at him, saying with an equal coldness, "I wasnae staring at your chest, ye vain mon. I was but noticing that your laces are badly frayed."

She was good, Alpin thought, as he watched her stand up. If his senses of smell and hearing were not so acute, he might believe she was as unmoved by the kiss as he pretended to be. He could still scent her desire, however, still hear it pounding in her veins. Pride led her now, and, he realized, he could use that to keep her at a distance, to stop her from tempting him with her warmth.

"Best collect your rocks ere ye hurry away," he said.

"They are rune stones," she snapped as she picked them up.

He shrugged as he stood up slowly. "They are nonsense, foolish superstition. I begin to lose patience with all these games."

"And I begin to lose patience with the air of defeat that fair chokes the air at Nochdaidh!"

"After so long, ye must forgive us for no longer believing in cures. And if the air here is so foul to ye, mayhap ye ought to go do your breathing elsewhere."

"Oh, nay, ye willnae get rid of me so easily. Fine, go and wallow in your self-pity. *I* am nay ready to quit. If ye dinnae wish me to fight for you, so be it, but I will continue to fight for myself and for the sake of any children I am blessed with." Seeing the look of fury upon his face, Sophie decided she had pushed him hard enough and she started back to her room. "And best ye get those weak laces seen to ere they snap. Ye could put an eye out, ye ken."

She shut her bedroom door quietly, resisting the urge to slam it shut. Seeing that Nella was still asleep, Sophie shook her head and put her rune stones away. She crawled into her bed and closed her eyes, knowing sleep would be slow to release her from the tumultuous feelings still gripping her. As she struggled to calm herself, she decided it was not the despair of holding love too briefly and losing it that she needed to worry about. If she was not careful, Alpin would drive her utterly mad long before then.

"M'lady, what troubles ye?" asked Nella as she walked through the village with Sophie. "Ye have been verra quiet."

She cast a fearful glance at Sophie's throat. "Did the laird drink too much of your blood?"

Sophie was abruptly pulled from her dark thoughts and stopped to gape at Nella. "Ye think the laird has been drinking my blood?"

"Weel, there is that mark upon your neck."

Clasping her hand over the mark upon her neck, Sophie grimaced. "I hadnae thought it so obvious." She sighed and told her maid about the confrontation between her and Alpin last night. "I assume 'tis something men like to do and, at that moment, it was quite, er, pleasant. I had thought I had hidden it."

Nella moved to adjust Sophie's braid as well as the collars of her gown and cloak. " 'Tis better now. Keep your cloak tied at the neck and it should remain hidden. Dinnae want too many catching a peek at it. If they ken 'tis a love bite, your reputation will be sorely marred, though I suspect most will think what I did."

"I fear so." She frowned as she caught sight of a crowd of people at the far end of the road. "A meeting?"

Two men ran past her and Nella, rushing to join the crowd. Sophie caught the word "murder" in their conversation and froze. This was the very last thing Alpin needed. Sophie was about to turn back toward the keep when one of the women in the crowd saw her, called to her, and drew everyone's attention to her.

"M'lady, ye must come see this," Shona the cooper's wife called. "This will make ye see the danger of staying within the walls of such a cursed place."

"I really dinnae want to see this," Sophie murmured to Nella even as she started to walk toward Shona, Nella staying close to her side. "For them to cry murder means 'tis nay a clean death. No death is pleasant to witness, but murder can leave a verra untidy corpse."

"Ye fret o'er the oddest things," Nella said as she nudged

her way through the crowd. "Dead is dead. Aye?" Nella abruptly stopped and shuddered. "Oh, dear."

Sophie took a deep breath to steady herself, stepped around Nella, and looked down at what had once been a man. She felt her gorge rise and took several deep breaths to calm herself, her hand cupped over her nose and mouth to shield herself from the scent of death. Aware that the villagers were all watching her closely, she carefully studied the corpse. She knew what they believed, knew the accusations and questions that would soon be spoken aloud, and she searched out every clue she could find to be used to proclaim Alpin's innocence.

" 'Tis Donald, the butcher's eldest lad," said Hugh the cooper. "Weel, nay a lad. A mon with a wife and bairns. The poor woman found him like this. Said he often came here to sleep if one of the bairns cried too much in the night. Since their wee laddie is cutting teeth, he was setting up a fair howl all night long. The laird must have been on the hunt, and poor Donald was easy game."

"The laird didnae do this," Sophie said, her voice steady and firm.

"But his throat was torn out."

"Nay, 'tis cut." She crossed her arms and waited as Hugh crouched down to look more closely. "A verra clean cut it is, as weel. Swiftly done with a verra long, verra sharp knife."

Ian the butcher wiped the tears from his ruddy cheeks and looked closer. "Aye, she be right. I couldnae have done it neater myself. But that just means the laird used his sword."

For one brief moment, Sophie considered the fact that the laird had been awake and wandering about last night. Then she felt both guilty and ashamed. Alpin would never do this. Even if he turned into a beast, she had the sad feeling he would cut his own throat before he attacked some innocent. The trick would be in convincing these people who considered every MacCordy laird cursed, or a demon.

"Did anyone see the laird last eve?" she asked. "I did—in

the keep, barefoot, cross and bellowing, and with nary a drop of blood on him. Now, I ken what ye think the laird is, that ye think he feasted upon poor Donald last eve. Look ye at the ground beneath Donald's neck. 'Tis soaked in his blood. If the laird did this, acting as the demon ye think he is, do ye truly think he would let all that blood go to waste?"

"He gutted the lad," said Hugh. "Mayhap the innards were what he craved this time."

Even as Sophie opened her mouth, Ian shook his head. "Nay. 'Tis another clean cut and I didnae see aught missing," he added as he covered his son with a blanket someone handed him.

"And that wound bled verra little," Sophie said, "as did the wounds to his head and face. Do ye ken what that means, Master Ian?"

"I think so. My poor lad was already dead and fair bled dry ere the other wounds were made. But why?"

"To make all of ye think the laird did this." Sophie patted the grieving Ian's broad shoulder. "If the laird had come a-hunting, had become the beast of the night ye all claim he is, he would not have left such an intact body. He wouldnae have let all that blood sink into the dirt. Nay, if he had become the demon ye fear is within him, he would have torn this poor mon apart, drank the blood, and nay cared if ye caught him bathing in the gore. This was done by someone else, someone who crept upon Donald as he slept, for there is nary a sign of a struggle, cut his throat, and then desecrated the body to try to hide their crime. Nay, worse, to try to fix all blame upon the laird. Poor Donald made someone verra angry."

"She just tries to protect her lover," spoke up a buxom young woman who suddenly appeared at Ian's side. "He has already made her one of his slaves. Look ye at her neck! He has been feasting upon her!"

Sophie felt herself blush deeply and clasped her hand over her neck. "Nay!"

"Och, aye," said Shona, and laughed softly. "Someone's

been feasting on the lass, true enough. 'Tis a love bite, Gemma, ye foolish cow. Now cease your nonsense and help your mon. He has a son to bury."

"I thought ye said it wouldnae show if I kept my cloak tied," Sophie grumbled to Nella.

"Weel, it would have, if ye didnae have such a wee skinny neck that pokes its way out of anything one tries to lash to it."

Sophie's response to that insult was lost as her gaze became fixed upon Gemma. It took all of her willpower not to cry out in accusation, to remain calm. She knew who had killed Donald, although she could not yet even guess why.

"Ian," she called, drawing the man's attention back to her, "until we ken who murdered your son and why, 'twould be wise to guard his widow and bairns."

She held his gaze and inwardly sighed with relief when he nodded. The brief look of fury that touched Gemma's round face only confirmed Sophie's suspicions. The problem was going to be proving the woman's guilt without revealing any of her own special gifts. She shook her head, then noticed Shona remained although everyone else had left, and the woman was watching her with an unsettling intensity.

"The laird didnae kill Donald," Sophie said.

"I ken it," replied Shona. "I dinnae ken what to think about the mon who lives in that shadowed place, but I *do* believe he didnae do this. Ye shouldnae hope that many will share my opinion, however." She smiled faintly. "Ye ken who did it, dinnae ye? Do ye have the sight?"

A scowling Nella stepped between Shona and Sophie before Sophie could reply. "Aye, she does, but if ye tell anyone I will take a searing hot poker to your rattling tongue."

"Nella," Sophie protested.

"Fair enough," said Shona, grinning at Nella. She stepped a little to the side, reached out, and touched the mark upon Sophie's neck. "Mayhap I have the sight, too, for I am that sure 'tis the laird himself who has been nibbling on ye. Best ye push the rogue away."

"He willnae hurt me," Sophie said.

" 'Tisnae him ye need worry on, but them." She nodded toward the keep.

Sophie stared at the people, horses, and carts entering the gates of Nochdaidh. "Who are they?"

"The laird's betrothed and her kinsmen."

"His what?"

"The marriage was arranged years ago. The deed will be done in a fortnight. He didnae tell ye?"

"Nay, he didnae." Torn between pain and fury, Sophie spoke through tightly clenched teeth, then started to march back toward the keep.

"Wheesht, she looked verra angry," murmured Shona.

"Aye, she did," Nella agreed in a mournful voice.

"Will she put a curse on him?"

"She isnae a witch," Nella snapped, then sighed as she started to follow Sophie. "Howbeit, she is so angry that the laird may begin to think another curse upon The MacCordy is the lesser of two evils."

Chapter Five

It was going to be a long night, Alpin mused as he sprawled indolently in his chair. He surveyed all the people seated at his table and decided it was going to be a very long night indeed. Except for Eric, who sat on his right and looked too cursed amused for Alpin's liking, everyone else did not appear to be feeling the least bit congenial. Since he had long ago lost the art of pleasant conversation, if he had ever even possessed such a skill, silence reigned.

Alpin looked at Sophie as he sipped his wine and inwardly winced. She had returned from the village to find him greeting his newly arrived guests. One look at her face told him she knew exactly who these people were. He was not accustomed to the look she had given him. People usually eyed him with wary respect or fear. She had looked at him as if he were no more than some impertinent spatter of mud that had soiled her ladyship's best dancing slippers. He had wanted some distance between them and now he had it. Alpin was not sure why he felt both guilty and desolate. He suspected she would leave now, just as he had been wanting her to, yet he was fighting the urge to hold her at Nochdaidh even if he had to use chains.

He looked at his bride next and watched her tremble so badly the food she had been about to eat fell from her plump white hand. Lady Margaret MacLane was pretty enough with her brown hair and gray eyes, her body rounded with all the appropriate curves most men craved. At the moment, she was ghostly pale, her eyes so wide with fright they had to sting, and her body shook almost continuously. She had already fainted once, and Alpin dared not speak to her for fear she would do so again.

And then there were his bride's kinsmen, he thought with a sigh. Most of them seemed oblivious to the tense quiet, their sole interest being in consuming as much food and drink as possible. The only time any of them was diverted was when he felt a need to cast a lecherous glance Sophie's way. Margaret's father also kept looking at Sophie, although curiosity was mixed with the desire in his gaze. A strong urge to do violence to the MacLanes was stirring to life within Alpin, but he struggled to control it. Slaughtering many of his bride's kinsmen was not an acceptable way to celebrate a wedding, he mused.

Unable to resist, he looked at Sophie again and tensed. She smiled at him, then smiled at Sir Peter MacLane, Margaret's father. Although Alpin had hated her silence, felt wretched over the hurt he knew he had inflicted upon her, he felt her sudden cheer was an ominous sign. She was planning some mischief. He was certain of it.

"There was a murder in the village today," Sophie announced. "Donald, the butcher's eldest son."

He was going to beat her, Alpin thought, and took a deep drink of wine.

"Are ye certain 'twas murder, m'lady?" asked Eric.

"Och, aye. His throat was cut. Ear to ear." Sophie ignored Margaret's gasp of horror and blithely continued. "His belly was cut open, too." Margaret groaned and her eyes rolled back in their sockets. "Oh, and his poor face was beaten so badly 'twas difficult to recognize him." Sophie calmly watched Margaret slide out of her seat to sprawl unconscious upon the floor. "If she is to make a habit of that, Sir Alpin, mayhap ye ought to scatter a few cushions about her chair." She smiled sweetly at Alpin.

Perhaps he would strangle her, Alpin thought. Slowly.

"Why was the laird nay called to make a judgment?" asked Sir Peter.

"Weel, most of the villagers thought he had already come and gone, that 'twas his work," Sophie replied, then looked at Alpin again. "Of course, I convinced them that ye didnae do it, at least those of them who would heed sense."

"How verra kind of ye," Alpin drawled.

"Aye, it was. I pointed out that all his blood had soaked into the ground and that, if ye were what they thought ye were, ye wouldnae have let it go to waste like that."

"Nay, I would have supped upon it."

"Exactly. And I pointed out that all his innards were still there, plus the wounds were done with a knife, nay with teeth or hands. He was also killed as he slept and I was fair sure ye wouldnae do that, either. Aye, I made it verra clear that ye were a noble warrior, too honorable, too forthright, too—"

"I believe I understand, Sophie," he snapped, feeling the sting of her reprimand even though he knew it was well deserved.

"How nice." Sophie stood up and smiled at everyone. "And, now, if ye gentlemen and the laird will excuse me, I believe I will seek my rest. It has been a most exhausting day, full of blood, tears, and treachery." As Sophie passed behind Alpin's chair, she reached over his shoulder and dropped the amulet she had made for him on the table in front of him. "For ye, m'laird."

"What is it?" he asked, fighting to ignore the hurt and anger he could sense in her.

"An amulet for protection. Ye can wear it or ye can keep it in your pocket. 'Tis why I was in the village today, to gather what I needed. I heard ye are planning to ride off to battle in three days' time. I wanted to be sure ye returned."

"And ye still give it to me after what has occurred today?" he asked softly.

"Why not? And who can say? Mayhap it will prove a charm as weel. Mayhap it will make your bride see ye as a charming, noble knight." When he looked at her over his shoulder, she met his angry gaze calmly.

"I should beat you."

"I shouldnae try it."

"How can I be sure this thing carries no curse?"

"As I told ye, a curse comes back upon the sender three-fold. I believe I have enough trouble to deal with already. And I also told ye that I am no witch. Ye should be verra glad of that, m'laird, for, if I were and I were the vengeful sort, I would be weaving one for ye that would make Rona's look like child's play." Knowing her anger was escaping her control, Sophie strode away.

Alpin watched her leave, Nella quickly following her. He picked up the tiny leather bag strung on a black cord and sighed. As he held it, he could feel her hope, her prayers for his safety. Despite her anger and her hurt over what she saw as a gross betrayal, Sophie still wanted to save him, still wanted to help and protect him. He ached to grasp at that support with both hands and hold tight, but was determined to resist that temptation. Sophie deserved better than he had to offer.

Looking at his bride as she pulled herself back up into her seat, he supposed she deserved better as well, but he would not stop the marriage. Margaret had no care for him. She feared him and would undoubtedly be terrified by the changes that would come, but she would not be saddened by them. Margaret would not be hurt when he did not give her a child or come to her bed. There was a chance he might even escape truly consummating the marriage, and that weighed heavily in her favor. It was a dismal future laid out before him, but he had never held any hope for another, better fate, and he would not condemn a sweet sprite like Sophie to share it with him.

Recalling her parting words, he almost smiled. Mayhap not so sweet. She had strength, spirit, and a temper. Even when she was threatening to curse him, he knew she was perfect for him. Alpin considered the fact that he could not hold tight to her the hardest part of the curse to endure, and the cruelest.

"Who is that lass?" demanded Sir Peter.

The first words that came to mind were *my love* and Alpin was stunned, so stunned it took him a moment to compose himself before he could reply with any calm. "She is who she said she is—Lady Sophie Hay."

"Nay, I mean what is she to ye?"

"Ah. Just another in a verra long line of people trying their hand at curing me of my affliction."

"So she is a witch."

"Nay, a healer."

"Then what is that she just gave ye?"

Alpin slowly placed the amulet around his neck. "Something she made to bring me luck in the coming battle."

"Then she is a witch."

"Many people, e'en the most godly, believe in charms for luck, sir. Lady Sophie is a healer, nay more."

Before the man could further argue the matter, Alpin drew him into a discussion concerning the upcoming battle. In some ways Sophie did practice what many would consider witchcraft, and those who feared such things were usually incapable of discerning the difference between good and bad sorcery. Alpin had the strong feeling she had other skills many would decry as sorcery, such as the sight, or some trick of knowing exactly what a person felt. One thing he was determined to do for her was shield her from the dangerous, superstitious fears of those like Sir Peter. It might even, in some small way, assuage the hurt he had inflicted. Or, he mused, he could allow himself to fall in the coming battle, ending her pain as well as his own. He sighed and forced himself to concentrate on the conversation. Fate would never allow him to escape his dark destiny so easily.

"That Lady Margaret is a worse coward than I, and that be saying a lot," muttered Nella as she sat before the fire in their bedchamber sewing a torn hem upon one of Sophie's gowns. "I wonder she hasnae washed her eyeballs right out of their holes with all the weeping she does."

Sophie lightly grunted in agreement, never moving from the window she looked out of, or taking her gaze from the activity in the bailey. For the three days Lady Margaret had been at Nochdaidh, the girl had done little more than cry, swoon, or cower. Not one thing Sophie had said or tried had calmed the girl. At times, Sophie had wondered what possessed her to try to help a woman who would soon lay claim to the man Sophie herself wanted so badly. She just could not abide being around all that self-pity and abject fear. There were enough dark, somber feelings thickening the air at Nochdaidh without Lady Margaret adding more by the bucketful. That very morning Sophie had finally given up on trying to help the girl.

"I tried to give the lass one of my amulets," said Nella, "but she just sobbed and crossed herself."

"Ah, aye. Despite the denials of everyone at Nochdaidh, as weel as our own, Lady Margaret is certain we are witches."

"Such a fool." Nella frowned at Sophie, set her mending down, and moved to stand beside her. "What is going on?"

"The laird prepares to ride away to battle. He must fight the men who have been pillaging Sir Peter's lands. A wedding gift, I suppose."

"I am sorry about that, m'lady," Nella said quietly.

"So am I, Nella." Sophie sighed. "My anger has faded, but my unhappiness lingers. I have come to understand that Alpin believes he is doing what is best for me by pushing me away."

" 'Tis best for ye to have your heart broken?"

"So Alpin believes. He think 'tis easier for me now than if I stay at his side whilst the curse devours his soul."

"Mayhap he is right," Nella whispered.

"Nay. I believe I have finally figured out how to break this curse. 'Tisnae amulets, rowan branches, or potions that will save him. At best they but slow the change from mon to beast."

"Then what *can* save him, m'lady?"

"Me." She smiled briefly at an astonished Nella. "Aye, 'tis me. I am the key to unlock the prison of pain Rona built."

"I dinnae understand."

"Rona's words were: 'Thus it shall remain until one steps from the shadows of pride, land, and wealth and does as his heart commands. Until all that should have been finally is.' Until MacCordy weds Galt, Nella. Until a MacCordy laird chooses love o'er profit." Sophie shrugged. "That wouldnae have to be me in particular, but I begin to feel that that is how it has come to be. Alpin cares for me, of that I have no doubt. Yet he turns from that and goes to Margaret, who will bring him land and wealth. He may do so for verra noble reasons, but 'tis still the wrong choice. Again. 'Tis Ciar and Rona all over again. I fear that the curse will ne'er be broken if Alpin does marry Margaret."

"Then ye must tell him. Wheesht, ye have wealth and land aplenty, too, if that is what the mon seeks."

Sophie shook her head. "He willnae heed me. Alpin denies there is a curse at work here, e'en though, deep in his heart, I think he kens the truth. He willnae allow me to enter what he sees as his private hell, to share in his damnation. And if I tell him of my wealth to make him choose me, will the fact that his heart welcomes that choice end the curse, or will it become just another choice of wealth and land? I dare not risk it, for I truly believe he must choose between wealth and love, turning away from one to embrace the other."

"It makes sense, yet how can a curse tell the difference? It has no thoughts or feelings."

"Something keeps it alive, year after year. Something keeps each MacCordy laird alive, keeps them breeding that heir to carry on the curse, and something keeps killing the love in the hearts of the men chosen by each daughter of Rona's bloodline. I dinnae understand how, just that this curse somehow keeps itself alive and will continue to do so unless Rona's demand is met."

"So what can ye do?"

"Weel, I have a wee bit more than a week to make Alpin love me enough to want me to stay."

"Aye. Unless, of course, he already loves ye and that is why he will make ye leave."

"That is the dilemma I face, aye. Not an easy knot to untangle."

Nella stared down into the bailey. "What is that strange cart? Do ye ken, it looks a wee bit like a coffin on wheels."

Chilled by the image, Sophie wrapped her arms around herself. " 'Tis what poor Alpin must shelter in if he cannae find and defeat the enemy ere the sun rises. 'Tis made of iron with holes at the bottom to let in the air and some light, yet keep out the sun's rays. Once beyond the shadows, heavy cloaks arenae enough protection any longer."

"Odd that none of the lairds simply walked out into the summer sun and let death take them. It would have freed them."

"I think the curse wouldnae allow it. It needs the heir. So a hint of hope, a sense of self-preservation, and the poor mon survives long enough to fulfill his sad destiny. Rona set her trap weel. Her magic was verra strong indeed."

"Yours be strong as weel, m'lady, but 'tis a good, kindly magic. Ye must try to have more faith in it."

"I think 'tis more important that Alpin have some faith in it. His surrender to a dark, sad fate runs deep, Nella, and I truly fear it will condemn us all."

"She watches ye," said Eric as Alpin mounted his horse. "I believe her anger has eased."

Alpin glanced up to see Sophie's pale face in the window of her bedchamber. "Then I shall have to think of something to fire it again."

Eric cursed softly. "Alpin, that beautiful lass cares for ye. Why dinnae ye—"

"Nay," Alpin snapped, glaring at his friend. "Cease shoving temptation beneath my nose. Look ye," he pointed at the iron cart as it rolled by, "I must carry my coffin about with me. 'Tis the rock I must crawl beneath if the sun rises whilst I am still afield. I go now to kill men because the father of my bride wishes them dead. And we both ken how I will revel in the slaughter," he added in a low, cold voice. "The scents of blood, fear, and death rouse the beast within me. I breathe them in as if they are the sweetest of flowers. It will take all my will nay to feast upon the enemy like the demon all think me to be.

"I can hear your heart beat, Eric," he continued. "I can hear the blood move within your veins." He nodded toward a young man several yards away. "Thomas had a woman recently. Dugald has dressed too warmly and begins to sweat. Henry's wife has her woman's time," he nodded toward a couple embracing by the wall, "but he bedded her anyway."

"So ye have gained a sharp ear and a keen nose."

"I have grown closer to the wolf than the mon, Eric. I have resisted marriage longer than any MacCordy laird, but duty beckons. The bargain my father made must be honored. And despite my plan to seed no woman, to breed no child, I am nay longer sure I can defeat my fate so easily. As the wedding draws nigh, I feel something stirring within me that can only be called an urge to mate. 'Tis as if I am descending into a state of rut."

"Then mate with the woman we both ken ye really want."

Alpin shook his head. "There is a coward within me who trembles at the thought of Sophie watching me descend into madness, become a beast who needs caging or killing. There is also a strangely noble mon within me who cannae condemn her to watching her child step into monhood and begin the fall into this hell. I will wed Margaret." He took one last look at Sophie, then kicked his horse into a gallop, fleeing her and the friend who tried so hard to weaken his resolve.

Chapter Six

Alpin strode into his great hall, saw who waited there, and cursed. Now was not a good time to face his timid bride and her family. The battle had been fierce and bloody, the smell of it still upon him. He knew how such ferocity, such blood-letting, made him look. His people were accustomed, but his bride and her family were not. He had retained enough of his senses to wash his hands and face, but it was obviously not enough, not if the wide-eyed looks of his bride's family were any indication. As he approached the head table where most of them sat, Margaret gave out a small sob, her eyes seemed to roll back in her head, and she slipped from her chair in a swoon.

"Considering the fact that I spend a great deal of my time in battle," he drawled as he stared down at his unconscious bride, making no move to lift her up off the floor, "this could prove to be a problem."

He heard a faint rattle and knew Nella approached. The woman looked at the men, who did not move, then looked at the girl on the floor. Nella crouched, grasped Margaret under the arms, and looked at Alpin. Her eyes widened, but then she frowned.

"M'laird, did ye ken that your eyes look just like a wolf's?" she asked, glancing around in surprise when several people gasped.

Leave it to Nella to simply blurt out what everyone else pretended not to see, Alpin mused. He felt a tickle of amusement creep up through the bloodlust still thrumming in his veins. A smile touched his mouth, much to his amazement, but he knew it was a mistake the moment he did it. Several muttered curses cut through the silence and he saw a number of the MacLanes cross themselves. Nella's eyes widened even more, but she looked more curious than afraid.

"Your teeth have grown, too, havenae they?"

"Aye. 'Tis what happens when I have been in a battle."

"Ah, aye, the beastie comes out. All that killing, maiming, and blood spurting stirs him up, eh? Are ye going to sit in your chair, m'laird?"

A little startled by her abrupt change of subject, Alpin shook his head. To his utter astonishment, the small, bone-thin Nella easily lifted up the several stone heavier and half a foot taller Margaret. Nella set the woman in his chair with little care for any added bruises or concern for Margaret's appearance. His betrothed was sprawled in his chair like some insensate drunk.

And what was this talk of a beastie? he wondered. The moment he asked himself the question, he knew the answer. It was how Sophie had explained his affliction to Nella. Nella believed in the curse as strongly as Sophie did. Sophie had obviously told Nella that the curse had put a beast inside of him. It was a nice thought, far better than the truth. The truth was that the beast *was* him and he could not exorcise it. Soon, he suspected, he would not be able to control it, either.

"Your food and drink are in your bedchamber, m'laird," said the buxom maid Anne, pulling him from his dark thoughts.

"Good," he said. " 'Tis time I sought my solitude."

"Shall I—" began Anne.

"Nay."

Knowing she was offering him the use of her body, he wondered at his reluctance. It had been far too long since he had had a woman and his body was taut and needy. Anne had serviced him in the past when he had returned from a battle, so he knew she could endure the wildness in him at such times. Then he saw the glint of fear and disgust in the woman's eyes, visible beneath the arrogance and anticipation. Whatever her reasons were for offering herself, one of them was certainly not desire. Inwardly shaking his head, he headed for his bedchamber. He wanted only one woman anyway, and he could not have her. Not only did she probably not understand how to prevent a child from taking root, but he could not subject her to a bedding by the beast raging inside of him.

A bath awaited him and he took quick advantage of it, scrubbing the scent of death from his skin. Although he ached to find the strength to turn away from the meal set out for him, he could not. His hunger was too great and he feared what he might do if he did not slake it in some way. Alpin tore into the meat barely seared on either side, his speed in finishing it born of both need and revulsion. He poured himself some of his enriched wine and stood by the window, staring down into the torch-lit bailey. A little of the ferocity within him eased as he fed the craving that so disgusted and terrified him. When would enriched wine and raw meat cease to be enough? he wondered.

He tensed as he heard someone slip into his room. The fact that the scent he picked up was Sophie's did not ease his tension at all. This was a very bad time for her to come to his bedchamber. He listened to her take a few hesitant steps toward him, then stop. Slowly, he took a deep breath, closing his eyes as he savored her scent. She had bathed; her warm skin smelled of woman, with a hint of lavender. To him she smelled of laughter, of warm sun and wildflowers, of hope. He could almost hate her for that.

Another scent tantalized him and he grew so tense his muscles ached as he opened his eyes to stare blindly out of the window. Sophie smelled of desire. Alpin hastily finished his drink, but it satisfied only one hunger. There was another now raging inside of him, fed by the hint of feminine musk. He breathed it in, opening his mouth slightly to enhance his ability, and the blood began to pound in his veins.

"Go away, Sophie," he said. "'Tisnae a good time for ye to be near me."

It took Sophie a moment to realize he had spoken to her. From the minute she had entered the room to see him standing there wearing only a drying cloth wrapped around his lean hips, she had been spellbound. She had cautiously moved closer to him, her palms tingling with the need to touch that broad, strong back. He was so beautiful, he made her heart ache.

"I felt ye return," she said, taking another step toward him. "I wished to see that ye had come to no harm."

"I am still alive, if ye can call this living."

She sighed, but decided not to try to dispute his words this time. "I felt—"

"What? The beastie in me? The ferocity? The bloodlust? Or," he looked at her over his shoulder, "just the lust?"

Alpin realized his error the moment he set eyes upon her. Her hair was down, hanging in long, thick golden waves to her slender hips. She wore only a thin linen chemise, the delicate curves of her lithe body easy to see. Her wide eyes were fixed upon him, more green than blue. Sophie was all soft, womanly sunlight, and he craved every small inch of her.

Sophie shook her head. "I felt that ye needed me, but, mayhap, that was just vanity."

He turned to look at her more fully. "Nay, not vain. I *do* need ye, but I willnae allow myself to feed that hunger."

"Because of Lady Margaret?"

"Nay."

"Then why?" She forced herself not to reveal how his sudden move toward her startled her, knowing how easily he could read it as fear.

"Why?" He nearly snarled the word, standing so close to her he had to clench his hands into tight fists to keep himself from touching her. "Look at me. I am more beast than mon."

He did look quite feral, she mused, with his eyes more yellow than golden brown, and they had changed in that odd way again to look more like an animal's than a man's. His teeth had also changed a little, looking far more predatory. Subtle though the changes were, they were alarming, but not because she feared he could hurt her. She had seen such changes in him before, although not this clearly. The changes were proof, however, that nothing she had done so far had lessened the tight grip of the curse.

"The mon is still there, Alpin," she said quietly.

"Is he?" He strode to the table and picked up the plate that had held his meal. "Does a mon eat naught but meat, meat barely cooked, simply passed o'er the fire until it becomes as warm as a fresh kill?" He poured the blood that still pooled upon the dish into his tankard, then filled it with more wine. "Does a mon drink wine heartened with blood?" He took a long drink before setting the tankard down. "And the mix grows more heartened with each passing year. The craving grows stronger."

He walked toward her again. "And what mon, save the most bestial, takes such delight in battle? I have blood upon my hands, Sophie. I have washed them but I can still smell it. From the moment I first swung my sword this night, my bloodlust raged. The smell of blood and death were a heady perfume to me. I ken not how many men I killed, and I care not. I can kill as fiercely with my bare hands as with my sword. And, this night, I killed a mon with my teeth," he continued in a hoarse voice. "I fell upon a mon and tore his throat open with my teeth. For a moment, as his blood heated my mouth, I was filled with a savage hunger. I wanted to drink it all. It was sweet and the mon's fear made it taste even sweeter. Is that the act of a mon?"

It was a particularly gruesome tale, and a very bad sign, but she placed her hand upon his arm and quietly asked, "Was the mon unarmed? Was he offering his sword in surrender? Was he crying out for mercy?"

His gaze fixed upon that small, soft hand that touched his skin, Alpin shook his head. "Nay. His sword was about to take Eric's head from his shoulders. That doesnae matter," he began.

"It does. Aye, the manner in which ye killed the mon is worrisome, for it means the curse still holds ye firmly within its grasp. Yet ye had to kill him or he would have killed Eric. This mon was armed and your enemy. Any mon would have killed him. And none of what ye have said truly answers my question, for I have kenned what ye are from the verra beginning."

"The *why* is because ye are a virgin, and so ye cannae ken the ways to stop my seed from taking root and use them. The why is because I can smell your desire and it has the blood pounding so fiercely in my veins, I near shake with need. 'Twould be no gentle bedding I would be giving ye. Nay," he continued in a softer voice, "I want to sink myself deep into your heat, Sophie Hay. Sink deep and ride hard. That isnae the way to take a virgin." He started toward the door. "And 'tis wrong to take a lass's maidenhead when I cannae wed her."

"Where are ye going?" Sophie was not surprised to hear how husky her voice had become, for his words, his seductive tone of voice, had stirred her almost as strongly as the sight of his strong body so meagerly covered.

"To one who kens how to keep her womb clean. Anne may not desire me, but she is always willing to service me."

" 'Tis the wrong time for me to conceive," Sophie said,

desperate to stop him from going to another's bed. She would lose him to another soon enough.

His hand tightening on the latch of the door, Alpin hesitated. "How can ye be sure?"

"I am a healer, Alpin. There is also a potion or two I can drink." Something she had no intention of doing, but he did not need to know that. "And when was the last time The MacCordy bred a bastard, or e'en a second child?"

Alpin slowly turned to face her. "Never," he replied, feeling somewhat shaken by the realization.

"Of course not. For the curse to continue unthreatened, there can only be one heir. Each Galt woman has but one daughter. Or, as was shown by my mother and aunt, one birth producing a female or twin females. Thus the curse can continue in us as weel. If there was a brother, then the first-born son of The MacCordy could have been slain ere he bred an heir, thus ending the curse. E'en a bastard son could have done so. Mayhap e'en a girl child."

"Bairns can die," he said as he started to walk toward her. "Many do. Too many."

"When Rona cursed your ancestor, she changed the fate of The MacCordy and of the Galt women of her bloodline. The curse was upon the firstborn son, the legitimate heir, therefore ye couldnae die or that fate would be altered. Mayhap, if a Galt woman of the line had died young, another would have been born to satisfy the curse, but I dinnae think it e'er happened."

"Ye speak as if the curse is a living thing."

She shrugged. "After so long, it may be in some ways. 'Tis our fate, our destiny, and such things willnae be denied, unless I can find the key to unlock its grip upon our lives."

He reached out and slowly dragged his fingers through her hair. Closing his eyes, he could hear the tempo of her blood increase, could smell her desire return and begin to grow stronger. By making him see that there would be no child born of their union, she had cut the only real tether upon his control. He could have her now. He *had* to have her now. Alpin grasped the hem of her shift and swiftly pulled it off her.

It happened so quickly, Sophie had no time to cover herself before he picked her up in his arms and carried her to his bed. He set her down and tore off his only covering, staring at her body all the while with a fierce hunger that made her feel beautiful. For the moment or two he stood there looking at her, Sophie took the opportunity to have a good look at him. That only added to her need for him. He was glorious, all smooth skin and taut, sleek muscle. And rather impressively manly, she thought, her gaze fixed upon his erection. She felt the rise of a virginal unease and ruthlessly smothered it.

Sophie was shocked when he settled his long body on top of hers, but not by the fact that she held a naked man. The feel of his skin against her, the hard contours of his body fitting so well with her soft curves, had her trembling from the strength of her desire. The feel of his mouth against the pulse in her throat did not frighten her, not even when she felt the light touch of his teeth. It made her breath catch in her throat as her need for him swiftly increased. As she ran her hands over his broad back, savoring the feel of his warm skin, she wondered if all of the heated dreams she had had were the reason why her passion was rising so swiftly and fiercely.

Then she frowned and tensed slightly, realizing that she had forgotten to shield herself from whatever memories and emotions were trapped within his bed. She did not want other passions Alpin had stirred in the bed affecting what they felt now. Sophie began to try to shield herself, only to realize there was no need. The only person she could sense had used this bed was Alpin.

"Um, Alpin?" She studied him when he clasped her face in his long, elegant hands and began to touch hot, soft kisses to her cheeks. "Ye have done this before, havenae ye?"

He smiled against her forehead. "A time or two, aye." He kissed the corners of her beautiful eyes. "It was a need I tried to ignore, for I feared breeding a child. The few times I weakened I went to the woman, or took her elsewhere. I didnae want the scent of mating upon my bed, for it would torment me, making it harder for me to subdue my monly hungers." He thought of one place he had taken Anne, inwardly grimaced, then began to tease Sophie's full lips with soft kisses and gentle nips. "Once in the bed ye now sleep upon," he heard himself confess and wondered what had possessed him to do so.

"Weel, ye arenae the only one. I think there have been many matings in that bed." She opened her mouth, inviting the deep, passionate kiss she ached for. " 'Tis why Nella now sleeps in the bed and I use her pallet. The bed was, er, unsettling." She twined her arms around his neck, threaded the fingers of one hand into his thick hair, and tried to hold his mouth to hers. "Are we going to go elsewhere soon?"

"Nay." He slid his hand up her rib cage and over her small, perfect breast, then savored her gasp of pleasure as it warmed his mouth. "I want your scent here. I want the scent of our loving to penetrate so deep that it will be years ere it fades. When I am again alone, I want to be able to breathe deep of it and remember."

Sophie was glad he kissed her then, and not simply because she so desperately wanted him to. She had been about to ask him where he intended to put his wife. Then she forgot all about his marriage, the uncertain future, and the dark past. Sophie was aware only of the feel and taste of him, the touch of his hands and his mouth, and the need he stirred within her. She sensed that he practiced some restraint, but she had none.

When he finally joined their bodies, she was barely aware of the brief, stinging pain signaling the loss of her maidenhead. She was so immersed in the joy and pleasure of feeling his body joined to hers, that it was a moment or two before she realized he was not moving. Looking up at the man bracing himself over her, Sophie mused that she had never seen him look so feral, nor so beautiful and arousing.

"The pain?" he began, finding speech difficult, as his every sense was fixed upon the feel of her, her heat, her scent, and his own blinding need.

"Was quickly gone." She slid her hands down his back and stroked his taut buttocks, sighing with delight when he convulsively pushed deeper within her. "Oh, my, ye do feel good." Sophie wrapped her legs around him. "More, please."

He groaned and kissed her even as he began to move. Sophie opened herself up fully to the pleasure he gave her. Soon it was questionable as to which of them was fiercer in their passion. Then, she shattered, swept away to a place of such intense pleasure that she lost all awareness. Just as she began to recover, Alpin drove deep within her, crying out as his own release gripped him. To Sophie's delight and astonishment, the feel of his seed, of his intense pleasure, sent her racing back to the blinding heights of desire. When he collapsed in her arms, she held him close, and felt sanity slowly return to them both.

Sophie was a little frightened by how deeply she loved this man, then told herself not to be such a fool. There was no controlling the heart in such matters. At the moment, she could see no future in loving him. She would leave, alone and heartsore, he would marry Margaret, and they would all remain prisoners of the curse.

The thought of such a cold future made her hug him closer, and she kissed the top of his head. When he lifted his head and smiled at her, she smiled back and knew she would love him always, no matter what the future held. She would hold that love close and cherish it. Unlike so many of her ancestors, however, she would not wallow in grief over what she had lost. She would find joy in her memories and she would continue to fight the curse, to try to find a way to break it.

Sophie kissed him, felt him harden within her, and silently swore that she would turn her love for him, returned or not, into a strength. With that strength she would find a way to end the curse, to give him the full, natural life he deserved, even if it was not a life he would share with her. It was what her love demanded of her, the least she could do in return for the joy he gave her, no matter how briefly it lasted.

Chapter Seven

Sophie sat before the fire to brush dry her newly washed hair and wondered what she should do next. As far as she was concerned, last night had set her course for her, but she was not sure if Alpin felt the same. He had not turned cold toward her, but there had been no opportunity or time to even speak to him. The MacLanes and the coming wedding had taken up most of his attention. She had caught a look in his eyes now and again, one of such passion it had caused her blood to run hot, but that did not mean he intended to make her his lover. Last night could have been seen by Alpin as no more than a weakening of his control, something he would now fight to regain. Sophie found that possibility very painful, but also understood it. He sought to protect her.

What she needed to decide was whether or not she would go to him if he did not seek her out. That would require her to swallow a great deal of pride, perhaps even subject herself to a harsh rejection as Alpin sought and regained his control. Then again, time was swiftly running out for her to make him love her enough to choose her, to have enough faith in her to know she would never turn from him no matter how

dark the future. If she was right about the way the curse
could be broken, then such cowardly behavior as fearing
how he might hurt her or damage her pride was almost as
great a sin as Rona's. All of their futures could rest upon his
choice of bride and, if she allowed him to set her aside, that
choice would definitely be Margaret. If she failed, she would
have years to nurse her bruised heart and stung pride.

For one brief moment, she felt guilty. Margaret was his
betrothed bride and a betrothal was as sacred as a marriage.
She was not only trying to take Margaret's soon-to-be husband away from her, but, in the eyes of many, committing a
sin very close to adultery. Then she shook her head, telling
herself she had no cause for guilt concerning Margaret. The
woman did not want Alpin. She was doing as her father
commanded, but made her despair painfully clear to all. And
if there was a penance for giving Alpin all her love when
they were not married and might never marry, Sophie knew
she would pay it gladly.

A sound at the door made her heart skip with anticipation. Alpin was coming to her. She turned and gaped, the
sharp sting of disappointment swiftly pushed aside by a
wary fear. It was not Alpin but one of Sir Peter's men entering her room and hastily barring the door behind him. She
did not need to ask why he was there; the reason was clear to
see in his expression. It was a chillingly lustful look, the sort
of lust that he would satisfy whether she agreed to service
him or not. She had seen that look upon his face a few times,
but had foolishly thought he would never dare to act upon it.

"I suggest ye leave, Sir Ranald," she said, pleased with
the calm tone of her voice, for inside she was trembling.
"My maid will soon come and will be sure to set up a cry if
the door remains barred."

"That bone-thin bitch Nella?" Sir Ranald chuckled. "Nay,
I dinnae think so."

"What have ye done to Nella?" she demanded, suspicious
of his certainty that they would not soon be disturbed.

"Just a wee tap to send her to sleep. Sat her up against the wall outside your door. Anyone sees her, they will think she nodded off to sleep whilst guarding your door."

"She sleeps in here and all ken it."

"Just as they all ken ye are far more than the laird's healing woman, aye?"

"Dinnae be such an idiot." As he approached, she started to step away, wondering if she had any chance at all of reaching the door, unbarring it, and fleeing before he could grab her. "And if I am more than that, attacking me isnae verra wise. 'Tis certain ye have heard all that is said of Sir Alpin. Such a mon isnae a good one to insult or anger."

"Ach, he willnae do anything about a mon helping himself to a wee taste of a whore. And he cannae do too much to me, can he? I am cousin to the bride."

He lunged at her and Sophie darted out of the way. Several times she managed to elude his grasp, throwing everything she could get her hands on. It all barely made him stumble in his relentless pursuit. She managed to get to the door, felt a tiny flicker of hope as she began to lift the bar, only to have it painfully doused when he grabbed her by the hair and yanked her back.

Although she fought with all her strength, Sir Ranald soon had her pinned to the bed. The sound of her nightshift tearing sent a chill of panic racing through her veins. She had only enjoyed one night of passion in Alpin's arms. She could not allow this man to defile her, possibly damage her ability to feel desire ever again, or, worse, cause shame to cool Alpin's passion for her or hers for him. Sophie cursed Sir Ranald, desperately tried to break his hold on her, and screamed for Alpin in her mind.

Alpin sipped his wine and calmly watched Sir Peter talk. It was hard to conceal his contempt for the man. Sir Peter spoke of the vanquishing of his enemies as if he had done it all himself, even though all knew he had waited out the battle safe at Nochdaidh. The man was a coward willing to toss his daughter into the lair of the beast so that someone else would do his fighting for him.

"Alpin!"

He tensed and looked around, certain he had just heard Sophie call to him. A tickle of superstitious fear ran through him when he could see neither her nor Nella. No one else showed any sign of having heard her call, either.

"Alpin!"

It was in his head, he realized in shock. There was a touch of fear in the way his name was being cried out. Alpin did not know how Sophie got into his mind, but he felt every instinct he possessed, those of the man and those of the beast, come roaring to life. Something was wrong.

Sophie was in danger, he thought as he slowly stood up. He was certain of it. Then he saw that Sir Ranald was missing from the great hall. The man had often stirred Alpin's anger with the way he looked at Sophie. Alpin looked at the man who always sat with Sir Ranald, but that man refused to meet his gaze.

"Sophie," was all Alpin said as he ran out of the hall.

Eric had noticed the change start to come over Alpin, and, vaulting over the table, raced after him. He had no idea what had set Alpin's beast loose, but the way the man had said Sophie's name had sent a chill of alarm down Eric's spine. If some fool was hurting Sophie, Eric feared he was about to be faced with the awesome task of trying to stop his enraged laird from killing a man.

Alpin halted before the door of Sophie's bedchamber. He saw Nella slumped against the wall, but the sound of her heartbeat told him she was only unconcious, and he turned his attention back to the door. A cry of pain from within spurred him on. He slammed his foot into the door, twice, and heard the bar crack. Then he rammed his shoulder against the thick wood, breaking the door open so fiercely it crashed against the wall.

He scented Sophie's fear and the hot lust of the man pinning her to the bed. With a soft growl, he leapt toward the bed just as Sir Ranald looked to see what had caused the loud noise. The man screamed and tried to flee, but Alpin grabbed him by the throat and the crotch. He held the cursing, praying man over his head and then threw him against the wall.

A hand grabbed his arm and he easily shook it off. A small, still sane part of his mind recognized Eric's voice, but Alpin ignored his friend. He hoisted the now weeping Sir Ranald over his head again.

"Alpin, ye came in time."

That soft, husky voice calling his name cut right through Alpin's rage. The bloodlust still roared in his veins, however. He ached to kill this man who had touched Sophie, had hurt and frightened her. Yet, he could not do so in front of her. Still holding Ranald, Alpin walked out of the room to the head of the stairs and tossed the man into the crowd of MacLanes hurrying up the steps. He then returned to Sophie's bedchamber, walked to the bed, and reached for her.

Sophie did not hesitate. She flung herself into his arms, wrapping her arms about his neck and her legs about his waist, clinging to him like a small child. She sensed the fury and bloodlust which still pounded in his veins, but she felt only the comfort of his arms, the protection he offered her. As he walked out of her bedchamber, she caught sight of Nella and made a soft sound of distress.

"She lives. E'en now she wakes," Alpin said and continued on to his own bedchamber. "Eric will see to her care." He stepped into his room and barred the door behind him.

Eric helped a slowly rousing Nella to her feet, putting his arm around her to steady her. "Ye will be fine, lassie."

"Oh! My lady!" Nella cried, suddenly recalling who had attacked her and easily guessing why.

"The laird has her."

"Ah." Nella slumped against Eric, finding comfort in the burly strength of the man. " 'Tis a wonder, as I ne'er thought such words would cross my lips, but I am glad he has her." She squeaked in alarm, although she did not move, when Eric suddenly drew his sword and held it out to stop Sir Peter's advance on Alpin's bedchamber.

"He nearly killed my nephew!" snapped Sir Peter, but he made no further move toward Alpin's room.

"Ye are lucky the fool still breathes. He was after raping the Lady Sophie."

"So he tried to have a wee tussle with the laird's whore. 'Tisnae worth breaking near every bone in his body."

Eric felt Nella stiffen with outrage and tightened his grip on her. "Ye should try thinking ere ye speak, Sir Peter."

"Curse it, he shames my daughter, insults her by carrying on e'en whilst the wedding preparations are made." He took a step toward Alpin's room, only to stop and draw a sharp breath when Eric pressed the tip of his sword more firmly against his chest.

"If ye take another step, I will gut ye where ye stand. Ye will leave the laird and Lady Sophie alone, and, if ye are wise, ye will say naught. Your lass has made it verra clear she doesnae want this marriage, so I doubt she cares what the laird does as long as he doesnae come too close to her. Still, I suspect there will be a marriage done. E'en if the laird comes to his senses, ye can probably make some other arrangement to ensure he still fights your battles for ye." Eric met the man's glare calmly and watched him stalk away, back down the stairs. "A fool as weel as a coward," he muttered.

Nella looked up at Eric. "Did that bastard hurt my lady?"

"Nay," replied Eric. "Alpin reached her in time, although I cannae say how he kenned she needed help."

"There are a lot of things I dinnae understand about all of this, about the curse, e'en about some of the things Sophie can do. Dinnae think I e'er will." She looked around him, her eyes widening when she saw the battered condition of the door. "The laird did that?"

"Aye. The bloodlust was running high in him. If your lady hadnae spoken to him, I think he would have torn that fool Sir Ranald apart." He saw Nella frown in the direction of Alpin's bedchamber. "He willnae hurt her."

"I think I begin to believe that. Weel, at least that he willnae hurt her in body, but I think he will sorely bruise her heart." She sighed and looked back at Eric. "She loves him, ye ken."

"Aye, and I think he loves her. Unfortunately, that will probably ensure that he sends her away."

Nella nodded. "And thus doom us all."

"I thought we were all doomed anyway."

"My lady thinks she kens how to break the curse, but I shouldnae tell ye. There cannae be any help given. It has to be by free choice, unaided and undriven."

"I swear I will hold fast to what ye tell me," vowed Eric.

"She thinks she is the key to unlock the curse. She thinks he has to choose her o'er Margaret with her lands and her dowry."

Eric stared at Nella for a moment, then cursed. "Of course. 'Tis there to see in the last few lines of that bitch's curse. 'Tis so clear, I wonder that we didnae all see it the moment we heard it. Heart o'er gain. Sophie o'er Margaret. And ye are right. It must be *his* choice, one made without prodding or trickery. Wheesht, lass, ye have set a heavy burden upon my shoulders."

"Aye, 'tis a hard thing to ken and nay be able to act upon," Nella said.

"Exactly. I can see hope within our grasp, but I must stand silent. All I can do is pray that Alpin acts as he must to free us all."

Nella looked back at Alpin's door. "Pray that as he holds her close, he comes to need that verra much, indeed, so much that he decides to cast aside that noble plan to free her for her own sake." She shook her head. "Pray, for all our sakes, that your laird has one blinding moment of selfishness which lasts long enough to ensure there is nay turning back."

Alpin watched the firelight caress Sophie's skin as she stood before the fire and washed herself. Each time she dampened the rag in the bowl of water and ran it over her skin, he felt desire tauten his insides. She was so beautiful, so graceful, it made him ache. He was not blind to the bruises upon her skin, however, and had to fight back a strong urge to hunt Sir Ranald down and kill him.

That rage and bloodlust had still held him firmly in its grip when he had first brought her into his room. Alpin could vaguely recall stripping them both and climbing into his bed with her in his arms. He had held her while she had wept. At some point during that emotional storm, she had fallen asleep. Still holding her close, he, too, had dozed, waking when she had slipped from his arms. And, despite the fact that he wanted her back in his arms, he was thoroughly enjoying the view.

Sophie blushed when she dried herself, turned to go back to bed, and caught Alpin watching her. She hurried to the side of the bed, gasping with surprise when he suddenly moved, grabbed her, and pulled her into his arms. The man could move with astonishing speed, she thought, as he tucked the bedcovers over them both. She wrapped her arms around him as he nuzzled her neck.

"I can still smell him," Alpin muttered, then tightened his hold on her when she tried to move away. "Stay."

"But if the smell troubles you," she began even as she relaxed in his arms.

"It but restirs the urge to tear him apart."

"He didnae, er, finish."

"I ken it. I fear I would be able to smell that, too, and that would stir a rage I couldnae control."

"Oh. Do ye ken, I think having such a keen sense of smell must be a burden at times. Some of the scents wafting through the air arenae verra pleasing."

He smiled against her neck, then lightly nipped the life-giving vein he pressed his lips against. There was a dark part of him that hungered for a taste of what pulsed through that vein, but he did not fear it. He knew that, as long as he retained even the smallest scrap of sanity, he would not hurt Sophie. She was his sunlight, that bright warmth he so yearned to enjoy again, but which would only bring him death now. She was the flowers that no longer grew in his shadowed world, the laughter that so rarely echoed in the halls of Nochdaidh, and the hope they had all lost but yearned to regain. And, he realized, she could reach the man still inside of him even at the height of his bloodlust.

"I am sorry I wept all over ye," Sophie murmured. "'Tis odd, for, whilst that fool was attacking me, I was mostly furious. Then, ye came, and I was safe, yet I wept."

"He hurt you." Alpin raised himself up on one elbow and began to gently touch each bruise upon her silken skin. "And, 'tisnae how one acts after the danger has passed that matters. 'Tisnae unknown for men to collapse, trembling and terrified, after the battle is done. I heard ye call to me," he said quietly as he lightly kissed a bruise upon her throat. "In my mind I heard ye call my name."

"How wondrous strange. I did call your name—inside my head. Weel, our families have been bound together by Rona's curse for o'er four hundred years. Mayhap that has something to do with it." She threaded her fingers through his hair, holding him close as he kissed the bruises upon her breasts. "They dinnae hurt," she said when he frowned at a bruise as he traced its shape with his long fingers.

"The bastard left his mark upon your skin."

Sophie placed her hands on either side of his head, turned his face up to hers, and brushed a kiss over his mouth. "So I stink of him and am marked by him. There is a solution to that problem."

Alpin settled himself between her slim legs and gently nipped her chin. "And what would that be?"

"Ye could replace his scent with yours," she replied softly as she stroked his long legs with her feet. "Ye could put your own mark upon me."

"Such a clever lass. Ah, but it could take a wee bit of time and effort."

"Oh, I do hope so," she whispered against his mouth before kissing him.

Chapter Eight

It took every ounce of Alpin's will to leave Sophie while she still slept. Today was his wedding day, and knowing he could not hold her in his arms all night again made him want to crawl back into the bed and cling to her like some frightened child. He should make her leave, but he could not bring himself to say the words. Alpin feared the darkness in his world would be complete if he could not at least see her now and again. There would be no more lovemaking, however, he swore as he forced himself to walk out of his bedchamber. Today marked the end of their stolen idyll and he had to draw that line deeply and clearly.

Once in the great hall, he fixed his attention upon the final wedding preparations. Since the priest refused to enter the gates of Nochdaidh, they would have to go into the village. That had required Alpin to gain special permission to be married after sunset, claiming some difficulty with sensitive skin. Embarrassing, but it had worked. A heavy purse sent along with the request had helped. That money had undoubtedly helped the church dismiss the dark rumors about him as well. So, he mused as he looked at his pale, trembling bride, he was free to marry.

As the day dragged on, Alpin fought the urge to go to Sophie. His mood grew darker with every passing hour, every badly smothered sob of his distraught bride. Alpin did think it odd that Eric seemed to share his mood. It was not until they gathered in the bailey to begin the ride to the church that Alpin realized he had not seen even a fleeting glimpse of Sophie or Nella all day.

"Where is Sophie?" he asked Eric as the man rode up, leading the horse Alpin would ride to the church.

"Gone," Eric replied while Alpin swung himself up into the saddle.

"Gone? Gone where?"

"She and Nella left to return to their home a few hours ago. Lady Sophie said 'twas best, for ye would be tied to Lady Margaret by vows said before God and that was a line she didnae want to cross. Feared she might be tempted if she stayed here. I sent three of the lads with them. Couldnae let them travel alone."

"Nay, of course not," he muttered, blindly nudging his mount into following the others to the village.

Alpin was stunned. He had wanted Sophie to leave, had thought it for the best. Yet, now that she was gone, he felt more desolate than he ever had before. This was how it should be, yet it felt all wrong. He certainly did not feel noble. When a man gave up what he wanted for the greater good, for the benefit of someone else, should he not feel some pride in himself, some warmth in the knowledge that he had done the right thing? All he felt was cold; chilled to the very bone.

It made no sense, he thought as he blindly obeyed someone's command to kneel next to his weeping bride. Sophie had only been in his life for a month. Most of that time he had tried to avoid her or he had been yelling at her. How could the loss of one tiny, irritating woman make him feel so shattered inside?

He took his bride's sweaty, shaking hand in his and looked at her. She was desolate and terrified, yet he had barely spoken two words to her in the fortnight she had been at Nochdaidh. Sophie had seen him at his worst and had never faltered. Could he have wronged Sophie in a way by thinking her too weak to endure what might yet come?

"Sir Alpin?" called the priest. "Your vows? 'Tis time to speak your vows."

Alpin looked at the priest, then looked back at Margaret. "Nay," he said as he slowly stood up. "Not to this lass."

"This was agreed to with your father," yelled Sir Peter as he glared at Alpin. "Your sword arm for her dowry, the land, and the coin. Ye cannae simply say nay."

"Aye, I can. I suspect we can come to some agreement if ye feel a need for my sword arm. But not this way."

"But, the land, the wealth? Your father was eager for them."

"I dinnae want the land or the coin. I want," Alpin thought of Sophie, "smiles." He looked at Margaret, who had prostrated herself at the feet of the priest, kissing the hem of his robe as she muttered prayers of thanksgiving. "I want courage. I want someone who will stand beside me, nay cower or faint each time I enter the room. I want to be loved," he added softly, a hint of astonishment in his voice. "I intend to be a selfish bastard and go get what I want and hold fast to it."

"Thank God," said Eric. "She rode southeast. She and Nella refused to ride anything but those ponies, so they should be easy enough to catch if we ride hard."

Although he was curious as to why Eric looked so elated, Alpin decided now was not the time to discuss that. "I thought to leave ye here to make sure the priest will still be here and ready when I return."

"Nay, I ride with ye." Eric ordered a man named Duncan to watch the priest, then turned back to Alpin. "Ye will have to ride hard to get her, bring her back here, wed her, and get back within the walls of Nochdaidh ere the sun rises. Thought I would ride with Nella and leave the lads to follow at a slower pace."

"Nella, is it?" Alpin grinned when Eric blushed, then started out of the church, idly noting that his people looked uncommonly cheerful. "Nella who rattles because she wears so many amulets and charms? A bit timid."

"Aye," agreed Eric as he and Alpin mounted their horses, "but, if ye recall, 'twas timid, wee Nella who put herself between your sword point and her ladyship's heart that first day."

"Ah, so she did. Timid, but no coward." Alpin nudged his horse into an easy pace for, despite his sense of urgency, he had to go through the village with care.

"And, nay matter what happens, she is now, weel, accustomed to Nochdaidh. She will stay."

"Do ye think I am being too selfish?" Alpin asked quietly.

"Ah, m'laird, mayhap, but isnae every mon? But, 'tisnae some weak miss ye go after. She kens it all, e'en a lot of our dark history. Why dinnae ye just let her decide?"

Eric was right, Alpin thought, as they reached the edge of the village and kicked their mounts into a gallop. Sophie was a strong, clever woman who knew exactly what he was and what he could become. She even knew they would have to make some hard decisions concerning a child. It was time to place the decision in her small, capable hands.

"I am sorry, m'lady," Nella said as she sat next to Sophie near the fire the men had built.

"Aye, so am I." She glanced at the three young men from Nochdaidh who stood to the far side of the campsite deciding how they would divide up the watch. "At least this time we travel with some protection."

"True. 'Tis a comfort of sort." Nella sighed and idly

poked a stick into the fire. "I had hoped the laird would see the truth."

"Weel, what *we* understand to be the truth."

" 'Tis the truth. I ken it deep in my heart. The words at the end of that vile curse say it clear. And I believe the fact that 'twould be a Galt woman and a MacCordy mon would make the curative power of the match e'en stronger."

Sophie nodded. "It was verra hard to say naught, but that also had to be." She smiled slightly when she saw how carefully Nella watched her. "Dinnae fret o'er me. I may have hoped for something different, but I anticipated such an ending. And, aye, I suspect I shall trouble ye with some bad days, but, at the moment, I am numb. 'Tisnae just that I have lost the mon I love, but I fear I have lost all chance of ending Rona's curse. And mayhap my pain is already eased by the knowledge that I will still have his child to love."

"His what?!"

"Hush, Nella. His child," she whispered.

"Nay. How can ye tell so soon?"

"Trust me, Nella. I am certain. I felt it the moment the seed was planted. 'Tis odd, though, for Alpin was certain no MacCordy laird had e'er bred a bastard. Who can say? Mayhap the end of the curse will come through this child. Mayhap 'tis fate at work here."

"And mayhap your kinsmen willnae bring the roof down with their angry bellows?"

"Ah, there is that. Weel, we shall deal with that trouble when it presents itself. Best we get some sleep now," Sophie said as she moved to the rough bed of blankets arranged for her and Nella. "We didnae cover much distance this day and I should like to get an early start in the morning."

"Alpin?" Sophie heard herself say as she abruptly sat up.

"M'lady? Is something wrong?" asked her guard, Angus.

"A dream, I think."

Since Angus had chosen the first watch, Sophie knew she had only slept an hour or two. She looked around but saw no sign of Alpin. Yet she could not shake the strong feeling that he was near at hand. Just as she was deciding that she was letting false hope lead her, Alpin and Eric rode into the camp. She sat stunned as Alpin dismounted and walked to her bed to stand over her.

"What are ye doing here?" she asked. " 'Tis your wedding night."

"Nay, not yet," Alpin replied and held out his hand. "I have come to give ye a choice, Lady Sophie Hay."

"A choice?" she asked as she put her hand in his and let him tug her to her feet.

"Me and all the darkness that surrounds me, or freedom and the sunlight."

"What of Lady Margaret?"

"The last I saw of her, she was kissing the hem of the priest's robes and thanking God for saving her from an unholy union."

"Then I choose you," she said, so choked with emotion that her voice was barely above a whisper.

Alpin's only outward reaction was to nod and brush the back of his hand over her cheek. The look on his face, however, told Sophie he was deeply moved, as did the faint tremor in his hand. She knew she would get all the emotion she could handle later when they were alone.

There was little time for her to think about the big step she had just taken. She and Nella were told to collect their cloaks and mount the horses. The three young men from Nochdaidh were ordered to return at their own pace. Then they were racing over the countryside, Sophie clinging to Alpin and Nella to Eric. A little unsettled by how swiftly they moved through the night, she closed her eyes.

The promise of dawn was in the sky when they reined in before the tiny stone chapel in the village. Sophie was so unsteady when they dismounted, Alpin had to carry her into the church. She nearly laughed when he roused the people sleeping in the church with a lot of yelling and a few well-placed kicks. It became even harder to hide her growing amusement as a yawning priest married them, Alpin briefly kissed her, and she was hurried out of the church. The sight of the rapidly lightening sky sobered her quickly, however, and she said nothing as she was tossed into the saddle, Alpin mounted behind her, and they raced to the keep.

"Why is Nella crying?" Alpin asked the moment they were safely within the walls of the keep. "I had thought she had come to trust me, or, at least, nay fear me."

Sophie ached to tell him what she thought this marriage might accomplish, but bit back the words. She could be wrong. It would be cruel to convince him all would be well now, only to discover nothing had changed. One look at Nella's wide-eyed expression told her that her maid was thinking much the same.

"My arse hurts," Nella blurted out.

There was a moment of heavy silence. Sophie could feel that Eric and Alpin were struggling as hard as she was not to laugh. She finally croaked out the word "bath" and headed toward her bedchamber, Nella quickly following. If she understood Alpin's strangled words correctly, he was also going to bathe and wanted her to join him in his bedchamber in one hour. Just the thought of what would ensue when she joined him in an hour had Sophie's blood running so hot she doubted she would need the fire to heat her bathwater.

Alpin stared at the meal set out upon a table near the fire. Coward that he was, he had eaten the meat prepared for him and had quickly had his plate removed. Sophie might understand and accept him for what he was, but he still shied away from complete exposure. It was one of the things he had been reduced to that he himself found hard to bear.

Sensing her approach, he turned to face her as she entered the room. She looked beautiful in her thin, lace-trimmed nightshift, and he found her scent to be a heady perfume. She also looked delicate, soft, and innocent, and he felt doubt assail him. Surely it was wrong to drag such a warm, gentle soul into his world of shadow and blood?

"Ye cannae change your mind now," Sophie said as she moved to the table and helped herself to a honey-sweetened oatcake.

"Ye dinnae belong here, locked into the darkness," he said.

"I belong with ye, Alpin, be it in shadow or in sunlight so bright it makes our eyes hurt." She looked at the food on the table, then back at him. "Ye cannae eat any of this?"

"Nay. There is nay longer a taste to it for me, and the act of eating it only serves to stir up a strong need for the other."

"Do ye miss it?"

"Och, aye. I yearn to sit at a table weighted with food of all kinds and eat until I cannae move. I yearn to stand in the sunlight and nay fear the warmth of its light. I yearn to have people look at me without fear, without crossing themselves or making the sign to ward off evil. I yearn to see the flowers grow in the bailey."

Sophie moved to wrap her arms around his waist and rest her cheek against his chest. "Ye shall have those things again."

He gently gripped her by the chin and turned her face up to his. "Ye sound so sure of that."

"One of us has to be."

Alpin smiled faintly. "When I knelt beside the Lady Margaret, that undying hope of yours was one of the things I thought of. I may ne'er share it, but I wanted it. I thought of smiles, your smiles and your sweet laughter. I thought of how ye dinnae fear me, e'en when I am bellowing and ranting. And when the priest asked me to speak my vows, I looked at my trembling and weeping bride, and realized I couldnae say them to her. She was terrified of me and repulsed. If ye hadnae come into my life, I probably would have accepted that, for 'tis what I have become accustomed to. But ye gave me a thirst for more, Sophie. I suddenly kenned that I yearned to be loved," he added in a near whisper.

"Oh, ye are, Alpin." She hugged him tightly and rubbed her cheek against his chest. "I love ye."

He felt the warmth of those words flow through his veins. Holding her close, he rested his chin on the top of her head. He started to smile when, after a few moments of silence, she began to grow tense. His smile widened to a grin when she slipped her hand inside his robe and pinched his waist. It was probably a little unkind to tease her so, but he was sure that she knew exactly how he felt.

"Alpin," she muttered crossly.

"I love ye too, Sophie mine. Ye are the sun that warms the cold shadows of my prison." He frowned slightly when he felt a slight dampness seep between her cheek and his chest. "Are ye crying?"

" 'Tis just happiness, Alpin."

"Ah, I thought your arse might hurt." He laughed at her startled look, picked her up in his arms, and carried her to his bed.

"Time for the wedding night? Or, rather, dawn?" she asked with a smile as he set her down on the bed and shed his robe.

After tugging off her shift, he sprawled in her arms. "With ye in my bed, my wee wife, I think I could actually grow to like the dawn."

"What are ye doing awake?" Eric asked Nella as she joined him at the table in the great hall.

She cut herself a thick piece of bread. "Hungry. I shall get some rest after I eat." Nella cut a thick slice of cheese, set it on the bread, and stared at the food in her hand. "Do ye think it will work?"

"Ah, fretting about that, are ye?"

"Arenae ye?"

"Some, aye. It seems as if it ought to, but this trouble has plagued us for so long, I find hope a hard thing to grasp."

Nella sighed. "So do I. I have heard all the tales of the sad lives of the Galt women and, though it makes sense that this is the answer, it just seems too easy."

"Ye think there ought to be some spell done, herbs and smoke and magic words?"

"Aye. A ceremony of sorts, I suppose. Ah, weel, mayhap the marriage itself was all the ceremony needed."

"It has its own power, true enough. Weel, ye eat and then rest, lass. Ye will need your strength."

"Oh? Why?"

"Because if Sophie is right and this ends the curse, there will be a wild celebration. If it doesnae, if she is wrong, she will be needing a lot of comfort."

Chapter Nine

Alpin stretched, poured himself a tankard of cider, grabbed a couple of honey-sweetened oatcakes, and walked to the window to stare down into the bailey. He felt at peace for the first time in his life and it was a good feeling, one he savored and prayed would continue. A day and a night spent in the arms of his passionate little wife undoubtedly had something to do with that, he thought as he washed down the oatcake with a drink of cider and started to eat another one. He was loved and it soothed a lot of the pain he had suffered in his life. There were troubles ahead, but he no longer feared the future as much as he had.

As he finished his third oatcake and washed it down with the last of the cider, he realized there was a lot of activity in the bailey. It looked as if every resident of Nochdaidh were out there. He nearly gaped when he saw what he was sure were Eric and Nella dancing around like fools. It was a little late to still be celebrating his marriage, he thought as he turned to look at Sophie, thinking to rouse her to come and see what was happening.

The sight of her distracted him for a moment, even though

only her head was visible above the covers. She looked so young, sweet, and delicate as she slept, but he well knew the strength beneath that soft beauty. Her thick hair was splayed out over the pillow and coverlet, looking more golden than ever with the morning sun gilding its length.

His empty tankard slipped from his suddenly nerveless hand as Alpin realized what he had just done, what he was seeing. Alpin stared at the tankard as he accepted the wonder of having eaten oatcakes and drunk cider. The only hunger the act of eating had roused in him was one for more oatcakes and more cider. The sunlight was filling his room. He had seen all his people so clearly because they had been hopping and twirling about in the sunlight.

"Sophie," he called, realized his voice was little more than a soft croak, and cleared his throat. "Sophie!" he yelled.

When she just groaned and turned over, he ran to the side of the bed. He yanked the covers off her, grabbed her by the shoulders to pull her into a seated position, and shook her slightly. This time he was not finding her inability to wake quickly and be alert very endearing. Alpin knew he was in a precarious state of mind when he got a clear view of her lithe body and did not crawl back into bed with her, just snatched up her nightshift and yanked it over her head. He ignored her muttering as he dragged her over to the window.

"Look out there and tell me what ye see," he ordered.

Sophie struggled to do as he asked. As she slowly woke up, she realized Alpin was acting strangely, could feel his tense agitation. She frowned down into the bailey, wondering just what she was supposed to be looking at.

"Weel, I have to say that the people of Nochdaidh are some of the worst dancers I have e'er seen," she muttered and heard Alpin both laugh and curse. "And your mon Eric is the worst of all. He is leaping about in the sun like some sort of drunken—" Sophie's next words became locked in her throat. "Jesu, Alpin, the sun is shining on Nochdaidh," she whispered after a moment, then looked at him. "Did ye get hurt by it?" she asked worriedly as she looked him over.

Alpin sagged against the wall and put a shaking hand over his eyes. "Nay. I but sought to get ye to tell me whether I was dreaming or not." He reached out and yanked her into his arms. "The sun is shining o'er Nochdaidh, Sophie."

"Aye, and your people are hopping about like toads on hot sand," she murmured and held him tightly, feeling almost as unsteady, disbelieving, and elated as she sensed he was. A minute later, she jumped in surprise along with Alpin when the door to their bedchamber was flung open so hard it crashed into the wall.

"Alpin, the sun shines again!" yelled Eric, then grunted as Nella ran into the back of him.

Nella stepped around Eric. "Did ye see, m'lady? It worked! Praise God, it worked! I kenned ye were right." Her eyes slowly widened when she suddenly realized Alpin was naked. "Oh, my." She cursed when Eric clapped a hand over her eyes.

"For mercy's sake, Alpin, put some clothes on," Eric grumbled.

Even as Alpin moved to yank on some clothes, he eyed Sophie with a growing suspicion. "What worked, Sophie?"

"That ye chose her o'er the Lady Margaret," Nella replied and gave up trying to remove Eric's hand from her eyes.

"Sophie," Alpin pressed. "What plot or trick have ye been weaving?"

"No plot or trick, Alpin," she replied, then sighed. "I was fair certain I had puzzled out the key to unlocking the curse." She repeated the last lines of Rona's curse. "Do ye see? 'Twas right there, right before our eyes."

"And ye didnae think I ought to be told about what ye had learned?"

"Nay learned, Alpin, only suspected. It had to be your free choice, and I feared that if I told ye about it, the choice might not be so verra free. I also feared I might be wrong, and, if I convinced ye that I had found the answer only to have naught change, it would be cruel."

Alpin stared at her for a moment, then yanked her into his arms and heartily kissed her before striding out of the room. Sophie grabbed his shirt, yanked it on over her nightshift, and hurried after him. When she, Nella, and Eric reached him, Alpin stood unmoving, staring at the doors leading outside with his hands clenched tightly at his sides. Sophie stepped closer and took one of his hands in hers.

"The last time the sun's light touched me, it nearly killed me," Alpin said quietly.

"I dinnae think it will this time, my love," Sophie said, then drawled, "We will pull ye back inside if ye start smoldering."

"Wretch," he murmured, then, taking a deep breath and keeping a firm grip upon Sophie's hand, he strode outside.

Sophie stayed close by his side as he went down the steps and cautiously moved out into the bailey. She stood quietly, feeling his tension and fear fade as his exaltation grew. His grip on her hand grew tight enough to be a little painful and she looked at him. His face was turned up to the sun, his eyes closed, and tears seeped from beneath his eyelids. Sophie moved to hug him, pressing closer when he wrapped his arms around her and rested his cheek against the top of her head.

"I fear to believe it," he said as he fought to compose himself, since nearly all of the people of Nochdaidh were there watching him.

"Weel, how do ye feel?"

"I think I might actually be feeling something that has long been missing from Nochdaidh—hope."

"Trouble, m'laird," said Eric, moving to stand beside Alpin.

Looking at the crowd of villagers rushing in through the gates carrying torches and crude weapons, Alpin drawled,

"Mayhap I spoke too soon." He kept his arm around Sophie's shoulders as she turned to face the crowd.

The embarrassment Sophie felt over being seen so strangely attired by so many people faded quickly as she realized what had brought the villagers to Nochdaidh. Several smiles and small waves from a number of the women in the crowd told Sophie she would have allies if she chose her words carefully. The confusion that had beset so many of the crowd as they realized Nochdaidh was no longer shrouded in shadow and the laird was standing before them looking nothing like a demon would also aid her.

"This is my fault," she told Alpin. "I neglected to solve poor Donald's murder. I shall see to this."

"Shall ye now?"

He had to bite back a grin as she stood straighter and frowned at the villagers. She wore only his loosely laced shirt over her nightshift, her feet were bare, and her hair was hanging loose and obviously unbrushed. Her appearance seemed to have taken some of the fight out of the mob, who were already confused by the sunlight warming the bailey, so he decided to let her rule for a while. She knew more about the incident than he did, and all his men were subtly moving into a defensive position around the crowd, ready to act if the mood grew dangerous again.

"I suspect ye havenae come to congratulate me on my wedding," she said, crossing her arms over her chest.

"M'lady, we have come seeking justice," said Ian the butcher as he stepped to the fore of the crowd. "The killer of my son must pay."

"Did I talk to the wind that day? I believe I said the laird had naught to do with it."

"If ye will pardon me saying so, 'tis clear ye are under the mon's power. Who else could have murdered my lad? He had no enemies. We cannae find a single mon who disliked him."

"Then he will be kindly remembered, and that should comfort ye. But what about a woman?"

"My lad was true to his wife and, ere he wed her, he was a lad of strong morals. And he was a big, strong lad. What lass could kill him?"

Sophie shook her head. "One cutting his throat as he slept, just as I told ye was done. Aye, and one of those strikes upon his head may have come first to make sure he didnae wake whilst he was being murdered."

"But, he wasnae one to play with the lasses," Master Ian protested.

Although Gemma felt no guilt over her crime, Sophie sensed that the woman was afraid and her rage had not been satisfied with the spilling of poor Donald's blood. That was the woman's weak point and Sophie prepared herself to strike at it hard. "That doesnae mean there was no lass who wanted him to play." She sighed and shook her head. "A vain woman he turned aside, mayhap? Some woman who could-nae accept that he, or any mon, could resist her charms. Or that Donald would resist her allure to hold fast to his sweet, loving, beautiful wife—"

"Who couldnae satisfy any mon!" Gemma yelled, then paled as she realized what she had done.

Sophie could not believe the woman had broken so quickly, then stepped behind Alpin as chaos ruled. Only the quick, occasionally rough intervention of Alpin's men kept Gemma from paying for her crime at the hands of the mob. As she was dragged off to the dungeon to await judgment, she screamed out enough confirmation of her guilt to hang her. Sophie slowly approached a desolate Master Ian, noting out of the corner of her eye a plump widow of mature years who was having difficulty resisting the urge to do the same. Master Ian would not be alone for long.

"I am verra sorry, Master Ian," she said, patting his arm. "Did ye love her then?"

He shook his head. "Loneliness and lust, m'lady. The downfall of many a mon, I suspect. Only, my weakness cost my lad his life."

"Nay, Master Ian, ne'er think that. Ye did no wrong, nor did your son. The guilt is hers alone." She leaned closer to him and cast a pointed glance toward the widow tentatively edging closer. "Learn from your weakness if ye must. I think the lesson might be that a good cure for loneliness isnae always to be found in the young or the bonny." She squeaked with surprise when Alpin suddenly grasped her by the arm and pulled her back to his side. "I was comforting the poor mon."

"Ye were matchmaking," he murmured, but frowned out the gates as a troop of horsemen came riding into view. "A busy day."

Sophie noticed that the villagers quickly slipped behind the men of Nochdaidh, then she looked at the approaching men and softly groaned. She should have taken time during the long, lusty night she and Alpin had just spent together to tell him a few of the truths she had kept to herself. Recognizing the four young men leading about a dozen others into Nochdaidh, she knew a lot of those truths were about to be revealed.

"Ye ken who these people are?" asked Alpin, feeling Sophie tense as the four handsome young men leading the others dismounted but a yard from them and eyed Sophie with a mixture of annoyance, shock, and amusement.

"My brothers," she said and pointed to each as she introduced them. "Sir Adrian, Sir Robert, Sir Gilbert, and Sir Neil." She took a steadying breath, knowing things could become a little chaotic, and took Alpin's hand in hers. "This is my husband, Sir Alpin MacCordy, laird of Nochdaidh." She winced when they all stared at her for a moment, then all cursed.

"Ye married this mon?" demanded her brother Adrian. "Do ye ken the tales we have heard about him?"

"Aye," Sophie replied. "He lives in shadows, he drinks blood, he is a demon, he can change into a beast, and other such things."

"Ye left without a word—"

"I left a note."

Adrian ignored her and continued, "And Old Steven was sure that ye had been abducted. He had the men of Werstane searching and sent us word. We have spent weeks in the saddle looking for ye, going to Dobharach and e'en Gurby, then back to Werstane where we heard a chilling legend that made us think ye might be fool enough to come here." He put his hands on his hips and scowled at her. "And we were right."

"I had a plan," she ignored the groans of Nella and her brothers, "to solve our troubles. Weel, my possible future troubles. 'Twas no legend, Adrian. Ye see, our ancestor—" She gasped when Alpin suddenly clamped a hand over her mouth.

Although shocked and wondering just how many secrets his wife had, Alpin kept enough of his wits about him to stop her tale. A bailey crowded with curious and avidly listening people was not the place to start speaking of magic, witches, and curses. It would be too easy for people to start thinking Sophie was a witch as well.

"I think we'd best go inside," he said. "Eric, is there room for everyone?"

"Aye," Eric replied. "The MacLanes left yesterday."

Sophie grabbed Nella's hand and hurried to her room to get dressed. By the time she joined the men in the great hall, however, she knew by the look upon Alpin's face that she was too late to soften the shock of some revelations. She grimaced and took her seat at his side.

"I believe there are a few things ye neglected to tell me, wife," Alpin drawled.

"Weel, mayhap one or two wee things," she murmured.

"Wee things like Dobharach, Werstane, and Gurby—your lands? Or that ye have enough money to build a gilded cathedral? Or that ye have enough men to raise a small army? Ah, and let us not forget the eight brothers."

" 'Tis all that bounty which made us fear she had been

abducted," said Adrian. "She is a rich prize. Of course, since she lied to ye—"

"I didnae lie," protested Sophie. "I just didnae tell him everything." She waited a moment for the men to stop rolling their eyes and muttering insults about a woman's trickery, then proceeded to tell them all about Rona's curse and how she had been determined to find a way to end it. "And, so," she put her hand on Alpin's, relieved when he turned his hand to clasp hers, "I couldnae tell the truth or he may ne'er have made the choice, or would have made it for all the wrong reasons. If I was to be the choice o'er wealth and land, then he couldnae ken that I had any." She breathed a sigh of relief when Alpin lifted her hand to his mouth and kissed her knuckles.

Adrian shook his head. " 'Tis so difficult to believe, yet hard to argue against. Too much of the history of both families follow the paths set out by the curse." He looked at Alpin. "Do ye think the curse has truly been broken?"

"It would seem so. I think 'twill take more than one sunny day for me to feel certain, however."

Those words troubled Sophie for the rest of the day, even as she enjoyed the company of her brothers. Even the pleasure of watching Alpin eat a normal meal, openly savoring each bite like a child given a sweet, did not fully ease her growing tension. It was not until she eased into bed beside Alpin that she realized he had noticed her troubled mood. He did not immediately pull her into his arms, but turned on his side and watched her closely.

"Why do I get the feeling ye are keeping another secret?" he asked. "More lands? More wealth? More brothers?"

"Nay, I believe I have enough of each, dinnae ye?" she asked, giving him a weak smile.

"Aye, more than enough. So, what are ye hiding?"

Sophie sighed and stared down at the small ridge beneath the blanket made by her toes. "I am with child." She winced when she felt his whole body spasm with shock. "And, aye, I am sure, e'en though 'tis verra early in the game."

Alpin flopped onto his back and stared blindly up at the ceiling. "Ye said ye had potions ye could take."

Moving to sprawl on top of him, Sophie framed his face in her hands. "Do ye truly wish me to rid my body of our child?"

"Nay," he said quickly, his heart in his words, but then he grimaced. "But, the curse—"

"Is gone. Think, Alpin; I conceived ere ye chose me." She saw the glimmer of hope return to his eyes. "And I think ye also ken that I, er, feel things. I feel no taint in this child I carry. Have faith, Alpin."

He wrapped his arms around her and held her close. "I do have faith in ye. Ye will just have to have patience if I waver. After all, 'tisnae easy to forget four hundred and thirty-five years of darkness."

"The darkness is gone now. Ye chose love, Alpin, and drove the shadows away."

"Aye, I chose love." He tilted her face up to his. "And I shall teach our children the importance of all I have learned."

Sophie brushed a kiss over his lips. "And what would that be?"

"That a mon's real wealth isnae measured in lands, coin, or fighting men, but in the giving and receiving of a true and lasting love."

A Hell of a Time

Jackie Kessler

Acknowledgments

A zillion thanks to:
Heather Brewer (vampire author extraordinaire),
Caitlin Kittredge (where wolf? There wolf!),
Renee Barr (who, to date, has read everything I've
ever written, poor thing), and
Brett Kessler (always, forever).

Chapter One

"You really don't want to do this," I said to the woman be-hind me with the knife. Never mind that the blade was a cute thing that had popped out of a pen; the serrated edge felt pretty freaking un-cute against my throat.

"Shut up," she hissed, pulling my hair back to expose more of my neck. "This is all your fault."

"Mine?"

"You took it from me. You stole it from right under my nose."

"But I didn't," I said, trying to be the voice of reason with a lunatic who wanted to slice me open with a penknife. And before seven in the morning, no less. "I was ahead of you on line."

"It was mine! I've been dreaming about it. I've waited all week for this, saved up for it. And you ruined everything."

Her fist tightened in my hair, and my roots whimpered. I clenched my teeth, biting back a curse. All I'd wanted was to surprise Paul with a treat, and this was my thanks? Getting accosted in the store by someone who'd missed their morn-ing dose of sanity? Bless me, I was never, ever doing anything out of the goodness of my heart, ever again. Served me right; altruism wasn't exactly my strong suit.

Squeezed against her ample body, her knife at my throat, I said, "Lady, it's just a doughnut . . ."

"A marble-frosted doughnut," a voice oozed. "With sprinkles. *Mmmm.*"

Oh, crap.

My bravado melted like chocolate in the sun, and my heart careened in my chest. I didn't need to smell brimstone to recognize a demon of Gluttony—none of the other nefarious ones sound like flies having an orgy in a honey pot. But now that my mind was blaring "Demon! Demon! Demon!" at DEFCON 1, my senses couldn't help but hone in on the creature of Hunger: around the cloying sweetness of powdered sugar and the rich scent of coffee from the doughnut shop, I smelled hints of rotten eggs. Despite the fear turning my mouth sour and coating my tongue, I began to salivate. My stomach knotted, and all at once I wanted to stuff my face and run like fuck.

Maybe worst of all, I couldn't even let myself react to the Glutton's presence, because technically I shouldn't have been able to sense it—not even the woman it was trying to influence knew it was there. Just me, thanks to my connection to Hell.

Sometimes, being a former demon truly sucked.

"A *marble-frosted* doughnut!" the woman screamed in my ear. I flinched, then grunted when the knife bit into my neck. "With sprinkles!"

"And she took it from you." I heard the demon sigh mournfully. "You'll never feel its sweetness on your tongue, never feel its buttery deliciousness slide down your throat. All that pleasure, gone. All because of her."

Shit. With one of the evil goading her on, the woman might really slice me over a breakfast food she probably didn't even spell properly.

"You took it from me." She pressed the knife up until it

hit the bottom of my jaw. *Fuuuuuck*, that's sharp. If I swallowed, I'd have a second mouth. Right, this is me, not swallowing. The woman whispered in my ear, "Gone. All because of you."

Behind the counter, the clerk had her hands up in a placating "Don't Do Anything Bloody" gesture. "Ma'am, I'd be really happy to get you another doughnut."

"Hey, take mine," I said. "It's only a little dirty from getting dropped on the floor."

The woman snarled, "You'd have me eat *germs?*"

Great, gluttons were fussy eaters. Who knew? "I'm sure the five-second rule gets extended under extenuating circumstances . . ." The jab to my throat shut me up. Gleep.

"Why don't you let the lady go," the clerk said, "and show me which one you want? On the house?"

"I want the marble frosted. With sprinkles."

"Ma'am, the shipment we got this morning was light on that particular kind. But I've got chocolate frosted, chocolate glazed, chocolate cream—"

The woman bellowed, "Did I say I wanted chocolate? No. I want my marble-frosted doughnut, with sprinkles! I've saved up my points, and I've waited all week, and I'm not going to miss it because this skinny slut got here first!"

My eyes bugged. *Skinny?* That bitch!

"You should kill the slut," the demon suggested. "Show the doughnut vendor how serious you are."

Hooboy.

Crazy Lady was sweating, and I was unpleasantly close to her armpit. Maybe if we weren't having a heat wave in December, she'd be wearing a coat over her shirt and the odor wouldn't be so eye-watering. Then again, if we were having a proper New York City winter, I never would have burrowed out from under the covers to go on a doughnut run and wouldn't be in this situation. "I should kill you," she said to me, and I felt her spittle hit my ear like froth. "Show you just how serious I am."

"I have no doubt that you are dead serious." Okay, Jesse. Think. How do you get the knife away from her?

Crap, I had no idea. Four thousand years as a succubus had sort of made me dependent on magic for self-defense. Not so helpful now that I was a human with no magic other than a flaky ability to sometimes see auras. A human who would die very easily if Crazy Lady slit my throat. Mental note: learn karate.

"Ma'am," said the clerk, "please, put the knife down . . ."

"Not until I get my doughnut!"

"What's all the noise . . . oh. Oh, shit!" That from a pimply faced kid who came trouncing out of a back room, who now froze as he saw Crazy Lady and the knife. I felt the woman shift behind me, probably turning her head to see who'd arrived. And her hand gripping my hair loosened its hold, just a little.

Opportunity, meet door.

I grabbed her knife hand across the wrist and yanked her arm away from my neck. Or tried to; tough to untangle yourself from a large attacker when you're just five-foot-four. At least I'd gotten the blade off of my skin, but her thick arm was still wrapped around me, now at mouth-level.

The Glutton roared: "Kill the bitch!"

Crazy Lady tried to force the knife back to my throat, but I did what any good bitch would do: I chomped down on her forearm. Hard.

She let out a whopper of a shriek and released my hair. Bracing against her arm, I stomped on her foot: one-hundred-ten pounds of pissed off (and slightly terrified) female compressed into a three-inch heel. *Scrunch!*

The shriek tapered into a high-pitched wail, and she dropped the knife.

I spat her arm out of my mouth, then pivoted away from her and grabbed the weapon from the floor. I held it up in front of me, and never mind how badly my hands were shaking—I had the knife, and Crazy Lady was blubbering in a heap, moaning about her arm and getting a rabies shot. All was good, except for the salty, vaguely chickenish taste in my mouth. Maybe I was misremembering, but people had tasted better when I'd been a creature of the Pit.

Off to the left, the demon hissed.

Shit. Amendment: all was good, except for the evil entity squatting near the woman. Biting my lip, I kept my gaze on Crazy Lady and forced myself to ignore the quivering mass of demon that I wasn't supposed to see. See no evil, fear no evil . . .

Oh, screw that. I'd been evil long enough to know there was plenty to fear.

"Wow. That was so cool!"

Glancing over my shoulder, I saw the female clerk punching numbers on her cell phone—the police, I assumed—and the pimply faced kid staring at me like he was in love. Aw, that was sweet. His eyes widened, and with a huge grin he said, "Hey—you're Jezebel!" He turned to the other clerk. "This is Jezebel, the stripper!"

Ah, the lovestruck young thing was an adoring fan. I flashed him a smile, but it didn't sit right on my face; my muscles didn't want to work properly. And my hands wouldn't stop shaking. Being afraid as a human wasn't nearly as much fun as it had been to cause fear as a demon.

The other doughnuteer held up a "Give Me A Second, Will You" finger and spoke crisply into her phone: A customer in her store went nuts, attacked another customer with a knife, no one's dead but could you please cart the woman away pronto?

Yeah, that was about the size of it, minus the demon. I turned back to face Crazy Lady, who was weeping, cradling her bitten arm and staring forlornly at the doughnuts behind the counter. Out of the corner of my eye, I watched the Glutton watch the woman. It could still try to influence her, even though it looked like all the fight had gotten zapped—or bitten—out of her. My jaw throbbed, and I tasted salt on my tongue. Blech.

"Cops're on the way," the female clerk said.

"Terrific." I most definitely didn't miss the irony that I'd nearly gotten killed while getting breakfast for my cop boyfriend, who was still in bed. Some days, I think God really loves to fuck with me.

"You want to press charges, ma'am?"

"No," I said, "that's okay. She's got enough troubles." And based on how the demon was watching her with hunger in its glowing eyes, she'd have a Hell of a lot more troubles once she died. But that wasn't my problem.

"Are you still dancing?" the pimply kid said.

"Yeah, at Spice."

"Over on Lex?"

"That's the one."

The female clerk said to him, "You go to strip clubs? Ew."

"What? They play the game there on the plasma screens."

"That's like saying you buy *Hustler* for the articles."

"*Playboy*. For the interviews."

As the two clerks bantered over the merits of skin mags, I peripherally watched a massive shape reach for the fallen marble-frosted doughnut. Yes, munch on the yummy cake, and leave me alone, there's a good demon. . . . It slobbered up the pastry, then smacked its lips and belched. Then it let out a contented sigh.

I leaned back against the counter and blew out a very relieved breath. Looked like Jesse Harris wasn't on the menu this morning. Yay, me.

That's when my body said, "Holy fuck in Heaven, you were nearly killed just now over a freaking *doughnut*," and my legs decided to stop working. I slid down to my haunches and focused on not hyperventilating.

"You're really a stripper?" the clerk asked me, leaning over the counter.

"Actually," I said from the floor, "I prefer 'exotic dancer.'"

"And your name's really Jezebel?"

"Stage name." Among other things.

Crazy Lady was rocking on the floor, babbling about the evils of processed foods. She still didn't see the Glutton spitting-distance from her, picking its fangs. And it didn't really notice me; to it, I was just another flesh puppet, one blissfully ignorant of the nefarious ones walking among the humans.

Thank Gehenna for small favors. Even if it couldn't claim me for Hell—I was many things, but a glutton wasn't one of them—it could still try to play mind games with me. And my nerves were too shot to try to match wits with a demon. All I wanted to do was get back to Paul's apartment, bury myself in blankets, and forget this morning happened. Well, after a quickie, anyway. (I had my priorities.)

The clerk cleared her throat, yanking me out of my daydream of me diving into bed with Paul there to catch me. "Ma'am, may I have the knife, please?"

"What? Oh, yeah." I slowly pulled myself up and forced myself to turn away from the woman sitting on the floor and the demon loitering near her—digesting, as far as I could tell. It still hadn't noticed me. Score one for the ex-succubus. Sliding the penknife to the clerk, I said, "Uh, so, can I get two doughnuts and coffees to go?"

"We're out of marble frosted."

"I'll live." Thankfully. "Give me two double chocolates."

The doughnuteers gave me my order for free, which turned out to be a box of a dozen, plus two ultrasaurus-sized steaming cups of liquid caffeine. Paul would be thrilled; he had a big appreciation for doughnuts and coffee. I thanked the clerks as I carefully balanced the cups and the box. No way was I staying to talk to the police; I didn't want to be introduced to the criminal justice system. Besides, my very own cop was waiting for me.

"Be seeing you," said the lovestruck young thing as I walked away. Aw. He really was a sweetie.

As I shied around Crazy Lady, the Glutton hiccoughed, then looked right at me. Eep.

Grinning around a mouthful of fangs, it said in my mind: *Be seeing you.* Then it disappeared in a cloud of sulfur.

Shit.

I really need a vacation.

Chapter Two

In my four thousand years as a succubus, I'd driven corrupt leaders to the edge of insanity with a touch of my hand. I'd driven hardened criminals to distraction with a throaty purr. I'd even driven hypocritical preachers from their flocks with a lick of my lips, all in the name of Lust. But as terrific as I'd been at my job, there was one driving thing that I'd sort of overlooked.

"Let me drive."

Paul flashed me a smile. "Sorry, hon. Not without a license."

Humph. If I didn't love him madly, his letter-of-the-law attitude would really get tiring. Downside of falling for an honest cop. Putting on my Bambi Eyes, I said, "Please?"

"Nope."

"You're not allowed to be immune to the magic word."

"Sure I am. Immunity comes with the badge."

Ooh, I could make him come with the badge. . . . A winning smile on my face, I reached over the gear shift to brush my fingers across his thigh. Trailing my hand up, I squeezed lightly. Even through the heavy fabric of his jeans, I felt his muscle tighten in response. Yum.

Voice thick, he said, "Feminine wiles won't work, Jess."

"No?" I stroked the bulge beneath his fly. "Feels like they're working."

"Unless you want me to crash the car, you should stop doing that."

"You should pull over."

"The sooner we get there, the sooner we have a bed to do it in."

"Bed? Who needs a bed?"

"And you're still not driving. Not until you have a license."

Crap.

"Come on," I said, dropping my hand into my lap. "It's just a laminated piece of paper that tells people who I am." More like who I was claiming to be, but only Paul knew that. Well, him and Caitlin Harris, but considering she was the witch who'd turned me into a human three months ago, that was sort of a given. Oh, and a handful of infernal entities and one angel also knew about my status on the mortal coil. And then there was the King of Hell.

Huh.

Right, check that: Paul was one of only a select few who knew the truth. To everyone else, I was, and had always been, Jesse Harris: twin sister of Caitlin, and the only exotic dancer in the known universe to hold a state ID. Caitlin had recently explained to me that she hadn't given me a license because she didn't drive. Me, I thought it was punishment for how I'd stolen her looks. (And her wallet.)

"Sorry, hon," Paul said, not looking at all sorry. Yummy, yes. Sorry? Not so much. "It's the law. You're not allowed to drive without a license. Period."

"Don't see why," I grumbled. Friggin' stupid human laws. At times, they made infernal rules seem Heavenly. "I can drive fine."

"Yeah? When's the last time you drove?"

"Not that long ago." I batted my eyelashes innocently. Hell knew I was telling the truth: I'd held the reins of many a stagecoach in my time during my stint with Belle Starr. Granted, this was going back more than two hundred years. But in the scheme of things (i.e., four thousand years), it was just yesterday.

"Drove a *car*," Paul said. "Specifically, an automatic."

"Well, if you're going to nitpick . . . never."

He grinned at me, a delicious lopsided grin that practically begged me to nibble his lips. Sweet Sin, he was so gorgeous, from his too-long sandy brown hair that curled around his ears and neck to his small sea-green eyes to the adorable bump on his nose—one day, he'd have to tell me how he'd broken it. And oh, his strong, kissable jaw . . . to say nothing of his neck, his shoulders, his chest, his . . .

My nipples hardened, and I tingled way down low. *Rrrr.* I blew out a slightly hot, slightly bothered breath. Paul Matthew Hamilton: a man who could turn his smile into foreplay. One of the many reasons I adored him.

In the midst of my adoration, he said, "Just sit back and relax, hon. We won't get to the Catskills for another two hours."

Feh. Some days, I really missed my demonic powers. My current talent to (sometimes) see auras was a piss in the ocean compared with the innate abilities of a fifth-level succubus. One little touch of infernal magic, and Paul would have been putty in my hands, eager to do whatever I wanted.

Ah, who was I kidding? I wouldn't have done that to Paul, even if I were still a succubus. I loved him. I'd never force him to do anything. Well, not counting the time I'd tricked him out of Hell. But that was different: I'd been on a rescue mission. When you're saving someone, you're allowed to use whatever you've got in your stash: manipulation, deception, a battle-axe, what have you. It's in the rulebook, under "Greater Good."

Crossing my arms, I pouted and tried to swing my leg, but even someone as short as me had trouble doing a petulant kick in a Honda Fit. Argh. "Not allowed to drive. Not allowed to give you a handjob. You sure know how to show a girl a good time."

"I promise, as soon as we get there, I'll show you a toe-curling good time."

Ooh. "Really?"

"Just me and you, hon."

"And chocolate?"

"All the better to nibble between your breasts."

I loved my man.

Okay, I could survive until we got to the cabin for our romantic, spur-of-the-moment weekend getaway. After I'd told Paul about what happened in the doughnut shop, he'd made some phone calls and rented us a private spot in the Northern Catskill Mountains, where we'd have a mini-vacation. Thanks to the unexpected December heat wave (relatively speaking; low seventies doesn't really impress someone who's had to do laps in the Lake of Fire), he was able to find something without too much trouble. Or maybe he'd called in a favor or two. However he'd done it, we now had a cabin for the weekend, and he and I both had Monday off of our respective jobs.

It was going to be a perfect vacation. Free of work-related stress. Free of New York City crowds and noise. Free of supernatural freakiness. And full of lots of sex.

Grinning as I thought of all the wicked things we'd be doing later today, I fiddled with the radio. Snatches of music filled the car as I sampled songs, seconds of refrains blending into one another until Paul said above the cacophony, "Hey, keep this one on."

I sat back, frowning over his selection. Mick Jagger's voice crooned out of the car's speakers as he sang that late at night when you're sleeping, poison ivy will come creeping all around. "The Coasters do it better," I said.

"The Rolling Stones can do no wrong. Mick Jagger's like a god."

"Sweetie, I've met plenty of gods in my time. And I say with authority that Mick Jagger is no god."

"Don't insult Sir Mick. Was a time when I wanted to be him when I grew up."

I chuckled, picturing Paul singing into a microphone. "And here I thought you were strictly MTV generation. Were you even a twinkle in your daddy's eye when they recorded this?"

"So I grew up with alternative and grunge. Doesn't mean I don't appreciate classic rock." Paul let out a happy sigh. "Me and my dad saw the Stones at Shea Stadium in 1989. Best concert. Ever."

"Spoken like someone born way after Woodstock."

"Heathen. Sir Mick's the best front man in the history of rock."

"Maybe," I allowed. "But he still sounds like Madonna after smoking five packs of cigarettes."

Paul pulled his gaze from the road to give me a look that was so over-the-deep-end solemn that it was hard for me to keep a straight face. "Jesse, I love you with all of my heart. But don't make me choose between you and my rock hero." Then he winked at me, and it was all I could do to not grab him by the hair and plant a soul-stirring kiss on his mouth.

Restraint *sans* bondage. I was proud of myself for broadening my horizons.

The song wound down, and I idly hoped that the next one would be something appropriate, like "Sympathy for the Devil." (Not that I actually trucked with the Nameless Evil, but still, it would have been neat.) Instead, Dion came on, lamenting about falling in love with "Runaround Sue." Oh well.

Paul started singing under his breath. I smiled as I listened; he had a good voice—deep, rich. Full of passion.

Passion, like when his hands roam my body and explore

every curve, like when his mouth works on my flesh and teases me and . . .

. . . and then, there was dampness. One of these days, I'd remember to wear a panty liner.

I crossed my legs and tried to ignore how my body was all set to go. No luck; stealing glances at my man behind the wheel—just look at the way he's moving his head to the music, at the blissful smile on his face as he sings—was enough to heat my blood, speed up my heartbeat. Enough to make me want him.

Oh, and how I wanted him. *Now*.

No. No sex until we get to the Catskills.

My body refused to listen to my voice of reason. My body wanted Paul, wanted to feel his hands on my breasts, feel his mouth on my . . .

Distraction. I needed a distraction. Biting my lip—yow, too hard—I glanced out of the window and watched a blur of trees as we zoomed by. Heading north on the Palisades Parkway wasn't nearly as exciting as, say, watching grass grow.

Or watching Paul's face as I licked him from root to tip . . .

Nipples—down, girls! Desperate to stop thinking like a sex-starved succubus, I said, "Let me drive."

"Does 'broken record' mean anything to you?"

"You know what a record is?"

"I even know what an eight-track is."

"Impressive. Come on, sweetie. I know my way around a car." Especially the backseat. How hard could it be to get behind the wheel?

"Doesn't matter," he insisted. "It's against the law."

"The spirit of the law is that only experienced drivers can drive. And if there's one thing I've got, it's experience."

"How do you figure that?"

"I've seduced racecar drivers. And car thieves."

"Sorry. Doesn't count."

"You know," I said primly, "it was more fun being a demon. You mortals have way too many restrictions."

I'd been hoping for a laugh, or at least a smile. But Paul's voice was strangely flat when he said, "*We* mortals. That includes you now."

"Only by a couple months."

"Doesn't matter. You have to do what the humans do. And that means following human laws."

"But not all humans follow those laws." If they did, Hell wouldn't be nearly as crowded as it was.

"This human does." He shot me a look, heavy with meaning. His eyes glistened like stardust on the ocean, and his jaw clenched. Angry—Paul was angry.

Shit. How did that happen? I'd wanted him to laugh. . . .

Looking back at the road, Paul said, "If you're serious about being part of my life, that means you have to follow the law too."

I blinked. What did he mean, *if* I was serious? "It's not like I'm asking you to make life more interesting by randomly shooting people just to see where the blood splatters."

"There's a happy picture."

Oops. Could I help it if I'd always be a demon at heart? "Sorry."

"I promise, if you get your learner's permit, I'll be happy to give you driving lessons. But I sure as hell am not going to let you drive for the first time on a major highway."

"This is New Jersey. No one would notice if I go too fast." I knew I'd drive fast. Speed turned me on.

"No."

I should have stopped. He was done playing; that was all but tattooed on his forehead. But being a passenger was boring. Demons might be used to waiting, but I wasn't a demon anymore. And I was learning that patience was a virtue I'd never hold. So I pushed. "Come on," I said. "I want to drive."

A pause, during which I thought that maybe Paul would

relent and let me sit on his lap and put my hands on the wheel. Then he said, "You know, Jess, it's not just about what you want, or what makes sense to you. Not anymore. There's other factors to consider." He slid a glance at me. "And other people."

Ouch.

"Demons aren't known for being thoughtful of other people," I said, backpedaling. "I've had lots of time to get used to being self-centered."

"Get unused to it. You're not a demon anymore."

Crap. This was not the smoothest beginning to our sinfully romantic weekend. I knew I still had a lot to learn about being in a (shudder) monogamous relationship, let alone about being human. But it was becoming very clear that at the rate I was going, the only driving I was going to do was drive away the man I loved. All because I was a selfish former nefarious entity.

Well then, I'd just have to stop being selfish. I could do that.

The song on the radio ended, and a commercial came on about how to get rid of weeds. "You're right, sorry," I said, trying to sound contrite, but it came out like I was constipated. Mental note: work on apologizing convincingly. "You drive."

"Fine."

He was still bent out of shape. I needed a peace offering, quick. If a handjob was out, then a blowjob wasn't even a possibility. Hmm . . . Fiddling with the radio, I hit a station playing a Madonna tune. "There you go," I said, smiling. "Sir Mick."

Paul laughed, a full-bellied sound that warmed my heart, and I knew all was right with the world. For now.

I planned on stretching out that "now" as long as I could. Settling back in the passenger seat, I decided that no matter what else happened this weekend, I absolutely would not make waves. No more complaining. No more whining about what I wanted. Paul and I would have a lovely time, filled with romance and sex and soulful looks—a weekend completely free of all things Evil. I'd make sure to help him think happy things about our future together, instead of constantly remind him about my infernal past.

No problem.

Chapter Three

There was absolutely nothing sinister about the cabin from the outside. It stood proudly in the sunlight, its logs a warm chestnut. Cheery yellow curtains framed a large window. Even the slope of the roof was inviting, turning the structure into a happy, welcoming retreat. Flowers decorated the landscape with joyful pinks, innocent whites, bright reds. Nothing marred the view of lush trees peppering the mountains. Nope, nothing sinister here.

Bummer.

Well, at least it was secluded, which automatically gave it a quiet sense of foreboding. To me, that was more of a homey touch than the curtains blowing happily in the breeze. A whiff of fear was the perfect potpourri.

No. Bad ex-succubus. Humans don't get a rush out of being afraid. Out of being alone.

Alone on thirty acres of land, with only a cabin, a hot tub (huzzah!), a small pond, and roughly a gazillion trees to keep me and Paul company. The place was an advertisement for mass murderers and pissed-off ghosts. I grinned. *Sweet.*

No! Come on, Jesse, stop thinking like that! You. Are. Not a succubus. Anymore. Scary things equals bad.

I sighed as I stepped out of Paul's car, my body cheering its newfound freedom. There had to be a happy medium between being human and appreciating the darker things in life. Rolling my shoulders to work out the kinks, I wondered if I could get away with going Goth at thirty. (Caitlin was thirty; therefore, so was I, no matter how many millennia I'd racked up when I was soul-free.) Or maybe I should become an adrenaline junkie.

"This," Paul said from behind me, "is going to be terrific." He clamped his hands onto my shoulders and started rubbing.

"Absolutely." I leaned back against his torso, my head on his chest, a smile already playing on my face from the feel of his fingers pressing into my skin. I inhaled deeply, taking in his scent over the smell of the mountain air and fresh-cut grass and flowers—the heady bouquet of gunmetal and musk that was all Paul. *Mmm.*

One of his hands left my shoulder to point at the lake off to the left. "Me and my dad used to go fishing in a pond like that one every summer, out in Cape Cod. I should've brought my pole."

How could I pass that up?

Grinning, I reached behind me and down to stroke the length of his fly. "You already did."

He took in a shuddering breath. "Not what I meant."

"I know." Stroke.

"You're being evil."

"Habit. Besides, you said we'd have a toe-curling good time when we got to the Catskills." More stroking, with a little squeeze. "Should we let the toe curling commence?"

"Well now." His hands slid down to my breasts, cupped them, flicked his thumbs over my nipples—which even now were trying to burst free of my bra and blouse. "What a fabulous idea."

"I try to get fabulous ideas at least once a day. . . ." My voice trailed off as he kissed my neck, my jaw, nibbled on my earlobe. Oh, sweet Sin, the way he makes me feel . . .

"Let's get the key," he murmured, "and go take a tour of the cabin."

"All three rooms?"

"One of them's the bedroom."

"You're on."

Hand in hand, we walked around to the front of the cabin. A metal lockbox was posted by the door; twenty-first century version of the key under the welcome mat. Paul pulled out a scrap of paper from his pocket, then started punching in numbers. When he pulled at the handle, the box didn't open.

"Huh." He reread the note, then typed in another code. Pulled. Still nothing. "Thing's stuck. Hang on a second. . . ."

As he fiddled with the box, I walked to the garden on the right. Roses, mostly, with only the occasional delphinium scattering white among the scarlet. Pretty. Then again, I've always had a fondness for red.

So why was my stomach knotting?

Had to be indigestion. We'd stopped for lunch at a rest stop, and it was questionable whether the byproducts used in the frankfurters had any real meat in them. Or maybe it was from eating too many doughnuts earlier. Sure—an overdose of caffeine, à la chocolate and coffee would be enough to turn anyone's stomach into a roiling mess.

But no matter how I rationalized it, staring at the bleeding reds of the roses was making my stomach cramp. Great. I'd wanted sinister, but instead I got squeamish. I was a seriously messed up former malefic entity. Maybe I needed a support group.

"Got it!"

I turned away from the garden to see Paul triumphantly displaying a metal key. "Good."

"You okay? You look pale."

"I'm fine," I lied, smiling brightly and fighting the urge to swallow a Midol. Ugh. Stupid roses. Maybe I'd pluck them all, stuff them into vases and watch them die over the weekend.

Paul returned the smile as he pushed open the front door. "Shall we?"

"Let's."

We paraded into a world of brown: wooden walls, wooden floors, wooden ceiling. Nice, if you were a termite. The tree-like feeling was sort of a given for a cabin in the mountains, but there was only one kind of wood I truly enjoyed, and Paul was sporting it. As we breezed through the large room, I noted the fireplace in the corner, complete with a small pile of logs and a wood hatchet leaning against the wall. My vision of floral genocide would work well with the room: the mantel would be a perfect spot for the roses, with the added bonus of their green leaves bringing out the forest-green sofa and loveseat. Very, very feng shui.

Look at that: human for only three months, and I was already getting the hang of home décor. If I ever decided to hang up my G-string, maybe there was a career for me as an interior decorator.

We nearly ran into the small bedroom. It was quite standard: bureau drawers, nightstands, banded rug on the floor . . . and a queen-size bed, complete with a patchwork quilt and two huge pillows. Grinning, I said, "Room service."

"What?"

"Here's the room. Time to get serviced." I practically threw Paul onto the bed, then launched myself on top of him, straddling his hips. Good bounce to the mattress; firm, but not too stiff. Promised to take a licking and keep on ticking. Then again, by the time Paul and I were done for the week-

end, the bed would be begging for mercy. And so would
Paul. Just the thought of his naked body got my juices flowing. *Growl*. I fumbled with his zipper.

"Aggressive," Paul chuckled. "I like."

"Sweetie, I'm going to make you love."

"Sweet love?"

"That too." With a wink, I pushed him down onto his
back. His head landed on one of the overstuffed pillows with
a soft *whumph*. I took a moment to enjoy how his eyes sparkled
like sunlight on the ocean, the way his mouth quirked into an
utterly scrumptious grin. "And now," I said, smiling as I
perched over him, "I'm going to slurp you up like an ice-cream
cone."

"You're lactose intolerant."

"Don't ruin the mood."

"Jeummm."

I assumed he said my name, but with my tongue in his
mouth, it was hard to tell. He laughed for a moment before
he opened wide. That's my guy.

Our kiss deepened, and I felt myself flush and my body
tighten with need. Just the touch of his lips on mine was
enough to bring my blood to boil, but now, as we kissed, and
kissed, the love between us stretched into something passionate, something hungry, and as our tongues danced I
imagined I could almost taste his soul.

My Paul.

His hands moved along my face, tracing the outline of my
jaw, my cheeks, his calloused fingers not at all rough on my
skin—moving back now, those thick fingers laced through
the dark curls of my hair, brushed them back as he pulled
away from my lips and stared deeply into my eyes. Smiled at
me like I was his everything.

Sweet Sin, I love him so much.

I sealed my mouth against his, bruised his lips with mine
as I kissed him again. His hands moved down my back, and
up, back down again to caress my ass. *Umm*ing into his

mouth, I broke the kiss to suck on his bottom lip, then trailed a path with my tongue down his chin, his jaw, his neck, the stubble there scraping against my flesh.

Softer, now: curls of chest hair tickled my nose as I kissed along the neckline of his T-shirt. His body shivered beneath mine, and the former succubus in me shivered in return from the way he reacted—not fear, no, never that between us, not fear but something just as intoxicating, just as addictive.

Desire.

Sliding back up, I bit the curve of his neck and shoulder—salty and meaty and so very sweet—then softened the sting with wet licks. Jesse Harris, vampire in training.

Paul's hands flowed around my hips, glided their way up my waist to trace the swells of my breasts. He squeezed once, twice, then pressed my mounds together and lifted his head to them, nuzzled them. Kissed them. Ripples of pleasure broke over me as he suckled me through my shirt, as he teased first one nipple and then the other with his mouth.

Maybe the sex had been more creative when I'd been a demon. But unholy Hell, it felt so much better as a mortal.

Around his wet kisses, Paul worked on the top button of my blouse, and then the next one, maddeningly slow. And then the next. Panting, I bit my lip as my body ached for him. I wanted him in me. *Now.* As if he sensed my growing frustration, he reached behind me in slow motion to unhook the clasp of my bra. My breasts peeked out as the material binding them loosened, the underwire pushing them up, eager for his mouth.

Grrr—he was taking his sweet time with the undressing process. Worse, he gently moved my hand away when I tried to help set my boobs free.

"Let me," I breathed. "I'm a professional stripper."

"Uh-uh. This weekend, I'm the one who's taking off your clothes."

"Paul—"

Then his mouth was on my exposed nipple, and my protest

died a cheerful death. Groaning, I arched back and closed my eyes, lost myself in the way he made my body hum.

Yes, love, oh bless me yes, I love your lips on me, your hands on me, I love the feel of you beneath me, on me . . .

He kissed his way up my chest, my neck, kissed his way to my ear, where he whispered, "Be right back."

Huh? I opened my eyes and asked, "Everything okay?"

"Just have to get the condoms out of my travel bag."

"Screw the condoms."

"Nope. I'm screwing you. But first a pit stop to the car to get my bag." He untangled himself from me and dashed out of the room, his erection leading the way.

Argh.

I flumped down onto the bed, my body already missing his touch. Figured that the man I'd fallen in love with was disgustingly sensible. Mental note: find alternative method of birth control . . .

Evil.

. . . ideally something less latexy . . .

Evil thing in my place.

Um, what?

Blinking, I propped myself up on my elbows and looked around. I could have sworn I'd just heard a voice. And not one of those funky phantom background voices I sometimes hear on the phone or catch as audible flotsam in the City. A real voice, like someone had whispered something right in my ear . . .

Except, of course, there was no one in the general vicinity except me and Paul.

Huh.

I nibbled my lip, idly wishing I still had my shieldstone against evil: a spiffy necklace that I'd, cough, borrowed from Caitlin when I'd first become human and had to hide from my infernal brethren. Then I rolled my eyes. I was psyching myself out. Even though I was just human, I could still smell a demon's presence.

And if it were close enough to mentally whisper sour nothings, it would be close enough for me to see it.

Glancing around the bedroom again, looking for signs of anything nefarious—glowing red eyes, or inhumanly muscled men clad in cheesy gym shorts—I saw only the bureau, the nightstands on either side of the bed, a door in the far corner that was probably a closet, and a large window that let in a shining ray of sunlight.

On the windowsill, a creeper of ivy rested.

I stared at the leafy vine, wondered whether the cabin owner minded that the property was overgrown. Greenery was supposed to be on the outside; I was quite sure of that.

A chill blew up my spine, and I crossed my arms over my breasts, suddenly feeling exposed. Watched.

Riiight.

I shook my head and let out a laugh. Big, bad former malefic entity daunted by a plant; story at eleven.

See, this was why I needed a vacation in the first place. I was so used to paranormal crap interfering with my life that I started to look for the bogeymen in the shadows. And I knew from experience that bogeymen preferred dark alleys to solitary cabins in the mountains. (Trolls were all about the mountains. And they didn't venture out in the daytime.)

As the last of my chuckles faded, Paul walked back into the bedroom. Huzzah—on with the sexin'! I posed on the bed, my boobs awaiting his attention, not to mention the rest of my body. But when he didn't throw himself on me, I frowned. Belatedly, I noticed the set of his mouth, the crinkle of his brow. "Paul? What is it?"

He sighed. "We have a problem."

"What's wrong? Where're the condoms?"

"And that would be the problem."

"They're not in your travel bag thingie?"

He sat down hard on the bed, raked his fingers through his hair. "No. Damn it! I know we had a few left. Where the hell are they?"

"Don't know. Maybe we used them all back home. But that doesn't mean we can't have fun right now." I stroked his crotch, and he let out a sound caught between a gasp and a groan. Leaning against him, I purred, "I believe I mentioned slurping you like an ice-cream cone." I unfastened the button of his jeans.

"Or," he said, his breath hitching, "we can hop into the car right now, get supplies. Then come back and go at it like rabbits."

I blinked. Was he really saying no to a blowjob? Guys could *do* that? "But . . . this is for you."

"Hon, this weekend is for both of us. Come on," he said, gently taking my hand off of his fly, "we'll be there and back in no time."

"Who needs condoms? I'm happy to go with the rhythm method."

"Uh-uh. Rhythm has a way of turning into a nine-month baking project." He pressed my hand to his mouth, kissed it. "I'd sooner take a chance on the prayer method."

Gah! "Them's fighting words."

"You've never had to go through a pregnancy scare."

"You were pregnant?"

"Cute." His eyes darkened, and some of the playfulness left his face. "This was back in college. She got her period and all, but until we knew for sure, those were the longest days of my life."

I assumed the "she" was his ex-fiancée, but I didn't ask to confirm. His past lovers didn't matter to me. Words to live by . . . especially since I fervently hoped the same applied to him regarding my miles-long list of former clients. A succubus racked up a lot of belt notches in four thousand years. I said, "Do you know how unlikely it is for you to knock me up the one time we have sex without protection?"

"I'd rather not tempt fate. Besides . . ." He leaned me back against the bed, and before I knew it his hand was down my pants and under my panties, his fingers brushing against my clit.

Ahhh . . .!

"I'll make it worth the wait," he said, his voice husky with promise. "A quick run to the store for supplies. Then back to bed." The brushing turned to stroking, and my eyelids fluttered as small shocks tingled down my thighs and over my belly. "What do you think?"

Think? Who could think when they were getting fingered? My throat tight, I said, "You can be very persuasive."

"I learned from the best."

"Flatterer. Ooh!" That last as he reached inside of me, crooked his finger and . . .

. . . and . . .

And he pulled out of me.

No! Come back!

Kissing my nose, he said, "More later. First, the store."

A long pause as I felt my orgasm slip away, going, going . . . gone. "Paul," I said, "you officially suck."

"Like I said. More later."

"You suck and you're evil."

"I learned that from the best too."

Aw. He was such a sweetie.

But as we left the bedroom, I thought I heard my own words echo in my mind.

You're evil.

Chapter Four

"That was marvelous," I purred, feeling content and warm and blissfully happy.

"Worth the wait?"

"Bless me, yes. It was the best I've ever had."

Paul grinned. "Better than chocolate?"

"Love, it was positively orgasmic."

Seated across from me at the small kitchen table, Paul chuckled. "Now *that's* a compliment. Keep it up, and I'll make fajitas every night."

"Mmm." I licked my lips slowly, let my lips get wet and shining. "Sounds good to me."

He leaned in close and kissed me, his tongue darting out to dance with mine. *Mmm*, again. A taste of cayenne and guacamole, and then Paul pulled away, leaving my lips tingling and lonely. "Glad you liked," he said. "But you're still on clean-up duty."

Crap.

"Chin up, camper." His eyes sparkled with mischief. Humph—he was enjoying this, the creep. "You know the rule: The one who cooks doesn't clean."

"But there's no dishwasher here." I was the epitome of reason. Can't wash dishes if there's no dishwasher.

"Sure there is." Paul took my hands in his, then lifted them up. "Right here. Two of them, in fact."

"Funny guy. Tell you what," I said, pulling his hands to my mouth and kissing his fingers, one by one. "If I'm going to get soaked to my elbows in soapy water . . ." A pause as I sucked on his index fingers, then I said, "How about first we go all the way and get in the hot tub?"

"You're stalling . . ."

"I'm horny."

"Hell of an argument." His voice gave way to a groan as I applied more suction and stroked the sensitive pad of his thumb. "Yeah, hot-tubbing sounds terrific. I'll just get into my suit."

I popped his finger out of my mouth. "You know we're alone for roughly a million miles, right?"

A flush of red stained his cheeks and ears, and he grinned sheepishly. "I know. But I don't care how remote the place is. Some things I can't do. I can't soak in a tub naked if it's outdoors."

Or indoors, I guessed. He was so adorable when he was embarrassed. I thought he was insane to be self-conscious about strutting around in his birthday suit, but I was the all-new, all-improved Jesse Harris: I would respect his decisions (even if they were stupid ones) about what to wear (or, one could hope, not wear), and I wouldn't force my worldview down his pants. So I just smiled and nodded like Paul wasn't completely off his rocker.

"I'll just be a minute," he said, standing, and I reluctantly let go of his hand. "Be right back."

"I'm going to go check out the tub," I called, watching him as he walked into the bedroom. The way that man filled out his jeans should be illegal. It was definitely, happily immoral. Sin poured into denim. Yum. Feeling a grin eat half my face, I headed to the front door, already unfastening the buttons on my blouse.

Crickets serenaded me as I stepped outside of the cabin, and pinpoints of white speckled the indigo sky like tiny spotlights. Paul had lit the tiki torches before dinner, and those flames danced along the path now, leading the way to the hot tub like super-size flambéed bread crumbs. My skin pebbled as I stripped off my shirt; it was still warm for the season, but the temperature had dropped by a good twenty degrees since we'd arrived. Perfect night for tubbing in the buff. (Or anything in the buff, as far as I was concerned.)

Dropping my blouse to the ground, I walked past the flower gardens, catching the scent of roses and something deeper, something not quite loam or grass. Humming "Poison Ivy" (the Coasters version; sorry, Sir Mick) under my breath, I popped the button of my jeans and pulled down the zipper. *She comes on like a rose . . .*

A tickle by my ankle, and gentle pressure.

Fucking mosquitoes. It's December in the mountains; the little flying leeches should be in Australia or Zimbabwe or—

My foot snagged on something, and with a yelp I fell forward, barely stopping from eating dirt by smacking my palms on the ground to absorb the impact. Ow. Screw me on Salvation Day, why was it that I could easily parade around in five-inch heels on a waxed floor, but I wiped out in sandals on grass?

I started to pick myself up, but something pressed against the back of my head and pushed, hard.

Forget about eating dirt—now I was breathing it. Earth clogged my nose, rubbed against my lips, my teeth. I didn't start to panic until I lifted my head up and something shoved me back down. Struggling to get up, I opened my mouth to shout for help. But instead I swallowed soil and grass as something ground against the back of my head like it was trying to squish a bug underfoot.

Someone was trying to kill me.

Over the sound of my heart galloping and my blood pounding in my ears, I heard leaves whistling in the nighttime wind, the sound like floral laughter.

Laughing at me.

With a snarl, I pushed up, hard. Something gave a little, and I gasped in a breath of grassy air. The back of my head wailed that it wasn't an eggshell, please don't fucking crack it, thank you very much. Before I could tell my head to shut up, something damp and ropey wrapped around my mouth. I bit down to try to tear through the gag, and someone yelped.

Hope I severed one of your fingers, you psycho! See how freaking scary you are with your hand gushing blood and your digit dangling like a limp pecker!

I sawed my teeth, tasted something like ranch dressing on my tongue. The yelp transformed into a shriek, and the rope dropped away from my mouth.

Ptui! I spat out a gob of thick, white liquid.

What the . . . ?

That sure as Sin wasn't blood. Pus, maybe? Great, did I just take a bite out of a Boston Strangler wannabe with some nasty infectious disease?

I lost a good second staring at the whatever-it-was before I remembered that someone was trying to kill me. Get the fuck into the cabin; analyze the white viscous loogie later.

Pushing myself to my knees, I drew in a breath to shout for Paul. And then my head was slammed down and my face hit the ground hard enough that sparkles burst behind my eyes.

Ooh, pretty.

I watched the sparkles dance in the growing darkness, leaving trails of red and purple in their wake. My body relaxed, and I felt myself floating. Nice. Peaceful. Staring at the pretty, pretty flashes of color, I realized that I wasn't breathing. The sparkles bloomed into splotches of color like wildflowers.

It dawned on me that I really *should* be breathing, that not breathing was all sorts of bad. Humans need to breathe. I'm human now. Insert oxygen.

Shaking away the pretty sparkles, I forced myself to inhale. And wound up swallowing dirt. And then I started to choke.

Forget bad. This was pretty fucking terrible.

I struggled to turn my face away from the spongy ground, but all that did was push the soil into my mouth and nose. The sparkles burst into life again, more colorful than before, dancing hypnotically and telling me that all I had to do was watch them, and then all my troubles would float away.

A hint of laughter in the wind, like a whiff of flowers.

No. No freaking way was I going to just lie down and die. Especially not when someone else was getting off on it.

I reared back, trying to throw my attacker off of me, but no luck—whatever was pressing my head into the ground held me tighter than a vice. Plan B, I needed a Plan B. . . .

Screw the plan; my body was on autopilot and well into Survive At Any Cost mode. My hands flailed out to grab whoever was trying to get me to take a dirt nap. Instead of a person, my fingers clamped around the rope holding me down by the back of my head. I dug in deep, feeling something squish under my nails.

Get . . . off!

I yanked with desperate strength until the rope pulled free.

Oh, Gehenna, thank you . . . air! Sweet, sweet air!

For a few precious seconds, I just breathed. And over the sounds of my gasping, I heard someone screaming in pain. Scrambling to my feet, I spun to face my attacker . . . and saw a vine snaking into the rose garden.

That's it: no hulking behemoth of an assailant, no sicko with a rope, not even a guy in a hockey mask. Just the vine, thick as a python, slithering away from me.

No. No, no, no.

This was my vacation away from all things supernatural. I

rode in a car for three fucking hours to get away from shit like this.

Something was squirming in my hand.

I blinked at the torn leafy strand clutched in my grimy fingers, white sap oozing from its tattered ends as it quivered. Ugh. I opened my hand, and the tendril dropped to the ground, trembling and curling like a slug on a salt lick. Then it disappeared in a pop of pollen. Golden-green motes shimmered in the air and gently floated down and touched the upturned earth, and then they vanished.

Three hours. Without being allowed to drive. To get away from shit like this!

A sound like a slurp made me look up in time to see the monstrous vine disappearing into the ground, leaving the roses in the garden undisturbed. Gone—with no sign it had ever existed.

And I swear to the deepest pits of Hell, the blessed flowers were laughing at me.

No. Fucking. Way.

I leapt into the garden and pawed through the dirt, uprooting the roses as I hunted for the murderous vine. The flowers fought back: Thorns riddled their stems like boobytrapped chastity belts, and soon my hands were laced with small cuts and streaked with blood. I barely noticed; I was on a mission. I was going to find that reject from the set of *Tarzan* and rip it apart with my bare hands. Rather like what I was doing to the roses, which weren't laughing at me any longer.

Roses are red; pluck them, they're dead.

When digging up the flowers didn't produce the vine, I started burrowing in the ground like a mole on cocaine, my hands cutting through the soil in double time. Come out, come out, wherever you are. . . .

"Jesse?"

I froze, then slowly looked up to see Paul, gloriously naked save for his bathing suit—which was far too baggy; I had to buy that man a Speedo—and staring at me as if I'd lost my mind. For a second, a nimbus of gold-tinged white circled his head like a helm.

My White Knight.

Gasping in a startled breath, I blinked away the image, leaving just Paul, very human and very vulnerable . . . except I knew, just knew, that whatever insanity was happening here, Paul was safe. Shielded. I didn't have to worry about him—at least, not about killer vines strangling him while taunting roses watched and giggled.

Mental note: my flaky aura talent sometimes had its uses. Now, if only I could figure out how to control it . . .

I licked my lips (and tasted dirt), then said, "Hi."

"What in the world are you doing?"

Tell him the truth, I told myself. You're supposed to be honest with each other. You're supposed to have no secrets. You love each other.

Right, but I'm also not supposed to make waves. I'm not supposed to get in his face about the supernatural. Not this weekend. Not when he's the one reminding me that I'm supposed to be one of the humans. "Um. Gardening?"

"Uh-huh." His eyes narrowed as he looked me over. Voice flat, he said, "In the dark?"

"I . . . didn't want to get sunburned?"

"Really." He paused. "Gardening means destroying someone else's roses?"

Oops. I glanced down at the dying flowers, which didn't look like they'd been laughing at me, let alone harboring a murderous vine the length of a human's small intestine.

Bless me, I didn't know what to say.

Tell him the truth, a tiny voice whispered again. And I knew I should. Paul has put up with a lot from me lately, and he's also been through a lot—the man had gone to Hell and back, literally, all because of me. I could tell him the truth, and he'd believe me. He understood that weird things happened sometimes to a former demon.

His voice, a memory just a few hours old, echoing in my mind: *You're not a demon anymore.*

Biting my lip, I debated what to do. If I told him about the attack, he'd probably destroy the rest of the garden himself, then throw me into the car and drive us back to the City. He was a hero; that's what the heroes did—defeat the bad guys and get the helpless maidens to safety.

But I wasn't helpless. And I'd never been a maiden.

And even if Paul did save me from some lurking evil here upstate, I was positive that his back would be up the entire ride home, and longer—he'd be reminded, once again, about my infernal baggage.

How much of my baggage could he handle before his back broke from the strain?

You're not a demon anymore.

No, I was a normal human (for the most part). Normal humans don't have vegetation trying to kill them. Not unless there's E. coli in their spinach.

I couldn't tell him the truth. But I didn't want to lie to him. Shit. I didn't know how to handle moral dilemmas; I was more used to a black-and-white point of view.

Paul said, "You're not going to tell me, are you?"

My mouth opened, closed. Opened again, and no words came out. Not knowing what else to do, I shrugged, hating that no matter what I did, it wouldn't be the right thing.

His gaze bore into me as he searched my face, and I saw in his eyes that he was begging me to tell him the truth.

Please don't make me.

A long moment as we looked at each other, the silence stretching into something fragile and breakable. Finally, Paul sighed—resigned, maybe, or disappointed. "If you change your mind, you know where to find me."

My eyes wide enough to make anime artists fall in love, I said, "In the hot tub?"

His lips twitched into a half-smile. "You're sort of filthy."

"I'll dash into the shower. Won't take a minute."

"Okay." He helped me to my feet, and something inside of me went all mushy as his large, strong hand held mine. "The owner's going to have kittens when he sees what happened to the flowers."

"We can say a goat ate them."

"Don't think there are wild goats in the Catskills."

"Or a deer."

He arched a brow, questioning.

I said, "What? Bambi eats flowers. Not including the skunk. Wise move on the baby deer's part, if you ask me."

Now the smile came out to play, and I knew the moment had passed. "Go," he said. "Get clean. I'll meet you in the tub."

I flashed him a thank-you smile and dashed into the cabin.

In the bathroom, I stripped off my bra, pants, and underwear, then turned on the water. When it was sufficiently hot, I flipped the switch to turn the shower function on, and then jumped in, pulled the curtain closed, and made with the lathering. Liquid brown sluiced off of my body, revealing pink skin with the occasional greenish-blue bruise. I didn't want to think about what the colors my face must be showing, now that the dirt was washed away.

How would I explain my injuries to Paul? *Yeah, it's from the gardening. One of those weeds was a real killer. . . .*

I blew out a frustrated sigh as I shampooed my hair. If I still had my powers, my true infernal powers, this would be a non-issue—I'd bamf up a new body, and Paul would be none the wiser. Not a lie, exactly; more like skirting the truth. Not at all the same thing.

Bless me, I missed my magic.

The water washed over me, and I closed my eyes, pretended I still had some power—enough, at least, to give Paul the Jesse he wanted. I imagined me sparkly clean: curly black hair that gleamed with blue highlights, large green eyes set in a heart-shaped face, slight overbite when I smiled. Short at five-four, lean yet curvy, decent breasts, cute waist, great legs. Not a runway model by any stretch, but sexy. Maybe that was the succubus in me shining through.

If only it were as easy as wishing the bad stuff away. Caitlin probably could have cleaned me up with a blink, but I wasn't about to call my pseudo-sister and beg a favor. Witches loved to have people (and entities) owe them favors. Not a good habit to fall into. So I'd just have to deal with looking like roadkill.

At least I could look like unstubbly roadkill. I reached for my disposable razor and then perched on one leg and extended the other straight out, bracing against the shower wall. Water lapped at the ankle of my standing leg, tickled against my flesh. Just a once-over to make sure I was still smooth, then it was off to the hot tub. The razor scraped over my knee.

On my other leg, the ticklish feeling spread up my calf.

What the—?

Glancing down, I saw a vine wrapping around my standing leg.

I had enough time to clearly think: Unholy Hell, not *again*. And then the vine yanked my foot out from under me, and I crashed to the ground. My head slammed against the porcelain tub, setting off fireworks of color behind my eyes.

Owwwww.

Fuck me, that hurt. A lot. My vision blurred, and everything grayed as the water streamed down on me.

Come on, Jesse. Focus.

Lifting my head up, I was hit with a wave of dizziness that made the shower rotate to the left. Ugh, focusing isn't fun. My stomach clenched, and the fajitas I'd eaten threatened to exit the same way they'd entered.

Over the nausea, I felt the vine wrapping around my leg, working its way up my thigh.

I swallowed thickly and begged my belly to behave. It agreed, at least until after I ripped the floral tentacle out by its roots and flushed it down the toilet; after that, it was re-gurgitation time. I told my stomach it had a deal.

The leafy tendril skittered over my hip and arched up like a cobra. Oh, my, look at the mouth with all the teeth. My throat constricted and dried up, so I couldn't tell the mutant plant that it really had no business being here, because Venus flytraps aren't native to the Catskills. Maybe it was lost.

The vine grinned at me—and bless me for an angel if those weren't really needle-fangs in its mouth. It whispered in my mind: *Evil thing in my place.*

This from the poster child for shower scum. "Didn't see your name over the doorway."

Its grin stretched wider, and it reared back, hissing over the spray of water from the showerhead.

Uh-oh . . .

It lunged, and I jerked to the right just as its teeth snapped exactly where my neck had been a second before. The plant smacked against the tile wall, and for a moment it hung there, shaking its bulbous head as if to clear it.

I clung to the shower curtain, half out of the tub. Couldn't run, because the thing was wrapped around my leg. And shit, that leg was probably even more bruised and swollen be-neath the vine's tendrils. I'd never be able to explain it to Paul. Assuming I even made it out of here alive.

My stomach roiled from the thought, but my fear was bubbling into rage. Getting eaten by a psychotic plant was not on the agenda. And in the shower? No freaking *way*.

Lips peeled back in a snarl, I grabbed the vine just under its fang-filled mouth. It squirmed in my grasp, wet and slick, but it couldn't bite me. In my other hand, my fingers tight-ened around my disposable razor.

Over the spray of water, I shouted, "I am not plant food!"

I smashed its bulb-head into the wall, then sliced the razor down and peeled off a long, wet strip of mottled green skin. It screeched and pulled free from my hand, unwrapping itself from my leg in record time. By the front of the tub it hissed at me, its maw open wide, displaying its long, sharp teeth.

"Back at you." I held up the pink disposable razor like a dagger. "Try it again, vegetable, and I'll potato peel your ass!"

It paused, swaying back and forth as if it were considering me.

My head throbbed in time to my heartbeat, and my leg felt like a Doberman had used it for a chew toy. Breathing heavily, I waited for the vine to move. I wouldn't be able to pull back the curtain and leap out of the tub fast enough to get away. Even if Paul could hear me, I wouldn't want him fighting this thing. Not unless he had his gun with him. And last I checked, the only weapon that had been tucked into his swimsuit wasn't his gun. No, it was just the toothy plant and me.

Oh, you little piece of slime, if I still had my powers, you'd be a stain on the wall.

Maybe it saw the thought in my mind or on my face, because it cocked back and spat a challenge.

I love you, Paul. Sorry I'm leaving you with a big mess to clean up.

My teeth bared in a feral grin, I whispered, "Come on, then. Let's go."

A knock on the door, then Paul's voice: "Jess? I forgot the towels. Can I come in?"

The plant hissed, then shot down the drain.

I blinked, counted five seconds, then slowly approached the front of the shower. Glanced down the drain, ready to leap away (and probably slip and break my neck) if even a hint of green appeared. Nope, it was gone.

"Jess? Can you hear me?"

Keeping my eye on the drain, I turned off the water. I thought I heard a hiss from somewhere down below, but that could have been the runoff swirling down the pipe.

Another knock. "Hon? Can you grab towels for the hot tub?"

Paul.

The vine was afraid of Paul.

"Sure thing," I said, overly bright, still staring down at the drain. "Hang on, I'll be right there."

That's when I noticed that my leg wasn't bruised. For that matter, my fingertips weren't sore. My nails were perfect.

Biting my lip, I stepped out of the shower and quickly wiped down the mirror over the sink. My reflection showed that my face and neck were also a healthy pink. And now that I thought about it, my head was no longer auditioning for *Stomp*.

Blinking, I remembered how I'd wished that I still had my magic, how easy it would be for me to just bamf up a new body.

And here I was, looking like I'd spent a few hours at a spa—with no sign of the struggle in the garden, let alone the battle of the bath.

So either I had imagined everything . . . or I had my demonic powers back.

Chapter Five

Considering that one of the gravest punishments the Pit uses on underperforming demons is the Trial by Lake of Fire (the first demon to leap out of the burning liquid gets drawn and quartered for a century), you'd think that a hot tub would hold little appeal for a former resident of the Abyss. But there are three differences between getting dunked in the Lake and going tubbing: you control the heat in a hot tub, you don't get a hundred years of agony if you want to call it quits, and the bubbles soothe away your tension instead of sear away your face.

Sighing with pleasure, I settled back against the edge of the tub. "This is nice."

"Yeah." Sprawled across from me, Paul let out a sigh of his own. His eyes were closed, and there was a look of sheer joy etched onto his face. "I could get used to this. Think I can sneak a hot tub in the apartment?"

"George won't even let you have a washer/dryer." The super, when he wasn't hopped up on coke, was a stickler for the rules. "You'd have to bribe him."

He shrugged, smiling. "Can't do that."

"Damned ethics?"

"Exactly."

"Well . . . maybe George would agree, if you let him have a go at the tub."

Paul opened one eye and looked at me. "Would you want to walk in on that?"

I pictured pear-shaped, hairy George lounging naked in the bathroom. Actually, I wouldn't mind seeing him *au naturale*. Me, I liked men without clothing, no matter what the shape of their bodies. But I figured Paul wouldn't approve, so I hedged and said, "Um."

"Right."

The frothing water slowly worked its magic on me, relaxing me and making me feel fuzzy and warm. Who cared about possessed plants or the possibility of me once again wielding the powers of Hell? At this moment, all that mattered was that Paul and I were together, soaking away our troubles.

Paul and me, together. The thought made me smile. After everything we'd gone through, after all of the changes, we were still an "us." I used to think that the idea of soulmates was laughable; I knew what happened to souls at the end of everything, and having a mate wasn't one of the options. At least, not in Hell. But being here with Paul—and bless me, just being in the same place as him, even without us touching, was enough to make my heart beat faster—convinced me that sometimes, people are meant to be together.

Me and Paul. Together.

Me, a one-time succubus who'd loved thousands of evil mortals and took them all to Hell when they died, a creature who once knew how to drive men to their knees with only a look, who caused desire so intense that it rocked humans to their souls. Me, a human who had once taken incredible pleasure from mortal terror.

My Paul, my White Knight. He was brave. Good. A hero who put others before himself and yet wasn't a doormat. An officer of the law, who loved with a passion as fierce and bright and powerful as magic itself. A paladin from another time. A man meant for Heaven, if there ever was one. Without a doubt, Paul was meant for Paradise.

So at the end of it all, where did that leave a one-time succubus?

Chewing my lip, I sank deeper into the hot water until it covered my shoulders. I wasn't marked for Hell; that much had been painfully clear when I'd confronted the King of the Abyss a couple weeks ago. I could handle that.

So what that I'd never go home again? I'd always have fond memories of cookouts in the Lake of Fire, of orgies in the Red Light District. Of certain entities who'd made me laugh, of others whom I loved. I'd walked (cough, run) away from the Pit, from those friendships, from everything I'd enjoyed as a demon. And I was okay with never going back.

The thought made my chest tighten. I took a deep breath, then exhaled, slowly. It was okay to miss it, I told myself. Humans did that sort of thing. Mortals had regrets. Probably due to the limited lifespan.

My heart thumped on, perfectly healthy. Unbroken.

See that? I was human, complete with all the messed up, stupid emotions that went along with it.

Besides, it was all moot. I couldn't go back, even if I really wanted to—and certainly not to the way it was before. The reason I'd run in the first place was still there . . . and during the time I'd left, the Underworld had changed dramatically.

For that matter, so had I. Doing Hell as a mortal was worlds different than doing it as a demon. For one thing, it was sort of a one-way ticket. For another, humans don't fully appreciate the art of fear and horror; they're too busy being terrified and suffering agonizing punishment. Not being marked for Hell was a good thing. A Good thing, even.

But could a former demon, even one with a spiffy mortal soul, find a home in Heaven?

"Hon? You okay?"

Paul's voice pulled me from the quagmire of my thoughts. I clung onto the sound and let his question save me from drowning in philosophy. I really didn't want to think about a happily ever afterlife, not when there was a real life to live. "Hmm?"

He smiled softly, and when he spoke, his voice made me think of hot chocolate sliding down my throat and warming my belly. Yum. He said, "I asked if you were okay."

"I'm fine." I smiled to prove I wasn't a liar.

"You look like you're going to cry."

Shrugging in the bubbling water, I said, "Just thinking."

"About what?"

About Heaven, and whether I had a place in a realm that redefined ennui. About Hell, and how a land that had been home to me for thousands of years was now relegated to my nightmares. "Nothing important. Silly stuff."

He slid over until he was next to me, and he wrapped his arms around me. I leaned into him, my head pillowed on his damp chest, and listened to the steady beating of his heart. When he spoke again, I felt his voice vibrate against my cheek. "You know you can talk to me."

"I know. It's just . . ." I didn't know how to finish the thought, so I shrugged against him and said nothing else.

He stroked my hair, which felt really nice, especially with the heated water lapping at me. Enjoying the feeling, I closed my eyes and smiled. This, right now, was what I wanted: Paul holding me, comforting me, Paul cocooning me in his arms and wanting to know what I was thinking.

It occurred to me, sitting there in the hot tub, that even this one moment of us together wasn't really about us: it was about what I wanted. I wanted Paul, and I had him. He wanted me to tell him the truth—about what had happened in the garden before, about what I was thinking now—and I wouldn't.

No matter what I'd told myself before, I'd always be self-ish. What can a demon really share except pain?

But I wasn't a demon, not anymore. I wasn't evil.

In my mind, the plant creature hissed: *Evil thing in my place.*

No, I was *human*. Just human. Most people wonder what's in store for them after they die. I was no different. No more insider knowledge for me. I sighed against Paul's chest. Maybe the wetness on my cheek was from the water.

"Sometimes," Paul said softly, "I forget how hard it must be."

"What is?"

"For you. Adjusting."

I stiffened against him. This was exactly what I didn't want to discuss with him. Might as well wear a sign that said "I Used To Fuck A Lot Of Men Before I Took Them To The Lake Of Fire—Ask Me How!" Not exactly the best way to convince Paul that he and I had a future together. So I insisted, "It's not hard. I'm mortal. It's what I wanted. What I chose." *You're* what I chose.

"I know." A pause, filled with him running his fingers through my curls. Then he asked, "Are you homesick, Jess?"

Yes. Satan spare me, yes. But there was no point to admitting that. "My home's with you. I wouldn't want it any other way."

He touched my chin with his finger and tilted my head up until our gazes locked. What I saw brimming in the sea green of his eyes nearly brought me to tears—so much feeling, so willing to share it. "I want to make you happy, Jess."

I let out a startled laugh. "But you already do. Don't you know that?"

Paul smiled at me, a radiant, loving smile that slowly melted my worries. "Let me make you happy."

I opened my mouth to tell him again that he did make me happy, that whatever pleasure I'd experienced before him was nothing compared with his *realness*, with his love, but he silenced me with a kiss.

Oh, Paul.

My mouth opened, and his tongue darted between my lips, teasing me, grazing my teeth, touching my own tongue and making me shiver with need. I *uhmmm*ed and he ate the sound, devoured it whole with lips and teeth and tongue. His hands, caressing my face now, holding me as if he were afraid I'd slip away.

I'll never leave you, love. You made me stop running.

My arms wrapped around his neck as we kissed, and kissed, and sweet Sin, I could kiss him until the world ended. Our mouths sealed together, he lifted me up and set me on his lap. Yes, this is where I belonged, here with my man, in his arms. I moved my hips and said hello to the erection pulling his swimsuit taut. He pulled me closer, closer until my breasts were crushed against his chest. Water churned around us, bubbles rolling and breaking in a backbeat as our hearts thumped sweet nothings to each other.

He broke the kiss to nibble on my lower lip, then worked his way down my neck, now my collarbone, down to the swell of my breast. With every touch of his lips, my blood heated; with every lick of his tongue, my breath hitched until I was panting. And then he latched onto my nipple, and my body whooped for joy as shocks of sheer pleasure shot through me. Too used to the thin walls in his apartment, I bit back my cry, swallowed it as Paul sucked.

I changed for you, tamed myself and taught myself to unlearn, and I swear by all that's unholy I would do anything for you . . .

Wet kisses, hot and demanding. His teeth, grazing the sensitive nub of my nipple, hinting at pain, promising delight. Too much, and not enough—my sex tensed and begged for release, begged to feel him thrusting inside of me.

I had to have him, now, feel him inside of me, filling me. Now, as my body coiled tight, tight, so very tight and ready to burst. Now, as he brings me to the edge . . .

Rocking hard against him, the material of his bathing suit

bunching beneath the bare skin of my thighs, I said, "Take it off."

As a reply, he moved to my other nipple and lashed it with his tongue. Groaning from his touch, I arched back as he suckled me, his mouth hot and wet on me and his lips sizzling on my skin . . . oh love, how you make my body clench with need, how you make me burn . . .

"Take it off," I said again, my voice a husky whisper, insistent.

His hands flowed around me, moving from my back to my breasts, cupped them. Squeezed, gently, as if he could feel how much they ached. He broke suction and I voiced my displeasure, my nipple missing the warmth of his lips. Laughing softly, he massaged away my protest, his deft fingers rolling my peaks, sending liquid bursts of heat through me. I squirmed in his embrace, wanted more. Wanted him. "Paul."

Watching me react to his touch, he smiled, self-satisfied and knowing. His voice commanding, he said, "Stand up."

I did. My skin pebbled in the cool mountain air as water streamed down my body, the heated bubbles of the tub breaking against my thighs. With a grin that was deliciously wicked, he nudged my legs apart, then planted his hands on my hips. And then he dove down.

Oh . . . !

My fingernails clawed into his shoulders as he licked me, his tongue making magic and his mouth loving me and worshiping me, and my sex throbbed as his lips worked on my folds, probed deeper, and unholy Hell, the way he makes me feel . . .

Then he flicked his tongue against my clit, and I gasped in delight. There he stayed, stroking that spot wetly, firmly, and I bucked as my core tightened and *tightened* and bless me it feels so good so good it almost hurts almost as he strokes me and more and oh *yes* there again and again and—

The orgasm ripped through me, and I shrieked my joy to the Pit and the Sky and the four corners of the world. Paul growled his approval as I came, as he feasted on me, his sounds of triumph mixing with my cry, our voices echoing in the night and the moon shining spotlight as I shivered over him. My mind trumpeted his name, my man, my lover, the one who I loved with all my heart. All my soul.

My Paul.

He coaxed the last drop from me, and my knees sagged, braced on his shoulders. Kissing my inner thigh, he pushed down on my hips and lowered me back into the water, onto his lap. He wrapped his arms around me, and I leaned my head on his chest, a lazy smile stretching across my face. "Thank you," I murmured. "Oh, thank you."

"You're very, very welcome."

Between the pulsing aftershocks rippling through me and the heat of the water, it would have been easy to float off to sleep, safe in his embrace, my body cushioned on his. But first I absolutely had to return the favor, had to share this feeling of pure bliss with him.

"Do I make you happy, Jess?"

"Oh yes." Reaching down, I caressed the bulge of his erection, still blanketed by his bathing suit. "Let me show you how happy you make me."

He groaned a reply as I squeezed, slowly stroked him up, stroked him down.

And up, firmer now. "You said you can't soak in a tub naked if it's outdoors."

"Uh-huh."

"What about getting a blowjob in a tub, naked, out-doors?"

He breathed, "Willing to give it a try . . ."

Heh.

Keeping a steady movement on his shaft, I tugged down his suit with my other hand—first over his right hip, then his left. And then over his ass, pausing to grope him and cup his cheeks. I stopped stroking his cock to yank the suit down to his knees. Obscured by the rolling bubbles in the water, his penis seemed to ripple and shimmer in the heat of the pool.

Both of my hands now on his ass, squeezing. He moved beneath me, looking at me with such longing that I wanted to spear myself on him and ride him until he exploded inside of me. But no—he'd want a condom, and there was no way I was breaking the mood.

And as much as I enjoyed the feel of him in my hand, I'd much prefer him to melt in my mouth.

I tickled him behind his balls, then dragged my fingers over his cheek and across his hip until they brushed against his pubic hair. Playing there for a moment, I watched his eyes darken and heard his breathing quicken, and even with the desire so plain on his face, I also saw, felt, something deeper and truer and stronger than lust, something more powerful than magic and as eternal as a soul.

Love.

My love. My White Knight.

Let me love you, Paul.

My fingers wrapped around his cock—no bathing suit between our flesh now, just him in my hand, just him, full of blood and passion. My chin dipped in the water as I kissed his tip, and I smiled as he gasped my name. I took him in my mouth.

"God, Jesse," Paul said again, my name a ragged prayer. "Oh God, Jesse . . ."

Deeper. Deeper still. My head bobbed beneath the water as I sucked him down . . .

. . . and water shot up my nose.

Gah!

Pulling away from Paul, I spluttered to the surface and snorted out water. My nostrils burned and coughs spasmed through me, making it impossible take a full breath.

My face flushed, but it wasn't from my violent coughing. Fucking stupid human body! I used to finish clients (especially the rich and shameless) in hot tubs and pools, and I never, ever had to stop because I was drowning. I'd left that to them, after they'd come inside of me and then fade off to sleep as their bodies shut down, their souls already bonded to me . . .

But that was forever ago. Now I was just human. Stupidly, helplessly, pathetically human. My throat tightened, and something cold and damp blanketed my heart.

Paul's hand, strong and tender, on my shoulder; his voice, full of concern: "Hon? You okay?"

Coughing, tears streaming down my cheeks, I shook my head and shrugged out of his grip. *Don't look at me like this.*

His telepathic skills were obviously on the fritz, because he hugged me and murmured nonsense words until I could take a breath without feeling like my lungs were doing the backstroke. My nostrils were raw, almost singed, and every inhalation was like brain freeze. How could ordinary water burn like the Lake of Fire?

Blinking away tears, I found myself gazing at the garden. At the new roses, shining like spilled blood in the moonlight. They swayed in a sudden breeze, and I heard their floral laughter in the wind.

My neck tensed, but I forced myself to relax; no way was I letting Paul know something was wrong. Whatever nastiness was out there, it would leave Paul alone. And as long as I was with him, all I had to do was ignore their flowery taunts.

The roses giggled, their thorns gleaming.

My lip curled in a sneer before I schooled my face to impassivity. *I swear to my Sire and to Hell Below, I'm going to pluck every last one of you and press you in the phone book.*

I must have jerked in Paul's arms, because he started to massage my shoulders. "It's okay," he said, his voice soothing, his hands slowly easing away my rage, my utter embarrassment. Paul said again, "It's okay, Jess. You're all right."

I sighed, let my body go with the movement of his hands. "I'm stupid."

"No, you're not. You just swallowed water."

"Like I said."

"It happens, hon."

"It shouldn't." Mental note: breathing is not optional, even in the midst of fellatio in a hot tub. Well, I sure as Sin wasn't going to let a little thing like almost drowning kill the mood. "Let's go inside, sweetie. Somewhere less watery. We'll pick up where we left off."

"You know what I'd really like?"

"What?" I said, ready to take notes. I'd do whatever he wanted, even dress up like a Catholic schoolgirl.

His hands flowed down my back. "To curl up next to you. To lie with you spooned against me."

I turned to look up at him, to see him smiling, his eyes warm and loving. "But what about you?"

"What about me?"

"Don't you want to finish?"

"What I want more is to just be with you."

My brow crinkled. "You don't want sex? But . . . isn't that against the rules? Or at least a penalty?"

He laughed softly, brushed his hand against my cheek. "I don't play that game. Don't you know by now that it's not just about the sex?"

There was no way for him to know that his words pierced me to my core. I was, had been, a creature of Lust. It was *always* about the sex. But then again, love was different. Bless me, love was hard. I looked down, wondered what to say.

"Jess," he said, "I don't need to finish tonight. What I need is to be with you. To hold you. To feel you next to me."

"But . . ." I took a deep breath, said, "But why don't you want me to make you feel good? Did I do something wrong?"

"God, of course not." His hand, under my chin, nudging my head up until I met his gaze. "Hon, this isn't about me.

What you need tonight is for me to hold you. Let me give you what you need."

"Paul . . ."

"Something happened before. Something scared you. Let me make you feel safe again." Panic shot through me, but when I opened my mouth, he said, "You don't have to tell me. You can, if you want. But if you don't, that's okay. We all have our demons." He chuckled and beeped my nose. "Some are sexier than others."

I swallowed the lump in my throat. "You . . . you really mean that?"

"Of course I do."

The succubus in me wailed that he was insane, that no matter what, it was always about the sex, and this wasn't what happened during a romantic weekend getaway. But the rest of me muffled the succubus with a ball gag and locked her in a box filled with sex toys to keep her busy. Because I couldn't think of anything more romantic than lying in Paul's arms, listening to the sound of his heartbeat as I fell asleep. "How do you know just what to say?"

"White Knight boot camp. They trained us well."

I hugged him as if my soul depended on it, and he held me close, and for that wonderful moment, everything was right and normal and good. "Love?"

"Hmm?"

"Does this mean I don't have to do the dishes?"

He laughed again, and I felt myself fall even more in love with him. "Come on, hon. Let's go to bed."

Chapter Six

I really had every intention of just snuggling with him. But there in bed, lying next to him—skin on skin, his breath tickling my ear—was more than enough to make my nipples tighten and my sex thrum, and when he shifted behind me I felt his erection hard against my back. I wiggled my ass, and he pulled me close, pressed his arm over my breasts.

"Love," I said in the dark, "know what I really need?"

"What?"

"You." I unwrapped his arms and moved his hands until they cupped my breasts. "I need to feel you inside of me. I want to swallow you."

A pause, filled with his heavy breathing. Then he said, "You don't have to." His voice was husky, a thing of caged passion.

I had to set it free.

Rolling on my hip, I faced him, touched his face, his jaw, stroked the curve of his neck. "Of course I don't have to, love. I want to."

His fingertips dusted my nipples. "Jesse . . ."

"Less talking. More moaning."

I nudged him back so that he was lying against a throne of pillows, then straddled his hips. As I ran my hands over his chest, his curls of hair still damp from the hot tub, I let my gaze linger over his naked body—over his broad shoulders and muscular arms; his sculpted torso and narrow waist; his erect cock, thick and eager, curving up as if to ask for a kiss.

So I kissed him.

No interruptions this time; no burning need for me to breathe against the water or for him to cover himself with a condom. Just him and me, his flesh in mine, my lips and tongue driving him crazy with desire.

How could he think I wouldn't want to do this? Didn't he know how much I loved making him come? How much pleasure it gave me to see him lose himself in rapture?

His hands fisted in my hair, moved with me as my head bobbed. With every wet stroke of my mouth, he panted, a sound like a grunt or a growl—a delicious sound that made my sex tingle and my nipples ache. This was for him, yes, but it made me feel so good. Sex: the gift that keeps on giving.

My fingers grazed his sac and dangled behind, and he let out a strained laugh as I tickled him there. Back to his balls now, kneading lightly, and his laugh stretched into a moan. Sucking him, I switched hands and tripped my fingers along his thatch of pubic hair. As he rocked beneath me, I broke suction to lick his shaft, to run my tongue along the rim of his head. To nibble the sensitive skin of his inner thigh.

And then I took him deep in my mouth.

"Jesse . . . oh God, Jesse . . ."

Deeper now, and still deeper, and he groaned, his body tensing, muscles bunching.

Yes, love. Lose yourself in me.

With a cry to shake the rooftop, he burst inside of me, and I drank him down, every drop. I sucked him until his body stopped quivering with aftershocks, and then I sucked him more. When he was completely spent, I finished him with tiny kisses on his tip.

Paul, I love you so much.

He wrapped me in his arms and whispered his thanks, and I whispered mine—for before, for now, for always. We lay there in the dark, bundled in each other, and I smiled, feeling blissfully content.

Feeling safe.

Chapter Seven

Demons don't dream. They rest. Some may sleep. But they don't need to mentally shed themselves of the things that have been preying on their minds all day. Benefit of not having free will.

But humans . . . well, humans need to dream, otherwise they go crazy. Start hearing things, like roses laughing at them, or seeing things, like demons in a doughnut shop or a monster in the shower.

So it figured that because I have so much weird shit in my daily life, my dreams were upsettingly normal. No creature with knives on his glove out to shred me like confetti; no undying mental case in a mask trying to melt my skin off in a Jacuzzi. That stuff I could handle. (Actually, that stuff used to get my sweet spot.)

Sitting in bed, I wiped angrily at my eyes and did my best not to wake up Paul. I should have slipped out to go to the bathroom, or even the living room, but I couldn't bring myself to be alone right now. After the day I'd had yesterday and the horrible dream I'd woken up to now in the blackest hours before the dawn, I didn't want to leave Paul's side. Maybe it was insecurity, or fear. Or pure selfishness. I had no idea; my personal knowledge of human emotions only went so far. But whatever it was I was experiencing, it absolutely sucked angel feathers. And I didn't know how to make it stop.

To prove the point, the dream replayed in my mind. It started off well enough—we were in bed, not sleeping. Fucking like fallen monks trapped in a sorority house. I was riding Paul as if he was my White Stallion as well as my White Knight, a sexual centaur of hero-worshiping proportions.

My fingers entwined in his, my body thrilled with his every thrust, with the feeling of him inside of me, filling me. No barriers between us—no condoms, no words. Just him and me, together. I screamed in ecstasy as we came.

After the echoes died, we lay together, our limbs entangled as our sweat began to dry. Smiling as I settled against him, I felt content. Safe.

And then he asked me what had happened out in the garden.

"Nothing," I said, flustered. I didn't want to talk about it, didn't want to remind him, yet again, that to be with me meant dealing with supernatural insanity. The whole point of getting away this weekend was to leave that sort of thing behind.

Around me, his arms tensed. "When are you finally going to trust me?"

"I do trust you."

"Like hell."

"I *do*," I said—no, I shouted, because who the fuck did he think he was? Shrugging out of his embrace, I propped myself onto my elbows and glared at him. "I told you the truth about my history, my role in the Underworld. I told you how I'd become human. What more do you want from me?"

"Trust isn't a one-time thing, Jezebel," he said, my infernal name sounding foreign on his tongue. "It's an ongoing commitment."

"I don't know what you're talking about."

"Don't you?" He stared at me, his gaze cutting me to the quick. "Something was going on back there, something more than you suddenly deciding you hate flowers."

I bit my lip to stop the words from escaping. I couldn't tell him. No making waves this weekend, nothing to remind him about my past. That was the deal I'd made with myself. Humans did that: they promised themselves that they'd do things, or would stop doing things, and they swore to change their evil ways. Humans lied to themselves.

Yet another difference between demons and mortals—demons lied to others, but never to themselves. They just weren't wired that way.

"It was nothing," I said.

"Bullshit."

"Let it go."

"Why don't you trust me?"

Just tell him. He'd understand.

Unless he wouldn't. Unless he'd push away from me and would run off to find himself a normal human woman, one who wasn't chained to Hell. Feeling angry and betrayed for no reason I could think of, I said, "I just wigged out on the garden, Paul. Can't we just have a nice weekend without you psychoanalyzing everything?"

"Can't you let me save you?"

"From what? Bible thumpers?"

He looked away, saying nothing, his broad shoulders screaming his tension. After a long moment, he sighed—a low, mournful sound that stole my breath and filled my eyes with sudden tears. "Jezebel," he said, and the name made me cringe. "I love you with all of my heart. But don't make me choose between my ideals and you."

"I don't understand," I said, my throat thick around the words. "Choose? How'm I making you choose?"

"If you won't let me save you, then there's no point to any of this." With that, he rolled over and went to sleep.

And my dream ended with me waking up, lying naked in the dark, wondering for a moment if we'd really fought. No, there was no intangible wall between me and Paul, nothing ugly filling the silence.

Except the seeds had already been planted, hadn't they?

Why don't you trust me?

I do, love. I swear.

But you didn't say that to me, did you? That was just my own guilt, taking your form in my mind. Right?

You're not going to tell me, are you?

Those words had been real. Not an accusation, but a declaration.

I watched him sleep, smiled to see such a peaceful look on his face. At least his dreams were good ones. His dreams probably ended after the great sex. No fucked-up post-coitus discussion to ruin the afterglow.

What was the lesser of two evils: me telling Paul the truth because he wanted to know and deserved to know, or me hiding the truth because I didn't want to keep reminding Paul about my ties to Hell?

Feh.

Blowing out a frustrated sigh, I lay back against my pillow. The whole free will thing, I decided, really blew moose chunks.

Over the sounds of Paul's snores and the whirling hum in my mind of words unspoken, something slithered and stretched, like a creeper of ivy working its way up a wall, trying to reach the sun.

Chapter Eight

A quick kiss on my nose, and Paul's obscenely chipper voice: "Morning, camper!"

Gah. I rolled onto my side and buried my head under the pillow.

"Uh-uh," Paul said. "Rise and shine."

If he told me to give God the glory glory, I'd gouge his eyes out. "Go away."

"Nope."

Then the bastard tore the pillow away and started tickling me. I squealed like a stuck pig and tried to bat away his hands. But he was too quick, and he prodded laughter out of me, even though I wanted to curse his name. (Or call Caitlin and have her do the cursing; witches did that sort of shit.) In between manic fits of giggles, I spluttered out a "Stop!!!"

"Stop what? This?" More tickling, on my waist, my armpit, my hip.

"Yes!"

"Will you get up if I stop?"

Tears leaked between my closed eyelids as I agreed.

"Good. Come on, hon. Coffee's waiting." I felt the bed rise as he stood up, heard the floor creak as he walked out of the bedroom.

That . . . that was positively evil of him! Guess I was rubbing off on him. "There are better ways to wake me up," I called out.

No reply, other than a hearty chuckle. Humph.

Pulling myself up until I was sitting, I stretched my arms up, tried to convince my body that it was really time to wake up. My body wanted no part of it. Go back to sleep, it told me. I glanced down at the bed and sighed. It did look very comfortable. Inviting. But no, Paul would just wake me up again. And I was sure that he wouldn't be as lenient the next time.

My head throbbed, and my eyes felt grainy. And, blech, whatever had died in my mouth overnight hadn't removed itself after. Right, time for my toothbrush. I swung my legs over the side of the mattress and stood.

And my knees buckled when I saw the creeper of ivy sprawled on the windowsill.

It rested there, unmoving. Certainly not saying anything. I swallowed thickly and took two big steps away from it, until I was standing by the foot of the bed. Still no reaction from the green vine.

Of course not. It was just a plant.

I looked down at my hands. Pink and healthy. The skin showed no signs of having been pierced with thorns the evening before. Even my nails looked freshly manicured. And my arms and legs were perfect: no discoloration, no broken skin. For that matter, no razor stubble.

Maybe I really had made the whole thing up.

The throbbing behind my eyes kicked up a notch, and I sank back down on the bed and cradled my head in my hands. I was losing my mind. There were no man-eating (woman-eating?) plants with needle-sharp teeth. No taunting roses. No mysterious return of my powers.

Right?

Gamely, I reached inside myself, tried to touch the place where my infernal magic had once been. Nothing. Or maybe I was doing it wrong; it's not like I'd needed a Magic 101 course to teach me how to use my power—it had just happened. I'd intuitively known what to do. Demons were creatures of nefarious magic, so using that magic was as natural to them as . . . well, as breathing was to humans.

I sighed. Oh well. It would have been nice if I could have magicked myself taller. And maybe take away the overbite.

From the other room: "Jess? You didn't go back to sleep, did you?"

"Who, me?"

"Because I've got a bucket of ice water, and I'm not afraid of using it."

"Bathrooming, then I'm on my way." Casting one last, long glance at the vine on the windowsill, I dashed into the bathroom. Doing my business, I noted that the curtain had been drawn around the tub. Paul must have straightened it out last night before going to sleep.

I flushed. Washed my face. Scrubbed my teeth. Eyed the curtained tub the entire time.

Either it watched me in return or it hung there, inanimate. Like a shower curtain was supposed to do.

I spat water into the sink. Listened to it flow down the drain. Worried my lip with my teeth as I watched for movement behind the curtain.

Just get it over with.

Steeling myself, I tore back the curtain, a cry of challenge on my lips . . .

. . . which fizzled into a wordless exhale of breath, a lame *pfft*. Nothing: just a porcelain tub, with a showerhead above. The drain even had a slotted lid over it to prevent too much debris from spiraling down the pipe.

No powers. No plant from the lowest depths of Hell. I

was going crazy. Gooseflesh dotted my arms, and I hugged myself to try to keep warm.

Right. Have a breakdown later. Paul's waiting.

Normally, I would have padded to the kitchen dressed only in wicked intentions, but I thought the shivering wracking my body would ruin the effect. I hastily dressed—white matching bra-and-panty set (white lingerie always makes me giggle), green crop top, cargo pants—before venturing out. No makeup, though. Shaking hands plus eyeliner equals one half-blind exotic dancer.

The smells of cooking food permeated the hall and living room. Eggs, from the smell of it (and not the rancid sort I'd grown up with). Bacon too. Yum. Paul was in the kitchen, working by the stove and singing a Rolling Stones tune. "Satisfaction." When he saw me, he left the pans a-sizzling to grab my hands and dance with me around the small table. "Hey hey hey," he sang to me.

Hello, Sir Mick. I pressed Paul close and turned the impromptu foxtrot into something more sensual. Grinning, I sang back, "That's what I say."

We kissed good morning. Yes, this was much better than getting tickled. (Slap and tickle was another matter entirely.) A little tongue, and then small, sweet pecks. "Coffee's in the pot," he said, then he attacked my neck.

My body decided that it was time to wake up after all. *Mmm.*

Paul nipped my earlobe. "Have a seat." Then he was back at the stove, leaving me wanting much (much) more.

"You're in a playful mood," I said.

"Well rested. Ready to face the day."

"Any chocolate in the eggs?"

"Even you wouldn't like that."

"Try me."

"Later." He winked at me, then started filling plates with food.

We ate—Paul with enthusiasm, me picking at breakfast. He was a great cook, but the food just didn't taste right to me. Even the coffee seemed off. Maybe that's because I was so freaking exhausted that I could barely get the cup to my lips without spilling.

"Didn't sleep well?" Paul said.

"Am I that obvious?"

"My keen detective skills at work."

"The yawning give it away?"

"And the circles under your eyes."

Shit—I should have done the makeup thing after all.

His gaze roamed my face, and I tried not to blush under his scrutiny. He said, "Couldn't get comfortable?"

I shrugged, toyed with my food. "Bad dream. Felt real."

"Hate those."

"Yeah." I darted a glance at him, then took a sip of coffee. "We fought. In my dream, I mean. You were upset with me."

"Why?"

"Because I wouldn't tell you something." When he arched a brow, I smiled tightly, added, "I was no sweetheart, either. Told you to stop psychoanalyzing me. You told me if you couldn't save me, there was no point."

"Sounds like I was a real prick. What was I supposed to save you from?"

Succubus-eating flora. I shrugged again, non-committal. "Just a dream."

He reached over to cover one of my hands with his. "You know, considering that we came up here to get away from stress, there's an awful lot of stressing going on."

"I operate well under pressure."

Lifting my hand to his lips, he gave it a quick kiss. "Tell you what. When you're done with your breakfast, we'll take a walk. A nature hike will do wonders for your mood."

"How do you figure that?"

"Well, there's lots we can do outdoors." He waggled his

eyebrows, and I couldn't quash my giggles. "Yep, we can do that too."

"First the hot tub, now alluding to sex in the wild. My, my. Paul Hamilton, you're becoming an exhibitionist."

Chuckling, he lifted his coffee cup. "I like to keep you on your toes."

Chapter Nine

Two hours later, we were traipsing along a foot trail, following its various bends and twists, wandering amidst the maples and beeches and birches, their leaves a surprising yellow-green. More than once, I had to remind myself that it was still December—that the trees should have been barren and chill, their dead limbs jutting like rotten teeth. Even a weeklong heat wave shouldn't be enough to bring May to the woods in the Catskill Mountains.

Maybe I was just down on all things floral.

Paul certainly didn't seem to mind the off-season landscape. If anything, he took the unnatural spring in stride, thrilling with every cavern warmed with bright flowers. When he found a stream, he actually laughed with delight like a little boy, pointing and almost capering. Satan spare me. Fighting the urge to roll my eyes, I smiled at Paul's joy. It felt like a grimace on my face as I stared at the flowing water. Yay, nature.

No, stop that; be happy. This is all part of the romance, remember?

Huh. I'd pictured the romance having a lot more . . . well, romancing.

But look at how eager Paul is: the bounce in his steps, the easy movement of his long legs. Look at his grin as he turns back to make sure I'm right there and enjoying the view (and as long as he was walking in front of me, I certainly was enjoying the view—bless me, what he does to those jeans . . .). I blew out a sigh, laughed softly. Paul was truly enjoying this. That's what mattered.

And hopefully, he wasn't kidding before when he'd hinted at us fornicating in the woods.

We followed the stream, Paul marching like an intrepid explorer and pointing out the various plants and trees, me close behind, not caring one whit about the trillium and violets. "For a city boy," I called out, "you sure know your way around the forest."

He looked over his shoulder at me and grinned. "I'm an enigma."

Heh. "Wrapped in a mystery?"

"What other kinds of enigmas are there?"

Passing a large tree with a split trunk, we found a fallen birch a few feet from the stream. We sat on the dead trunk facing the water, surrounded by colorful flowers that seemed to mock the empty tree. Or maybe that was just me projecting my worldview onto a bunch of violets. Death and life; color and ash. Kumbayah, and all of that.

Paul draped an arm around me, and I rested my head on his shoulder, listened to the sounds of his breathing and his heartbeat over the soft gurgle of the stream. Wind rustled in the trees, carried the woody perfume of the forest.

"This is nice," I said.

"Glad you like." Even though I didn't see his face, I heard the smile in Paul's voice. "It's been forever since I've gone hiking."

"Jungles of New York City don't count?"

He kissed the top of my head. "Maybe back when I was a rookie. But I was in Boston then."

"The jungles of Boston don't count?"

"Nope. They're nothing like walking the trails in the Berkshires."

I pictured Paul roughing it, decked out in hiking boots and sporting an oversized backpack. "Did you wear lederhosen?"

"Wishful thinking on your part."

"You bet. You've got great legs."

We shared a laugh, then settled back, my head now on his chest, both of his arms wrapped around me. "What about you, hon? You enjoy the great outdoors?"

"Sure."

"That said with all the enthusiasm of a substitute chemistry teacher."

I didn't get the reference, but I did get the gist. "Well, it's lovely and all. But . . ." I shrugged.

He prompted, "But what?"

"But I've always preferred the wonders of architecture to the wonders of nature."

"You're more about the concrete than about the creeks?"

"There's only so many times you can look at the trees and the grass and the purple mountains and be like, ooh, look at all the majesty. But buildings? *People* made those. From nothing." I shook my head in wonder. "*That's* magic. The things that people make . . . it's utterly breathtaking."

"Buildings." Paul laughed softly, and I felt the sound vibrate in his chest. "I had no idea you were into architecture."

"Don't know if I'm into it," I said. "But I definitely appreciate it."

"Frank Lloyd Wright fan?"

Divorced twice-over, tragedy and murder in his home, post-mortem turmoil over his corpse—who wouldn't be a fan of that? "Absolutely."

He stroked my hair, then kissed the top of my head. "You must have seen a lot in your time. Building-wise."

My mouth opened, closed. Opened again, and I said before I could stop myself, "I'm not sure how to answer that."

"What do you mean?"

"I don't know what you want to hear."

"What I . . . ?" His voice trailed off, and his arms stiffened around me.

"Yesterday," I said. "You reminded me on the ride up that I'm not a demon anymore. That I had to be more human."

"Jesse, I never said that." He sounded horrified, but I couldn't bring myself to look at his face to know for certain. "I'd *never* say that."

My voice soft, I said, "But you don't want me to be a demon, do you?"

"You're *not* a demon."

"But I was. For a long, long time. And I know it upsets you." I took a deep breath. "So I'm trying. Really trying to just be human. But how'm I supposed to tell you about my past without . . ." My voice broke, but I forced the rest of my words from my mouth. "Without reminding you of what I was?"

For a long moment, he didn't reply. When he finally spoke, his words were careful, measured. "You want to know what really upset me yesterday on the ride up? It wasn't you talking about being a demon."

Frowning, I shrugged out of his arms and turned to face him. "But you said—"

"What I said was you had to follow human laws. That's what bothered me, Jess. When you made it sound like human laws are beneath you."

Shit. I looked down at the leaf-covered ground. "I didn't mean to do that."

"I know. Hon, please look at me."

Biting my lip, I met his gaze. His eyes were warm, loving,

and the smile on his face could have melted the icecaps. He said, "I'd never ask you to be something you're not."

"The former demon thing doesn't bother you? Really?"

"Hon, I'm more okay with that than I am with you being a stripper."

My eyes bugged. "You want me to stop *dancing?*"

"No!" he said, his lips twitching like he was fighting back a smile. "Really. You're happy doing it. And I want you to be happy. I'm okay with other guys drooling over you. Sort of. I can't really complain, as long as I'm the one you come home to."

I smiled—it felt a little sheepish, and a lot relieved. "You're the one I'm sleeping with."

"Thank God."

"He has nothing to do with it."

Laughing, he pulled me close. I hugged him in return, felt the tension leak away from my shoulders and neck. Whatever I'd done to deserve Paul Hamilton, I was glad I'd done it. Gehenna knew, he deserved much better than me. But far be it from me to tell him that.

"You know," he said, "since you're into architecture, when we get back to the City, there's lots of places I can take you. I'm guessing you haven't done New York City as a tourist."

"You'd be right." I'd done lots in New York City—specifically, I'd done it lots with clients in New York City. But I had never really stopped to appreciate what the land had to offer. Hard to do when you've got to make a quota.

"Okay," he said, pausing for a moment. Then his words came flooding out: "We're going to the Statue of Liberty, the Empire State Building, the Chrysler Building, Rockefeller Center, the Flatiron—"

I giggled from his enthusiasm. "And what'll we do the next day?"

"Easy: the library, the Plaza, the MetLife building, Carnegie Hall . . ."

"And Macy's?"

"For the architecture, not the shopping, right?"

"If it were for shopping," I said primly, "I would have said Bloomingdales."

He hugged me tight. "Hon, there's so much I want to show you."

I couldn't think of anyone else I'd rather have to show me.

We stayed like that for some time, just holding each other. And then the holding turned to petting, and the petting to stroking, and soon our hands were exploring each other's bodies, searching for hidden treasures. His mouth on my skin, setting me on fire with every kiss. My tongue blazing trails on his jaw, his neck.

Our limbs entwined, we rolled to the spongy ground. Paul took the brunt of the impact, his breath a grunt as his back hit the matted leaves. He'd cushioned my fall with his own body—my man, ever the White Knight. His hands cradled my waist, and I slid down until I positioned my hips over his. Sitting up, I smiled down at him, sandwiched between my legs, my hands on his chest.

"God, you're so beautiful." His voice was thick, heavy with lust, and his eyes darkened as he gazed up at me. "Your eyes, your smile . . . God, Jesse, everything about you. Everything. Looking at you now, with the sunlight in your hair . . . God."

My shoulders bobbed as I laughed softly. I was short, had an overbite, and without makeup I was second-glance pretty. "You're a silly, sexy man."

"I'm madly in love."

A goofy grin spread across my face, and my heart felt too big for my chest. "Me too."

I leaned down and kissed him—softly, lovingly, only the barest hint of how my body ached for him. His tongue slid past mine, brushed the roof of my mouth. Tingling warmth, all along my arms, my breasts; a liquid heat pulsing through my belly and thighs. Rougher, now, his lips more insistent, bruising mine with passion.

When he stiffened beneath me, I thought that maybe he'd jumped off the ledge before I'd even gotten my bungee gear on. Then he pulled away, cocked his head to the side.

"Sweetie? What is it?"

"You hear that?"

I listened, but all I heard were the sounds of the woods, of the stream, of Paul's ragged breaths. "Hear what?"

Frowning, he shook his head. "Never mind. Probably a bird or something." But he kept listening, as if he didn't quite believe his own words.

Now that he mentioned it, that was the one thing I hadn't heard on this little nature hike: the sound of animals. No rabbits or woodchucks, no raccoons or chipmunks, no squirrels or foxes or deer. No butterflies or grouses; no hummingbirds or bluebirds. None of the creatures that should have been at home in the Catskills. Plant life abounded, but outside of the greenery, nothing.

Just flowers . . . and a monster vine with lots of fangs and an appetite for former demons.

Pure silliness, I told myself, taking a deep breath. Enough with the creepy woods mentality. There was no possessed plant eager to chomp on me like I was a super-size portion of fertilizer. The roses in the garden hadn't been laughing at me. I'd imagined it all—the sad product of too much stress and not enough sleep.

Of me wishing I had my demonic mojo back. Of me feeling so freaking uneasy in my all-too-human skin.

Fucking *stop* it, Jesse. There's nothing bad here looking to harm us, nothing trying to eat us in a distinctly non-sexual way.

I am not afraid.

To prove just how not afraid I was, I kissed Paul, hard, pushing my tongue between his lips and breathing him in as if I could suck out his soul. He kissed me just as hard, fighting to claim my mouth with his. Not likely, love—my heart belongs to you, but no one owns my lips.

But I must admit, the man put up a heroic fight. Yum.

Just as I was considering sweet surrender, his mouth retreated from mine. I kissed his chin, licked my way up to his ear, all the while hoping he was going to launch a new frontal attack somewhere in the vicinity of my nipples.

"You really don't hear that?"

What, the sound of my buzz slipping away? Sure did.

I pulled back and propped myself on his chest, resting on my elbows. Gazed at him. Smiled as I remembered the image of him in the garden, a golden white helm on his head. "What's it sound like?"

He squinted, as if that could help him hear better. "Like . . . I don't know, maybe a person calling out."

"We keep going," I purred, "and I guarantee you'll hear a person calling out. Loudly. Multiple times."

A quirk of his lips, but the humor didn't touch his eyes. "Not us. Someone else."

"Sweetie, maybe there are other people with the same idea as us: get away for the weekend and go to the mountains." Lowering myself until my mouth was a bare two inches from his, I said, "You're distracted. But I bet I can keep you focused."

His smile pulled into a wicked grin. "You can try."

Ooh. I do so love me a challenge.

My tongue poked out, touched his lips. Traced the line of his mouth. Licked a path along his jaw, tripping over the rough stubble. One hand on his shoulder for purchase; the other between us, on his broad chest, moving down until my fingers were playing over the snap of his jeans. He *ummed*, the sound deep and sexy, and utterly arousing.

Rrrr.

I sat up, squeezing his hips with my inner thighs. "So," I said, rocking slowly, "are you still distracted?" I reached behind my back, under my shirt, and unfastened my bra.

His gaze locked on mine, desire transforming the seagreen eyes into a stormy ocean of color. "Hell no."

I licked my lips, slowly, and thrilled to hear his breathing quicken in response. "You sure? If you want, I can stop," I said, shrugging out of one strap.

"Don't you dare."

Smiling demurely, I pulled the bra out from my left sleeve and dangled it over Paul's head.

"White," he said, his voice a rasp. "Nice."

"Glad you like. If you want, I'll put it back on."

"I like this better." He reached up, sliding his hands beneath my top to cup my breasts.

The bra dropped to the ground. "Me too."

Then his fingers were circling my nipples, toying with them. I closed my eyes and rode the waves of pleasure, moaned when Paul pinched me lightly. Heat bloomed in me, set my body on fire. My sex throbbed as I rocked over him. Wanted him.

A growl sounding in my throat, I leaned down to attack his neck. My lips on his skin now, tasting the salty musk with its hint of gunmetal. Tension coiled in my belly, urged me on, faster, faster now, working my way back to his mouth. In me, love—I need you in me.

But when my lips met his, Paul gently broke the kiss. He said my name, his voice turning the word into something tender. My passion quieted, its effects softening to small tingles in my chest and crotch, the heat banked but not extinguished. His hands cupped my face, caressed my cheeks, brushed my hair from my eyes.

And in that moment, amid our smiles and lover's gazes, the world stood still. Here, in the woods, Paul and I together: a soundtrack of wind in the leaves, of ripples in the water; of things moving beneath the earth, burrowing, digging; a pulse riding through me, through us, connecting us as our heartbeats danced to the rhythm of all living things. This feeling, surging through me, drowning me, making me feel drunk and ecstatic and immortal. So much stronger than lust, than rapture.

Oh, sweet Sin. I love him so much.

Paul's hand, soft on my cheek. "Is everything okay? You look like you're going to cry."

"Happy cry. You make me happy, love."

He started to say something, but then he turned abruptly to the right, his head cocked, his eyes squinting. Tension rippled through his shoulders, and even though I knew, *knew* everything was all right, I shuddered as icy tendrils snaked their way up my spine. My voice pitched low, I said, "Again?"

"Yeah."

I listened, nearly popped a blood vessel in my effort to concentrate, but I didn't hear anything.

He turned to face me, his smile attempting to belie the unease sketched in his face. "Tell you what—let's take this back to the cabin. Hot tub, bed, kitchen table. Your choice."

"Sounds good to me. The great outdoors is vastly overrated." I smiled, big and false, wondering what Paul was hearing that I didn't. No matter; it was time to go. I stood up and offered a hand, which he took.

On his feet once again, he said, "I believe this is yours?" Dangling from his right index finger, my bra waved in mock surrender.

"Thanks." I took my clothing from him and put away my boobs. Go back to sleep, girls. I'll wake you up when it's time to play. Better yet, Paul will wake you.

We walked back along the path, not exactly hurrying, but we sure didn't pause to take in the scenery. Silently, we passed tree after tree, shrub after shrub, with Paul leading the way. No pointing out the various flowers this time. Fine by me. I wasn't the sort of gal who preferred to stop and smell the roses; I liked them good and dead. And maybe lacquered into jewelry.

Still no birdsong. Creepy.

Cool.

Cheered by the sense of foreboding, I tried to hum the

theme song to *Halloween*, but I can't carry a tune to save my life. So I settled on going "ch-ch-ch-ah-ah-ah" under my breath. More fitting for the woods, anyway. Didn't matter; Paul didn't notice. He was probably lip-syncing a Rolling Stones tune.

A sudden aroma of oak and moss, cloying, dizzying. And then I crashed into Paul, who had stopped short. Rubbing my sore shoulder, I was going to say something about him installing brake lights, but the set of his shoulders made me pause.

His voice tight, he said, "That wasn't here before."

"What wasn't?"

"That."

Helpful. Stepping around him, I saw a huge oak tree up ahead blocking the footpath. No, forget huge—this sucker redefined ginormous. Easily twenty feet thick, the main trunk stretched up about fifteen feet before splitting into about ten sections. Each smaller trunk branched out, bowing like Atlas in an effort to hold the sky aloft. Between the tangled limbs and the thick coat of scarlet leaves, the tree blocked most of the sunlight. Ivy shot through the bark, and as I stared at it, I thought of the ivy creeper on the windowsill in the cabin's bedroom.

My stomach dropped down to my ankles, and my breath caught in my throat. I squeaked out, "You sure this wasn't here?"

Eyes locked on the tree, Paul nodded.

Looking at the leafy green tendrils wrapped around the thick trunk, I decided that the spiffy sense of foreboding I was feeling wasn't that much fun after all. Actually, it downright sucked. And was sweaty. Ignoring the trickle of perspiration on my brow, I rubbed at the gooseflesh on my arms, swallowed to work some moisture back into my dry throat. "Don't suppose you brought the axe from the fireplace, by any chance?"

"Sorry, left it in my other jeans."

"Okay. Guess we walk around it then." And we'd give it a wide berth; the thing looked like it would happily eat small children.

Stepping off the path, we slowly crept around the massive tree, hand in hand. I held my breath as we walked, waiting for something Very Bad to spring out at us. But nothing out of the ordinary happened; it was rather anticlimactic when we reached the other side without getting attacked by giant spiders.

Safely back on the path, Paul and I exchanged a look, then we burst out laughing.

"Psyche," I said through my giggles. "My White Knight looked like he was going to shit his pants."

"Me? You were terrified. I thought you were going to squeeze my hand off."

"Uh-uh. Me big, bad former demon. Trees like that used to be my fangpicks."

"Fangpicks?"

"What? I had fangs."

Still laughing, we started walking again. And then I heard it: a woman's cry, a thing of terror and pain riding the air.

Before I could open my mouth, Paul bolted down the path, racing toward the sound.

Chapter Ten

"Paul," I shouted, "wait for me!" No luck; he was already gone.

Well, screw me on Salvation Day. That was pretty fucking inconsiderate of him—dashing off to rescue some damsel in distress while leaving me here. Alone.

Stop that. You're not supposed to be that selfish, remember? There are other people to consider. Paul had said so yesterday on the drive up. And he was right. He always put other people first, especially when they were in trouble.

I blew out a sigh as I thought about him doing the altruistic thing. Really, I shouldn't be surprised. You can take the cop away from the job, but you can't take the job away from the cop. Paul had to save someone at least once a day, preferably twice before lunch. He was just wired that way. A smile quirked my lips as I thought about my man racing off to do good deeds. Paul Matthew Hamilton, hero. That would look awesome on a business card. Maybe I should buy him a costume. Something sinfully red, with a big H on it for "Hamilton" or "Hero." Or "Hung." Heh.

The smile faded as I realized that Paul had really heard

someone before, when the two of us were getting down and dirty by the stream. He'd heard someone calling out, and I hadn't. Maybe his hearing was better than mine.

Maybe something didn't want me to hear it.

My stomach knotted as I thought about all the things that could have hurt someone here in the woods, things that Paul was blindly running to meet. Cue music from horror film.

He's going to be fine, I told myself as the wind picked up. Absolutely fine. Shivering, I wrapped my arms around my body. I'd seen his aura last night, and it had shown me that he was safe here. Protected.

Unlike me.

Looking around, I thought that the trees seemed much closer together than before. Watching me. Waiting.

Uh-huh. Sure they are.

I forced myself to laugh and to stop squeezing my elbows like they were the "oh shit" bars in Paul's car. Wow, look at my hands shake. I was right and properly mind fucking myself, wasn't I? Paul was just helping some intrepid soul with a sprained ankle. Or a bear trap.

Or monster spiders.

A twig snapped behind me.

Pivoting, I cocked a fist back, ready to punch and scream and bite. My heart careening in my chest, I glanced around, looking for any sign of anything out of place.

Nothing—no animals scurrying, no serial killer stalking. Just the mother of all oak trees, squatting in the path, its distended limbs looking like snakes swollen with food. The wind caught its branches, and they waved at me. Scarlet leaves rustled and blew, flashing like a matador's cape.

I released a breath I hadn't known I'd been holding and shook my head at my own ridiculousness. All things considered, I definitely preferred being the one to inspire fear than to actually feel its effects. Being scared sucked angel feathers.

Feeling stupid, I turned around, ready to go after Paul.

And gasped as I found myself completely surrounded by trees—dozens of them, right in front of me, behind me, to my sides, blocking the path. Trapping me.

Shit shit *shit* shit shit.

I tried to shout, but my mouth refused to work. My throat tightened, and I couldn't draw a full breath. Probably due to my lungs collapsing in shock and my heart trying to break free of my ribcage.

Okay. Panic after escape. Step one: escape.

Maybe I could squeeze between the trees . . .

A cracking, crumbling sound like squeezing freshly baked bread. Sweat popped on my brow as I watched tree limbs weave together to pen me in, caging me like a rabid beast. And that's when my mind screamed "Overload!" My vision went a bit soft around the edges—blurry, like watercolors running together.

Oh, *this* is what it means to be going crazy. Good to know.

Feeling like I was floating, I watched thick roots burst from the ground and wrap around my legs. The press of something rough and cold against my back pierced through the dream-like skein enveloping me, but not enough to force my body to move. Ticklish pressure around my middle, like a green caress, and then a squeeze that stole what little breath I had. Something grabbed my hands and pinned them back hard enough to make my shoulders scream.

Not liking this at all. Now would be the time to snap out of it, Jesse.

My body told my brain to fuck off, it was too busy being petrified to even consider fleeing.

A feeling like ants crawling over my arms made me shiver, and that's when I felt something slip under the skin of my wrists, light as a mosquito's kiss. The sucking sound is what really shook away the last vestiges of numbing fear and catapulted me into adrenaline-fueled terror. That, and the tingling numbness spreading up my arms.

I tried to pull free, yanked as hard as I could, but something clawed through my hair and slammed my head back. I felt the thud reverberate through my body before I heard the sound. Then the world slipped a bit, and everything went pleasantly gray. Dreamlike.

Quiet sips over the erratic thumping of my heartbeat. Spreading numbness through my hands and arms, edging over my shoulders.

The steady pounding in my skull slowly shredded the sheen of gray enveloping me. I opened my eyes. And squeezed them shut when the pain kicked in.

Fucking *ow*.

Evil thing.

My eyes snapped open. Helpless, hurting, I stared as one of the trees yawned forward. Its shape rippled, shifted, and suddenly I was drowning in a heady perfume—a deluge of oak and wine and roses. My eyes stung, watered. Wincing, I tried to turn away, but whatever had tangled in my hair held me tightly. I wanted to cry out for help, but fear had deadened my tongue. And the numbness that had started in my wrists was spreading up through my shoulders and neck.

Bless me, I was so freaking scared that I couldn't speak.

This was a stupid way to die.

And if I had to wait in Heaven for Paul for a human's lifetime, with only hymns and crossword puzzles to entertain me, I'd fucking lose my mind.

I can't die. Not like this. There had to be a way out.

Through my tears I saw the approaching tree transform into a sensual creature of wood and ivy, lushly feminine, curving. Eyes as green as spring; a mouth like ripe berries— and a flash of a brown ring emanating from her, first clinging to her like a fungus and then mushrooming over her and over me, behind me.

Then it was gone, leaving the wooden woman crowned in all of nature's terrible glory.

Between her appearance and the aura, I placed her: a dryad.

No, more than that. Through my growing terror, I pictured the monstrous oak that had blocked the path. She wasn't a free-range sort of wood nymph, able to loll about and frolic in the glen between bouts of fucking all the satyrs. No, this creature was a hamadryad—a living embodiment of an oak. Based on what I felt against my back, she'd bound me to her tree, like an insect stuck in a spider web.

Great, full-circle to monster spiders. And based on how she was licking her blood-red lips, maybe my analogy wasn't so far from the truth. Was that . . . drool? Gah.

Come on, Jesse—think!

My mind whirled as I watched her sway in the wind, mouth gleaming, the bark of her hair catching the breeze. The wood nymphs were all bound to Hell, as were most of the non-celestial entities in Creation. Technically, she bowed to the King of the Abyss.

Which was really shitty news for a former succubus who didn't hold the King's favor.

She reached out, and tentacle-like roots stretched from her fingers . . . headed toward my face. My brain threatened an aneurism when I saw suction pads on the tips of those roots.

Desperate, I shouted: "Why?"

The suckers paused, hovered inches away from my mouth. In my mind, a voice like twigs scraping: *Why what?*

"Why are you doing this?"

A long moment, during which I was sure my heart was going to just say "Fuck this, I'm done" and stop beating. Then the wooden tendrils lowered, revealing the hamadryad standing directly before me, spitting distance. Now if only I were a cobra . . .

Evil thing. She tapped a wooden finger against her chin, and the slurping sounds around me halted. The numbness in my arms and neck remained, but at least the feeling wasn't spreading any farther. A temporary stay of execution. Yay, me. *This is my place. You trespass.*

I remembered the mutant Venus flytrap hissing at me in the shower about how I was an evil thing in its place. My voice a squeak, I said, "We didn't know."

We? The hamadryad arched a leafy brow. *No "we." Your man is welcome here. He is Good. Nature always welcomes the Good.*

Was that a purr in her mental voice? Oh, Satan spare me, the vegetable had the hots for my man. Paul, stay far the fuck away from here. "I'm not evil."

You lie.

"No, it's true." I'm not lying, lied the liar. Try again, Jesse. "I'm not a demon anymore. I'm human." Blissfully, thankfully, painfully human.

You reek of Evil.

And she stank of Pine-Sol, but who was I to judge? "I ran away from Hell. Got turned into a human. I've even got a soul. I'm not meant for Hell," I insisted. "Even the King says so."

I don't recognize your King's sovereignty.

Hooboy.

Your King forced my kind to leave the Land, millennia ago. Your King forced my sisters to reside in Hell, as if we were mindless creatures of coal, or damned like creatures of clay. Her mouth twisted into a snarl, and her eyes shone with hatred. *I refused to bow, little demon. I bow before no man or god.*

Girl power, nymph-style. I licked my lips, said, "I respect your choice."

Your King did not. He punished me.

Yeah, that sounded about right. Gehenna knew, I understood her desire not to bow before someone she didn't acknowledge as her liege lord . . . and the consequences such an action brought. "Hell's not so big on free will. But I'm all for it. Live and let live." I even managed a big smile.

Your King bound me to my tree, tied me to it so that my pride is now my punishment. I remain in the Land, but I can't stray farther than ten thousand paces from my oak. I am trapped, little demon. Forever.

I understood feeling trapped as well. That's why I had to run away, why I had to take a chance as a mortal. But the hamadryad didn't have such an option. She'd bucked the system, and paid the price. My voice soft, I said, "I'm sorry."

Her eyes narrowed to slivers of jade. *Do not pity me, little demon. I take my pleasure when I can. Many Good people come here, and when they slumber I visit them, and they worship me as I was meant to be worshiped.* Smiling, she ran her hands over her curves, her palms scraping over the bark of her flesh. *They love me, and I love them. All of them.*

"Sounds like you've got a good thing going here," I said. "Your own space, plenty of lovers. What could be bad about that?"

Plenty? Yes. But there are those I can't touch, even when I truly want to. Those who have declared themselves to another are beyond my magic. Her eyes sparkled with jealousy, and I felt my stomach lurch. *Seeing them in love is so . . . infuriating. Tantalizing. Like your man, little demon. He looks delicious. But I can't have even a taste.*

I swallowed thickly, said a silent thanks to whatever deity cared to listen that Paul truly loved me. If he hadn't, the wooden bitch would have raped him in his sleep. Big difference between the succubi and the nymphs: the succubi fucked only evil people, those already damned to Hell, while the nymphs fucked anything on two legs (or, when they weren't picky, four).

And then, there are times when the Evil come to my place. Evil humans, whom I play with. Evil creatures, whom I destroy. A flash of wood as she grinned, displaying splinter teeth. *I despise all things of Hell. Such as you, little demon.*

"I'm not of Hell," I said weakly. "Not anymore."

It doesn't matter. You have encroached onto my terri-

tory, you who were bred from Evil. You flaunt your love for your Good man, taking him in my place when I wish to touch him. You insult me.

"I meant no insult."

I will take great pleasure in destroying you, in sucking away your essence and feeding on your flesh. She nodded, satisfied. *And that, little demon, is why I am doing this.*

My heart dropped to my ankles as I realized her diatribe had ended. Look at the bright side, I told myself as I tried not to panic. An aspect of Mother Nature wanted to kill me, but at least she was polite and had told me why. Getting eaten by a rude beastie took all the fun out of it. . . .

Hold the phone.

Blinking, I realized that the hamadryad had paused in her attack to answer my question. Other than the grandiose villains in movies doing their award-winning monologues, that sort of thing simply didn't happen; it was much more proficient for creatures to slaughter first and philosophize after, usually over an after-dinner mint to disguise the heavy stench of blood.

So why had she paused? Maybe she had to answer direct questions—a geis of some sort? Or maybe she was lonely? In love with the sound of her own voice? Practicing for Toastmasters?

Her hand on my cheek wrenched me out of my thoughts. The bark of her flesh was both supple and rough, a tree that bent with the wind but remained upright in a storm. Power thrummed beneath her skin like earthworms undulating in the soil. *You may thank me now, evil thing, for luring your man away so that he will not witness your death.*

Oh goody. Mental fingers crossed for the geis possibility, I said, "Why ten thousand paces?"

She cocked her head, regarded me like I was an interesting bug she was about to crush. *What do you mean?*

Geis, one; succubus-eating plant, zero. "Why not, say, ten paces? Or ten million? Why ten thousand?"

For that answer, you would have to ask your King.

Shit. "We're, um, not exactly on speaking terms. Maybe you could tell me? You know, just between us girls? What do you think?"

She chuffed laughter, the sound like leaves rustling. *You are amusing. Most who trespass don't speak but to scream. You fought me, and now you talk with me.* Smiling, she nodded. *Yes, I shall enjoy eating your heart.*

Eek. "You know," I said, sounding incredibly, insanely calm, "instead of eating little old me, have you considered taking your righteous ire out on lumberjacks?"

Brows of ivy rose up on her face, perhaps in surprise.

"Or maybe taking up eco-terrorism?"

Yes, quite amusing. And now, my amusement is done. No more questions, little demon.

Her hand flowed over my mouth, gagging me. I bit down hard enough to make my teeth vibrate, but all that did was hurt my jaw; the wood nymph didn't even blink. Her hand tipped up my chin so that our gazes locked. The slurping sounds began again—no delicate sips this time. Hungry sounds. Tingling numbness crept along my jaw and down my neck, kept spreading, over my face, my scalp.

Unholy Hell, she's drinking my blood.

I shall water my tree with your life and use your empty carcass as a nest for birds.

Shouting against the wooden gag, I struggled against my bonds, shook my head to try to wrench it free. My mouth locked, I screamed at her with my mind: *I am not plant food!*

The hamadryad smiled, patient and knowing, like a parent talking to a child. *Yes, little demon. You are.* Her voice echoed in my mind, no longer harsh and scraping. No, her words were soft as rose petals as they caressed me.

I blinked, fought against a wave of dizziness. Light-headed now—it felt like the world would spin away if my hair weren't tangled in the tree. Bad hair day. Bad day, period. My head began to throb again. When had it stopped hurting? No matter; the pounding was back, bigger than before, drumming in my brain and echoing in my body. In my ears, my heart thumped in a counter rhythm, loudly. Fitfully. And I couldn't take a full breath, as if my body was shutting down.

She was killing me.

You freak of nature! If I still had my powers, I'd chop you into itty-bitty splinters!

The slurping changed into sucking, strong and rhythmic, and I felt myself rocking with the sound. Getting sleepy.

I'd turn you into furniture. Not the quality kind, either. The shoddy stuff that falls apart as soon as you sit on it.

Yes, yes, she said, bored. **Now the threats. So common. I'm disappointed, little demon. Until now you were fairly uncommon.**

Exhaustion, dragging me down, making my eyelids heavy . . . No, fight it!

And . . . I'd split you apart. Like . . . like firewood. Like . . . wood. Like . . .

What was I saying? Something . . . about wood . . . So hard to think. I felt my body dimly, as if someone had tucked it in a thick blanket. As if I were already dreaming.

No, not a dream. This was real.

Focus.

It occurs to me that you have yet to thank me for sending away your Good man. She rained a smile on me, and the sucking sounds paused. **Do you thank me?**

I couldn't even raise my eyes to glare at her. *Go fuck yourself.*

More amusement. Very droll. Think on this, little demon: after you are dead, your man won't be bound to you. And then he will be mine.

No. I won't let her touch him. Not Paul.

I wanted to shriek my declaration to the Pit and to the Sky, but my mental words were a bare whisper: *You can't have him.*

I can. I will. She patted my cheek, and my eyelids fluttered. *Go to sleep, little demon. Because you amused me, I'll wait until your body is cold before I take him.*

Clenching my fists, I sliced my fingernails into my palms. Pain, hot and sweet, jolting me awake.

I said you can't have him.

Reaching inside myself, into that place where my power once danced, I scrabbled for anything, for the last vestiges of life that fueled me, that kept my heart beating. Autopilot; I knew I didn't have any real power left, not since I'd gotten a soul, but I couldn't just let her kill me and take Paul.

Not Paul. I won't let her touch him.

Digging frantically, I found something deep inside, pulsing weakly like a fading star: a hint of magic. I grabbed it and squeezed, and with a snarl I screamed: *I won't let you touch him! I swear by Pit and Paradise, I'll kill you first!*

You . . . oh. Frowning, she looked down. Her hands trembled, dropped, and the wooden tendril gagging me slipped from my mouth. The roots around my wrists loosened, but they didn't let me go.

Gasping for air, I tried to summon the strength to scream my lungs out for Paul. Big, bad former demon needs a shitload of help, pronto! Instead of a bellow, I let out an emphysemic wheeze. Fuck me raw! I needed a panic button, because Gehenna knew, I was starting to panic. Starting? Make that diving into full-blown panic.

Stop. Catch your breath, Jesse.

Focus.

Panting, shaking from fatigue and blood loss, I told my heartbeat to slow down. It didn't listen to me; it was auditioning for cardiac arrest. Dumb heart. It would be really stupid if I didn't die from the hamadryad after all but from fear. . . .

Hey, I wasn't dead yet.

I stared at the hamadryad, was puzzled to see her leafy brows knit together and a thoughtful look carved onto her face. I followed her green gaze down, trying to see what had stopped her from draining me.

There, on the ground, winking in the sparse sunlight, the wood hatchet from the cabin's fireplace gleamed. Its sharp blade had half-sunk into the soft soil, right by my feet.

My powers! I could have danced a jig, if I weren't about to be sacrificed to a carnivorous oak tree. Oh, who cared about that? I had my demonic powers! I . . .

. . . didn't have diddly squat. The axe may as well have been right back in the cabin for all the good it did me down there on the ground while I was still trapped.

I reached out with my mind, even made a "come here" gesture with my hand. Come on, axe! Come to Jesse! Let's slice and dice the overgrown vegetable and make some crudités!

The axe didn't move.

Fuck fuck fuck fuck *fuck!* So not appreciating the irony here!

Cute, said the hamadryad. She lifted her hand, and I watched it reform into a wooden hatchet that looked obscenely sharp. Gah. *But you need to work on your aim. Here, let me show you how it's done.*

And that's when I opened my mouth and screamed bloody murder.

Chapter Eleven

The hamadryad hefted her axe-hand over her head, poised to strike. *Silence.*

Or what, she'd kill me? Screw that six ways to Salvation. I kicked up the volume and screamed as if my life depended on it. Horror film directors would have creamed to hear me. Banshees would have been impressed.

Not the wood nymph. Instead, she swung.

Gah!

With the strength of utter desperation, I yanked my head to the left and down—and screamed even louder as my scalp caught fire. Fuuuuuuuuuck—that hurt!

Biting my lip, I forced myself to shut up, no matter how much it felt like my head had been pushed into a meat grinder; I didn't have the energy to shriek myself hoarse and still try to escape. But even with my mouth sealed shut against the pain, the screaming continued, filling the forest with the sounds of rage and sorrow.

Not my scream at all.

The hamadryad's voice echoed in my ears and my mind as she reached over my head, her hand trembling as she touched the tree—stroked it soothingly, lovingly. Tears streamed down her face, watering her skin. The blade of her hatchet hand was streaked with brown: bark and sap and mud, caked onto its edge.

I couldn't help myself; I was too scared and exhausted, and it really looked like I was going to die, so who really cared if I pissed her off? Grinning like a madwoman, I said, "Looks like I'm not the only one with sucky aim."

Demon, she hissed, cutting her gaze to mine. *You are going to suffer before I allow you to die.*

The vines pinning my hands around the tree trunk pulled, and I screeched as my shoulders almost popped out of their sockets. Through the red haze of my pain, I tried to touch my power again, to grab it and hurl it at her and fry her where she stood. I was going to fucking charbroil her and her little forest too. Have a little Hellfire, nympho!

Except nothing happened, other than my arms getting stretched to the ripping point.

Bad. Bad, bad, bad.

Black motes in my vision. Agony in my limbs. I screamed myself raw.

Paul, I'm so sorry.

And the funny thing was that I heard him calling my name, as if he were right there. Had to be a dream, because I was dying and Paul was somewhere else, chasing rainbows and red herrings and trying to save the world while I was torn apart. I was glad he wasn't here at the end of everything, because I didn't want him to see me like this.

No, the hamadryad said, over the sound of my screams . . . and bless me if she didn't sound as terrified as I did. The pressure on my arms let up, and I nearly passed out in relief. *No. Go away. This doesn't concern you.*

"You better fucking believe it does. Let her go!"

To my left: Paul's voice. My Paul. He's here. Oh, Gehenna, he's here.

I wanted to tell him to run, to get away, but my voice was

too hoarse for me to speak—and to be honest, I really wanted him to save me. Because I couldn't save myself, and dying was such a shitty option.

She hurt me.

"Good for her."

I wished I could see him, smile at him, touch him. But he stayed out of my line of sight. I swallowed, then groaned over the burning in my throat. Unholy Hell, I hurt all over. My head was one raw wound, and my shoulders felt like they'd been used to mop up acid.

"I said, let her go, now!"

The creature smiled, a thing of jagged wood. *Or what? You think your toy weapon can harm one such as me?*

"Happy to find out. Ever get shot before?"

If you try it, man, I'll rip the demon apart.

Standoff.

I knew Paul—he would do something utterly heroic, and completely stupid, and would lower the gun if she told him to. Because I was her fucking hostage. Mental note: being the damsel in distress truly sucked angel feathers; avoid at all costs.

Put your weapon down, man.

"Let her go, and I'll be happy to."

I said, put it down. Her smile took on a playful edge, and something wanton gleamed in her eyes. *Or raise a different one, one I will happily surrender to.*

I blinked stupidly, wondered if I was hearing correctly. She wasn't really flirting with Paul, was she?

Her hands flowed over her breasts, fondling the budding nipples. *Think on it,* she purred, one hand moving down to trace the curve of her belly. *I am all that is lush and fertile in Nature. I can make your body bloom.*

You are so *not seducing my man, you stupid vegetable!*

She grinned at me. *I'll even let you watch.*

"Psychotic plant-types aren't really a turn on," Paul said,

his voice flat. "We're done talking. Let her go, now. Or I start shooting."

You tell her, love!

The hamadryad turned back to face him, and something dark passed across her face. Her grin slid into an indulgent smile, and she puckered her lips. Blew him a kiss.

Magic, washing over me, drowning me . . . making me giddy.

Adrift in rose and wine and oak, I stared at the hamadryad, at this marvelous creature carved from the trees—her body, perfect in every curve; her lips, ripe and meant to be kissed. My nipples pulled taut against my shirt, and my sex thrummed, begged for her touch—

—and then the wave passed, leaving me breathless.

Whoa.

Shuddering, I squeezed my eyes closed. Fuck, she was good. And that hadn't even been directed at me.

No, not at me. Oh bless me . . . Paul didn't stand a chance.

Shaking off the effects of her power, I opened my eyes and pulled against my bonds, craned my head to the left to try to look at Paul. My head pleaded for decapitation and my shoulders whimpered as I forced them to move.

I couldn't see Paul . . . but I heard his ragged breaths.

Tell me, man. What do you see?

"You," he said, his voice low and reverent. "You're beautiful."

Oh no. Please, Paul. Don't.

Come to me.

Movement to my left, and then I caught sight of him peripherally, just a hint of his form.

"Your eyes, your mouth . . . all of you . . ."

Another step, and now I saw him, a dazed smile on his face.

Paul's voice, from my dream: *If you won't let me save you, then there's no point to any of this.*

Go ahead and make with the saving! No argument from me, I swear!

And another step. Paul, next to me now, close enough that I tried to touch him but my wrists were pinned and he slipped away. His arms dangled by his sides, his hands empty.

The gun . . . Where was the gun? Bless it all to Heaven, how was he supposed to save me without his gun?

"Paul." My voice was little more than a wheeze; I'd screamed myself hoarse.

He froze.

Trying to catch his gaze, I thought at him, even though I knew he couldn't hear me: *Please, love. You're stronger than this.*

His hands balled into fists; sweat popped on his brow.

Yes, fight her! You're not just a flesh puppet. You're my man. I love you. Fight her!

His smile peeled back, and a muscle worked in his jaw as he clenched his teeth. A step backward, dragging, pulling against the force commanding him to move forward. His shoulders shook. Chords strained on his neck.

The nymph chuckled, throaty and seductive. ***It's been a long time since I've had a strong man. I shall greatly enjoy the feel of you on my skin.*** Then she puckered up again.

No!

Frantic, I darted my gaze around, tried to find some way out. I had to help Paul, had to get him out of here before she got her roots into him. But I was trapped, my hands pinned, arms useless, my body bound against the oak tree. My feet were loose, but a fat lot of good that did—

And there, half-buried in the earth, gleaming like salvation at my feet: the wood hatchet from the cabin.

Tapping the last of my strength, I kicked out with my right foot, grunting from the effort—and slammed it against the flat blade of the axe, just enough to dislodge it from its scabbard of soil. It hit the ground and slid on the carpet of leaves, coming to a halt halfway between me and Paul.

The hamadryad skipped backward, staring at the axe as if the naked blade were the deadliest snake. When she looked up at Paul, there was a desperate sheen in her eyes. Yes, she was afraid of it! Come on, Paul, pick it up!

Don't touch it. Ignore it. Look at me, man.

Paul looked at her, and he smiled. Nothing dazed about the set of his lips now; it was a hungry smile. Predatory. Passionate.

What do you see when you look at me?

"You're beautiful. Powerful."

Yes, man. She preened, relaxed, and I felt my heart sink.

"A goddess," Paul said. "And yet, you still don't hold a candle to a former succubus."

I saw the shock in her eyes just before Paul snatched the wood hatchet from the ground and hefted it in both hands. "Let her go!"

She spluttered: *You dare?*

Instead of replying, he pivoted and swung at the beech tree to his left. The blade sunk in with a meaty *thwok*. Screeching to rend the sky, the hamadryad doubled over, her hands wrapped around her stomach.

I grinned from the sound of her cries. Such sweet music. I could dance to it, strip down and ride her agony like a bronco. Did reveling in her suffering make me a bad human being?

Fuck it—she'd started it. All I'd wanted was a romantic weekend getaway. She was the one who tried to turn my homemade porn flick into a snuff film.

As she wailed, the bonds around my wrists loosened—but not enough for me to shrug free. Hit her again, love! Bathe in her blood!

Okay, so I was a little bloodthirsty. The leafy bitch had stolen enough of mine to qualify her for vampirehood.

Paul yanked the axe free, and the nymph groaned. Hah! Take that, you little green skank! I hope you felt that slice across your scalp!

She hissed at him, throwing her hands back as if to strike. Paul swung again, hitting a tree to his right. Bark flew and the hamadryad screamed, clutching her head as if her brains were leaking.

The ivy squeezing me like a boa constrictor slipped down to my hips. With a grunt, I pulled against my bonds, pulled until my shoulders nearly dislocated from their sockets. Close, so close, but my arms were still trapped. That bitch! If I were free and not feeling like I'd been a welcome mat for a Mack truck, I'd fucking pound her into mulch!

Just thinking about me making like a weed whacker softened the spikes of pain in my head into dull aches. My scalp itched maddeningly, and tingling warmth spread like balm over my neck and back. The power of positive thinking. Imagining me plucking the hamadryad by the roots and boiling her in a pot full of potatoes and carrots, I yanked again—too hard. A hot bolt slammed between my shoulder blades, and I leaned back against the oak, gasping, trying to ride out the pain.

I am so never getting captured ever again.

Paul dislodged the axe. This time, the nymph was ready for him—as soon as the blade was free, she threw her hands forward.

"Paul," I hollered, my voice loud and clear and not at all hoarse, "look out!"

He whirled as the ground shook. To his credit, he looked only slightly freaked out when two enormous vines erupted from the ground: his eyes widened, his mouth dropped open, but he didn't piss or puke or bolt. The plants hissed as they rose, looming over him, drooling as they gnashed their monstrous teeth.

Paul stood rooted to the spot for two very long seconds, staring at the swaying bulbous heads. Then his eyes narrowed and he lifted his axe high, hiked it over his right shoulder like a baseball player waiting for the right pitch.

The two plants lunged forward, teeth bared, and Paul shouted as he swung. A thick *snikt* and a roar cut short—and one of the green heads bounced on the ground as its long body collapsed in a heap.

The other plant reared up and attacked, aiming for Paul's face. Ducking under the snapping jaws, he sliced up with the axe and cut through its body. He spun out from the falling vine, swinging the axe in a wide arc until the edge landed solidly in a birch tree. The *thunk* of contact rang in the air, followed swiftly by the hamadryad's wail.

My bonds shed off of me like snakeskin.

I pressed myself against the oak's trunk, gathered my strength as I felt my rage bubbling through me. The hamadryad had tried to kill me, a lot, which was bad enough. Worse, she'd attempted to seduce Paul with her mojo, the cheating bitch, and then tried to kill him.

The world, painted in shades of red.

Snarling in my fury, I launched myself at the nymph. She spun to face me just as I crashed into her. We both tumbled to the ground, with me landing on top of her. My fists flew, and I punched her twice in the face—yuck, spongy—before she bucked me off. I hit the ground on my back, grunted as I scraped over roots. Ow, ow, ow!

Skidding to a halt, I rolled onto my stomach and pushed myself up onto my hands, spat out dirt. The hamadryad brought her arms back, and the woods rippled with her magic. Shrubs, vines, trees, roots—all sorts of forest life shuddered with her power and surged forward.

But not toward me.

I risked a glance at Paul, who was doing his best lumberjack impersonation. Teeth clenched, knuckles white, he slammed the axe into trunk after trunk, ducking under tangles of thorny vines and jumping over snaking roots, dodging the swinging branches and deftly avoiding the slower-moving trunks. Some of the wooden soldiers had scored home; he was bleeding from dozens of scratches on his face and arms, and his hands looked raw and swollen.

"The oak," I shouted around a mouthful of bark. "Hit the big oak!"

Paul's eyes narrowed, and he charged out of my line of vision.

Your fault.

I turned back to face the hamadryad, who was stalking toward me, her face twisted into a hurricane of emotion. *This is all your fault.*

"You started it!"

You're nothing but a pathetic evil thing.

"My father is bigger than yours!" I spun and kicked out, smashing my foot against her shin. She staggered back, then dove to the side when I threw myself forward. Landing hard on the ground, the breath whooshed out of me. Wheezing, I turned and saw a monstrous root charging at me. Fuck! I pivoted aside just as it smashed down into the earth, burying itself in the ground.

Crouching, I tried to catch my breath. Times like this, I really, really, *really* missed my magic.

Your death cries will rock me to sleep for ages.

My shoulders trembling with adrenaline, I shouted, "What's the square root of pi?"

She blinked, said, *What?*

With a roar I sprang up and introduced my right fist to the nymph's chin. Her head rocked back and her legs buckled, but she stayed on her feet. Then I slammed my left hand into her face. The bitch crumpled to the ground in a distinctly ungodly heap.

Oh, fucking *ow!*

Hands throbbing, I sank down on my haunches. And listened to the sounds of Paul's axe sinking again and again into the nymph's tree. Grinning, I closed my eyes and just breathed. The air smelled of cut grass and fresh blood. Yum.

The hamadryad sobbed and begged for mercy.

A strong hand on my shoulder. Paul, standing over me, his sea-green eyes flashing with love and rage and other emotions I couldn't catch. He was covered in dirt and sweat, with ugly scratches littering his arms and face. His shirt had been shredded enough to qualify it for a rag, and his jeans were completely filthy. His body hummed with energy as he radiated strength like an avenging angel. He was gorgeous.

His voice husky, he said, "You okay?"

"I'll live."

Please, the nymph cried. ***Don't hurt my tree anymore. Please.***

Paul helped me up, and I absolutely didn't lean against him for balance. I just really wanted to feel the press of his skin against mine. Really. He stared down at the broken thing that was an aspect of nature, the axe in his hands as she awaited his judgment.

"Get out of here," he said. "Get out, and don't come back."

I can't, she whispered. ***I'm bound to my tree, bound to my place in the Land. Bound to these ten thousand paces.***

Strained silence as Paul considered her words and I focused on standing on my own two feet. Holy fuck in Heaven, I hurt in places I didn't even know I *had* places.

"You agree to leave us alone?"

Yes, she breathed. ***Oh, yes. I'll leave you both alone. I swear it on my name.***

What?

"Paul," I said tightly, "you're not really going to let her go, are you?"

He sighed, squeezed my shoulder. "Look at her, hon. She's beaten. I'm not going to hurt her when she's already hurt."

"But she tried to kill us!"

"Yeah. But she's done now. She'll leave us alone, and we'll pack our things and go home."

He had to be kidding. "I tried the live-and-let-live tactic before, but she didn't want to hear it then."

"I'm thinking she's okay with it now." To the hamadryad, he said, "Right?"

She nodded, her eyes wide and shocked.

Unbefuckinglievable. "I thought that even law-abiding citizens were still okay with a healthy dose of vengeance."

Paul shook his head. "There's a world of difference between vengeance and justice."

Oy. My White Knight seriously needed to get in touch with his inner demon. "What're we going to do, arrest her?"

Cutting his gaze away from the nymph, he looked at me, tried to tell me something with his eyes. Then he took a deep breath, let his shoulders slump as he sighed. He was exhausted—a fine tremble worked in his arms, and beneath the cool cop exterior, his face looked ready to crack. "Let it go, Jess," he said softly.

"But . . ."

I bit down on my words. This wasn't just about me. Even if I thought—knew—that she deserved to be flambéed over an open fire, there were other people to consider. Like Paul, who absolutely wouldn't hurt someone who's already down. Like the hamadryad herself, imprisoned forever, all because she had refused to sacrifice her freedom.

But she tried to kill us.

A little voice asked me, *Wouldn't you be more than a little crazy if you'd been bound to an oak tree for tens of thousands of years?*

Argh. Stupid freaking human conscience.

I blew out a frustrated sigh and crossed my arms. "Fine. But she's so lucky you're here. Otherwise I'd take that axe and solve all her dandruff problems."

Paul smiled—sweet Sin, how I love his smile—and kissed my forehead. "Come on, hon. Let's go home."

And we would have just walked away and left the hamadryad

to lick her wounds, but as soon as we turned our backs, something wrapped around my throat and squeezed.

I grasped at my neck, but my fingers couldn't find any purchase; the vines wrapped there like a living choker necklace were slick with wet soil. They squeezed, and I crashed to my knees. Couldn't breathe. They squeezed again, and black flowers bloomed along the edge of my vision.

A final squeeze . . . and then the vines slid off.

Gasping, coughing, I drew in sweet, sweet air, grimaced as it burned my throat. When I finally looked up, I saw Paul standing over the hamadryad's body, the axe shaking in his hands, its sharp edge slick with ichor and earth. By his feet was a growing pool of white, the thick liquid seeping into the soil.

The nymph's head had come to rest at the base of her oak tree. And bless me if her mouth wasn't fixed in a peaceful smile.

Chapter Twelve

Paul and I stared at each other, the dead hamadryad between us, her body filling the silence louder than any words. He was breathing heavy, a look of fury and despair on his face.

"Thank you," I said, my voice a strangled gasp.

He nodded grimly. Straightening up, he blinked at the axe, then threw it to the ground. Wiping his hands on his jeans, he strode over to me. White fluid had splattered on him, stained his tattered shirt and splashed his jaw. He was rumpled, filthy, and bleeding, and I wanted to pepper him in kisses. Instead, when he helped me up, I held him tight. That's what he needed right now: me, holding him. Letting him know that we were safe again.

He was rigid in my embrace, and painfully silent.

"Paul?" Oh fuck me, it hurt to speak. "Love, it wasn't your fault."

"I know." His voice was a harsh rasp, grating like sandpaper over my ears. "I never." He took a deep breath, and I pulled him closer to me, because I would be damned to Hell before I let him slip away. He said, "I never killed someone like that. Not like that."

"I'm so sorry."

With a sigh he wrapped his arms around me, rested his chin in my hair. "It wasn't your fault, either. It . . . uh-oh."

I stiffened. "Uh-oh?"

"The oak. It's changing color."

Still wrapped in his arms, I turned to look at the powerful tree. Its upper branches had a distinct yellow cast, and they seemed . . . well, droopy. "Um . . . sunlight hitting the tree-top?"

"I don't think so . . ."

Patches of bark skidded off and littered the ground. A sound like gunshots, and then two branches cracked. They tangled in the multitude of other limbs, which were changing color as we watched. Another cracking sound, and my eyes widened as a black fissure crept up the base of the tree, spread to one of the trunks. A heavy groan, and I gasped as the powerful tree leaned dangerously forward.

"Shit!" Paul grabbed me and started running, with me tripping over my feet to stay with him.

A mighty rending sound behind us, like a dragon farting.

Paul shoved me and I flew forward, landed hard on the ground with Paul right on top of me.

A *THOOM!!!* to rock the rim of Creation, and then it rained bark.

My face pressed against the dirt—*again*, my mind shouted, *again*, and unholy Hell, I never wanted to taste soil again in my life or afterlife—and my body vibrated with the tree's death throes. Even after the sound of its booming crash faded to an empty echo, I stayed down, trembling, feeling the leaves beneath me age and crumble to dust.

Finally, long after the woods had quieted, Paul and I sat up. We were covered in dirt and blood and bark, with bits of ichor smeared haphazardly here and there. "Um," I said. "Timber?"

Paul blinked, and then he burst out laughing, the sound

loud and deep and so very right. Hugging me, he said, "You've got to work on your timing."

"You bet."

Then Paul was kissing me, and I melted into his embrace. We stayed like that for a lovely slice of forever before he slowly pulled away.

"Jess?"

"Hmm?"

"She said you'd hurt her. She didn't mean here, did she?"

"Ah. Um. Well, probably not . . ."

He arched a brow.

"She sort of attacked me last night. In the garden. And, um, the shower."

"Uh-huh. And you didn't tell me . . . why, exactly?"

Biting my lip, I wondered what to say . . . and then I decided to stop thinking about it and just say it. "I thought I was just hearing things, or maybe I was just sleep-deprived and hallucinating. I didn't want to worry you over nothing."

"Over *nothing?*"

"You have to admit, it's not exactly normal to have vines sprouting up and getting all carnivorous."

Paul shook his head, and even though his mouth was pulled in a frown, his eyes were laughing. "Promise me," he said, cupping my cheek, "that the next time you think you're just hearing things, you'll tell me right away."

I smiled sheepishly. "I just wanted to have a nice weekend, without the supernatural weirdness."

"Speaking of which . . ." His gaze searched my face. "How'd you get the axe in the first place? You told me you didn't have any demonic powers anymore."

"Um. Those reports may have been slightly exaggerated."

"Jess . . ."

"I don't know! Really! When I got my soul, that was it— no powers, no nothing. Well, except for seeing auras."

He repeated, "Auras?"

Shit. "Only sometimes. But that's flaky and not at all helpful. Except for showing me that you were safe here this weekend."

He blinked at me, then pointedly looked at his bleeding, swollen hands, then at my battered body, before shooting me a disbelieving look.

"Well, you sure aren't dead, are you? That counts. And seeing auras once in a while is nothing like bamfing up an axe or healing my bruises. That . . . bless me, it just happened." Please believe me.

"Healing your bruises?"

"Last night, in the shower. I think. Please, I'm telling the truth," I said, my voice soft and small. Fuck me, it sounded like I was going to cry. I just kicked serious nymphly ass. I shouldn't be crying.

After a long moment, Paul sighed . . . and smiled. "If it's okay with you, we'll add your powers to the 'Mysteries to be uncovered' column."

Oh, Gehenna—thank you. "After the weekend's done?"

"Oh yeah."

"So, the big bad evil is gone, and the peasants are rejoicing."

"Peasants?"

I cupped my breasts, flicked my thumbs over my hard nipples. "Rejoicing."

His eyes darkened, and his smile hinted at many wicked things. "I see."

"So how about we head back to the cabin, get ourselves very, very clean . . . and then very, very sweaty?"

"That sounds like a terrific plan." He wagged a finger at me. "But swear to me, right now, that if you hear or see anything out of the ordinary, you'll tell me."

Bless me, I love my overprotective man.

"I'm done hiding things."

"Promise?"

"Promise." Well, except for the Announcement that wound up making me run away from Hell in the first place. But Paul didn't need to know about that.

Shit.

I amended, "At least, I'll really try."

He looked like he wanted to say something, but instead he sighed, exasperated.

"Demons don't trust humans," I said, "not any more than humans trust demons. I know, I know—I'm not a demon anymore." Even if I still (maybe) had access to (some of) my demonic powers. "But four thousand years is a long time to get set in my ways. Like you told me yesterday, I have a lot of unlearning to do."

Paul's shoulders bobbed as he laughed quietly. "Lucky for you," he said, "I'm happy to play teacher."

Ooh. "Can I be the teacher's pet?"

"Hon, I'm planning on it."

He offered his hand, and I took it, squeezed, swore that I would never let him go.

And that was one promise I meant to keep.

CITY of DEMONS

Richelle Mead

Chapter One

There is a time and a place for a skimpy white nightgown. A misty island in the middle of winter is not one of them, but I'd certainly done stupider things to get a guy's attention.

"Hey," I yelled for the third time. I leaned one hip against the doorway, hoping to offer a better view of my figure. "You're going to freeze to death out there."

The man I addressed was sitting back in a lawn chair, posture easy and relaxed, with his long legs propped up and a laptop balanced in front of him. In the distance, early morning fog hung across the still water, nearly obscuring the dark shapes of other islands. After several more moments, Seth Mortensen—who dubiously carried the title of my boyfriend—slowly looked up from the screen and focused on me. Soft sunlight glinted on his brown hair, giving it a slight coppery glow.

"I don't know," he said thoughtfully, eyes lingering on my chest. "You look like you're the one who's freezing."

I petulantly crossed my arms, careful to leave my breasts and their attention-seeking nipples visible. "Are you coming inside or not?"

"I have a coat. I'm fine."

"You promised me breakfast."

"I just need another half-hour to finish this chapter."

"That's what you said a half-hour ago."

"I mean it this time." He looked back down. I was losing him. Damn it. This nightgown was one of my best. "Half-hour."

"Fine," I snapped. "Take all the time you want. I don't care. I'm going to go take a shower. A really long, slow, and sensuous shower."

No response.

"With lots of hot water and soap to make sure I get *every inch* of me clean. I'll probably have to do a lot of rubbing."

No response.

With a huff, I spun around and went back inside the bedroom, slamming the door loudly behind me. The cottage we were renting on Orcas Island only had this one bedroom, and it was small, with a messy, quilt-covered bed taking up most of the space. The front of the house had a kitchen smaller than my closet at home, and the bathroom here was tinier still. But this place had been ours for the weekend, and it was cozy and quiet and romantic. The kind of place you and your beloved could go to escape the world. To grow emotionally closer. To have mad, passionate, back-breaking sex.

If, of course, you could actually have sex with said beloved person without dire, soul-altering consequences.

With a sigh, I turned on the shower and waited for the water to heat up. I tossed my nightgown onto the bed and paced around naked, pondering not for the first time how an award-winning succubus could be so ineffectual—especially around a guy that was allegedly in love with me. Of course, the fact that said guy and I couldn't touch in any meaningful way kind of made things difficult. Being a succubus meant I was immortal and could shape-shift into any form I chose. The cost of that was that I had to steal energy and life from other people—through sex. So, yeah, that sort of put a damper on our romantic escapade here since I refused to consummate our love and shorten his life.

Halfway through my shower, the curtain jerked open. I yelped and saw Seth standing outside. He still had that same casual posture, but there was a glint of something very warm and very male in his brown eyes as he surveyed me.

"After writing *white nightgown* ten times, I decided it was time to quit."

"Well. You're too late. I took it off."

"I can see that." He didn't sound disappointed.

With deliberate slowness, I let my slick hands run down my body, wiping away the last of the soap. His eyes followed. Then, with feigned haughtiness, I snapped the curtain closed in front of him.

"Go away. I need another half-hour."

He opened the curtain right up again and reached into the tiny stall to shut the water off, oblivious to his own clothes getting wet. "You're done."

"Am not."

"Are too."

I pointed to the towel hanging on the bar. "Look, you've displeased me this morning. Immensely. But, if you apologize profusely and beg my forgiveness, I might let you dry me off. Might."

A wicked, playful look shone in his eyes, and I loved it. Seth was normally pretty shy and introverted. Seeing his dark and passionate side surface was always a treat. He grabbed the towel and stepped back, waving it tauntingly, like a matador.

"You aren't the one making demands here, Thetis." Thetis was his nickname for me, in honor of a shape-shifting nymph from Greek mythology. "If you beg, then I *might* let you have the towel."

"What kind of a threat is that? I can just shape-shift—"

"Is this a bad time, Georgie?"

My mouth clamped shut as I stared beyond Seth. There,

standing on the other side of the small bathroom, was my boss. Jerome was a demon—*arch*demon, in fact—who controlled all hellish activities in the greater Seattle area. He also looked like . . . well, John Cusack. Seriously—if you gave him a boom box to hold over his head, he would have been a dead ringer for the star of *Say Anything*. Out of instinct, I wrapped my arms ineffectually around my nakedness. It was very Garden of Eden.

"Please," Jerome said, rolling his eyes. "You have no idea how uninterested I am in your body."

Seth meanwhile had noticed my deer-in-the-headlights expression. He looked at me, glanced back to where I stared, and then turned back to me. "What's wrong?"

Jerome was invisible to mortal eyes. Only I could see—or hear—him.

"So what are you doing here then if you aren't spying?" I demanded. Seth opened his mouth to say something else, and I waved him off with my hand. He stayed quiet, suddenly realizing something immortal was afoot.

Jerome pulled a large manila envelope out of his black suit jacket. "I'm here to give you your plane ticket."

"My—what?"

"You're going to Los Angeles for me."

"Am I?" I attempted a little cockiness, but mostly I sounded confused. Because I was.

"Yes," he replied. "I was summoned for a tribunal. You're going to go in my place."

"What kind of tribunal?"

He waved his hands in a dismissive gesture. "Fuck if I know. Some duel. A demon got destroyed or some such idiocy, and they're having a hearing to figure out who did it."

I fell silent, processing the implications of what he was saying. "So . . . what? You got jury duty and you're pushing it off on me?"

"I'm reminding you that you work for me. And I'm telling you that you're going to Los Angeles."

More moments of silence. "They summoned *you*," I argued. "They aren't going to use me instead."

"They will. Hugh filed the paperwork this morning." The demon tapped the envelope, indicating the appropriate forms were inside.

"Why? Why me?" I asked.

"Because I have better things to do. And you always seem to be so interested in other people's business." He paused, face suddenly thoughtful. "And you might actually have something useful to offer."

That last sentence piqued my curiosity, but I didn't pursue it. "When am I supposed to go?"

"Tonight."

"I can't."

Jerome's dark eyes narrowed. "I'm sorry, Georgie. It almost sounded like you were defying me."

"I was. I can't go. Not tonight." I threw my hands up, indicating the cottage as a whole. "We have this for the entire weekend. It wasn't cheap."

He closed his eyes, and I had the distinct impression he was counting to ten. Jerome holding his temper was a rare thing. This might be a more serious affair than I realized. Meanwhile, Seth was simply watching and listening, no doubt trying to parse what was going on based on only hearing one side of the conversation.

Jerome's eyes opened. "Your weekend in a shit cottage on a shit island is none of my concern."

"I see," I said angrily. "So, it's okay for you to inconvenience me so long as it's convenient to you."

"Yes."

"No. I've done a lot for you lately. You owe me."

"I owe you nothing, Georgie. You're an unruly employee, and you're lucky I tolerate you."

That wasn't entirely inaccurate. Not only did I feel guilty about sleeping with Seth, I also didn't like to sleep with nice guys in general. They didn't deserve to lose their life energy and get wiped out. Of course, those were exactly the kind of guys Hell wanted damned, so my employers didn't appreciate me only going after corrupt men. I had "improved" recently for the sake of my career, but Jerome really had put up with a lot from me in the past.

"It's not fair," I growled.

Jerome snorted and spoke in a simpering voice. "Oh, oh. You're right, Georgina. It isn't fair. Thank you for helping me see the error of my ways."

I glared. "You're a real asshole, Jerome."

"That," he said seriously, "is the first reasonable thing you've said since I got here." He tossed the envelope onto the toilet lid. Seth jumped as it became visible. "This is neither an option nor a request. You *will* go to L.A. tonight."

Jerome turned, and I knew he was about to disappear. Anger and frustration flared inside me, mainly because there was nothing I could do. Suddenly, he stopped and sighed. He glanced back at me, annoyance all over him. A rectangular piece of white paper materialized in his hand. A plane ticket. He tossed it on top of the envelope.

"Take the human with you."

Jerome vanished.

After almost a minute of silence, Seth finally figured out that our visitor was gone. "You okay?" he asked.

"Yeah," I said shaking my head to clear it. "I think so."

Seth pointed to the papers. "What is that? What's going on?"

I took the towel from him without challenge and wrapped it around me. "This trip's about to take a different direction."

"Oh? How?"

"We're going to the City of Angels." I paused and reconsidered. "Or rather, the City of Demons."

The great thing about Los Angeles, at least, was that it was warm. And when you were just starting December in

Seattle . . . well, even smog and urban sprawl seemed like small sacrifices for sun and surf.

Our flight down was uneventful. Seth worked on his laptop. I browsed through the papers in the envelope, trying to figure out what I'd gotten myself into. When we'd landed and retrieved our baggage, I hailed our cab and gave the driver the address. Seth, still engrossed in whatever novel he was writing, didn't pay much attention to the ride. So, he was kind of surprised when we arrived and he stepped out of the taxi.

"A Marriott?" he asked, looking up at the building in front of us.

"Yup."

"But . . ." He frowned and took a suitcase from the driver. Seth's reticence in conversation usually came from a need to choose his words carefully. I could tell this particular moment called for special care. "You're going to some kind of demonic council, right?"

"Yes."

"And it's at a Marriott."

"Yes."

"Why?"

Luggage in hand, we walked into the lobby. It was wide and round, with a faux marble floor and a huge, gaudy chandelier that looked shabby and cheap. I was willing to bet its sparkling shards were made of plastic, not crystal.

"Why not?" I returned. "They've got to hold it somewhere."

"Yeah . . . but why not around a bonfire in the middle of the woods? Or at least a Masonic temple."

I walked toward the desk and crooked him a grin. "No room service."

Our room was nothing special, but that didn't matter. I'd gone into this weekend wanting to spend time with Seth, and now we could have it. Sort of. In fact, depending on how long this absurd tribunal went, we could be spending a lot of time together. But, the trial didn't start until tomorrow, so for now, it was just me and him. The thought filled me with happiness, and I was almost able to forget I was here against my will.

Feeling saucy, I patted the bed. "Want to break it in?"

Seth raised an eyebrow, and I immediately felt stupid. Of course we couldn't break it in. The joke had risen to my lips without thinking. Suddenly, like that, the bubble of joy burst, and reality slammed into me. It didn't matter if I was on a cold island or a queen-size bed with a plaid comforter. Seth and I could never reach the intimate levels we both craved. I don't know why it hit me so hard just then, but that's how it was. Sometimes I could deal with the hands-off nature of our relationship; sometimes it killed me. But, regardless, it was better than killing *him*.

Seth, noticing my mood change, smiled gently. The physical limitations we faced saddened him too, but he dealt with them with infinite patience. I'd told him he was welcome to get cheap sex anywhere since I was certainly busy myself with succubus "duties," but he never took me up on the offer. He always said he wanted to be with me and me alone. He wouldn't be budged. His strength continually amazed me.

Ignoring the awkwardness created by the joke, he shook his head. "I'm too tired to break it in. But you, Georgina . . . well, if you want to . . ."

The dangerous smile was back on his face, and I could feel a similar one coming onto my lips. We might not be able to touch each other without serious repercussions, but I could touch myself without any sort of loss.

And Seth . . . well, Seth loved to watch.

Chapter Two

The next morning, Seth and I headed downstairs to the trial. I stifled a yawn in the elevator and leaned my head against his shoulder. He slid his hand down to my lower back and brushed an absentminded kiss into my hair.

"This is going to be a long day," I sighed.

"Did you read up on the . . . case?" The catch in his voice showed how weird he still found all of this. I didn't blame him. When I nodded, he asked, "What's it about?"

The elevator reached the lobby, and I waited until we had stepped outside and were away from the other occupants.

"Murder," I said, yawning again.

Seth looked at me.

"Murder," he repeated flatly.

"Yup."

We started walking toward the hotel's meeting rooms. After several moments of silence, he finally spoke again.

"I can't believe you just yawned while saying that."

"It's not very exciting."

"It's *murder*. And aren't we . . . aren't we dealing with immortals here?"

We reached a long corridor and suddenly slammed into a wall of people. There were a few humans mixed in with the bunch, but most were immortals. Demons. Vampires. Imps. Even a few succubi and incubi. I rarely spent time around this many immortals, however, and nearly staggered from the force of all those signatures—auras, if you will. It was heady and oppressive. Like breathing in too much perfume.

I peered around them. "Jesus. This is the line to get in." I hated lines.

"Georgina."

I turned back to Seth. "Huh?"

"Murder? Immortals?"

"Oh. Well. It can happen. You know that."

"Yeah, but the last time it happened, you weren't this calm."

He had a point, and I shivered involuntarily, recalling the incident he referred to.

"Well . . . that time involved a serial killer taking out immortals at random. And who, um, had a crush on me. No one knew what it—he—was. This time, it's pretty obvious what happened. A demon destroyed another demon."

It was something demons did from time to time. And honestly, when you considered demons' selfish and prickly natures, it was a wonder it didn't happen more often. Sometimes demons would set up formal duels. Sometimes one would just get pissed and incinerate the other. Demons varied in strength, and two who were matched in power mostly just tended to circle and scuff each other up. When the power levels varied wildly . . . well, things ended pretty quickly.

Regardless of how it went down, destroying each other was *not* looked upon favorably among our masters. It was disorderly and annoying and created a lot of paperwork for the personnel department.

"If it's obvious, then why are you here?" Seth wanted to know.

"Because they don't know which demon did the, uh,

smiting. All the evidence shows a demonic attack; there's no question about that. What they have to figure out here is who the murderer is, so they can make an example of him or her."

"An example? Like capital punishment?"

"Not exactly. But trust me, you're really happier not knowing any more than that."

An imp standing in front of us turned around. He'd apparently overheard us.

"She means torture." He grinned at the two of us, revealing a mouth full of gold fillings. With his green suit and feathered derby, I think he was going for some kind of pimp look. Mostly it put me in mind of a porn star Robin Hood. *Robin of Cocksley*, maybe. Or perhaps *Friar Suck*. "Me? I'm guessing flaying, but my buddy Roger swears it's going to be disemboweling. I was just talking to this other guy in the bar last night, and he thinks Noelle's pissed enough that they'll actually flay *and* disembowel the poor bastard. Thinks they might even get some wraiths to do it—and you know how *those* little buggers are. They really get into ripping out intestines. Fuck, I don't even think they care about eating the entrails. They just play with them half the time. Spin 'em like lassos. Wear 'em like boas." He winked at me. "We're starting a pool. You want in, sweetheart?"

"No, thanks." I glanced over at Seth who wore the kind of shocked look accident survivors had. "Demons heal," I said hastily. "None of it's permanent."

He swallowed. "And so, they flay . . . or whatever . . . this guy, and that's that?"

Our new friend the imp answered before I could. "Well, you gotta understand that the flaying or disemboweling takes a long time."

"How long?"

The imp narrowed his eyes thoughtfully. "Oh, I don't know. Three, four centuries. Maybe five, depending on how bad a mood the judge is in."

"Five centuries?" Seth exclaimed. "And that works? Stops repeat offenders? Discourages others?"

"No." The imp and I spoke in unison.

"But it certainly makes them think twice," I said.

The imp stood on his tiptoes, trying to see the front of the line. "Yeah, some of the punishment's public, so it sets a pretty harsh example. Pretty cool, really. Too bad we'll have to wait days to see it. It'd be a lot easier if they just did a reading and got it over with."

"Reading?" asked Seth. "What's that?"

"It's something immortals can do to each other. It's a way of . . ." I grasped at words for something I barely understood myself. ". . . viewing someone's mind and soul. More than a viewing . . . it's almost like a union with them. You can see their experiences, know if they're telling the truth. You *feel* them."

"Whoa. Wouldn't that be a lot less trouble then?" he wanted to know. "And wouldn't it make sure the wrong person wasn't flayed?"

"It's soul rape," said the imp.

Seething Seth's puzzled look, I explained more delicately. "Letting someone look into your soul is pretty invasive. It completely exposes you—opens up everything inside of you. And from what I hear, it's a pretty horrible experience, so no one does it willingly. A more powerful immortal could force it on someone else, but even demons don't like to cross that line. It'd be like . . ."

"Soul rape," repeated the imp.

I could tell from his expression that Seth still didn't quite follow. "And so, even though that would reveal the truth right away . . . it's still easier just to go through this whole process?"

"Yeah," I told him. "Demons want to hide their souls. Besides, with the way they lie, one could look inside another and swear they saw something that wasn't actually true. So then they'd have to get more demons to find out what's real. Makes everything a mess."

"This is going to be some trial," muttered Seth, shaking his head.

"Technically," I said, "this won't be a trial at all—at least not in the sense you're used to. It's more like a . . . a tribunal, I guess. There are suspects—but they don't get lawyers. They just get examined by the prosecution and the jury. The jury decides who they think is guilty. A judge keeps everyone from killing each other in the meantime."

"No lawyers?" Seth considered. "Let me guess. You guys are the ultimate guilty-until-proven-innocent group."

"No. Well, I mean, yes, but that's not why. Really, in the grand scheme of things, this is kind of a small dispute. Anthony—the guy who got killed—was a minor demon. They threw together this tribunal because no one wanted to go to the trouble of having a formal hearing. If they did, then *that* would have a lot more procedure and whatnot. It'd probably take place in Hell itself too. Not a Marriott."

"I hear that," said the imp in disgust. "This place is a dive. Last time I went to one of these, it was at a Hyatt." He shook his head, clearly appalled at the collapse of Hellish civilization. "Fucking cheapskates."

When we finally made it to the head of the line, the demon working the door gave me a hard time. His eyes flicked coldly over the paperwork I handed him. He promptly handed it back.

"You aren't Jerome."

"I'm his proxy."

"A succubus can't be a proxy."

He started to turn to the person behind me, but I jabbed him in the arm with my finger. He glared.

"Well, obviously I can, or he wouldn't have sent me. Read it again."

I actually hadn't read the document. When Jerome had given it to me, I'd assumed everything was in order and devoted my attention to actually figuring out what this case was about. I had, however, seen my name on the last page and figured that was the important part. I opened to that sheet and pointed.

"See?"

"It's invalid."

"You didn't even read it!"

"I'm sure he read it," a voice nearby suddenly said. "Because surely, *surely*, Marcus, you wouldn't offhandedly dismiss a potential juror—particularly one sent by one of the more powerful archdemons in the country. Not only would that be rude and likely incur *his* wrath, it would also create chaos here when we realized we were down a juror. And that, my friend, would incur *my* wrath. Now, surely, *surely*, that isn't what you want."

All three of us turned to the speaker. He was a demon, like Marcus the bouncer, but even a mortal like Seth—without the benefit of reading signatures—could immediately assess the difference in strength. The newcomer radiated power, and it wasn't just his six-foot-five height and broad shoulders.

"Er . . . well . . ." Marcus jerked the papers away from me, suddenly unable to read them fast enough. He practically dropped them in the process and stared at the bundle a full ten seconds before realizing he held the sheets upside down. He flipped the stack upright, scanned through it, and then handed it back. "My mistake. You're cleared."

Seth and I walked into the crowded meeting room, the largest one the hotel had. It was one of the ballroom-size ones that wedding receptions were often held in. My benefactor fell into step beside us.

"My, my," he said pleasantly. "What is this world coming to when they let succubi sit on juries? It's like we have no standards left at all. Might as well put the suspects' names in a bag and draw a victim—er, culprit—at random."

We stopped walking, and a grin crept over my face. "They're trying to add a little class to these things, Luis, that's all."

He grinned back. "'Class?' Is that what the kids are calling it these days?" The giant demon leaned down and hugged me. "Nice to see you again."

"You too," I said.

Luis' gaze fell on Seth. "It's apparently a sign of the times too when succubi have human minions."

"He's my boyfriend."

Luis shrugged. "Same difference."

Rolling my eyes, I introduced them. "Luis used to be my boss," I explained. "Like Jerome. Only more fun."

"And sterner with unruly succubi," Luis added.

I thought about Jerome's recent behavior. "Debatable."

"Well, we can battle it out later." He glanced at his watch. "Right now, I've got to go take my place."

"Are you a juror too?" I asked hopefully. It might make this thing a little more entertaining.

He gave me an incredulous look, like I'd just insulted him. "Me? On a jury? Come on, you know me better than that. I'm the judge."

Chapter Three

The other jurors had reactions similar to Marcus the doorman's when they saw me.

"This isn't the Junior League, doll," one of them told me. "You can't just sit here and look pretty. This is serious business." The demon who told me this appeared to be drunk. Considering demons could sober up at will, he was purposely staying inebriated. Serious business indeed.

A few made uncomplimentary remarks about Jerome. One expressed jealousy over not thinking of sending a proxy herself. Most simply ignored me. The only one who treated me in a semi-friendly way was a guy who followed up his greeting with a proposition involving a whip, a waterbed, and peanut butter.

"I only use the organic kind," he added, as though that would make a difference.

Hoping he referred to the peanut butter, I ignored him and turned my attention to the rest of the room. Blue linen covered small round tables set with pitchers of water and surprisingly cute flower arrangements. I'd left Seth at a table with a bunch of incubi, figuring that would be safest. Most incubi (and succubi) swung both ways, but the incubi would be more interested in hitting on human women. I hoped. I'd mainly wanted to keep Seth away from vampires and imps. The former would go after his blood, the latter his soul.

The jury of thirteen sat at the front, facing the crowd from a long rectangular table. Luis sat at a raised table to our left, looking bored. On the other side of him, another long table held three very unhappy-looking demons. A few empty seats separated them from a demoness and an imp that I believed to be the prosecution.

After scanning the room, my gaze fell back on Luis. He had an elbow propped up on the table, letting his chin rest in one hand as he too studied the room. His chin-length black hair fell forward and shielded his face like a curtain. Seeing him stirred a number of memories, most of which were good. He'd been my archdemon long ago, back when I lived in colonial Massachusetts. I'd gone there because I'd liked the idea of moving to a fledgling group of settlements; it had seemed like an adventure.

Luis had been a good boss, ready with a smile and scrupulously fair. He did not tolerate any slacking, however. That easy smile could turn fierce in the space of a heartbeat, and those who angered him didn't get second chances. Fortunately, I'd performed my job well.

But in the end, even a cool boss like him couldn't change my mind on one thing: colonial America was a dive. I'd soon lost interest in it and requested a transfer back to Europe, deciding I'd check back on the New World in a few centuries or so. Luis had been sad to see me go, but he knew a happy employee was a good employee and had expedited my transfer.

Watching him now, I saw that same instant transformation take place. One moment he was slouching and bored; the next he was straight in his chair, banging the gavel and demanding attention.

The hearing started.

I realized then what Jerome had meant when he said I

might have something useful to offer. It soon became clear that I was the only juror paying attention. One leafed through a copy of *Harper's Bazaar*. Another played sudoku. Two talked in low whispers, falling silent like guilty schoolchildren when Luis barked at them to be quiet. One demon at the end of the table had his eyes open, but I was pretty sure he was actually asleep.

As I had told Seth, this was mostly an opportunity for the prosecution to lay out their suspicions and evidence. The demoness I'd spotted at the end of the table was indeed Noelle, poor Anthony's supervisor. Beauty among demons meant little since they could change their shape as easily as I could. Nonetheless, Noelle had chosen an especially gorgeous form in which to walk the mortal world, one I paid attention to for future shape-shifting inspiration. Not that I had plans to copy her identically, of course. Demons weren't big subscribers to imitation being the sincerest form of flattery.

Her face was a perfect oval, framed by tumbles of jet-black ringlets that fell almost to her waist. Her skin was smooth and clear, a coppery tan color that set off the blue-green of her large, long-lashed eyes. She wore an ivory skirt and jacket, stylish yet professional, matched with gold-buckled high heels I very much coveted. After Luis, she was probably the most powerful demon in the room. Something about her reminded me of him, like perhaps she too was eager to smile and laugh. But also like Luis, business came first. She certainly wasn't smiling now, nor did she seem likely to anytime soon. Those lovely eyes were narrowed with anger as she studied the three suspects. I'd heard that Anthony had been a particularly prized employee of hers.

Noelle did little talking, however. She left that to her imp, a shrewd-faced little woman named Margo. Imps were the administrative assistants of the demonic world, and I was willing to wager good money that Margo had been a real estate agent when she was human. She had the look of someone willing to say—and do—anything to get you to buy that haunted fixer-upper on the fault line.

Margo called up the first suspect, a demon slimmer than Luis but every bit as ripped. He had a shaved head and skin so dark there was no way he could walk out among humans without getting double-takes. Definitely not natural. Still, he made a striking, handsome figure, and I was a bit disappointed to learn his name was Clyde. It didn't fit. I wanted him to be named Nicodemus or Shark or something cool like that.

"So, Clyde," began Margo, "do you know why you're here?" She spoke in a voice of utter boredom, like he was so beneath her as to barely deserve notice. I raised an eyebrow at this. She might technically be in the position of power here in the courtroom, but at the end of the day, he was a demon and she was an imp. There was no question about who sat at the top of the universe's food chain.

From the look on Clyde's face, I wasn't the only one who'd noticed the condescension. The look he gave Margo would have sent me running.

"Yeah," he said in a rumbling baritone. "I'm here because you guys have no clue who took out Anthony and need a scapegoat."

Margo's smile was thin and utterly fake. "Oh, I see. So, you're here for *no* reason at all. It's completely unfair. You have no connection whatsoever to Anthony that would make you a possible suspect. No reason at all that you would have wanted to kill him. You were just plucked out of your everyday life and dropped into this room because the world is cruel and unjust. Poor, poor Clyde."

"Margo," said Luis, his smooth voice sliding through the room like a blade. He didn't even need the gavel to get attention. She jumped. "Stop your posturing and get on with this. If you want to get melodramatic, you can go join the community theater's production of *Our Town*."

I heard a few snickers, and Margo blushed. She turned back to Clyde, face sober as she became brisk and businesslike.

"You work here in Los Angeles?"

"Yes," he said.

"Noelle's been your archdemoness for almost a century?"

"Yes."

"Which is about the same time Anthony worked for her?"

"Yes."

"So," she continued, a bit of that swagger returning, "when Noelle needed to appoint a new lieutenant, it was pretty clear to everyone that it'd be either you or him, based on seniority."

The set of Clyde's face turned hard. "Yes."

"And when the time for her decision came and she picked *him*, that must have been terribly disappointing."

He didn't answer.

"Particularly since, by all accounts, you are—were— much, *much* more powerful than him. Am I right?"

Clyde remained silent, and I didn't blame him. An acknowledgment of how much stronger he was than Anthony just proved how easily Clyde could have destroyed his rival.

"Answer the question," said Luis in a firm voice.

Clyde grimaced. "Yes."

Margo made a great show of flipping through some papers, but I had no doubt she already had everything in them memorized.

"So . . . let's see." More paper flipping. Down the table, the juror I'd suspected was sleeping began snoring. The demon beside him hit him in the arm, jolting him awake. "Okay," said Margo. "According to what I have here, you had nearly double Anthony's power. That would have been a neat, easy kill. Over before anyone noticed it—which, from what we can tell, was exactly what happened."

"I wouldn't have destroyed him for that," growled Clyde,

his temper clearly rising. "Noelle made her decision. That was that."

"Not exactly." Noelle spoke for the first time, and heads turned. She had a sweet, lilting voice. Like music. Even some of the other jurors started paying attention. "You came to me after I appointed him, and you were *not* happy. In fact, I recall you saying some very . . . ugly things to me." She spoke crisply, all business-like. Even in the heat of an event like this, it was clear professionalism and calm were important to her. I admired that.

Although it was impossible to tell, I got the impression Clyde was blushing now. "I . . . was out of line, Noelle. I shouldn't have said what I said, and I apologize for it. I apologized then, after the fact." The words came out stiffly, but I got the impression they were sincere. Demons apologized. Who knew? "Although . . . not to place blame, but you were already upset when I walked in. You were in a bad mood, and it fed mine . . . and made what I said far worse than it might otherwise have been. Made me angrier than I normally would have been."

"You admit you were angry." Margo seized on this, a mongrel with a bone in her mouth. "Angry enough to insult and talk back to your archdemoness. Angry enough—according to witnesses—to 'exchange words' with Anthony too."

I could see Clyde's chest rise and fall as he took a few deep breaths before speaking. There was a temper there behind those dark eyes—again, not surprising for a demon—but he was working hard to stay calm.

"Yes. I had a few . . . confrontations with Anthony. He wasn't exactly humble about the promotion. We got into a few arguments."

"Because you were angry," reiterated Margo. "Angry enough to explode. Angry enough to kill him. You probably couldn't blow him apart fast enough, could you? Or maybe you ripped him up . . . tore him limb from limb or something before incinerating him. Anything to sate the bloodlust inside of you, right?"

He narrowed his eyes. "Honestly? It's been centuries since I had any bloodlust to sate. Funny thing, though . . ." He gave her a cold smile. "You're inspiring me to maybe rip something apart after all."

Luis sighed heavily and gestured to Margo. "Do you have anything else to add?"

The imp smiled smugly. "I think I've proven my point."

Luis glanced over at us. "Does the jury have any questions for the suspect?"

We all sort of sat there a moment, squirming under the room's attention. Then the demoness beside me raised her hand. Luis gave her permission to speak.

"So, did you call Noelle a bunch of names or something? What were they?"

"Yeah," piped up another demon. "Did you call her a ladder-climbing, self-serving cunt? That'd be a good one." While I admired Noelle's professional demeanor, it was obvious that others among us did not. I had the distinct impression my fellow jurors wanted to get a rise out of her.

Clyde's angry face registered momentary surprise. Luis snorted.

"Don't answer that," said Noelle, nodding to Clyde. Her face was still composed.

"Ooh," said my neighboring juror. "Then he *must* have called you a cunt, if you don't want us to know."

"I don't care if you know what he said," explained Noelle in exasperation. "But I'd rather you ask questions that are actually useful. This isn't *The Jerry Springer Show*."

"I agree," said Luis, giving my neighbor a censuring look. "Does anyone have any questions that will actually facilitate this matter?"

Silence. I have to admit, I felt kind of appalled. Demons were demons, evil by nature. But they also tended to be very efficient and business-like. The apathy around me was disheartening, even among our ranks. Whoever had thrown together this jury had picked low-ranking demons, ones who were completely self-absorbed and would never rise up in the ranks. They weren't shrewd like Jerome or commanding like Luis. They were bottom-feeders who'd be doing crappy jobs in Hell for the rest of eternity. They didn't care about this case. They were probably only here for the free food.

Tentatively, I raised my hand, needing to ask a couple of things that I honestly couldn't believe hadn't come up yet.

I thought I saw amusement in Luis' eyes when he noticed me. "Go ahead, Georgina."

The silence in the room grew even heavier. I don't think many of them had noticed there was a succubus on the jury until now. Even the center stagers—Noelle, Margo, and Clyde—seemed surprised to see me.

I put on my customer service face, hoping I looked as calm and confident as Noelle. "Where were you when Anthony was killed?"

Clyde didn't answer right way, and I could tell from his gaze that he was appraising me in a new way. I don't think he'd expected any sort of reasonable questioning in this courtroom. I don't think anyone had.

"I was at home, watching a movie."

"Was anyone with you?"

"No."

"No alibi," said Margo happily.

She was right, which didn't help his case. On the other hand, I felt pretty confident a demon like Clyde could have gotten some low-ranking vampire or imp to lie for him and play alibi.

"Any other questions?" asked Luis.

"What movie did you watch?" asked the drunk juror.

Luis glared at him, then flicked his gaze back to me. "Any *other* questions?"

I thought about it. "When was the last time you saw Anthony?"

"That morning. He was leaving Noelle's office while I was coming in."

"Did you talk?"

"No. Well, cursory greetings . . . and even that seemed to piss him off. He was angry and in a hurry. Was kind of an asshole." I had a feeling he might have elaborated, but Clyde probably realized trash-talking the guy he was accused of killing wasn't too smart.

I nodded and looked back at Luis. "That's all I've got."

"Why did no one ask those questions right away?" Seth asked me later, back in our room. There'd been a little more procedure, and then the court had recessed for the day. "Those are, like, the most basic courtroom questions ever. 'Where were you when this happened?' etc., etc."

I shrugged. "I know. None of them care."

"Yeah, but there's a five-century disembowelment on the line."

"They're demons," I told them. There wasn't more I could offer by way of explanation, and Seth seemed to understand.

"So, what about the other suspects?" he asked. "When will they be examined?"

"Tomorrow and the next day. Nobody wants to work too hard at these things, so they spread it out. In fact, most of the people watching are only here for the social aspect. It's the party of the century."

"Literally," muttered Seth.

I laughed and brushed my lips against his cheek. "Well, speaking of parties, there's one right now up in the penthouse. Wine and appetizers for dinner."

A wary look crossed his face. "And you want to go."

"It's a party. And not everybody here sucks. Luis is cool."

Seth was silent a moment, and I could almost see the wheels turning in his head. "Luis was . . . nice."

"So, you want to come with me?" I asked. "It'll be fun. I

saw you packed your Moon Patrol shirt, so you can even dress up."

He gave me a wry look at the shirt joke. "You know how I feel about parties *and* groups of immortals. This would be like . . ."

"A five-century flaying?"

"Yes. Exactly."

"Coward."

He caught me in his arms, pulling me to his chest. "Around this sort of thing? Yes. I make no pretense to bravery."

"What are you going to do instead?" Like I didn't know the answer.

"Are you kidding? There are five coffee shops around the corner with free wi-fi. I'll have a new novel done by the time you get back from the party."

I didn't doubt it. And honestly, I couldn't believe Seth had gone this whole day without getting any sort of writing done. It was truly a sign of his love for me.

But then, a wistful look appeared in his eyes, one that indicated that *maybe* writing wasn't the only thing on his mind. "But I'd much rather spend time with you," he said.

A pang of guilt thudded in my chest, and suddenly, I felt bad. This was supposed to be our getaway, and here I was, blowing him off for a party. But I did want to get a feel for this case and knew there'd be other opportunities for us to hang out.

So, I let him go on his way, with promises to get in touch later tonight. As for me, I set about figuring out what to wear to this shindig. I might not respect most of the demons here, but I wanted to be respected. I wanted to look like I could actually add some value to that jury. And, yeah, I just also wanted people to think I was hot. Demons are selfish. Succubi are vain.

I'd packed lightly on this trip so I wouldn't have to check luggage, figuring I could just shape-shift on whatever I needed. Standing in front of the mirror, I conducted my own fashion show, trying on and dismissing a dozen different combinations. As much as I would have liked for Seth to go to the party with me, I was kind of glad he wasn't here to see me trying on more outfits than a teenage girl.

Finally, I decided on a white charmeuse trapeze dress, the kind of dress that looks like a bag on anyone except a model. I had a model's body but still cinched the dress with a wide, black leather belt that better defined my waist. Part of my light brown hair I pulled up into a high bun, the rest I let hang down my back. I was admiring the effect of black stilettos when I decided the white was too stark. I shifted the dress red, decided that was overkill, then settled on a pale gold shade that complimented the hazel-green of my eyes.

"You should have stuck with the white one," a gravelly voice suddenly said behind me. "It made you look angelic."

Chapter Four

I spun around, swallowing a yelp. Who the fuck was in my room? I peered into the darkness. There, practically blending into the corner shadows, stood Clyde.

"Holy shit," I said, as the demon stepped forward.

He smiled. "Sorry to startle you."

"It . . . it's okay." I forced a smile of my own, trying to play cute succubus and not act like I was freaked out that a demon—possibly a demon murderer—had materialized in my room.

Then, it hit me.

"How can you be here?" I exclaimed. "Aren't you under arrest?" I took a step backward. "Oh, Jesus. You didn't break out, did you?"

Still smiling, he shook his head. "They don't keep me behind bars, Georgina. They—" He paused thoughtfully. "Do you go by Georgina? Or do you prefer Gina? Or Georgie maybe?"

"Georgina," I said. Bad enough there was already one demon in the world who called me Georgie. I'd told Jerome a hundred times not to call me that, but he never listened.

Clyde nodded, pleasant and cordial. There was no sign of the angry and frustrated demon I'd seen earlier. It was like we were already at the party, making small talk.

"Okay, Georgina. As I was saying, they don't lock me up. I'm bound to this area, though. I've got about a three-mile radius around this hotel that I'm confined to. I try to leave, and believe me, they know."

"Do they cut you off from your powers too?" I asked, by no means comfortable with this situation.

"Some, not all. If you're worried about me blowing you up or something, don't. Aside from the fact that I can't, it would really hurt my case if I destroyed one of the jurors."

Fair point.

"Okay," I said, feeling only a little better. I still had my arms crossed in a weak attempt at protection. "Then what are you doing here?"

"Just thought it'd be nice to get to know you," he said with a shrug. "Seeing as we've never met. A little chat to pass the time. I was very impressed with your performance in the courtroom today. I appreciated that you didn't ask my underwear size or my favorite color."

Disdain replaced the last of my fear. "You having chats with all the jurors tonight?"

I swear, that grin grew almost twice as wide and was reflected in his dark eyes. "You're too smart to be here, Georgina. You might be the only one who actually cares about how this turns out. Well, aside from me and the other two."

I shook my head. "If you're here to bribe me, it won't work."

"No?"

"No."

"Everyone can be bribed," he countered. "It's how you sold your soul in the first place. It's just a matter of finding out what you want now. The other jurors? They have plenty of things they want, things I can deliver on once I'm free and back in power."

"So, what? They're all on your side?"

"Depends on what Starla and Kurt offer them. Believe me, every demon on the jury who casts a vote will do it based on a bribe. The question is, which bribe will each one take?"

"That's . . . horrible."

"We work for Hell, Georgina. You want fairness, go to the other side."

"Luis is fair." I spoke without thinking.

Clyde tilted his head, studying me from another angle. "If you're thinking about running to him and telling on us, forget it. He knows what's going on, knows he can't stop it."

I chewed on my lower lip. I *had* been thinking of going to Luis.

Clyde came closer. "So, what do you want? What'll it take to get you to acquit me?"

"I told you, I don't want anything—nothing badly enough to free you if you're the one who did it."

His face hardened, a serious look crossing his features. "That's the point. I didn't do it, but that doesn't mean anything out there. They want someone to hang—literally and figuratively—and they'll take whoever's convenient."

He sounded sincere again, but I wasn't fooled. Demons were superb liars.

"Please go," I said, hoping he hadn't been lying about being unable to hurt me. That too had been convincing. "I'm not taking your bribe."

"You're a succubus," he mused. "You don't need money— that's what Starla'll probably offer you, by the way. But I'm guessing you've got plenty of your own—or can get it from some dying old man. Kurt . . . he's smart. He might offer something good. Not sure which way he'll go. But me . . . let's see. Pleasure. That's what you want."

I choked on a laugh. "Pleasure? Baby, do you know how often I get laid?"

He waved his hand dismissively. "Probably more than me. But that doesn't mean you like it."

It was true. I didn't always like it. Sometimes the act did it for me; sometimes not. But there was one part I always liked.

"I get my life from it," I said honestly. "And when that happens—that rush—that transfer. That's pleasure. That's amazing. Better than the sex."

"But wouldn't it be nice to experience sex that was better than the transfer?"

I stared incredulously. "You're trying to bribe me with sex? You're trying to bribe a *succubus* with *sex?*" Maybe he was the killer. He was clearly deranged enough. "That's the most—"

Clyde reached out and touched my forehead with his fingertips. I gasped at the jolt of power that shot through me.

Suddenly, I wasn't standing in the hotel room anymore. I was in another room, a room from antiquity, on a bed covered in plump pillows and silk sheets. The silk slid against my back, and Clyde's body slid against the bare skin on my front.

Our limbs were entwined, his mouth on mine in a kiss that was all fire. *He* was fire. His skin was literally hot—so, so hot. It was a demon thing. I seriously thought it would scorch mine, but my skin stayed whole and unmarred. He moved against me, bringing his mouth down and trailing more of those burning kisses down my neck. His lips found my breasts, taking turns with each nipple. He sucked hard on them, his teeth biting in a way that danced a very thin line between pleasure and pain. For now, it just barely kept to the pleasure side.

But his mouth and the fire of his skin weren't what drove me wild. They weren't what made me moan and arch my body up to his, pushing as much of myself forward as I could.

It was his hands.

Because everywhere they touched, they poured life into me—that beautiful, blissful silver life energy I stole each time I slept with a human. It was the glittering energy that filled the soul, the power that usually coursed into me at the end of sex and sustained my immortality.

But now, that energy was coming from the palms of his hands as he ran them over my body. He moved slowly too, dragging out that ecstatic agony. It was almost like he was massaging oil into my skin. That life covered me, saturated me, and soaked in. It was more than I'd ever gotten from a human—even the purest, noblest soul. Ten times more. Maybe a hundred. Who could tell? My body became one enormous erogenous zone. Really, there's no way to describe that energy to anyone who hasn't directly experienced it. It's, well, life. The universe. The touch of God.

One of those glorious hands danced down between my thighs. His fingers slid along my flesh, slipping through my wetness. His skin still burned against mine, and coupled with that continued flow of life, I almost couldn't handle it. I writhed under his touch, whimpering as his hands teased and taunted, promising much but not yet delivering.

I knew this wasn't *really* happening, but I also knew he wouldn't show it to me if it wasn't a possibility. This was his bribe.

"How . . ." I gasped out. "How . . . can you do this? How can a demon have this much life . . . ? Energy and souls . . . that's only for humans and angels to deal in."

He removed his hand so that it and his other one rested on my hips. Shifting onto his knees, he pushed into me. The pleasure and pain line blurred for me again, and it wasn't just because of his size and hardness—both of which were considerable. Nor was it the fierceness with which he thrust away—which was also considerable. It was that fire again, the heat that coursed through a demon's skin. It was like a flame spreading up and into me.

It hurt, yet I exulted in it. And as that fire continued to

sear me, his hands stroked my breasts and upper body with that glittering energy. It was pure delirium, cool and crisp in a way that compensated for the heat of his body. We were fire and ice.

"How can a demon have this much life?" he asked, echoing my question. He continued moving forcefully into me, each powerful stroke pushing me closer and closer to being suffocated by all that lovely life. The rapid pace appeared to take no toll on him. His dark face watched me thoughtfully, and if I squinted just right, I could barely discern horns on his head and flames in his eyes. They shimmered in and out, like a mirage. "You don't know? Haven't figured it out?"

Some part of my brain said if I thought hard enough, I *could* figure it out. But I didn't really want to think too much just then. "No . . . no . . ."

The words came out as a moan, and I felt only a little embarrassed at my loss of control. Wasn't I supposed to be the sex professional here? Fuck it, I decided. There was so much life energy in me now that I doubted any more could even make a difference. I was drowning in it, high on it. And I could tell by his motions that he was going to come soon. A demon exploding inside of you is like fire too, and while it hurts horribly, it's also insanely pleasurable at the same time—so much so that it almost always triggers an orgasm in return.

I was going to come, and it was going to be *good*. My body was practically ready on its own, but I wanted to wait for him to finish it.

"You're forgetting something," he said softly. His strokes were long and controlled. Very purposeful. He was close, and I had no clue what he was talking about anymore. Fire and ice. That was all I knew.

"Forgetting . . . what . . . ?"

He leaned over me, putting his face right next to mine, and I cried out as the shift in position allowed him to take me at a different, deeper angle. Fire and ice.

"The reason demons can have this much life . . ."

I was almost there. So close, so close. His voice was low. It was velvet on my skin.

". . . is because . . ."

I was on the edge, ready to fall over. Fire and ice.

". . . we used to be angels too."

Fire and—

He pulled out and sat back on his heels. Suddenly, all that pleasure, all that bliss . . . it was gone. Bam! I was empty and aching. It was like being thrown into cold water. All ice now, and not even the good kind. No more fire. I jerked upright.

"What the fuck are you—"

I blinked and looked around. No silk-covered bed. No Clyde, even. I stood alone in the hotel room, still in front of my mirror. The dress was white again.

"Remember this," a voice whispered through the air. "We can finish it . . ."

Chapter Five

I went to the party, a bit dizzy on the idea that I'd just had virtual sex with a suspected murderer. Naturally, I had had sex with actual murderers in the past . . . but, well, this wasn't something I wanted to make a habit of.

Luis found me right away and handed me a drink. "You okay? You look like you've seen a ghost. And I know that can't be true since they stay away from these kinds of soirees."

I shook my head and took down the drink. Appletini. A bit froofy for my tastes, but hey, it had alcohol in it. I wasn't about to knock that after what I'd seen today.

"Long story," I said evasively.

"Okay." He sipped his own drink. "So, how'd you like your first day in court?"

"It's . . . depressing. Nobody cares. Someone was asleep on the jury."

"Only one?"

"Luis, I'm serious."

"I know," he said unhappily. "And so am I. That's how these things work."

I stared off across the room, absentmindedly watching a

couple of demons who seemed to be . . . very close friends. One appeared to have an astonishingly long tongue. Like, Gene Simmons long. I looked away with a shudder.

"I realize we're evil and all that." I recalled Clyde's comment about me and my nature. "And yeah, I'm here because I gave in to temptation. So is everyone, even you guys. But, well, I don't know. I'd like to think there's some nobility in all this."

"There is, here and there. Some have given up and completely given in to their dark sides. Some are like you, still in possession of an annoying yet adorable sense of right and wrong. Semi-good people who only made one mistake, a mistake they regret, so they still try to live with some semblance of their old selves."

I frowned. "Are you like that? Regretting your one mistake?"

He laughed, finished the drink, and set it on a nearby table. "Oh, it's different for us. Mortals are faced with daily temptation—as well as the uncertainty of what's *really* out there in the world. Is there a God or gods? Is human life all there is before oblivion? Are you alone in the universe? I'm not saying that justifies falling, but it's certainly easy to do. If you believe there's no real higher calling in life, why not give in to temptation? Why not take the easy way out and seize your deepest desires? Maybe damnation won't be that bad . . . then, you realize it *is*. Some embrace it. Some, like you, hope that maybe holding on to that one spark of goodness will redeem you. Get you salvation."

"I don't think that," I said obstinately.

He winked. "Don't you, though? Somewhere, buried deep inside, is a hope that maybe things can change. Because again, mortals—or mortals turned immortals—just don't know for sure. Now us . . . higher immortals . . ." The brief amusement faded. Darkness clouded his features. "We know. We know the truth, what's out there, what's beyond life and the universe. We've seen divinity, seen the rapture . . . and we still turned away from it. It's lost to us. It's a fleeting dream, the kind you wake up from in the middle of the night, one that leaves you gasping and mortified because it's only a phantom . . . a fading memory that's forever denied, blocked by a wall through which there is no passage."

A chill ran down my spine. I was used to lighthearted Luis and all-business Luis. This Luis—troubled, philosophical Luis—was frightening. I could see the longing in his eyes, the remembrance of that which he still longed for and could never have again. It was a haunted look, a look filled with things too big and too powerful for a succubus to understand.

He blinked, and some of that otherworldliness faded.

"And that, Georgina," he informed me, bitterness in his voice, "is why so many demons have completely given themselves over. When you lose what we've lost, when your hope is gone . . . well, for most of us, there's no point in trying to reconcile our old selves with our new selves. It's too late."

"But not you. Not entirely."

"Hmm . . . I don't know. I don't know if there's anything good in me anymore."

"But you want to see this trial conducted fairly," I pointed out.

His smile returned. "Wanting to know the truth isn't necessarily being good. Maybe it's just curiosity."

I didn't believe that. I liked to think there was some glimmer of that angelic nature left in Luis. *We used to be angels too*. Clyde had proven that they still burned with the power of life. But maybe I was just being naive.

"And some of us," Luis continued, "seek the truth simply for vengeance."

He inclined his head over to a table set with food. There, Noelle and Margo conferred about something. From the grim look on the demoness' face, I could only presume it was about the murder.

"Don't be fooled by her alleged concern for a fair trial," Luis murmured in my ear. "And don't be fooled by her pretty face. She's dying to punish someone, dying to rip someone's head off with her own hands. Destroying one of her demons is an insult—and whatever other fancies you want to believe about us, never doubt for a moment that we're controlled by pride. Hers has been slighted, and she wants someone to pay."

"But does she want the *right* person to pay?"

"She'd certainly like that, less because of fairness and more because she hates the thought that whoever did this to her might walk away unpunished. But if we can't figure out who did it . . . well, she probably wouldn't be too picky so long as she got to watch *someone* suffer." He paused. "Plus, I think she . . . 'liked' Anthony. If you catch what I'm saying."

"Ah." Noelle's anger suddenly took on a whole new meaning for me.

He nodded. "That's also why she didn't ask to simply look inside them, I think."

He was referring to the same "soul reading" that Seth had asked about. If Noelle, who had brought this case to court, really pushed, she could have maybe convinced the authorities to force readings on the suspects. It might be taboo, but sometimes Hell resorted to it.

"She claimed something about how they didn't need to go those extremes and how the jury would decide in an efficient way," he added. "It sounded quite noble. But I think that's bullshit."

I thought about it. "Because if it turned out none of the suspects had done it and there were no other leads, she wouldn't get to take her revenge out on someone."

"Exactly."

Wow. He wasn't kidding. She really was out for blood.

I spent the rest of the party socializing with Luis and others, smiling and flirting in a way that came second nature to me. I had become something of a novelty—the only lesser immortal on a demonic jury—and a lot of people wanted to talk to me.

I also received a fair number of solicitations, but that was pretty common for a succubus. We were viewed as the call girls of the immortal world. Fortunately, none of tonight's offers involved peanut butter.

After the party, I found Seth in a diner a few blocks away, a place I never would have suspected of having wi-fi. He sat in a corner, focused entirely on the laptop in his usual way. His devotion to his work was infuriating at times, but it was adorable too. Watching him, I felt a sudden desire to run my fingers through his hair and make it messier still.

He hadn't noticed me entering, and when I had almost reached him, one of the waitresses stepped up to the table. She was young, lower twenties, with her blond hair pulled up into a high ponytail. Underneath the blah uniform, I could see a perfect hourglass figure. She had the good looks of a struggling actress, but I half-suspected she wasn't anorexic enough to meet today's starlet standards.

"You want more?" she asked, holding up a pot of coffee. The orange rim signaled decaf. Typical of Seth.

I waited for him to ignore her, but to my surprise, he looked up right away. He smiled at her. It was the cute half-smile that always made me melt.

"Sure."

She filled the cup, leaning over to do so. And then—I swear it—Seth's eyes hovered briefly on her cleavage before looking away. Impossible. Seth almost never checked women out. I stiffened.

"What chapter are you on now?" she asked.

"Thirteen."

"Thirteen? Are you taking speed with that decaf? You were on eleven last time I checked."

His smile twitched. "The muse is in a good mood tonight."

"Well, send her to my place. I've got a ten-page paper due tomorrow."

"Is that the history one?"

What kind of question was that? Had he learned her life story after only a few hours?

She shook her head, ponytail swaying. "English. Gotta analyze *Dracula*."

"Ah, yeah." Seth considered. "Vampire stories. Slavic dualistic concept of life and death, light and darkness. Harkening back to pre-Christian myths of solar deities."

Both the waitress and I stared. Seth looked embarrassed.

"Well. Not that Stoker used much of that."

"I wish you could write this for me," she said. "You could do it in five minutes. I can't believe you wrote all that. Where do you get all those ideas?" She grimaced. "That's probably a stupid question, huh?"

"Nah. Someone I know thinks that, but honestly, it's a good question. I just don't have a good answer, I'm afraid."

That "someone" he referred to was me, and I didn't really appreciate being delegated to a non-specific pronoun. The appropriate designation would have been, "My stunningly brilliant and beautiful girlfriend whom I adore beyond all reason . . ."

She laughed. "Well, if you figure out the answer, let me know. And let me know if you need anything else."

I swear, there was a subtle inflection in her voice when she said that, like she was offering more than just coffee. And Seth, amazingly, was still smiling at her, even regarding her admiringly. He'd also been almost comfortable in chatting with her. Usually his shyness took over with new people, and you could barely get two words out of him—and even those came with a heavy dose of stuttering.

I swallowed back my jealousy. Seth and I had our arrangement. He was perfectly entitled to go after cheap waitresses if he wanted. Besides, I was above such petty insecurities.

The waitress passed me on her way back to the kitchen. *Beth*, her nametag read. Alliterative with bitch.

Okay. Maybe I had a little pettiness.

I strolled over and sat down across from Seth.

"Hey, Thetis," he said. He smiled at me, but it was a leftover smile from Beth.

"Hey," I returned. "Think you can drag yourself away?"

"Let me finish this page, and I can. Cady's about to figure out who the culprit is."

"Too bad she can't help me with this trial."

He looked up from the screen. "No insights at your party?"

"Someone tried to bribe me." No need to get into specifics. "And Luis concurs that the whole thing is corrupt." I smiled. "You going to come back tomorrow to see more antics?"

He typed a few words. "No . . . if it's all right. That whole thing freaked me out. And I'm kind of on a roll here. This place has a good vibe."

"Yeah," I said carefully. "That waitress seems pretty nice."

"She is," he agreed, eyes still on the screen. "She reminds me of you."

I kept smiling, but I wasn't entirely sure if I should feel complimented or not.

Chapter Six

Whatever resentment I held toward Seth and the waitress faded pretty quickly when we got back to our room. He held me as securely as ever, kisses light on my skin and affection radiating around him like an immortal signature.

I let him sleep in the next morning as I blearily dressed and headed downstairs for day two of the trial. To my surprise, there were a lot less spectators than the previous day.

"They saw what they wanted to see and went home," Luis explained to me. We stood near the entrance to the room, drinking coffee. "A lot of this is just sensationalism. The thrill is gone, though some might come back for the sentencing."

I glanced over at the jury's table. "At least none of *them* left. I kind of expected it."

"Nah. They know better. There'd be serious consequences if they took off from something like this."

Apparently, though, none of the demonic jurors felt they had to do more than just be present. They proved just as negligent as yesterday. The suspect today was a demon named Kurtis.

"Kurt," he corrected Margo.

"Kurtis," she said, "can you tell us about your relationship with Anthony?"

"Relationship? We barely had one date. I'd hardly call it that."

A few people laughed at his joke. He'd chosen a lanky form and pale skin, with hair that kept falling into his face. If he was concerned about being accused of murder, he didn't show it. His chronic smile indicated how silly he thought all of this was, Margo most of all.

She glared at his impertinence. "What I mean, *Kurtis*, is how did you know Anthony?"

He opened his mouth, and I would have bet anything he was about to crack another joke. Just then, he happened to make eye contact with Luis, and the accused demon's face sobered a little bit.

As the story unfolded, we learned that Kurtis had once been Anthony's archdemon. This perked the jurors up a little bit. Archdemons, as the leaders and power players in our world, tended to be better at self-constraint. Luis, Noelle, and even Jerome were good examples of that. If archdemons did take on others, it was their peers—not underlings. If Kurtis had indeed destroyed Anthony, it would be a juicy scandal. An archdemon undergoing a five-hundred year flaying would be equally compelling.

"Nothing'll happen to him," murmured the demon sitting beside me, as though reading my mind. He was the one who was into peanut butter. "He's here because they wanted to make it look like they had a full group of suspects. You know, like they'd really researched all the possibilities. There isn't enough evidence against him."

I was surprised to hear something so astute from one of my colleagues. "That must be why he's so laissez-faire about all this."

"Yup." The demon's eyes studied Kurtis, then gave me a curious look. "What about Nutella? You into that maybe?"

When Anthony had worked for Kurtis, the two had apparently had a fair amount of tension between them. It wasn't entirely clear if Anthony had done something to warrant the antagonism or if it was just a personality conflict. Regardless, Kurtis had taken retaliatory measures against his unruly employee.

Margo was pretending to read her clipboard again. "So, let me get this straight. You burned him alive?"

Kurtis shrugged. "If you can call it that. I mean, it didn't do any permanent damage. And really, are we alive? Don't we just exist? Or, in his case now, not exist?"

"And you locked him in a box at the bottom of the ocean for a month."

"It was a roomy box."

"And you decapitated him."

"No."

Margo looked up from her clipboard, eyebrow raised. "I have several witnesses who say otherwise."

"I only partially decapitated him," Kurtis countered. "His head was still attached . . . technically."

Margo continued to go through a laundry list of assorted tortures Kurtis had inflicted on Anthony. Horrible or not, I had to admit the archdemon was pretty creative. Anthony had finally filed a complaint with higher authorities and gotten a transfer. He'd also gotten in very good with a high-ranking demoness. She'd made arrangements to ensure Kurtis was punished for his transgressions. No torture, though—well, at least not in the physical sense.

He'd been transferred to Belgium.

The mention of this dimmed Kurtis's humor a bit. The transfer was still a bitter point with him. It had happened four centuries ago, and he was no happier about his current locale than he'd been then. He'd apparently spent these last four hundred years being quite liberal in his slander and criticism of Anthony.

"And you're up for a possible transfer now, aren't you?" asked Margo.

"Yes," he replied.

"Hmm. Coincidental timing."

He snorted. "Hardly. Why would I destroy him now? You think I'd want to risk getting in trouble when my review comes along?"

"Or," said Noelle, suddenly speaking up, "maybe you wanted to make sure he wouldn't be able to influence the review committee."

Kurtis gave her a tight, mirthless smile. "That's your own wishful thinking, Noelle. You have no fucking clue who did this, and you'll take anyone you can find."

"I'll take whoever's guilty," she replied. She'd matched the steel in his voice but still wore her usual composure. "And I'll make sure they pay."

I left the proceedings that day with mixed feelings about Kurtis. With his history of violence and casual attitude about said violence, he did make a suspicious figure. On the other hand, I had to agree with him about the danger of taking out Anthony with the transfer hearing so close at hand.

Just like the day before, I was the only one to ask any real questions. I wanted to know when Kurtis and Anthony had last seen each other and if Kurtis had an alibi. He did, but again, I didn't doubt a demon could come up with any number of people to lie for him.

Post-trial parties held little appeal for me today, so instead, I decided to go straight to Seth's diner. The notion of just hanging out and doing something mundane like watching a movie had astonishing appeal. Besides, I was feeling guilty about my neglect.

When I stepped inside the elevator, I was surprised to see Noelle riding down as well. We stood there in that awkward silence elevator passengers often have, our eyes trained on the numbers as we descended. Daring a sidelong glance, I again admired her pretty features and remembered what Luis had said about her loving Anthony.

The words were out of my mouth before I could stop them. "I'm sorry about Anthony."

Her sea-colored eyes flicked from the numbers to me. Bitter amusement glinted in them. "You're the only one, I think."

I thought so too. "I . . . I know it's hard to lose someone you're close to."

"Close, huh? You've been talking to Luis. He might be the only other person who cares about this too." A small frown wrinkled her brow. "But I believe you. You do know what it's like. That's the thing with you lesser immortals . . . you're always around humans, getting caught up in their muddled emotions. Loving them. Losing them. Getting betrayed by them. You'd be better off staying detached from all that. Save yourselves a lot of pain."

I wanted to tell her that if she'd loved Anthony, then she wasn't a very good role model as far as emotional detachment went. Instead, I said something completely asinine.

"Well. I don't think you can really have happiness if you don't have pain too."

Something like a snort caught in her throat. Noelle's eyes swept me, and I felt as though she suddenly could see my life story without the benefit of a reading.

After several moments, she replied, "You must have a lot of happiness then."

I held back a glare and left the elevator when it opened, murmuring a polite good-bye as I stepped out.

I walked down to the diner and caught sight of Seth through the window. He sat at the same table, and so help me, that fucking waitress was there again. The door was propped open to let in the nice weather. I started to step through, hesitated, and then retreated. There was a small overhang around the side of the building, obscured from the rest of the street.

I sidled over to it and shape-shifted into invisibility. Returning to the front door, I crossed the threshold, hidden from mortal eyes.

Beth was laughing when I approached. "Really?" she asked. "You get love letters?"

"Sure," he said. The abandoned laptop sat before him. Didn't he have deadlines or something? "Not sure I really deserve it . . . but they show up more than you'd think. I've actually gotten poetry too."

"Like dirty limericks?"

"No, thankfully. Got some haikus once, though."

She laughed again. "The more you tell me, the more I really want to read your books. I've got to go pick up one."

Seth shrugged. "No need. Give me your address, and I'll send you a couple."

"Oh, no. You don't have to . . ."

He waved her off. "They send me boxes of them. It's not a problem."

"Wow, thanks." She grinned. She had a cute smile for a shameless tramp. "That'd be great. Maybe . . . maybe I could get you coffee as a thank you. I mean, coffee not from here."

Seth didn't quite catch it at first, then I saw the surprise register on his face. "Ah," he said. The social ease and banter he'd just had abruptly shut down. "Well. I . . ." He hesitated, and suddenly, *suddenly*, I wondered if he was hesitating over whether to accept rather than choosing words to refuse her. After what seemed like an eternity, he shook his head. "No. I can't. Not . . . no. Not really. I'm, um, probably busy."

Her face fell a little. "I understand." A moment later, she mustered a smile. "Well . . . let me check on some tables, and then I'll be back."

She sauntered off across the restaurant, and I wished that dress wasn't quite so snug on her ass. Seth's eyes followed her, a bit regretful.

Suddenly, I didn't want to talk to him quite so much after all.

I left the diner, my emotions in a tangle. I discretely shifted back to a visible form and headed down the street, moving toward the hotel but not really sure I wanted to go back there either.

"He likes her," a voice suddenly said beside me.

Startled, I turned to find Kurtis walking along with me. He'd appeared out of nowhere. I didn't bother asking what he'd just seen. Demons could move around with their signatures masked, and I supposed it was time for his bribe.

"No, he doesn't," I said immediately.

Kurtis laughed, the same unconcerned laugh I'd heard in the courtroom. "Of course he does. She's hot."

"He loves *me*," I said.

"Love doesn't stop people from betraying each other."

It reminded me a bit of my conversation with Noelle. We passed near a bakery, and he beckoned me toward it.

"Come on," he said. "Let's talk. This place makes great éclairs."

Which is how, five minutes later, I found myself sitting at a table and eating a cinnamon roll the size of a car tire with another potential killer.

Kurtis didn't speak until he was halfway through his second éclair. "So. Where were we? Ah, yes. Your naive belief that love can keep a man from cheating on the one he loves." He fixed me with a knowing look. "Honestly, I never thought I'd hear that from a succubus. You of all people should know better."

He was right. I did know better. I couldn't even keep track of how many men I'd lured away from the women they loved. Affection and reason tended to get a little murky when the body and its hormones took over.

"Seth's different," I responded.

"Of course he isn't. He's a man. He likes women, and that woman wants him so bad, her panties get wet each time she refills his coffee."

"Doesn't matter. She's not his type."

"She's the female type. And she's pretty."

"She's a waitress. Seth wouldn't go for that."

"She's a waitress using her shitty job to put herself through college. You saying a geeky guy like him wouldn't respect that?"

Yes, Seth would indeed respect something like that. But I still didn't want to go along with any of this.

"He still wouldn't do it."

"Why? Because he's getting it somewhere else?" He gave me a pointed look.

I honestly shouldn't have been surprised if he knew everything about me. Still, I had to ask. "How do you know that?"

Kurtis licked chocolate icing off his fingers. "How do you think, little one? That guy's got a soul brighter than a five-hundred-watt bulb. If he was sleeping with you, it'd show. And if you were going to do it, you'd have already done it."

"He's above physical needs." It was quite possibly the stupidest thing I'd ever said, more so than the happiness and pain comment in the elevator.

"No one's above physical needs. Not even demons. Look at Noelle and her insane obsession with all this."

I tossed my hair back, putting on my best bland look. "Well, I don't care if Seth wants to sleep with that girl. Not like he'd leave me for her. Besides, we have an arrangement. He knows he can get sex on the side if he wants. I don't care."

Kurtis threw back his head and laughed. "The fuck you don't. I don't have to be an angel to know you're lying. It would kill you if he slept with someone."

"It wouldn't," I said, even though he was right.

"Have you noticed that their names rhyme? It's pretty cute."

"Look," I said angrily, "will you just leave my personal life alone and get on with whatever bribe you're here to offer me?"

"Actually, your personal life *is* why I'm here. And I'm here to bribe you too."

"Yeah? With what? Your compelling relationship advice?"

"Nah. You wouldn't listen to it. I'm here to give you what you really want."

"Yeah. Clyde said the same thing."

"Clyde's full of shit," he scoffed. "*I* can give you the real deal. You don't want to hurt your guy? I'll give you a night with him, consequence free."

I stared. The room seemed to stop moving.

"You can't do that."

"Of course I can."

"How?"

"You belong to Jerome, right? I'll get him to block you off from your power for a day."

I blinked. I'd never thought of that. Hell, in its complicated love for hierarchies and chains of command, had a weird organizational system. An archdemon's underlings were connected to him in such a way that their divine powers were "filtered" through him. It kept him in control of his subordinates and also gave him a sense of their whereabouts and well-being. It was also sort of like a string of Christmas lights. Take out an archdemon, and it'd cut off his lesser immortals from their powers until a new system was established. I'd never considered the notion of an archdemon willingly blocking someone out of the immortal chain.

The appealing fantasy quickly shattered for me. "Jerome would never do that. He doesn't approve of my relationship with Seth."

"Jerome owes me a favor."

"He does not." I had a hard time picturing my boss being indebted to anyone.

"He does." Kurtis held his hand out to me. "I swear, if you vote for one of the other suspects, I'll make sure you have a night with your guy during which he'll suffer no damage to his soul."

I felt the slight crackle of a demon offering a bargain. They could lie and swear about the most extraordinary things . . . but they were bound to their deals.

I swallowed, a brief image of being naked with Seth flashing in my mind's eye.

"I can't," I said slowly. "I won't vote because of a bribe. How do I know you didn't do it?"

"Please. The evidence against me is ridiculous, and you know it. I could see it on your face at the trial."

"Then why are you worried? Why do you need to bribe me?"

"Because there are plenty of jurors who'd enjoy convicting me just for the fun of it. I need to make sure that won't happen."

Temptation, temptation. The story of my life.

"I . . . can't."

He shrugged. "If you say so. Keep an eye on your boyfriend and that waitress, and you'll see that I'm right about that. I bet he's a great *tipper*, and I bet if he starts getting it somewhere else regularly, he might find it isn't worth sticking around you. But, if you sleep with him sooner rather than later, you'll keep him from straying." He pushed his chair back and stood up. "Think on it. You vote for one of the others, and I'll make good on my promise."

His hand caught mine as he spoke, and a jolt shot through me. He'd sealed his vow.

I didn't know what to say; my mind was a blur. Kurtis recognized that and grinned. "See you around."

He walked out of the bakery, but I just sat there picking at my cinnamon roll, suddenly no longer hungry.

Chapter Seven

The third day of the trial brought out the last suspect, a de-moness named Starla. She was a tiny little thing, all doe eyes and long golden hair. She was also a new demon, one who must have recently fallen. She had apparently been a lesser-ranking angel in her pre-Hell days because she was relatively weak now as far as power went. So weak, in fact, that there was absolutely no way she could have blown Anthony away.

However, as the questioning went on, it became clear she might have blown him in another way.

"You had a romantic relationship with Anthony?" Margo asked. She said "relationship" like it was dirty word. She probably hadn't had sex in centuries, and honestly, if there was anyone I'd ever met who needed to get laid, it was her.

Starla was fragile looking, but she *was* a demon, weak or no. And even a weak demon was still a force to be reckoned with, particularly for an annoying lesser immortal like Margo.

"Yes," said Starla, her voice calm.

"So why'd you do it then? Jealousy? Lovers' quarrel?"

"I didn't do it."

"It's always the ones who are closest to the victim," continued Margo, glancing at us jurors. "This shouldn't be a surprise."

"I didn't do it," growled Starla.

"Were you afraid of losing him maybe? Sort of a 'If I can't have him, no one can' thing?"

"I didn't do it," the demoness repeated. "I *couldn't* have done it. You know that."

"You could have easily gotten someone else to," retorted Margo. "And while we'd like to find and chastise that person too, there's no doubt that you're the mastermind."

"Except that I'm not."

Margo brought out her idiotic clipboard again. "I understand that Noelle told you two to end your . . . relationship. She thought it was interfering with your work."

A flash of anger gleamed in Starla's eyes as she glanced briefly at her archdemoness. "It wasn't."

The imp shrugged. "So you say. But again, that would certainly lend credence to the 'If I can't have him . . .' theory, hmm? Someone like Anthony wouldn't have stayed lonely for long . . . there were certainly other ports he could have docked his ship in. But you? Who are you? Some minor, struggling little antisocial demon . . . so fresh from angelhood that you might as well still be wearing a halo. Not really worth anyone's attention unless it was someone who wanted to break you in. Anthony was your first, wasn't he?"

"That doesn't matter," said Starla tightly.

But apparently it did because it brought my fellow jurors to life. They showered her with questions, digging out as many personal details as they could. I could see Luis's ire growing, but it was Noelle who cut things off.

"We don't need to hear any more personal details," she snapped, sweeping the jury with those turquoise eyes. They radiated fury.

"I agree," said Luis. "If you guys can't ask anything useful, then don't say anything."

Unsurprisingly, the other jurors fell silent. I raised my hand. Starla regarded me warily.

"Did . . . do you have other friends? Aside from Anthony?"

She looked surprised by the question. "I have colleagues."

"Any that you're close to?"

"No."

Margo grinned broadly. "More proof as to why you'd have such a psychotic reaction to being separated from Anthony."

Starla glared at me as though I'd purposely just set her up. But I hadn't. Margo had called Starla antisocial earlier, and Starla herself admitted to having no close friends or colleagues. She could be lying, I supposed, but I didn't think so. The friendless thing only made her look more desperate; she wouldn't have purposely furthered that image by admitting to it. And if she *was* friendless, then I wondered who she could have gotten to kill Anthony. It was possible she could have made a business arrangement with someone. Maybe she had something to offer, but I doubted it.

Nonetheless, she found me afterward, just like Clyde and Anthony had.

"Wealth," she told me, standing with me in the hall by my room. "Money."

"Yeah," I said. "That's generally the definition of wealth."

She crossed her arms over her chest. "I'm offering you a great thing here. I mean, not like piles of gold or anything, but we're talking serious cash. Investments. Accounts in the Caymans. Stuff like that."

I shrugged. "I don't believe in bribes. And even if I did, I don't need the money. I've got my own stockpile. Besides, not like I couldn't find someone to give it to me if I wanted." It was exactly what Clyde had said.

I waited then for anger, for snippiness. What I didn't expect, however, was for her to suddenly start crying. I'd seen demons do a lot of things over the centuries. Torture. Destruction. Betrayal. Never, ever had I seen a demon cry. I didn't even know they could do it.

I started to reach for her in some sort of awkward attempt at comfort but thought better of it.

"Look," I said uneasily. "I'm sure there are other jurors who'll take the bribe."

She sniffed and shook her head, running a hand over her wet eyes. "No. Not from me. I don't have anything to give—not like Clyde and Kurtis. Everyone on the jury's stronger than me. There's nothing I can offer that they can't already get themselves."

"Well . . . I mean, I don't know. I guess you just have to wait for justice to run its course."

A harsh laugh cut off one of her sobs. "Justice? Here? There's no justice with this group. Even you can't be that naive."

I didn't answer. I knew she was right.

Starla exhaled heavily and leaned against the wall, tipping her head back. "For all I know, Noelle's giving bribes out for them to vote for *me*."

"Noelle wants to punish the person who did it," I pointed out.

"They're never going to find that out. There's both enough and not enough evidence on all three of us. No clear decision. In that case, she's going to just take it out on me. She *hates* me. Hates that Anthony . . ." She trailed off, and I was pretty sure she'd been on the verge of saying "love." Something else I didn't expect from a demon. ". . . that Anthony and I were involved. When she told him to end our relationship, he argued against it. He wanted a transfer, and she was going to try to block it; that's why he was so angry the day Clyde saw him. You can't imagine how jealous that made her—that Anthony would stand up for me. So, if she can't figure out who did it, she'll settle for seeing *me* punished. She'll do it out of spite."

"I'm sure she wouldn't . . ." But I wondered. Demons did stuff like that. And I'd seen Noelle's face when she talked about Anthony. His death had hurt her. When people get hurt, they tend to lash out to make themselves feel better. Torturing a romantic rival was just as good a way as any.

Like Noelle, Starla didn't need to use any powers to know what I was thinking. "You know," she told me. "You know she can do it. And you must know what it's like . . . being hated by other women."

A few moments of silence passed, then the demoness took a deep breath. She opened her mouth, swallowed, then said with great effort: "*Please*."

I stared. My mind couldn't handle any more demonic discoveries. "Please" wasn't in a demon's vocabulary. I was pretty sure they spontaneously combusted if that word crossed their lips. Maybe that was what had happened to Anthony.

"Please," she repeated, blue eyes wide. "Please help me with this. Maybe I can't offer you anything now . . . but someday I could do you a favor. Please. Just vote for one of the others."

Her pain made my own chest ache. "I want to . . . but I have to make sure . . . make sure I'm making the right choice . . ."

"It wasn't me," she said, eyes locked on mine. "I don't care what idiocy Margo was babbling about. That 'If I can't have him . . .' line is absurd. I l-loved Anthony. Why would I hurt him?"

I wanted to believe her. I wanted to believe in love and all the noble ideals it entailed. I shook my head.

"People do stupid things for love. Especially if they're afraid of losing the ones they love."

Starla stared at me for several more seconds, sighed, and then vanished.

Seth showed up later that evening, looking rather pleased with himself. I was lying on the bed, watching a reality dat-

ing show. The conversation with Starla had left me intro-
spective.

"You get a lot of work done?" I asked.

"Tons."

He set the laptop on the desk and lay down beside me.
His hand found mine, and he squeezed it contentedly.

We watched those poor, pathetic souls on TV for a while,
but soon, I couldn't take it anymore. With great effort, I kept
my voice as level as possible.

"Where'd you work today?"

Seth's eyes were on the screen where some girl ranted
about how her boyfriend had slept with her mother. Most of
her tirade was bleeped out.

"Hmm?" he asked. A moment later, he processed the
question. "That diner again."

The fucking diner. Fantastic.

"Ah," I said. "You must like that place."

"They have good pumpkin pie."

And good company, I thought. Beth's cute face and jaunty
ponytail flashed into my head. It was stupid. I had nothing to
be insecure about. She was nothing in the grand scheme of
things. Seth wasn't going to run off with her. Even if he did
want to do something physical with her, it'd be nothing.
Cheap, meaningless sex.

Suddenly, it was as though Kurtis was leaning over me
with his laughing face.

It would kill you if he slept with someone else.

Gritting my teeth, I reached for the remote and turned the
TV off. Seth glanced over at me in surprise. Shifting onto
my knees, I crawled over and straddled him.

"What's this?" he asked, amusement in his voice.

"I'm tired of watching other people's love lives."

I pulled my shirt off over my head and tossed my hair
back. Seth, still with a half-smile, watched me. His eyes
drifted down to where a black velvet bra held my breasts. A
cute little gold clasp unfastened in the front. I had better

breasts than that whore waitress, of that I was certain. Better shape, better size. Grabbing his hands, I slowly slid them up my stomach, careful to avoid the breasts themselves. It was always a delicate balance, this pseudo-making out. Too much, and we'd be courting danger.

My skin tingled as those fingertips slid across it. I brought his hands to the clasp, and he deftly unfastened it. Carefully, he peeled it away, and I wriggled it off my arms. His hands immediately withdrew, staying clear. Balance, balance. Always balance.

I slid off of him. Standing by the bed, I slowly and deliberately pushed my skirt down my legs. I wasn't wearing any stockings today, only a matching black velvet thong. It was my own creation. I'd searched high and low for one for a while. No luck, so I'd used my own resources. Shape-shifting was like a never-ending shopping trip.

My suitcase sat near the bed, and I rummaged through it, bending over as I did to give him a full view of my ass. Seth, I had long since discovered, wasn't a breast man or an ass man or anything like that. He was non-discriminatory. He appreciated it all.

Soon, I found what I wanted: a bottle of rosemary-scented oil that I'd brought along. Turning back to him, I poured some of the liquid on my hands, rubbing them until they were slick and shiny. I set the bottle down and brought my hands to my breasts, stroking them at an agonizingly slow pace—not unlike how Clyde had spread the life energy onto me. The memory made me shiver. The spicy scent of rosemary drifted around me as I leisurely rubbed the oil into my skin. My breasts took on the wet, gleaming look my hands had.

After several lifetimes of countless lovers, it always surprised me that I could turn myself on by doing this to myself. I think, however, it had less to do with my own skill and more with the act of being with Seth.

He still looked mildly amused, hands folded across his

stomach as he watched me. I met his gaze full-on, knowing mine was smoky and full of sex. His was alert and interested, though I could read little beyond that.

When my breasts and stomach were finally oiled to my satisfaction, I moved one hand down, slipping it inside the front of the thong. A cry that wasn't faked left my lips. I was warm and slick between my thighs, hardly in need of any oil. My fingers stroked me slowly, then found their way into me. In and out I moved them, attempting to quench a desire for him that would never really be adequately fulfilled. My moans came soft and low as I got myself off, my mind ablaze with images of Seth's body moving against mine.

I didn't realize my eyes were closed until I had to open them. Still touching myself, I regarded him curiously.

"How do you want me to finish it?" I asked in a breathy voice. "Keep standing? Lay down?"

His eyes traveled down, watching my skilled hand. Sometimes he would touch himself when I did this; sometimes he'd wait until afterward. Since his hands were still folded, I assumed it would be the latter.

"Actually . . ." he began, hesitation in his words. The half-smile was gone. "There's, um, no need."

My hand froze, oblivious to the rest of my body's outrage. "I . . . what?"

Sheepishly, he shrugged. "I mean, you're beautiful. Like always. Sexy. Really sexy. But, well . . . I'm not really into it tonight."

I stared, unable to speak. What kind of guy isn't into a succubus masturbating in front of him?

"You can finish for yourself, though, if you want," he added hastily, helpfully.

My brain started working again, and I pulled my hand out. "No . . ." I said slowly. "It's fine."

I shape-shifted away the velvet and oil. Jeans and a T-shirt took their place. Returning to the bed, I settled down beside Seth. This time, we didn't touch.

"I'm really sorry," he said. "I'm kind of . . . tired."

"It's fine," I repeated. I reached for the remote and turned the TV on again.

Neither of us brought the matter up again, but I was reeling. I'd just been rejected. This had never happened with us before. And what was up with the tired line? That was the lamest excuse in the book.

Beth, I thought. It had to be that goddamned waitress. But how, exactly? Had he fucked her in the diner's bathroom? I found that unlikely. Too unsanitary. Maybe she was just on his mind. Maybe that working girl image was what turned him on now, so much so that my seductive attempts were about as effective as a cold shower.

No, I thought. There was nothing wrong with me. I had no reason to feel insecure, not when it came to stuff like this. No way was he not attracted to me.

Seth turned his head to look at me. I must have had a troubled look on my face. He lightly brushed my cheek.

"I'm tired, Thetis. Really."

"It's fine," I said.

Chapter Eight

If Seth had any lingering feelings from last night, he didn't show it. He showered and packed up his bag like normal, called me Thetis, and regarded me with all the affection he normally did. I watched him as he moved toward the door.

"You going to that diner again?" I asked carefully.

He glanced up, face momentarily distracted. I could tell he was already getting sucked into the whirling plots of his stories.

"Hmm? Ah, no . . . they're closed on Sundays. Gonna go over to that coffee shop across the street."

"The one with the pig on the front? It looks horrible."

"Yeah. But just because it's not kosher . . ."

I groaned. "Oh my God. I really sleep with you?"

He grinned, one of the rare, genuine ones that flashed across his face like a sunrise breaking over the horizon.

"Yes. Happily."

He brushed a kiss over my mouth, then headed out. I stared at the door a few moments, felt a smile of my own cross my lips, and left shortly thereafter, suddenly feeling cheery about life again.

That cheeriness faded when I reached my destination for the day. The trial was over, the ballroom empty. No more court. Now it was time for the jury to deliberate.

Apparently, Hell had decided it couldn't spring to pay for another conference room in the hotel. The thirteen of us instead found ourselves crammed into one of the jurors' rooms. Admittedly, it was a nice room, but there wasn't enough space, and I chose to sit cross-legged on the floor. No one paid any attention to me, so I tried to make myself small as I listened to the conversation.

"I'm telling you, the internet is going to send more souls our way than the Inquisition and the Pill combined," one demon was saying. He had slicked-back brown hair and a weak chin.

Peanut Butter Guy shook his head. He looked remarkably alert today. "The internet's *taking* souls from us," he argued. "People don't have to sin in the real world anymore. They can do it virtually."

"Doesn't matter if they're actually doing it," said Weak Chin. "So long as they feel guilt from it. You don't think a married minister looking at gay porn isn't doing mental self-flagellation? Besides, the internet's a gateway sin. Experience it enough virtually, and eventually you crave the real thing."

"Let's not forget child predators," piped up a demoness who was idly flipping through channels. She had full lips painted glossy and bright with magenta lipstick. "You think they'd have as much access to thirteen-year-olds without the internet?"

"Oh, fuck," said Peanut Butter. "I love when Chris Hansen does those *Dateline* specials."

"Oh yeah," said Weak Chin excitedly. He appeared to have forgotten his earlier argument. "Did you see that one last week? With that guy they caught *again*?"

The entire room grew enthusiastic.

"That was fantastic! How could he let *Dateline* bust him twice? How stupid do you have to be?"

"Guys like that are keeping our coffers full."

"Yup, that and craigslist."

There was a pause, and then they all burst into laughter. I sighed.

Eventually, the rest of the jurors showed up. I straightened, figuring we'd get down to business now. Instead, the newcomers simply joined in on the internet conversation, which had now strayed into MySpace and stealing wireless internet.

After about a half hour of this, I took advantage of a momentary lull to ask, "Um . . . so, are we going to talk about the trial?"

Twelve sets of eyes turned to me. Silence.

I shifted uncomfortably. "I mean. Isn't that why we're here? To reach a decision?"

Weak Chin finally spoke. "Already reached mine. Clyde."

The demoness with magenta lips glared at him. "Starla."

"Kurtis."

"Starla."

They went around the room. Four, four, and four.

"What about you?" asked Magenta Lips.

"Um, well . . . I don't know. That's why I figured we'd be discussing it."

"Nothing to discuss," said another demon.

"How can you guys be so—" I stopped myself. "Oh. The bribes. That's why you're voting."

"Of course," chuckled Peanut Butter. "Why else?"

"I don't know . . . to get to the truth."

They all started laughing again. Even more than when craigslist had been mentioned.

"Darling, you've got a lot to learn."

"What do you expect? Putting a succubus on a jury."

"Well, yeah, but fuck. That was brilliant. Jerome's drinking mai tais somewhere while we have to put up with this shit."

"And a goddamned Marriott too."

I closed my eyes and took a deep breath. A moment later, I opened them.

"Okay," I said. "Even if you're voting by bribe, we still have to reach a unanimous decision."

They considered, and then, the whole room burst into noise. Arguments broke out as everyone tried to convince/ bully others into voting their way. It was dizzying. Most of them tried to do it by offering bribes of their own. There was more negotiating than in a game of Monopoly. Some, however, tried to do it by force. As I'd noted earlier, this wasn't the most powerful group of demons I'd ever seen, but they could compete with each other. As tempers rose, I felt power flare, filling the room like static before a storm.

I shrank back, briefly considered turning invisible, but knew it wouldn't matter with this group.

Finally, after a few more hours, our deliberation ended for the day. We dispersed, off to do our different things. No decision had been reached.

I left the room, nearly dizzy. Fuck. What had that all been about? We weren't going to reach a decision any time this millennium. I'd be stuck in Los Angeles forever. Seth would marry Beth and have ten kids. I'd have to move in furniture to the Marriott.

Speaking of Seth, I decided seeing him was exactly what I needed. That calm nature would help soothe my frazzled nerves and forget the day's insanity.

I'd reached the lobby when I felt someone walking with me. "How'd it go?"

I glanced over at Kurtis' laughing face. I sighed. So much for forgetting the insanity.

"Not so well."

"Hmm. Not surprised. Bribes have been flying fast and furious. What's the split right now?"

"Four, four, and four."

"Really? I'm surprised it isn't even more split."

I stared. "How could it be more split than that?"

"Write-ins." He grinned. "What's your vote?"

"I don't have one."

His eyebrows rose in mock astonishment. "Really? Even with all the lovely things you've been offered?"

"I told you. I don't go for that."

"How are things with your guy?"

"Fine," I said automatically. "We have a great relationship."

"But not the kind where you wrap your bodies around each other and break out the handcuffs."

"Will you stop this?" I asked. "I already told you I'm not going for any of that. You're wasting your time."

"If your relationship's so great, then why isn't he here?"

"Because he's working."

"With Golden Girl."

"No," I declared loftily. "He's not even at that diner today."

"Why? Are they closed?"

"I have places to be," I snapped.

"Of course you do. Off to beg for his attention, right? Make him notice you with your stunning wit and charm, hoping desperately to keep him captivated while his eyes and thoughts stray to other women . . ."

In normal circumstances, I never would have walked out on a demon. But Kurtis was powerless to hurt me just now, so I picked up my pace and stormed out the front doors. I knew he could have easily reached me again, but fortunately, he didn't.

I crossed the street over to the coffee shop Seth had gone to and paused in front of the window. He sat there working, no cute waitresses in sight. I breathed a sigh of relief.

My insecurity embarrassed me. There was no reason I should let Kurtis' words get to me. I knew that. I trusted Seth. I trusted his love. Yet . . . the demon had been effective. Not surprising, of course. He was, well, a fucking demon. And Seth *had* refused my advances last night.

I stared at Seth, willing the queasy feeling in my chest to go away.

Hoping desperately to keep him captivated while his eyes and thoughts stray to other women . . .

Not tonight, Thetis.

I swallowed. And then . . . I did the craziest thing I'd done in a while. I slipped into the coffee shop, carefully avoiding his line of sight. Not that it would have mattered. He was so engrossed, like always, that a marching band could have come through without him noticing. I went straight to the bathroom, shut the door, and changed my shape.

Into Beth.

A barista gave me a startled look when I stepped out. I think he'd seen me go in in my usual shape. But a few seconds later, he shook his head, apparently deciding he'd imagined it. That's how mortals were. They didn't expect the fantastic in their lives, so they tended to rationalize it when it happened.

Clad in blond, hourglass glory, I walked over to Seth's table.

"Hey," I said, hoping I had her voice right. I'd only heard her a couple of times.

There was a delay, as usual, then he looked up. "Hey," he said, clearly surprised. But he didn't look displeased. "What are you doing here?"

I shrugged. "Was walking by and saw you. I need some coffee . . . mind if I join you?"

He frowned. "I thought you didn't like coffee."

Fuck.

"Once in a while I do," I said evasively. "The only way I can get a real caffeine kick sometimes."

He nodded, thankfully not questioning it too much. After getting a cup of drip, I sat down across from him.

"So, how's progress today?" I asked.

"Slow," he admitted. "It happens sometimes."

A lapse of silence fell. I tried to think of something that idiotic fan girl would say.

"Slow for you is probably ten times faster than what I can write." Recycled material, but what could you do? Praying they hadn't had this conversation before, I asked, "How'd you get published in the first place?"

He smiled. "Slush pile."

"What's that?"

"It's where unimportant aspiring authors go when they're trying to get published. It often gets ignored. Or sorted by interns."

I frowned. "Then how did you get noticed?"

"Mmm . . . well, agents still go through it. They just take a while sometimes. Or sometimes you get a savvy intern."

"I thought only actors have agents."

"Everyone selling themselves has an agent."

"Is yours good?"

He nodded. "She's got me some great deals." He paused. "I'm not convinced she has a soul, though. The best ones never do."

"You know a lot of soulless people?" I asked glibly.

He flinched. "Um, yeah. Some."

Then, just like in the Robert Frost poem, two paths diverged in the woods. I could either make Beth sound completely idiotic and see if Seth would lose interest. Or, I could aim for compelling and captivating to see if he'd go for it.

I wasn't really good at idiotic.

"I dated a guy once who I'm pretty sure didn't have a soul." Beth's fictitious past rolled off my lips like it was my own. "He was a lawyer. I swear, I used to hear him mumble in his sleep at night. I think he was chanting Doors songs backwards."

"That's evidence of being soulless?"

"You seen Jim Morrison? That guy was so hot that there's no way he didn't have some deal with the devil."

Seth laughed genuinely, and I saw it. The interest in his eyes.

I pushed forward, chatty and funny, trying to do it in a way that was interesting but didn't sound like a Georgina clone. To my dismay, Seth forgot all about the laptop and displayed none of his usual reticence in conversation. He spoke to Beth as easily as if she were, well, me.

An hour or so later, I made my move.

"I know you've got a girlfriend," I said hesitantly. "And I know you couldn't do coffee the other day . . . but . . . I'd love to keep hanging out, and I'm really hungry. Do you think maybe you'd like to go grab some food? I'm starving, and I know a great place. And it'd be just as friends."

Seth's good humor faltered. "Well . . . I would . . . but, well, I've got to meet her later on. I don't have the time. I mean, but I would otherwise. It sounds fun."

This was true. Seth and I had made dinner plans. He had a legitimate excuse. But what if he didn't . . . ?

Stop this, Georgina, I told myself. *This trial's unhinging you. You're moving into psycho territory.*

"Okay. No problem," I said, smiling and open. I stood up. "Hey, I'll be right back."

I headed into the bathroom and pulled out my cell phone. I dialed Seth's number.

"Hey," he said when he answered.

"Hey," I returned, back to Georgina's voice.

"How's the jury thing going?"

"Ugh. It sucks," I grumbled. "Finally wrapped up for the day."

"Ah, cool."

"But, I've got some bad news. I got sucked into some dinner thing. I'm not going to be able to see you until a lot later."

A long pause.

"That's okay . . . I can fend for myself."

"I'm really sorry . . . I feel like I've been neglecting you."

"Nah, it's okay. Really."

"Cool. I'll catch you later."

We disconnected, and I walked back to the table, fully in Beth mode.

"Back," I said, returning to my chair.

Seth smiled. This time it was the bemused, pensive smile he got when he was thinking hard about something. Finally, I saw a decision snap into his eyes.

"So . . . hey. Maybe we can do dinner after all . . ."

Chapter Nine

The weirdness of technically being out on a date with my boyfriend and another woman wasn't lost on me. Nor was the fact that this sort of insane, paranoid behavior was typical of the kind of women you hear about on TV who drive themselves and their children into a lake.

"Georgina" never followed up with Seth on when "she" would be back later. This gave him no immediate reason to go home, and the night turned out to be a long one. The two of us ended up walking down the street to some cute little French café. It had outdoor seating, which was absolutely perfect for the balmy evening air. The tables were tiny and round, made of patina copper. Christmas lights, strung merrily along the roof's edge, twinkled down at us. Seeing them reminded me of my earlier metaphor about demonic power hierarchies. Kurtis only had to pull out one "light" in my string to give me a night with Seth, a night that could possibly stop insanity like *this* night from happening again. Pondering that brought the trial back to my mind. The thought of going back to the jury deliberation tomorrow made my brain hurt.

Beth's past still poured forth with ease, but then, I'd been making up identities my entire life. I also knew enough about Seth to adapt her perfectly to him. I could say exactly what he wanted to hear. Dinner flew by, the conversation fast and furious. Afterward, we wandered over to a beachside park and spent a long night continuing our conversation. A number of times, I had to remind myself to stay in character. Being with him and talking like this just felt so natural and so comfortable that it was hard to remember that he and *I* just weren't out on a normal date. He was with Beth. What was disturbing was that he treated "Beth" just as sweetly and familiarly as he would have treated me.

For all I knew, Seth might have stayed out all night, but I eventually made up some excuse about needing to go home and do homework. We didn't touch—no kissing or hugging—but Seth regarded me with genuine pleasure.

"This was really great," he said. "You're . . . very easy to talk to. Thanks for asking me out."

"Thanks for joining me," I replied. "It beat doing homework." I tilted my head curiously. "So, tell me again: how long are you in town?"

He shrugged. "Still not entirely sure. Another few days at least."

"Ah. Okay." I put on a look of demure shyness. "Well . . . I don't suppose . . . I don't suppose you'd want to maybe catch dinner again before you leave?"

He turned thoughtful, conflict in his eyes. "I don't know," he said. "I'd like to . . . but I mean, I don't know what my schedule's like." A palpably nervous pause followed. "Could . . . could I call you when I know for sure?"

Crap. No. He couldn't very well call Georgina's number.

"I lost my cell phone," I told him.

"Well . . . I'll probably be at the diner tomorrow. We could talk then."

Oh, yeah. Even better. The real Beth would be pretty surprised to hear about what a great night they'd had. Frantically, my mind whirled.

"A couple other friends have been coming in lately too, and my boss is getting annoyed that I keep talking to people during my shift. Might actually be better if you work somewhere else. I need to keep this job," I added, hoping I sounded like Pathetic Struggling Student Girl. "Why don't you just give me your number and I'll check in with you tomorrow?"

He scrawled it on a scrap of paper, and we walked off in separate directions. A few minutes later, I became invisible and caught up to him, following him back to the hotel. I let him go into the room first, waited several minutes, then walked inside in my usual form.

"Hey," I said, smiling. He was on the bed, watching some kind of improv comedy show. "You're still awake."

He smiled back. "Crazy night?"

I rolled my eyes and flounced onto the bed beside him. "You have no idea. What'd you do today?"

His eyes flicked back to the TV. "Wrote. Ate dinner."

Flirted shamelessly with another woman, I supplied.

"Same old, same old," I said instead. "Doesn't it ever get boring?"

He ran his fingers along my arm. "You're enough excitement for both of us."

I snuggled against him, and we watched TV in silence. When, after a little while, I made a few amorous suggestions, he again refused.

"No . . . it's not you. I'm just not up for it."

"You don't have to do anything," I teased. "*I* do all the work."

"I know, I know. It just doesn't . . . doesn't hold much appeal at the moment."

"Me naked and getting off doesn't hold much appeal?"

He held up his hands in innocence. "It's nothing personal,

I swear. It's just well . . . it's not the same as sex, as that union, you know? Don't get me wrong . . . I like it, and I'm not saying I don't ever want to do it again. But . . . I mean, it's icing. You and me . . . our connection is what matters. We know the physical doesn't really enter into it." His hand found mine. "It's just enough to be with you."

I sighed and hoped he was right.

I didn't bother asking Seth where he was going to work the next morning. I kind of wanted to forget last night; it had been stupid of me. Nothing I should repeat. I hoped he'd take "Beth's" advice and just go somewhere else. If he planned on going back to the diner, I didn't want to think about it and the ensuing complications when they checked their stories against each other's.

Besides, I had other complications to occupy me. That fucking jury. Until this deliberation process started, I'd been pretty sure there could be no professional experience more painful than the time my bookstore boss made us attend a seminar entitled *How to Turn a Minimum Wage Job Into Maximum Fun*. I'd left that class wanting to drill a hole in my head to end the pain. Suddenly, though, I could have sat through that whole god-awful workshop again rather than face my "jury of peers" once more.

To my surprise, I was the last juror to arrive. I glanced at the time, wondering if I'd miscalculated and was late. Nope. I was a couple minutes early—which meant the others had arrived earlier still. Casual conversation sparkled around the room, but I saw a few sets of eyes turn toward me as I entered and sought out my corner from yesterday.

Once I was settled, the demoness with magenta lips who'd envied Jerome's brilliant proxy idea immediately started business. Everyone fell silent and paid attention. My apprehension grew.

"So," she said briskly, "let's get this over with, shall we? Who has thoughts to share on the case?"

My peanut butter friend spoke up right away. "Well, it seems pretty obvious to me. There's no way Kurtis could have done this. He wouldn't want to screw with his review, and besides, he doesn't live anywhere near here." I wanted to point out that a demon could transport from Belgium to L.A. in a heartbeat, but the others were nodding along eagerly, like his reasoning made perfect sense. "And anyway, it's been a long time. I think he's given up the grudge. I mean, Hell, if that whole thing he did to Anthony with the boars and cannibals wasn't enough revenge for him, I don't think obliteration would be much of an improvement."

The others laughed appreciatively.

"You're totally right," someone piped up. "He had nothing to do with this."

"Agreed," said another.

From around the room, more confirmations of Kurtis's innocence followed. After several minutes of this, Magenta Lips moved us on to the next stage. I could only stare, wide-eyed, astonished at this brilliant show of order.

"Right then," she said. "What else do we think?"

The demon with the weak chin jumped in this time. "Well, Starla seems like the logical choice to me."

Starla honestly seemed like the least logical choice to me. Uneasily, I remembered her words about how she made an easy target. She had the least to offer in the way of bribes. I mustered the courage to protest her guilt but was cut off when the discussion took an even more bizarre turn.

"I agree," said a demon across the room. He put a lit cigarette to his lips, despite the little sign on the end table politely asking him not to smoke. "Of course, we all know she couldn't have actually done it herself. Which leaves only one explanation."

"Right," agreed Weak Chin. "Clyde."

"It *is* the only reasonable explanation," mused Magenta Lips. "Starla decides to kill Anthony, figures out the logistics, then gets Clyde to do it." Anthony had been incinerated. I didn't really know how much logistical planning that took.

"And we all know Clyde wanted to do it anyway," added Peanut Butter. "He probably didn't even need her provocation."

I looked from face to face, suddenly feeling terribly out of the loop. I felt like I was the understudy in a play. Everyone already had their lines down, and I was desperately unprepared.

Just as with Kurtis' acquittal, everyone in the room concurred with this theory. Immediately, twelve sets of eyes turned on me, their gazes smoldering—and not in a sexual way.

"What about you?" asked Weak Chin. "What do you think?"

"I . . ." I swallowed. "I think we don't entirely have enough proof to say for sure that Clyde and Starla worked together."

Peanut Butter scoffed. "Who needs proof? We have deductive reasoning."

"We need a unanimous vote," said the presiding demoness warningly. "*We're* all in agreement. You're the only one who isn't."

The faces that I'd hitherto seen bored and playful were suddenly hard and cold. Menacing. They watched me with angry expressions, daring me to disagree.

Something had happened last night, clearly. While I'd been out being psycho stalker girlfriend, Kurtis had apparently done some serious lobbying to get the jury to agree with this theory. The quality of the bribes had to be off the charts. It was funny, though, that he hadn't come to *me*. Of course, considering the deal he'd already offered, he probably figured there was no greater reward he could give me. He was right. He also probably figured there was no point in swaying me because I wouldn't be able to stand against all these angry demons.

And for a moment, I thought he was right on that too.

This group was scary as fuck. It would be so easy to agree with them, so easy to cast my vote for this unsubstantiated theory. I didn't want to have twelve servants of Hell hating me. I wanted to go home and end this insanity. I wanted to take Seth away from waitresses who might lead him into temptation.

And so, I think it was a surprise to everyone—including me—when the next words out of my mouth were, "I . . . don't think that explanation is right."

The following hours were horrible.

They yelled at me. They raged at me. They threatened me. None of them actually hurt me—the rules of this whole operation forbid it—but they came close. And sometimes, mental abuse can be worse than the physical kind anyway. I heard more creative options than Kurtis had come up with for Anthony.

I was almost in tears when salvation came in the form of Luis. He stuck his head in the room, having expected such a lazy jury to have recessed earlier. Seeing the demons gathered around me so threateningly, he arched an eyebrow and said, "Why don't we call it quits for the day?"

He escorted me downstairs, holding on to my arm. It was only when we walked into the bar that I realized I was shaking. We sat down, and he ordered me a vodka gimlet.

"You okay?" he asked, not unkindly.

I took a deep breath and told him what had happened. Little expression showed on his face.

"Clever," he finally said, once I finished the story.

"Clever?" I exclaimed, beckoning for a second drink since I'd inhaled the first in under two minutes. "That was fucking insane! Do you have any idea what they said to me? What they said they'd *do* to me?"

Luis shook his head, still looking unconcerned. "They're trying to scare you. And yeah, it's working, but you know they can't hurt you. You're protected under all the rules of this trial, and anyway, Jerome would string up any and all of them if they laid a hand on you. They're flies compared to him."

"It was horrible," I reiterated with a shudder. "I can't believe they all latched on to this idea. It's insane."

"Not really." Luis downed his own drink, bourbon and soda. "Kurtis has the most to offer, so his bribes would be the best. And this option also curries the most favor with Noelle. She hates Starla. Noelle would be happy to see her suffer. And Clyde was uppity when he got pissed off over the promotion thing. That had to have hurt her pride too. This way, he's taught a lesson about what happens when you talk back to your superiors."

I groaned. "So the jurors get their reward and earn brownie points with Noelle."

Luis nodded.

"What are the odds of the jurors changing their mind?"

"About as good as a snowball's chances in Hell."

I glared.

"Sorry," he said, looking chagrined.

I restrained myself with the second drink, instead stirring the ice around and around. "What can I do?" I asked bleakly. "I'm pretty sure Clyde and Starla didn't do this."

"You do the only things you can do. You either agree with the jury or stand against them."

I choked on a bitter laugh. "You think I can stand against them?"

"If anyone can, you can."

"Sure. That would be my 'annoying yet adorable sense of right and wrong,' right?"

He grinned. "It's what makes you so entertaining."

I turned back to my drink. "I can't stand against them. I'll go insane. And this thing will never end."

"Then cast your vote." I got the impression Luis's interest was now more in observing the moral snafu I was in, rather than seeing how the trial ended.

"Don't know if I can do that either."

He stood up and patted my shoulder. "Well then, darling. You're fucked. But if you survive all this, you can come work for me in Vegas anytime."

Luis left the bar, and I followed a few minutes later. As I did, I passed Kurtis. He smirked and started to join me.

"I don't want to talk to you," I snapped.

"I hear there was a little dissension in the jury." He chuckled. "But only a little."

I stopped and turned on him, forgetting for half a second I was squaring off against a demon more powerful than me physically and magically.

"I can't believe you did this! Arranged this. It's bad enough you wanted to bribe people, even if it made the wrong person suffer. But this? Now *two* people will suffer."

"I hear it's a pretty sound theory, though," he said glibly.

"It's horrible."

"We work for Hell, little one." When I didn't respond, he continued, "Besides, if it goes my way, I'll still make good on our deal. This is a win for you."

"I don't need your deal."

"Right. Because your boyfriend is proving true and stalwart against Blondie."

"He is."

Kurtis shook his head, still wearing that annoying smirk. "Georgina, Georgina. No wonder Luis likes you so much. You're adorable." He took a step toward me and lowered his voice. "I know about last night, and from what *I* saw, your guy didn't seem to do that good a job against your—I mean, *her*—charms."

"You followed me?" I cried. This got worse and worse. I bit back a stream of obscenities. "Well, it doesn't matter. He didn't try anything. He didn't offer anything."

"Well, it was only the first date," pointed out Kurtis.

"It wasn't a date."

He rolled his eyes. "Semantics. Okay, then. You think he could be so noble again? On the second da—whatever?"

"There isn't going to be a second da—whatever."

"Are you sure? Would he refuse?"

"Of cour—" I stopped because suddenly, I wasn't sure.

Kurtis laughed at my doubt and stepped away. "Go and see."

I watched him go. A thousand emotions rushed through me. Fear and frustration over the jury. Doubt and jealousy over Seth. Kurtis was a very good demon, I realized. And by good, I meant evil and despicable. Once again, he'd thrown me into the kind of state that's led mortals into temptation for millennia. My stress and anxiety from the jury debacle only intensified matters.

Which is why it shouldn't have been surprising when—despite my promises not to repeat last night—I called Seth and told him I'd be busy tonight. A half hour later, I found a lobby phone and called him as Beth, asking him for dinner again.

To my supreme dismay, he accepted.

Chapter Ten

I'd had pretty bad hand-eye coordination when I'd been a mortal, but centuries and centuries of practice will pretty much perfect almost any skill set.

"Whoa," said Seth, wide-eyed.

A Ping-Pong ball sailed from my hand and landed neatly into a glass filled with blue water. About twenty other glasses sat pressed together around the blue one, some with clear water and some with red. I eyed my target and launched another Ping-Pong ball. It too landed in the blue glass. It was the third time I'd hit my mark.

The guy running the game booth shook his head. "I don't see that very often."

Seth turned and grinned at me—or rather, he turned and grinned at Beth. We'd taken a cab to this small, beachside carnival and had spent most of our evening playing games and spinning around on rides that caused me only a little more nausea than jury deliberation had. After all that demonic bribery and intrigue, impersonating another woman in order to test my boyfriend seemed downright mundane.

"That was amazing," said Seth. "You play sports or some-thing?"

"Now and then," I replied enigmatically.

"Here you go." The game attendant shook his head again and handed me a large, stuffed dragon. I handed it to Seth, who already held a unicorn and a bear.

"You sure you're okay with all that?" I asked him as we walked away.

"Hey, I'm not winning anything," he replied, shifting his hold on the animals. "You're doing all the work. I figure I should just help out the best I can."

I laughed. It was such a typical Seth thing to say. If his arms weren't full, I might have been in danger of reaching out and holding his hand.

"I can't keep those," I told him. "You want to take them home?"

"No," he said promptly. "Too much trouble." I wondered if he was contemplating the difficulty in fitting them in his luggage or the difficulty in explaining to his girlfriend how he'd acquired another woman's midway winnings.

Fluffy clouds of pale pink caught my eye, and I honed in on a cotton candy vendor. I bought a clump of it, and Seth and I sat on a nearby bench so that he could deposit his burden and eat the spun sugar with me.

"Good God," he said, putting a piece into his mouth. "I can feel myself getting diabetes already."

I didn't respond right away, instead luxuriating in the way the billowy sugar melted away to nothing on my tongue. "You look like you're in shape," I told him a few moments later. "I don't think you're doing any permanent damage."

"Not at the moment, no. But I can't make this a regular thing. I swim and jog, but considering how much time I just, well, sit around . . . yeah. Gotta watch this stuff." He tore off another piece. "But not right now."

I chuckled. "I hear you. I have to go to the gym every day and . . ." I paused. What trendy fitness activity were mortal women doing these days? ". . . and pay homage to the elliptical machine. Pain in the ass—no pun intended. I mean, I hate those people who can eat anything they want and never gain a pound."

He nodded. "Yeah, my girlfriend's like that—" He cut himself off and abruptly looked elsewhere.

"It's okay," I said. "You don't have to avoid talking about her. We're just friends, remember?" Several awkward moments passed. We weren't making out or anything, but no one in their right mind was oblivious enough to think this outing had no romantic overtones. "So? What about her? Is she in really good shape?"

"Um, yeah," he finally said. The dangerous topic had triggered some of his usual hesitancy. "Really slim."

"Cool," I said. "And she doesn't work out or anything? She must have good genes."

Seth choked on his cotton candy a little. "Yeah. Great genes."

"How long have you guys been dating?"

"A couple months."

"Is it serious?" He didn't reply. "Look," I said hastily, "if you don't want to talk about it, it's fine, really . . ."

"No, no." He sighed. "It's just . . . I'm sorry. This is just kind of weird for me. Us. You and me." He gestured toward the happy people mingling around the carnival attractions. "This. I just don't . . . I'm just not sure . . . I don't know."

"You feel guilty?" I asked.

He considered. "Yeah. A little. I mean, we're in town for her . . . thing, so it's not like I'm neglecting anything of my own by being here tonight. I got my writing in. She's busy. And, um, I like hanging out with you, but the whole thing is . . ."

". . . weird," I finished.

"Yeah."

"I understand. I know it's hard . . . men and women being friends always are. And I don't want to cause any trouble for you. We can go now if you want." I paused meaningfully before going in for the kill. "I mean, especially if you guys are having problems or anything . . . probably best if we don't . . ."

Seth stared off at the gray line of the Pacific. "Not problems. Just a few kinks here and there."

I waited for him to say more, but he didn't. So. Seth didn't think everything was perfect with us. No surprise there. *I* sure didn't. Hearing him acknowledge it—to a woman he hardly knew—yanked painfully at something inside my chest.

But, he didn't seem like he was going to elaborate on it, which was good. He also didn't seem like he was going to get up and leave, however, so he wasn't taking my—Beth's— offer to end tonight's awkwardness. I tried to think of what some ostensibly helpful and secretly lustful woman would say. God knows I'd played this role plenty of times in the past. Nothing like a helpful confidante to pave the way for seduction.

"Anything you want to talk about?" He glanced over at me, and I offered a small smile. "Want a woman's perspective?"

He provided a small smile of his own in return and shook his head. "It's more than that. The prob—kinks we have . . . well, they're just little cracks here and there in what's otherwise a . . ." The wheels of word choice spun in his head. ". . . a work of art."

"Little cracks can eventually destroy a work of art," I pointed out.

"Yeah," he said wistfully. "But for now, it's so beautiful." More silence fell, and at last, Seth straightened up from the slouch he'd fallen into. "You know, maybe we should go. I'm sorry . . . I don't mean to . . ."

Relief flooded through me. Seth was walking away from this situation.

"No, no, it's okay," I assured him, crumpling up the cotton candy paper. "It's getting late anyway."

We stood up, and Seth gathered my winnings again. Frowning, he glanced down at them and then let his eyes drift off to the people walking up and down the midway, watching and playing games. I followed his gaze and knew him well enough to immediately know what held his attention.

A woman—mid-thirties maybe—was walking through. She had two grade school children, a boy and a girl, walking with her while she pushed a stroller holding a toddler. The boy was pointing toward one of the games. I couldn't hear what he said, but he sounded excited. They passed near us, and I heard his mother's words clearly.

"No one *ever* wins those things," she told him. "It's a waste of money."

They kept going and then paused in the shadow of a crazily spinning ride, so she could kneel down and fuss with the toddler's bottle.

"Be right back," Seth told me.

A smile crept onto my face as I watched him stroll over, bearing the stuffed animals. They were too far away now for me to hear, but I watched him speak to the woman and present his offerings to the children. My heart fluttered, and my insides turned wispier than the cotton candy. Seth was amazing. There was no one else in the world like him. No one as sweet. No one as kind.

"Do you know," a voice suddenly said in my ear, "how easily the bolts in one of those cars could come loose? And at the speed they're going . . . wow. Yeah. It'd be pretty bad for anyone in the car—not to mention anyone it hit on the ground."

I turned jerkily and looked into the cold eyes of Magenta Lips from the jury. Weak Chin stood beside her. A slight shimmer to their appearance told me they were invisible to mortal eyes. Damn. For half a second, Seth's sweet nature had made me forget about my woes. Now, here they were, right in front of me.

"And did you also know," Weak Chin added, "how many people in a crowd like this are armed? Guns, knives. So easy for things to go awry if some would-be thief tries to steal from someone. Hell, there doesn't have to be a crime involved. A trivial fight breaks out, someone pulls a gun, some bystander in the crowd is in the wrong place at the wrong time . . ."

"And yet, even *that's* not as dangerous as the ride back," mused the demoness. "People still don't believe those statistics about flying being safer than driving, but it's amazing what can go wrong on the road. Drunk driver. Brake failure. Really, it's a wonder mortals live as long as they do."

"Fortunately," pointed out Weak Chin, "*we* aren't mortal, so we don't have to worry about anything like that." He turned from me, and I followed his eyes to where Seth still stood talking to the family. "Poor bastards."

"Are you threatening me?" I asked in a small voice.

Magenta Lips' magenta lips turned up in a cruel smile. "Of course not, sweetie. You know the rules. We can't harm *you*. Wouldn't dream of it." But her eyes were on Seth now too.

"Look, if you guys think—"

"Oh, look at that," interrupted Weak Chin, glancing down at his watch. "We need to get back. Still got more deliberation in the morning, and I'm sure we'll all want a good night's sleep if it turns out to be as long as today's was."

"Well," said Magenta Lips crisply. "Let's hope it isn't."

They vanished. A minute later, Seth walked back over to me, smiling broadly. It was another of those full ones I loved so much, but I couldn't even appreciate it.

"Now *there* are some people who really value a good throwing arm." The smile faded as he peered at me. "Are you okay?"

No. No, I wasn't. I could barely focus on his face, and I felt cold all over, despite the warm weather. The two demons' words had ripped into me like shrapnel.

"I . . . yeah . . ." I swallowed. "Just not feeling so great all of a sudden. Let's go back."

* * *

I didn't sleep well that night. "Not well" meaning "not at all." I tossed and turned and alternated between staring at the ceiling and at Seth. Apparently he'd gained no sugar high from the carnival food because he'd been fast asleep when I'd arrived back in my normal body. He slept heavily and peacefully throughout the night, a content look on his face. He didn't look like a guy who couldn't touch his succubus girlfriend or who had a death threat hanging over his head.

Surely . . . surely they wouldn't do it, I thought. They were bluffing. Trying to scare me. They *couldn't* do it.

Except . . . they could. As a juror and demonic "property," I was untouchable. But nobody in Hell's hierarchy would care what they did to Seth. He was a mortal, one who didn't play much of a role in anything that concerned them. No one would raise an eyebrow if he died under mysterious—or mundane—circumstances.

The thought that they would try to do this to me made me ill. And yet, I knew I had no reason to feel so wronged. I was a fucking succubus. I worked for Hell. Everyone who was part of this insane spectacle had given in to temptation and sold their souls out for greed, jealousy, or some other vice. There were no morals here. No sense of honor. No need for justice. No one cared about Seth. No one cared if Starla and Clyde were guilty or not.

Except, of course, me.

When morning came, I went to the deliberation room like someone sleepwalking. The others had already gathered, just like yesterday. When I entered, they all looked up, and the sight of those smirks and knowing looks made my stomach roil. I averted my eyes, looked straight ahead, and sat in my corner.

"All right then," said Magenta Lips. An image of her eyes on Seth last night flashed into my head. "Shall we wrap this up? Who's in favor of convicting Starla and Clyde?"

"Me," said Peanut Butter.

"Me," said Weak Chin.

Around the room they went. And just like yesterday, it all came down to me again. Twelve demons, eyes boring into me. Maybe it was my imagination, but I thought I could smell brimstone in the air. I hunkered back into my corner.

Just say the word, an angry voice in my head said. *Agree with them. End this. Go home. Keep Seth safe.*

Seth. Seth was what mattered here. Whatever happened to Starla and Clyde wouldn't kill them. It would hurt. Oh, yeah. It would definitely hurt. Like, five centuries worth of hurt. But they'd survive. Not like Seth. Seth was mortal. One accident would kill him. And whereas both Starla and Clyde probably had a laundry list of *other* atrocities they deserved punishment for, Seth did not. Seth was good. Seth gave stuffed animals away to children. Seth came clean about his girlfriend with another woman he was attracted to. Seth did what was right.

Seth *always* did what was right.

The words hurt coming out when I spoke to the demons.

"I'm . . . not . . . convinced . . . yet . . ."

They'd been surprised yesterday to hear my dissension, but they were *really* surprised today. I don't think this many demons had been caught off guard since the Reformation.

The demon who'd lit a cigarette yesterday lunged for me. "Why, you little—"

Peanut Butter caught him. "Don't."

Another demon took up the cause. "But you heard her! She—"

"Yeah!" interrupted another. "Some succubus slut isn't going to keep me from being a lieutenant in Monaco—"

"Quiet," snapped Magenta Lips. Silence descended. Her eyes fell on me, and it was like frost spreading along my flesh. Her immortal signature swirled around me, cloying and fetid. Like greenhouse flowers starting to rot. "She's not convinced yet." Her voice was very calm, very steady.

"I'll convince her," growled the restrained demon.

The demoness gestured slightly to Weak Chin. "Explain our logic again, please."

He did. There was an edge of annoyance to his words as he spoke, but otherwise he wound through the whole string of bullshit reasons that they'd contrived yesterday. When he finished, he looked at me expectantly.

Seth, Seth, my inner voice whispered. *What are you doing?*

I trembled as I started to speak. "I—that is—"

The demoness cut me off with a raised palm. "No, don't answer yet. Just think about what we said. Let's break for lunch, and meet back in half an hour."

I gaped. The others shared my surprise. Lunch? We'd been here for fifteen minutes. But this group, as impatient as they were for me to succumb, also welcomed the opportunity for a break. They scurried out or simply vanished. As they went, I expected someone to hold me back and issue a few threatening words, but none of them did.

I headed downstairs alone, uneasy and perplexed. I didn't feel hungry, but I hadn't eaten all day, so I figured I should at least have coffee and a doughnut. In the elevator, I found Clyde waiting for me.

"Don't talk to me," I said wearily.

His face was hard. "I've heard what's going on. They're setting us up. Starla and me."

"Yeah, I kind of know that," I snapped. "I've had to put up with twelve demons yelling at me over it for two days now."

"We didn't do it," he said fiercely.

"I know, I know. No one did it." God, I wanted to be anywhere else. A warm beach or my bed would have been optimal, but honestly, I wasn't picky at this point.

"You can't let them convict us. It isn't fair." Fear and desperation hung in his voice, surprising me. He always seemed so tough, like a five-century disembowelment wouldn't faze him at all.

"Fair? Fair?"

We stepped out of the elevator. On the other side of the lobby, I saw Seth about to leave for the day. He'd paused to talk to the concierge and caught my eye. I held up a hand to tell him to hang on, and then I turned back to Clyde.

"I'll tell you what isn't fair," I said. "You see that guy over there? That's my boyfriend. He has nothing to do with any of this. He just came here to keep me company. But since I decided to take the high ground with your case, those bastards on the jury are threatening to kill him if I don't vote their way. *That's* not fair."

Clyde's face grew less angry. A sober, grim look took over. "They wouldn't do it."

"Wouldn't they? And anyway, even if they don't and I still manage to keep up with this nobility, I'm never going to sway them. This'll just keep going. Kurtis's bribes are too good. He offered me . . . well, something I've always wanted. And he apparently promised to make some other demon a lieutenant demon in Monaco. God only knows what else is on the table."

Clyde snorted. "He's lying then. Kurt's powerful, but he can't do that. You think he'd still be in Belgium if he could pull strings for a Monaco transfer?"

Great. Fake bribes. As if this thing wasn't bad enough.

"Well, even so," I argued, "that demon on the jury sure believed it. That's all that matters."

"So . . . you've given up."

"You act like you're shocked by that!" I exclaimed. "Why is it okay for everyone around here to have black souls, yet somehow *I'm* held up to a higher standard?"

He'd grown solemn again. "Because there's something in you that isn't gone yet. A glimmer of goodness."

"A glimmer of goodness?"

"Yes. And around here, that means some—"

That's when the chandelier fell without warning.

There was no shaking, no trembling. No sign that it was starting to slip. *Bam!* The same chandelier hanging over the lobby that I'd mocked for cheapness came crashing down and hit the hard floor in a spectacular explosion of glass. Shards of all sizes spread out in a glittering radius throughout the room. Apparently it wasn't plastic after all. It was like watching a production of *Phantom of the Opera*, except with better special effects.

We couldn't suffer any real injuries, but Clyde grabbed my arm instinctively and jerked me back. We stared at the mess, stunned. People were shouting. Somehow, inexplicably, no one had actually been directly under it. It was a miracle—ironic, considering most of the hotel's current guests. The spraying glass had done a fair amount of bodily damage, however, and almost everyone around the lobby had sustained some kind of cut.

Including Seth.

I broke out of Clyde's grasp and tore off across the room, circling around the wreckage. Seth still stood by the concierge's desk. He'd dropped his messenger bag and held a two-inch shard of glass in his hand. Blood coated one end of it, and I saw the complementary slash in his cheek.

"Oh my God," I gasped. "Are you okay?"

He grimaced. "I think so. Are there any more? It doesn't feel like it."

Tiny pieces of glass and a fine crystalline powder covered a lot of his clothing, but I saw no more stuck in his skin, fortunately. It was warm out, but undoubtedly out of habit from Seattle, he'd headed out today with a flannel shirt over his Lynda Carter T-Shirt. The long sleeves had protected him, as had the thick fabric.

I studied the cut on his face with dismay, resisting the urge to touch it.

"You should get that looked at." Clyde had walked up behind me.

Seth shook his head. "It's not going to need stitches or anything. Lots of people worse off than me here."

"You're so lucky that's all you got," I breathed, looking

around the lobby at others who'd undoubtedly need medical attention. No one seemed to be dead or anything, just scratched up. This whole trip's increasing rate of awfulness was astounding, but Seth being hospitalized because of a falling chandelier would have defied belief. "I can't believe—"

I stopped. My eyes had fallen on four people standing directly opposite me. Four people who hadn't been injured at all. Four demons. Four jurors.

They watched me, malice in their eyes. Magenta-colored lips twitched into a knowing smile. Suddenly . . . suddenly I knew.

I turned back to Seth, my heart turning to lead as I squeezed his hand. Clyde, having noticed what I'd seen, looked at me with widened eyes.

"Georgina—"

I shook my head. "I'm sorry," I said, meaning it. "But glimmers of goodness really don't mean anything at all."

Chapter Eleven

Kurtis found me in my room later that day, after the jury had turned in its unanimous vote. He simply appeared out of nowhere. I was lying on my bed, staring at the ceiling while on TV, Oprah gave away a car to someone in need.

"I can't wait to go home," I told him nastily. "At least then I'll get some privacy. No one seems to respect it around here."

He leaned against the desk and tossed his messy hair out of his face. "That's why I brought you these." He reached into his pocket and produced a set of keys. He threw them over, and I caught them. The keychain's tag had an address on it.

"What are these?" I asked.

"Condo by the beach," he said. "I snagged it for you. Figured you'd want someplace nicer than this for your big night tonight."

I closed my eyes and groaned. "No. I don't want it."

"You earned it. I keep my promises."

I remembered what Clyde had said about Monaco. "Not all of them. You promise things you can't deliver on."

He frowned. "No. I keep my promises. All of them."

I shook my head. "Whatever. It doesn't matter. I don't want your blood money."

"You might as well get something for selling out your principles," he said cheerfully. "Besides, you're never going to get this chance again. And you can save your crumbling romance at the same time."

"It's not crumbling. Seth told me—er, her, that he couldn't do anything that made him feel guilty about us. We don't need to have sex for me to keep him around." But oh, good God, did I *want* to have sex. It was hard to lie there and tell Kurtis I was throwing his gift back in his face.

"I don't believe it. If that waitress offered—if he was in a position where he really *could* do it with her—he'd do it. That is, he'd do it if he still wasn't getting any from you."

"He doesn't believe in cheap sex. Staying faithful to me is part of his morals, and unlike everyone else around here, there are still some people in the universe who hold to their beliefs and actually have a sense of right and wrong."

Kurtis straightened up. "Sweetheart, everyone sells themselves out in the end. Keep the keys. The reward's still yours, whether you waste it or not. But—be warned. The clock's ticking, Cinderella. Offer expires at midnight. Of course, then you'll be just in time to see the show."

Ack. There was going to be a public display back at the hotel of Clyde and Starla's first round of punishment. I had no idea what exactly that would be, but it was going to be horrible and disgusting. After that, they'd be sent off to somewhere in Hell for the remainder of the sentence. The spectacle tonight would satisfy the sadistic and sensationalist natures of those who had journeyed to the trial. The perfect encore. I had absolutely no interest in going.

Thinking of that horrific display—as well as Kurtis's smug condescension—suddenly made something inside me snap. It made me sick that he could do this, sick that he could bribe and flatter others into getting whatever he wanted. I jerked myself upright from my defeatist sprawl.

"You don't think he could do that? Resist? Well, here's a deal for you. What if I can prove you're wrong? What if I can prove that Seth really does hold to his standards in the face of temptation?"

He rolled his eyes. "Whatever."

"You see?" I said, attempting the same smugness he managed so well. "You *aren't* sure. You're not the great judge of human nature you claim to be."

Those laughing eyes suddenly hardened. It was never a good idea to mock a demon. "Careful, little succubus. You don't want to go down this road. Take your boon, fuck your guy, and leave it at that."

I lay back against the pillows. "Okay. I get it."

"Get what?"

"That you're all talk. You really don't know for sure that Seth would succumb."

"In the face of that woman half-naked and going after him? Yes, darling. He'd succumb."

"Then let's bet on it."

"What do you want?" he asked warily.

"The truth. I want the truth from you about whether you really killed Anthony."

He shook his head. "I've told you a hundred times I didn't."

"Yeah, and you promised Julius a house in Monaco." Kurtis blinked. "I don't believe anything you tell me. When I say I want the truth, I want *the truth*. You know what I'm talking about. I want to see inside you."

"What's that going to accomplish? Even if you found out I'd done it—and I didn't—it wouldn't hold as evidence."

"I know. But *I* just want to know, once and for all, the truth about just one thing in this whole tangled mess. Let me look inside. Just to be certain about *something*."

He stared, actually caught off guard. As I've noted before,

to look inside another immortal was no small thing. It was traumatic, for both parties. Powerful. I honestly didn't know the full extent of what I was asking, but I liked the shock on his face, and honestly, after days of deceit, I just wanted something *real*.

"I'm not letting a succubus look inside me."

"Doesn't matter if the whole thing is a moot point."

He glowered. "What do I get if you're wrong about him?"

"What do you want?"

He considered, then a slow smile swept over his face. "I want you to fuck him."

"I—what?" My growing confidence promptly withered into confusion. I jingled the keys. "Isn't that what I'm already supposed to do?"

"No. I mean, fuck him after the gift expires. In all your power. Break that kindly naive notion you have of sparing his life and soul."

I felt the blood drain from my face. Sex with Seth? With no protective promise? No. No way could I do it. I'd promised myself that the instant this relationship started. I couldn't steal his energy for my own gain, couldn't shave off part of his life to feed my immortality. The thought made me queasy, and Kurtis could see that.

"Guess *you're* not so confident about him after all," he chuckled.

My heart hardened. I was angry about this trial, furious about what I'd been forced to do. And I was pissed as hell at Kurtis and his high-handed, arrogant attitude. Just once, I wanted to make some demon uncomfortable.

"It's a deal," I said.

"Really?"

I sat up. "Yup. Let's work out the details."

You couldn't ever make an open-ended or vague deal with a demon. Otherwise, they'd find any loophole possible to wiggle out of their end. So, Kurtis and I hashed out exactly what would be required to win the bet, what I'd have to do, and how each of us would have to pay up. By the time I was done, I felt like I'd done a pretty good job at covering all the contingencies. Probably not as good as if I'd had an imp present . . . but I felt certain it would suffice.

When we finished, Kurtis and I shook hands. Power crackled around us, sealing the deal. He vanished.

I climbed out of bed then and glanced at the clock to see how much longer I had succubus freedom.

It was time to go seduce my boyfriend.

The cold insanity of what I was going to do hit me a little while later. I was a total hypocrite. I'd made all these claims about the honesty and goodness between Seth and me, yet here I was about to entangle him up in a web of trickery which involved me deceiving him in order to test his fidelity—fidelity, by the way, which he wasn't even really forced to adhere to.

But I'd made my deal with Kurtis, and now I was in. So, I tried not to dwell on my guilt and instead attempted to focus in on how I would win this bet. After all, if I did, almost everything else would become irrelevant. Seth would prove faithful, I wouldn't have to sleep with him (how wrong did *that* sound?), and Kurtis would have to suck it up and do something he didn't want.

Still, I felt kind of bad blowing off Seth for the night. To make matters worse, I even did it a little coldly. I wasn't mean or anything, but I was definitely brusque with him in the hopes that my attitude would make him accept another Beth invitation.

It did. Of course, who could say? Maybe he still would have accepted if I'd been perfectly nice. Regardless, after "Georgina" took off for another party, "Beth" called Seth with an offer to come watch a movie we'd talked about at the carnival.

"Look," I said on the phone, "if it's too weird . . . I understand. I mean, I got what you were saying last night, and really . . . I don't want to cause trouble for you or anything. I mean you and your girlfriend probably already have plans, but I thought I'd check since my roommate actually just rented it . . ."

There was a long pause, and I could perfectly picture the look on Seth's face. "I don't have any plans . . ." More silence. I held my breath. "Okay. What's the address?"

I gave it to him, rented the movie, and got to the condo ten minutes before he did. That turned out to be a good thing because it took me about that long to recover from the shock of the place. Maybe Kurtis hadn't been bullshitting. When he delivered on his promises, he *delivered*. The condo had two floors and sat right on the edge of a stretch of gorgeous, private beach. Wood floors and leather furniture gave the place a swanky, sexy feel, and a fully stocked bar completed the image of a pimped-out bachelor pad—or in my case, bachelorette pad.

Of course, I realized the problem right as I let Seth inside. He stared around at the luxurious accommodations, at the six-figure sculptures and teak end tables.

"I thought you were short on money?" he asked in amazement.

"Er, I am," I replied. "This is my roommate's . . . place. Her family pays for it, and I rent a room from her." I didn't add that that room would technically have to be the bathroom since there was only one bedroom in the place. I had checked it out in my initial examination. The room had a round bed and mirrors on the ceiling. Honestly, Kurtis might have been trying too hard.

Seth looked a little skeptical, but I distracted him by asking about the cut on his face. Later, I found popcorn and tea in the fully stocked kitchen, and we settled down on one of the sleek black sofas to watch the movie. It was an independent film I'd seen several years ago and thought was amazing. I'd wanted him to see it for a while now; I never thought it'd be under these circumstances.

As we watched, I covertly maneuvered myself nearer and nearer to him. I used reaching for the popcorn as my excuse and pulled off the moves like a pro—because, well, I was a pro. Eyes on the screen, he didn't even realize what I'd done until the lights came up and we were sitting thigh to thigh and arm to arm. We weren't exactly groping, but we'd clearly moved past something platonic.

Seth noticed then, and he shifted himself away a little—but not too far away.

"What'd you think?" I asked.

He leaned his head back against the couch. Those long-lashed, amber-brown eyes stared off thoughtfully as he processed his opinions. In some ways, it wasn't hard playing Beth. Seth made both of us melt.

"Pretentious," he finally said. "But it had some good points."

"Pretentious?" I exclaimed.

We launched off into a critical analysis of the movie, very much like the ones we usually got into. I became so consumed that I didn't even notice the time passing until my eyes ran over the clock on the DVD player. Ten-twenty-seven.

The clock's ticking, Cinderella. Offer expires at midnight.

I hastily wrapped up the movie discussion, even conceding a few points to him. Moving on to the next stage, I brought us into personal matters.

"I'm really glad you could come over tonight," I told him, leaning against the couch in a way that made the space between us more intimate. "I was really afraid to call after last night . . . I mean, not that it was bad . . . but well . . ."

"Yeah, I know. But I'm glad you did call. Nothing else was going on."

Seth's eyes studied me in an appraising way. Then, as

though realizing what he was doing, he averted them in a way common to him.

"You keep saying you've got a girlfriend," I teased, "but I'm starting to wonder if that's just a line to keep me away. You always seem to be free."

He flinched, undoubtedly reminded of the way I'd abandoned him tonight.

"Oh, she's real . . . mostly. She's just been really, um, busy."

"Is she, like, working tonight?"

His brow furrowed slightly. "She might very well be," he muttered in a dry tone.

"What's she do?" I asked innocently.

"Um . . . she's in . . . customer service . . ."

"Wow. I didn't know jobs like that ran so late."

"Well, it's a conference kind of thing . . ."

"Oh, yeah. That's right. So, she's, like, schmoozing. Like . . . working the room?"

"Something like that."

"Why aren't you with her? Seems like you could go to parties with her, even at a work function."

"I'm not much of a party type," he said. "Especially these parties."

I tilted my head and met his eyes with a knowing look. "Is that really the truth?"

"What do you mean?"

"I don't know. With the way you keep seeing me . . . and the way you talk. It just kind of sounds like you're avoiding her."

"Er, no, no," he said. "It's not that . . ."

"But you said you have kinks. Maybe you're avoiding her and don't realize you're avoiding her."

"No, I don't think so . . ."

"Oh? Well, then, what are these kinks? You guys have trouble talking to each other? Not much in common?"

"Nothing like that," he assured me. "We have lots in common."

I arched an eyebrow. "Sex?"

His mouth opened to form a protest, but he stumbled on it.

"Ah," I said sagely. "I see."

"No," he said firmly. "It's not what you think . . ."

I studied him—face and body—and made it very obvious that I was doing so. I nodded with appreciation, liking what I saw.

"Well," I finally said. "It must be on her end. Nothing wrong with you. And here I'd had this image of this slim, gorgeous model with great genes."

"She *is* gorgeous," said Seth. I was happy to see him come to my defense.

I frowned. "Then . . . wait. Do *you*, like, have problems . . ."

The faintest flush showed in Seth's cheeks. It was a rare phenomenon, one I would have found adorable under other conditions.

"No," he said. "No problems like that."

"Then . . . will she not . . . ?"

Again, he took too long to answer.

"Oh," I said.

Silence fell. I could hear the ticking of a shiny, silver-rimmed clock on the wall. Eleven-oh-seven.

At last, I spoke. "I don't want to be harsh here or overstep my limits . . . but well, she's an idiot."

He shook his head. "It's complicated."

"Is it? I mean, you say you guys have stuff in common. You're gorgeous. She allegedly is. You want to do it . . . I mean, if she's got some hang-up . . ."

"It's not that, not exactly."

I sighed. "Look, I won't lie. I like you. I *really* like you. But even if I wasn't interested in you like this, I'd still be telling you you're crazy. You shouldn't waste your life on someone like that, shouldn't waste your sex life . . ."

Again, he shook his head. "It's about more than sex."

I shifted closer and put my hand on his bare arm, trailing my fingers along his skin. He jumped but didn't stop me.

"When was the last time?" I asked.

"The last time what?"

"You know."

No answer.

"Seth," I said in exasperation, still touching him. "This is crazy. Do you hear yourself? You make it sound like you can go without sex for the rest of your life. Can you? Can you go without being kissed? Can you go without having someone's hands slide up your chest? Can you go without touching a woman? Can you go without throwing her down and peeling her clothes off? Can you go without being wrapped up with—*in*—another person? Having that union? That passion?"

Seth was staring at me like he had no clue who I was. That was reasonable since I was pretty sure I'd slipped out of Beth's personality and into my own. At the same time, I think my words and the lust in my voice had kindled something in him. I could see it in his face—a doubt over what he'd been trying so hard to believe all this time and a yearning for what he'd wanted.

That was all I needed to see. I made my move.

Pushing myself over him, so a leg draped over his lap, I kissed him. In the fraction of a second before our lips touched, I realized it was fully possible Kurtis had screwed with me this whole time and that I was about to suck away part of Seth's life.

But I didn't.

There was no rush of power, no flow of his thoughts or energy into me. It was just a kiss, an ordinary kiss like any two mortals might have. Well . . . except that it wasn't ordinary. Not for me at least. It was *Seth*. Me kissing Seth. And so help me, he was kissing me—Beth—back. His lips were as warm and soft as they'd been every other time we'd had our brief kisses, but this time we didn't pull back. It was . . .

amazing. And that was when I learned that whatever shyness Seth might show in conversation did *not* translate to physical actions.

He returned the kiss with intensity, lips and tongue caressing my own, filled with an untamed energy that just barely managed to keep control. I pulled myself completely onto his lap, straddling him, and wrapped my arms around his neck. His own arms encircled my waist.

"How long?" I asked between kisses, my voice breathy. "How long since anyone's kissed you like this? Been on you like this?"

He didn't answer, but the hands on the small of my back caught the edge of my shirt and lifted it over my head. I'd dressed casual tonight—plain black T-shirt—but the bra underneath was red, and the hourglass figure made it look great.

I yanked his own shirt off and felt the heat in my own body increase as I took in the smooth, lightly tanned skin of his chest. I'd seen it many times, of course, but now—being able to kiss it and *really* touch it—I looked at in a totally different way. I leaned in and kissed him harder, pressing my breasts up to his chest. His hands were on my back again, but when they didn't unfasten my bra, I did the honors.

I saw his gaze travel from my face to my breasts, instinctual male desire filling his face. Pushing him over, I forced him to lie back as I crawled on top and continued straddling him. My hands found the edge of his jeans and unbuttoned them. Then, I took a hold of his hands and placed them on my stomach.

"Don't you want me?" I asked. "Don't you want to touch me?"

I didn't know who exactly I was speaking for anymore, Beth or Georgina, but it didn't matter. I'd forgotten the whole reason for this. All I knew was that we were going to do it. Seth and I were going to have sex. I had about forty-five minutes—forty-five precious, golden minutes—in which we could do anything we wanted with no consequences.

And what *I* wanted right now was for Seth to run his hands over me. He wasn't, though I could still see the longing all over him. And when I laid down on top of him and ground our hips together, I could *feel* the longing. I kissed him again, furiously, and then pulled my mouth back just a breath so that I could speak.

"We're going to do this . . . and it's going to be good. Very good. You . . . inside me. Good, so very—what?"

Seth suddenly struggled up, pushing me—not harshly— off of him. Once he was free, he stood up and backed away from the couch. He ran a hand over his eyes.

"Oh, God. I can't believe this is happening."

"It's happening," I told him, practically panting. "Come back—"

"No." He shook his head. "I can't."

"But you—you started to—"

"I know, I know," he groaned. He buttoned his pants. "I got caught up."

"You wanted me," I growled. "You still do." I stood up too and wriggled out of the jeans I wore, pulling my panties off in the process. Standing before him naked, I fixed him with a challenging glare. "Tell me you don't. Tell me you don't want to have sex with me."

Those serious brown eyes swept the length of me, of all my curves and smooth skin. The desire was still written all over him, but a hard glint in the depths of his eyes showed he was fighting it. The flesh was willing, but the spirit was weak—or rather, the spirit was strong.

"I'm sorry," he said, reaching for his shirt. "You're very beautiful. *Very* beautiful. And hanging out with you is fun. There's something about you—it's almost like—well." He shrugged the thought away, though I had a good feeling what it had been. "But I can't. I can't do this. I'm sorry. I shouldn't have come here tonight."

"But . . ." My lower lip trembled as I attempted confusion

while still looking sexy. "She won't . . . she won't give you what you want . . ."

"I want *her*. I want to be with her."

"You can still have her," I argued. "And tonight you can have me. Then you can go back, and she'll never know. She probably wouldn't even mind."

"*I* would know," he said. He pulled the T-shirt on and smoothed it. "That's what matters."

"I don't . . . I don't understand . . . there are no strings attached . . ."

"I love her," he told me, moving toward the door. "I can't explain it any better than that. I'm sorry." He turned away. The door opened, then closed.

I stood there in the living room, naked, staring at where he'd last been. Kurtis materialized beside me.

"Well, well," he said, following my gaze to the door.

"Was I convincing enough?" I asked. Part of the conditions had been that I couldn't do a half-ass seduction job.

"Very," he said wryly. "So much so that I'm guessing there wasn't actually a lot of acting going on."

I tore my gaze from the door and looked at the demon. Clothing and my Georgina shape materialized onto me. "But he did it. He resisted and held to his beliefs."

Kurtis smiled. "Disappointed?"

I thought about it, thought how it had felt—however briefly—to have complete access to Seth. The possibility of actually having sex was tantalizing and bittersweet. Of course, if we'd done it, it wouldn't have really been *me* and Seth. It would have been him and . . . an illusion. That wasn't how I wanted sex to be with us.

"A little," I answered. "But not enough." I sighed. "This was stupid of me. Testing him like that. I never doubted him . . . not really. I don't know why I had to prove it."

"People do stupid things for love," he told me. I'd said the exact same thing to Starla. "They do stupider things when they're jealous."

"What are you, a shrink?"

"Just an observer of humankind."

I sighed again. "I wasted a once-in-a-lifetime chance tonight."

He cut me a look, and I noticed then how agitated he appeared. "Maybe not."

I glanced back. "What do you mean?"

"I told you, I always keep my promises." With a resigned sigh, he extended his hand. "Ready to look inside?"

Chapter Twelve

I jerked back, suddenly uncertain. This whole bet, just to satisfy my curiosity over whether or not Kurtis really had killed Anthony, had paled somewhat in my eyes. I'd proven he was wrong about Seth . . . but what did that really matter when compared to how stupid I'd been in the first place about Seth?

Kurtis' eyes widened. "What's this? Cold feet? After everything you went through?" He shook his head, amused. "What is it with you? Don't you accept any rewards?"

"I don't know . . . I'm just so . . . I shouldn't have done this tonight . . ."

"Oh, good grief," he groaned. He was playing lax and silly, but I could see how the idea of me looking inside scared him. "After I braced myself for this all night?" He made a big show of looking at the clock. "Well, decide fast because I don't want to miss the main event."

My anger kindled once more at being reminded of poor Starla and Clyde meeting a potentially undeserved fate. "Okay. Let's do this."

He attempted his cocky smile, but I could see the sweat

on his neck and along his hair. His pupils were large. Wow. He was afraid. Really afraid. I wondered if I should be too. Closing his eyes, he held out his hand again. I grabbed hold of it and . . .

I was in.

I was in a place of white light, dizzying and blinding. It was filled with something—something I simply couldn't perceive. It was like a blind person staring at the color red. I could not comprehend what I was missing because it appealed to a sense I didn't have. In a flash, that surreal moment was over, and I stood on familiar territory, with sights and sounds I could comprehend.

I was on a battlefield at night, mud and bodies lit by a full moon and a star-clustered sky that had never seen city lights. Scraps of fighting still lingered around me, on the periphery of the battlefield. Groans of the dying filled the air. I looked around, disgusted.

Then I was in a city, an ancient city I didn't recognize, a city that had existed ages before my mortal life. I watched the town's life unfold, watched as the tyrant who ruled it trampled the citizens and abused them for their labor, denying them food and life when it was convenient. In the end, it didn't matter because a raiding army eventually came and destroyed the town, killing, raping, and enslaving its residents.

Scene after horrible scene flew past me in fast-forward. It was like the proverbial life flashing before your eyes. Humanity suffered, and I watched it through Kurtis' eyes, felt his pain and frustration, until finally he couldn't take it anymore. Then the white screen was back, the whiteness that meant nothing to me and everything to him. He tore it asunder, and it was like tearing himself in half. Then, there was no more light, only blackness and a hole in his soul.

After that, Kurtis' demonic career unfolded before my eyes, and I watched him commit atrocity after atrocity— some worse than the ones he'd broken with Heaven over—

simply because he didn't care anymore. I felt his pain, felt his emptiness, felt his apathy. The events blinked past me in seconds, an abridged version of a timeless life.

I saw his time with Anthony, saw the tortures that had been described in the courtroom. And as the present tumbled forward, I felt Kurtis' anger toward his former employee cool—and I felt his surprise when other demons hauled him off to the trial. I felt his frustration and fear, his desperate attempts to lobby and bribe for his innocence. His relief when Clyde and Starla took the fall.

And then, it was all over, and we were standing together in the condo.

Kurtis hadn't killed Anthony. He'd been telling the truth.

I broke contact and reeled from what I'd seen. I understood then why this wasn't done very often, even to prove a point. It was enough to live with the power of your own soul—or, in my case, of your leased soul—but to experience the emotion and intensity of another's was too much. The fact that I was a lesser immortal viewing a higher immortal made it that much more powerful.

I staggered backward and fell to my knees, arms wrapped around me. Kurtis grabbed an exquisite blue glass bowl, veined in gold, and held it to me.

"You gonna be sick?"

It certainly felt that way. I leaned over, feeling the bile rise in my throat as I squeezed my eyes shut. The room spun. I carried a lot of pain with me, almost a millennium and a half's worth. But I knew then, knew without a doubt that it was nothing compared to the scope of what angels and demons went through. Even the shadow of what he felt was wreaking havoc with me.

Swallowing, I pushed the nausea down and looked back up at Kurtis. His long face was serious, his eyes infinite and knowing, even as he shuddered and tried to master his own reaction. The experience had been rough on him too. Rougher.

Looking away, I breathed a grateful sigh that the sensations were already fading, that horrible loss of an angel who'd turned his back on Heaven because he was angry at the way the powers-that-be let humanity suffer.

"I'm sorry," I gasped out.

"For what?" he asked, a sardonic smile on his lips. There was a tight set to his face that said even if he had a chipper persona, he would still feel the effects of me reading him for some time.

"I don't know." I could have been apologizing for anything. For making him open up. For what he'd given up in anger millennia ago. For what he'd had to do in the intervening time. For being accused of a crime he didn't commit.

Kurtis seemed to understand. He set the bowl down and helped me up, even though he was a bit unsteady himself. "Will you be all right?"

"I think so."

"Look at that," he told me. "Eleven-thirty. You have time to go back to your guy."

He was right. I had thirty minutes, thirty minutes in which to go back to Seth as myself and share a few precious moments with no treachery or subterfuge. Now that I knew Kurtis was innocent, the sting of his bribe had faded.

Suddenly, I frowned. The memories of looking in his head were disappearing rapidly, but while inside of him, I'd seen the events of the trial through his eyes. I'd seen him approaching other jurors, making his offers.

"Monaco," I exclaimed.

"What?"

"You didn't offer Monaco."

He tilted his head and studied me. "You might have gotten hit harder than I thought."

"No! When you offered people bribes, you didn't offer to transfer that guy to Monaco. Clyde said you didn't have the power."

"Of course not," snorted Kurtis. "You think I'd be in Belgium if I could arrange that?"

"Who did then? Who offered bribes to acquit you and convict Clyde and Starla? Someone else was working with you. But, I mean, not *with* you." I could say that with some conviction because I knew for sure now he'd had no ally that he'd been aware of.

Kurtis frowned, face lost in thought, then it cleared. "Noelle."

"She's powerful enough?"

"Oh, yeah. Absolutely. Makes sense too. There wasn't enough evidence to have a clear decision, so she pushed for a quick ending and got her cathartic revenge. Punished two people who were pissing her off in the process. Very neat. Nice way to do it if you can't nail the right suspect."

It made sense. Starla and Luis had confirmed the same ideas. And yet . . . something wasn't making sense . . .

I blinked. "That's because the right suspect wasn't up there."

Kurtis' face registered mild surprise. "Oh?"

"It was Noelle. Noelle killed Anthony."

"Her own employee?" he scoffed. "Not likely. Especially since, as his supervisor, she could legally inflict any number of punishments." He grinned. "I of all people know the loopholes there. Besides, she had the hots for Anthony."

"So did Starla. A lot more than the hots, actually. Yet everyone thinks casting her as a murderer makes sense."

"Okay, you get points for that, but what else have you got, Sherlock? You can't just go accuse a major archdemon of murder." He made a face. "Unless it's one who's been sentenced to Belgium."

Scraps of conversation from the last few days began fitting together in my head. "Noelle was jealous of Anthony and Starla. He'd refused her advances, and it must have driven Noelle crazy that he preferred a new, weak demoness over her. She tried to split them up, right? Said it was interfering with his work. And that's when he lashed back. Starla told me how he wanted to transfer. Probably figured he could still date or whatever Starla without work problems. But Noelle said she was going to fight it—she didn't want to lose him. She loved him. And they had this huge, horrible blowout that made them both really mad. Clyde passed Anthony on his way out, and Anthony was furious. Then Clyde talked to Noelle, and she was livid too."

"So she kills Anthony over an argument?"

"No," I said. "Well, yes. More than that. The argument was the culmination of a lot of things. His rejection of her. The fact that she was likely going to lose him. Remember Margo's comment? 'If I can't have him . . .' That was Noelle's line of thinking."

Kurtis let out a low whistle. "That's quite a theory, little one. And a lot of circumstantial evidence."

"It's why she's been so angry over all this. It's not revenge. It's anger at herself for what she did—and fear to close this up fast and cover her own tracks. That's also why she didn't push to look inside any of you guys. She made it sound like she didn't want to violate you, but really, it was because she knew you'd all be proven innocent."

"Well, you've made some good leaps, I'll give you that." He pointed at the clock. Twenty minutes until midnight. "But there's nothing to be done for it, even if it's true. It's almost time. That group's in a frenzy by now, waiting for the torture. They're probably selling balloons and hot dogs. No one's going to listen."

I stared blankly at the window. "Luis would."

"*Maybe* he would." When I didn't answer, Kurtis laid an almost friendly hand on my shoulder. "Look, you really might be on to something, but it's too late. You're burning up time. At the very least, get in one kiss with your guy. Chase after this theory, and you blow any moment you have with him."

Kurtis was right. And I had already blown most of what time I could have had with Seth. I'd wasted it in the guise of another woman. But if I acted soon, I could have him now as me. I could have him, and Starla and Clyde would suffer. I'd noted before that they'd probably committed enough other crimes to deserve punishment, but it occurred to me that like Kurtis, they might have initially fallen from grace for more than just selfish reasons.

I looked up and met Kurtis' penetrating gaze. "Will you transport me back to the hotel?"

He was right about the spectacle. The ballroom-turned-conference-room was packed. The whole gang was there from the first day: imps, vampires, incubi, and demons. Kurtis and I pushed our way through the excited crowd. People slapped him on the back in congratulations as we passed. They made lewd comments to me.

Near the front of the room, a demon in black sharpened long, bladed instruments. Near him stood Starla and Clyde. The two "guilty" demons didn't move, though no visible bonds held them. They were frozen, trapped through some magical means. I averted my eyes from them.

"Help me," I told Kurtis. "Help me find Luis."

It was an impossible task. There were too many bodies mingling and moving. Luis was a big guy. I'd hoped I might find him simply by virtue of him being taller than others, but that seemed unlikely now.

Kurtis stopped walking. "He's not here."

I stopped too, nearly running into an annoyed vampire. "How do you know?"

"He's one of the strongest here, stronger even than Noelle. If he were in this room, we'd feel him, even above all this."

He was right, I realized. We fought our way back out. Once outside, Kurtis stood and looked around like a hound sniffing the wind. "Got him."

We found Luis sitting in the bar, stirring his bourbon over ice. He appeared to be the only one of the demonic congregation who wasn't in the other room making balloon animals or getting face tattoos. Feeling us enter, he looked up in surprise.

"You have to help us," I said. Immediately, I sat down and spilled the whole story, laying out the evidence—circumstantial though it was—about why I believed Noelle was the killer.

Luis listened with an unreadable face. When I finished, he pretty much said the same thing Kurtis had. "There's no way to prove it."

"But it makes sense! Luis, they're five minutes away from punishing the wrong people."

"Georgina." Luis sighed. "Unfair things happen every day in the universe whether you live on Earth, in Heaven, or in Hell. If you're right, it's unfortunate, but well . . . that's that."

"I thought you wanted the truth," I accused.

"Then I have it. Your idea makes sense. Noelle did it."

"But it's not justice!"

"I didn't come for justice." He gave me a kind, sad smile. "I'm not the one with 'an annoying yet adorable sense of right and wrong.'"

"I don't believe that! You must still have *something*."

"Look, I'm not happy that Noelle could get away with this, but it's too late. And this isn't a Christmas special where I suddenly see the error of my ways. I'm a fucking demon. I spread evil in the world. I *am* evil."

I figured fighting that would just get me accused of more cheery good will. And honestly, I did believe Luis still had a sense of right and wrong . . . but if his life had been like Kurtis', he had good reason for apathy.

"If you call her out," I said finally. "You'll get accolades. Big promotion."

Luis' face registered surprise, then broke into a grin. "You're bribing me now?"

I looked between him and Kurtis. "I hear that's how it works around here."

Luis's smile faded. "There's no way of proving her guilt."

"Well," mused Kurtis. "There's one way . . ." He'd perked up at the mention of promotion. I think he hoped being in on Noelle's takedown could help his Belgium transfer.

He and Luis locked eyes, and something passed in those glances.

"No," said Luis. "She wouldn't agree."

"You're strong enough . . ."

Luis grimaced. "If I do that, and she's not guilty, *I'm* the one who gets flayed."

"She is guilty," I said, having no clue what they referred to, only that something big was on the line. "Luis, *please*."

The clock ticked. One minute until midnight.

Luis studied me for a long time. He exhaled and stood up. "I can't believe I'm about to do this."

Kurtis gave him a friendly punch. "Don't worry. I've got your back."

"Really?"

"No."

Powerful presence or no, not many people noticed when Luis entered the ballroom. At least, not until he grabbed Noelle and slammed her against the wall.

Dead silence filled the room, except for Noelle's outraged cries as she fought against him. But he held her pinned with more than physical strength; she couldn't match his magical power.

"Are you out of your fucking mind? What the hell are you—?"

She quieted and blanched as he pressed his hand to her forehead. He paled as well, and I heard a collective gasp around the room. I realized then what he was doing. He was looking *in* her, just as Kurtis had allowed me. Only, Luis was doing it by force. It was a mental, spiritual rape of sorts.

I shuddered, remembering how it had been for me being the one to look inside. It had been a hundred times worse for Kurtis, and unlike Noelle, *he'd* consented. As she grew paler and paler, I could only imagine how it must feel for her to undergo that. No, scratch that. I couldn't even comprehend it.

The two demons broke apart in less than a minute. I wondered if that's how much time had elapsed when Kurtis and I had done it. I'd relived an eternity in my mind while it happened.

Luis and Noelle stood there, gasping, staring at each other. Both looked ready to pass out.

"Holy shit," exclaimed Luis. "You did do it."

Noelle frantically shook her head, black curls swaying, as she tried to hold on to the wall for support. "No, no." She looked desperately at the crowd. "He's lying! He's lying!"

Luis was visibly trying to recover himself. He grabbed nothing for support, but he had the look of someone who'd been gut-punched. "You want to let someone else look and prove me wrong?"

"No!" she cried. In power, she was second only to Luis here. None of the other gathered demons could actually force her as he had. She would have to allow it—unless an outside demon was summoned. "You can't prove anything, Luis. You're lying. You're—"

"I can prove it," he interrupted. "You showed me. I saw it inside you. I know where to go and—"

"No, don't. Don't."

He shrugged. "Your call. You tipped me off. I know how to get evidence now and prove it. I'm the one passing judgment. Make me go hunt down the proof, and your sentence will be . . . bad. Or, confess now, and your sentence will be . . . less bad."

A silent battle took place. I had no idea what evidence Luis had seen inside her, but her expression showed that she did not want it made public. Realizing she was fucked either way, Noelle finally nodded.

"All right. All right. Yes, I confess. I did it. I killed Anthony and set the others up. There. Are you happy? Are you fucking happy?"

Those gathered went crazy. They *loved* the new turn of events. It might have even been better than a flaying for them. As chaos broke out in the room, I heard Kurtis chuckling behind me.

"Sweet," he said. "I am *so* out of Belgium."

"What, for helping with this?" I asked.

"Yup. Well, that and I hear there's an archdemon opening in L.A."

Chapter Thirteen

Seth and I flew back to Seattle the next day. A lot of demons had wanted to talk to me, but I needed to get out of that hotel as soon as possible. In fact, I'd hightailed it out of the ballroom once Starla and Clyde had been freed. I hadn't stuck around because I had a feeling Noelle was simply going to be swapped into their place for the evening's entertainment.

Sitting beside Seth for the two-and-a-half hour flight home brought all the *other* events of last night back to me. As we held hands and recounted the bizarre trial events, he in no way acted as though he'd faced temptation and won last night. I in no way acted as though I'd been the cause of that temptation and had subsequently lost the one chance we might have had for physical intimacy. The fact that my exploits had led to two demons' freedom was little comfort.

"She really killed him?" asked Seth in amazement.

"Yup."

"But she loved him . . . or something, right?"

"Yup."

"Then how could she have done that?"

I stared at his profile, at the cheekbones and brown eyes I loved. I thought about losing him, how I would feel if he chose another woman. I wouldn't be driven to kill him, of course, but . . . well, I could empathize with the pain.

"Because people do stupid things for love," I murmured sadly, thinking of my own sins.

He turned and met my eyes, compassion shining in them. "You okay?"

I hesitated, and for a brief moment, the instinct was there. I almost spilled everything I'd done in my silly Beth obsession. After all, Seth and I had recently had big discussions about honesty in relationships. He was a big believer in telling the truth, and I wanted to live up to his ideals. Yet, the words stuck in my throat.

"Fine," I said instead. "Just worn out . . . long week."

"Yeah," he said. "I hear you." His gaze turned inward, and I had a feeling he was thinking of the condo. He opened his mouth, like he too might say something, then closed it. I was pretty sure I knew what had been about to come out.

"So," I said carefully. "Where'd you go this morning?" He'd gotten in some writing before our plane left. "The pig café?"

He smiled faintly. "No. I went back to that diner . . ."

"Oh?"

"Yeah . . . weird thing. That waitress you saw . . . she was working, and I told her I was leaving and . . ."

My smile was frozen on my face as I attempted to play blasé. "And?"

Again, I had the feeling he was about to tell me about last night, and again, he held back. "I don't know. Just weird. She was acting really strange when I talked to her . . ."

Like, say, when he talked to her about events she had no clue about?

"What do you mean?" I asked.

He shook his head, letting it go. I wondered if he'd tried to apologize to her. He probably thought her obliviousness was feigned as retaliation. "I don't know. Like I said, she was just being weird."

He squeezed my hand, and we settled back into our seats. Both of us held our own secrets, our own guilt. Neither of us had the courage to bring them up. I wondered if that's how all couples were, hiding small, silent sins.

Nonetheless, I couldn't resist asking, "Weird, huh? Wait . . . didn't you say she reminded you of me? Are you saying *I'm* weird?"

Seth laughed. He brought my hand to his lips and kissed it. "Thetis, there are no adjectives for you. And the two of you are nothing alike."

"Really? I mean, you acted like we were twins or something."

"I did no such thing."

"You *did*," I teased. "It was like you couldn't tell us apart."

He sighed and rolled his eyes at my joking. "I told you, you're nothing alike. You don't act alike. You don't think alike. You don't talk alike."

"Or look alike," I added.

"Right," he agreed. After another squeeze of my hand, he released it and opened up his laptop.

Watching, I figured I should be glad he didn't suspect anything. I'd gotten away with my blunder, my test of his fidelity. I should feel glad. Except I didn't.

"People do stupid things for love," I muttered under my breath.

Seth glanced at me. "What'd you say?"

"Nothing."

BITTEN

Lynsay Sands

Prologue

The room was nearly pitch black. The weak glow of moonlight coming through the only window gave little illumination, but that didn't matter. Darkness was their friend for this trap.

Keeran crouched behind the chest that had been positioned to block him from the view of anyone entering the room. Hand clenched around his sword, muscles tensed, he stared with fixed attention at the crack of light coming in under the bedchamber door.

A rustle reached his ears as his father shifted in his own hiding place on the other side of the chamber. Keeran turned his eyes in that direction, but while he could see the dark shape of the bed between them, he could see no sign of his father in the gloomy corner beyond it. Keeran knew he was equally invisible to the older man.

Another rustle. It was the barest of sounds, but he recognized it for a sign that the older warrior was restless. They hadn't been hiding there long, but Keeran was restless as well, eager to claim vengeance for the deaths of his mother and sister.

His gaze returned to the dark corner and Keeran silently cursed his father for refusing to remain at his side as he had wished. After losing both his mother and sister in quick succession, he'd wanted to keep his sire close as they awaited the beast they were sure would strike again this night.

His mother and sister. Keeran felt grief try to claim and weaken him, but staved it off. He needed anger now to strengthen him, so deliberately reflected on the events that had led up to this night.

Keeran had returned from more than a year fighting the king's battles to find Castle MacKay in an uproar and his mother dead. It was his father who had told him the tale of what had come to pass. Some weeks past, young village girls and boys had begun to die, found pale and bloodless, two marks on their throat as if bitten. Panic had been quick to set in among the MacKay clan. Since the attacks had all taken place at night, parents began locking their children away the moment the sun went down, but this did little to slow the deaths. Two more young girls turned up dead in their beds, both only feet away from their sleeping parents.

As clan chief, Keeran's father was expected to both stop these deaths and to avenge them. He immediately set up a night watch to patrol the village, then gathered a group of men to hunt the source of the attacks. It was the third night of the hunt that Keeran's father came across what appeared to be a man feasting on the neck of one of the warriors assigned to patrol the village.

Geordan MacKay had told Keeran that for a brief moment, he had been so overwhelmed by the horrible realization that the ancient myths of night-walking beasts who fed on the blood of men were true that he had been unable to move. Vampires existed. But he had soon shaken off his temporary paralysis and attacked, taking the creature by surprise and hacking off his head before the vampire could straighten from his last victim.

News of the kill had spread quickly, and the clan had

gathered to greet him as Keeran's father had made his triumphant ride into the bailey, the headless vampire across his horse before him. They had all cheered when he held up the head, jaws open, deadly teeth exposed. A huge bonfire had been started and the body and head unceremoniously dumped on it to be sure the creature could not return to life. Then they had celebrated his death and the return of safety to the MacKays well into the morning.

Keeran's father had thought his troubles over then. He had killed the vampire plaguing his people. They were safe now. And they had been. At least the people in the village. But the very next night, his wife had fallen victim to the bloodless death. Geordan MacKay had awakened in the morning to find her lying pale and still beside him. Obviously, there was a second vampire, and this one had possessed the gall to kill Lady MacKay while she lay sleeping beside her husband. The horror was not over.

Keeran had arrived home the afternoon of his mother's death and joined the hunt for this new beast that night. That hunt proved fruitless, as did the next night's hunt, and the next. In the dawn after the third night, the men had returned to the news that Keeran's sister was dead. This new vampire had got past the patrols and guards that had been set everywhere and had killed her in her sleep, as had happened with their mother.

It had been obvious at that point that this second creature knew that Geordan MacKay had personally killed the first vampire and was now seeking vengeance. That being the case, Keeran had been the next logical victim. Father and son, both furious and grief-stricken, had redoubled their efforts to hunt down this new threat, but after nearly a week of searching, the laird of the MacKay clan had decided they should change their approach. They would lay a trap.

His plan had been simple. They would stuff straw under Keeran's bedclothes, hoping the creature would think him asleep there. Then each would take position on either side of the bed so that no matter which side he approached from, one or the other would be positioned to come up from behind and tackle him.

His father's plan had seemed a good one at first, but that was before they had doused the fire in the hearth, snuffed out the candles, and been plunged into stygian darkness. Suddenly blind, Keeran had feared they wouldn't be able to see the vampire to attack him when he came. But his father had insisted they would see him enter by the torchlight in the hall spilling into the room when he eased the door open.

With no better plan to take this one's place, Keeran had acquiesced and backed into his assigned corner. It was a relief to find that his eyes did adjust to the darkness and that, aided by the weak moonlight coming in through the window on the opposite wall, he could make out the dark shape of his bed.

Realizing all at once that this was no longer true and that the room seemed even darker than before, Keeran turned his gaze toward the window. It appeared that a cloud had been passing over the moon. Even as he looked, it moved away, allowing the faintest light back in. Keeran was just relaxing when another sound reached his ears.

Stiffening, he shot his gaze to the corner where his father stood invisible in darkness. Had that been a moan? He held his breath, straining to hear until his head ached with the effort. Keeran heard no other sound, but icy cold was creeping over him and he had the sudden uncomfortable sense of being the hunted rather than the hunter.

"Father?" he called in a bare whisper of sound.

Silence so thick it seemed to have a life of its own was his only answer. Keeran felt the hair on the back of his neck prickle. Had the beast got in? Nay. Light would have spilled into the room from the door had anyone entered. Still, his senses were on alert and his instincts were shrieking that there was trouble.

"Father?" he said, louder, to combat the sudden eerie sensation of being alone and exposed.

When there was no answer this time, Keeran eased up from his crouching position and moved carefully around the chest toward the door. They had removed all the rushes from the floor except for a foot-wide space around the bed. This had been to ensure they would be betrayed by no footfall as they crept up on the vampire when he appeared. Keeran was grateful for this forethought as he made his silent way to the door.

Relief coursed through him when he felt the wood of the door beneath his seeking fingers. Pausing just to the side of it, he listened for a moment, then pulled it open and thrust it wide.

Light immediately spilled into the room. Blinking as his eyes tried to adjust, Keeran turned to the corner his father had taken, prepared to apologize for the skittishness that had made him open the door, only to freeze as the man's crumpled figure came into view. For a moment, Keeran was bewildered as to what the older man was doing lying there slumped against the chest he should have been crouched behind, but then he saw the blood dribbling from two small puncture wounds on his neck. He also noted that—while pale as death—Geordan MacKay was breathing, taking in short, gasping breaths.

Instinct sent Keeran hurrying across the room toward his father. He had just reached the foot of the bed when movement out of the corner of his eye made him stop his forward motion and turn. In his concern, he had forgotten the monster they had been lying in wait for. It was a fatal mistake.

Keeran's sword was raised by the time he completed the turn, but the sight of the woman who stepped calmly out of the shadows so stunned him that he froze to gape.

She was slender, pale, and petite. She was also one of the loveliest women Keeran had ever seen. Her face was a pale oval, with perfect features framed by midnight hair that cascaded over her shoulders and out of sight down her back. His gaze stopped briefly on her large, lovely eyes, then dipped down to her sweet, blood red lips and stayed there. Keeran might have stared at her all night had a sound not drawn his attention to his father again.

" 'Tis her. She is *Vampyre*. Kill her!"

Keeran felt as if he had been punched in the stomach at these words. He turned back to the woman, expecting a denial. Surely this beautiful creature could not be the monster they sought? But he found her smiling an unholy smile. A shudder ran through him as she licked her lips and he realized the crimson color had been his father's blood. This *was* the beast who had killed his mother and sister and had now felled his father.

Red-hot rage immediately coursed through Keeran. He started to bring his sword down, but found she suddenly held the razor-sharp blade in a grip as hard as the steel she grasped. Keeran could neither raise nor lower it. Without hesitation, he drew the sword toward her as if her hand were a sheath. She didn't even flinch as it sliced into her flesh. Neither did she bleed, he realized. Only the dead didn't bleed.

Before he could attempt to hack at her again, the woman's open hand shot out at him. He barely had time to note the move, let alone block it. Her cold palm slammed into his throat with incredible force, then her fingers closed with a strength no human could possibly muster. She followed that with a lightning-swift blow to his chest that sent him to his knees as the air was punched out of him. The woman then stepped forward, dragging him around by the throat at the same time so that she stood behind him and they both faced his father.

The sword had dropped from his hand when she had punched him. Now weaponless, Keeran could only grab at her hand, trying desperately to tear it away. His shock at his inability to do so had his eyes bulging as he attempted to suck air down the throat her vicelike grip seemed to have sealed closed. He was a warrior: strong, hard, and twice her size, and yet she was stronger.

"Hellbound creature!" Geordan MacKay gasped, and the woman holding Keeran as easily as if he were a rag doll laughed. It was a tinkle of amusement, more suited to a ballroom than this tense moment.

"Undoubtedly." She sounded amused, but her voice turned cold as she added, "But you shall go to your Maker knowing that I am taking your son and heir there with me. 'Tis a fitting punishment for your killing my mate, would you not say?"

Keeran saw his father try to rise from his slumped position at this claim, even as he himself attempted to break the grip on his throat. Neither of them succeeded. His father fell back with a weak moan of despair even as Keeran felt the sting of the beast's death kiss on his neck. That first nip was all the pain there was to his death. Then ecstasy exploded where the sting had been, spreading from that spot through his whole body. Much to his shame, Keeran felt his body respond as if to a lover. Then cold began to creep over him and his vision began to narrow. His last sight before the encroaching darkness claimed him was of the tears leaking from his father's regret-filled eyes and rolling down his pale cheeks.

When awareness returned to him, Keeran found himself lying abed and not knowing how he'd gotten there. He rolled weakly onto his side, then stilled at the sight of his father lying dead in the corner, a stake through his heart.

"He is dead. It is done."

Keeran's eyes shot to the window where the woman stood, shrouded in the gray light of predawn. She had awaited his regaining awareness before making her next move, and he suspected it would be to stake him, too.

"Nay. I'll not put you to rest," she announced, apparently able to read his mind. "Your father shall suffer more in his heaven knowing that you walk the earth, taking life to sustain your own as I do."

"Never!" Keeran spat, repulsed by the very idea.

"We shall see." Her smile was cold and cruel. "You will find you will do much to end the pain of hunger when it strikes."

Realizing now that she did not have the mercy to kill him, Keeran turned his gaze aside, wishing she would just go away. He wished to be left to his misery and mourning. But while he could avoid looking on her monstrous beauty, he couldn't shut out her voice.

"The dawn comes. You should seek shelter ere it arrives and sends you to hell in a blazing glory. A most unpleasant experience, I am sure."

Keeran jerked his gaze back to her, prepared to spit out that he would rather die than live this walking death as she did, but he was just in time to see her slip through the window and out of sight. Now he understood how she had entered without alerting them, and realized that they hadn't had a chance. Neither of them had even considered she might enter through the window. Keeran's room was in the tower, too high for any mortal being to reach. They had underestimated the creature.

At least now she was gone.

Keeran relaxed on the bed with every intention of staying right where he was and allowing the sun to show him the mercy she would not, but when the first rays of light began to creep through the window and touched his feet, it felt as if someone had set a torch to his boots. It affected him even through his clothing. Jerking his foot out of that finger of light, he tried to sit up but found he was yet too weak.

Cursing himself for not staying where he was even as he did it, Keeran managed to roll off the bed, hitting the floor with a body-jolting thump. This gave him some respite from the sun's rays, but he knew it would not be for long. Unshuttered, the window would soon allow the light in to fill the room. Yet he was too weak to gain his feet, let alone walk somewhere that the light could not reach him, and he refused to call out for help. He would not have his people see him this way. As far as they were concerned, their clan chief, Geordan MacKay, and his son and only remaining heir, Keeran MacKay, had died this night. He would have it so. He would not remain among them to sully them with his presence.

His gaze slid to the side and landed on the chest he had hidden behind. Mustering the little strength he had left, Keeran managed to crawl inside it. Relief flowed through him when the lid dropped closed, enshrouding him in a cocoon of darkness. It was quickly followed by shame that he had not had the courage to stay where he had been and allow the sun to destroy the monster he had become.

Chapter One

Emily spat the invading water from her mouth and coughed deeply, wrenching against the ropes around her torso as her body tried to expel the liquid that had made its way into her lungs. When the fit was over, she sagged weakly where she stood, forcing herself to keep her eyes and mouth closed. Both instinctively wanted to open.

Despite being ceaselessly pounded and buffeted by the wind, Emily felt starved for air; she longed to open her mouth and gasp in oxygen. She also yearned to open her eyes, but there was little to see. She was trapped in cold, wet darkness, alternately suffocated by the hard slap of the wind and pounded by the battering waves. Were it not for the solid surface of the mast at her back and the ropes digging into her body, she would have thought she'd fallen overboard and was drowning.

Emily almost wished she *were* drowning; at least then there would have been a foreseeable end to this torture. As it was, she was being beaten by waves that crashed over her, first slamming her back against the mast as they hit, then pulling at her, trying to rip her away from where she was lashed as they washed away. She was in agony, every inch of her flesh screaming at the abuse of the icy water and tearing ropes. No doubt by now the bindings had more than rubbed her raw. She imagined she was bleeding through the cloth of her gown, the ruby red drops washed away by each succeeding wave. And it seemed to her that this had been going on for an eternity, long enough that she began to fear she had been drowned by the brutal waves and was now in some form of purgatory. A punishment, no doubt, for her lack of proper concern when her uncle had been washed overboard. Was lack of grief at the death of a family member enough to see you in hell? she wondered. Despite knowing she shouldn't, Emily blinked her eyes open and lifted her face to the sky. She was immediately blinded by another wave.

The storm had come on quickly. One moment it had been a bright and sunny morning, just coming on noon, in the next the sky had turned an ominous green that had gone darker and darker until all signs of daylight had disappeared. Emily had known from the sailors' reactions that this was to be no normal storm. The mood among them had quickly become as heavy as the clouds overhead as they hurried to batten down everything onboard. She'd understood why when the ship had begun pitching wildly about. Then the rain had started, followed by the lightning that had briefly and intermittently lit the sky enough for her to see the great walls of water that the ship struggled through. Even the brief glimpses she'd had of those mountainous waves had left her gaping in horror. She had begun to pray.

Had this been a passenger ship, Emily would have ridden out the storm in her own cabin. No doubt she would have been lashed to a cot to keep from flying about and been blissfully ignorant of the true violence of the battle they faced. But this was one of her uncle's cargo ships. There were no cabins. She'd spent the first part of the storm clinging to the side of the ship beneath a small wooden shelter, but as the storm had intensified in fury and she'd found it increasingly difficult to keep her footing, the captain had insisted on lashing her and her uncle to the mast. Her father's brother had insisted Emily be taken first, and she had been touched by this very first sign of familial caring from the man. Then he had ruined it by shouting that if they managed to get her safely to the mast, he would risk the journey.

It had taken seemingly forever for the captain and the first mate to get Emily to the mast. The wind had kept grabbing at the long skirts of her gown and trying to whisk her away. By the time they had lashed her to it and gone back to collect her uncle, the wind had been a living thing, grasping and greedy. Worse yet, on their return the ship had been cresting one of the enormous waves that had been assaulting them for hours. The men had not been able to reach the mast before they were picked up by a rogue wave that crashed over the ship. Her uncle and the first mate had been swept overboard like so much flotsam. The captain had been smashed into the side of the ship with a violence that had left him injured, but alive and still onboard. Emily had known at that point that—barring a miracle—they were all lost. Her opinion had not changed in the eternity that had passed since then as she had first watched the seamen struggle to fight the storm, then watched them being overwhelmed by it until it had grown too dark to see at all.

The time since then had been interminable, filled with the crash of waves, the sting of rain, and the never-ending, howling wind. At first, there had also been the occasional screams of sailors being washed overboard, but Emily had not heard any for the last little while. She was beginning to think that she was the only soul left alive onboard, and didn't know how long that would last. While the ship was still afloat, she was in dire danger of drowning where she slumped against the ropes binding her.

A sudden low crack and groan pierced the howling in Emily's ears. It was accompanied by a shudder that ran through the boards under her feet and the mast at her back.

Emily lifted her head and tried to penetrate the black, her heart thundering somewhere in the vicinity of her throat as she struggled to understand what this meant. It sounded as if the ship had hit something. This couldn't be good.

Another wave battered her body and Emily moaned as her head cracked violently against the wooden mast. For a moment, the gloom was illuminated by stars dancing behind her eyelids and she was wretched with pain. It was then that the wind and water were abruptly cut off. She could still hear the wind, but it no longer beat at her as it had. Emily didn't open her eyes until a hard form pressed itself against her.

Blinking her eyes open then, she was surprised to find that there was some light where until now there had been only darkness. The storm was apparently easing and some small moonlight was struggling through the clouds, enough that she could make out the ruffled front of a white shirt before her nose. Then that cloth and the body beneath it were pressed against her face and she felt arms close around her. Before she could quite understand what was happening, the ropes that had held her in place for so long slipped away. Stiff and weak from hours spent in the punishing wind, Emily felt herself crumpling downward, then was caught under the arms and lifted up.

"Hold on to me." The words came to her clearly, though she almost thought she had imagined them, for surely even spoken into her ears she should not have heard them so clearly in this wind? Nevertheless, Emily did her best to obey the instruction, but her limp arms were incapable of following direction. She lifted helpless, apologetic eyes to the face looming above hers and was briefly caught in its dark beauty. Sad, gray eyes that seemed to reflect the moonlight peered out at her from a pale, chiseled face that was both handsome and somehow tragic. Emily knew instinctively that this man had suffered untold sorrow.

Her thoughts died an abrupt death as another fierce wave

crashed over the boat, slamming both her and her would-be rescuer back against the mast. Her head cracked against the wood once more, this time a violent slam that made the night explode in a blinding light that faded as quickly as it had appeared, taking consciousness with it.

Emily blinked her eyes open and stared into obscurity. For a moment, she feared she was still on the ship and that the storm had merely passed, but then she realized this couldn't be. She was dry, lying down on a relatively soft surface, and covered by what felt to be a mountain of blankets. She was saved! That glad thought was followed by the question of *how?* and a brief picture of a pale, handsome face beneath wind-tossed hair flashed in her mind.

Emily sat up abruptly and winced at the tenderness in her stomach, a reminder of her ordeal through the storm. She suspected she'd be tender for some time to come.

"And should be grateful to have escaped so lightly," she reprimanded herself, then gave a start at the rusty sound of her own voice. Her throat was raw and sore, though whether from the seawater she had swallowed or from her own shouts she just didn't know. Whatever the case, she determined to be grateful for this little reminder of her experience as well. No doubt, the men who had been washed overboard would have welcomed the opportunity to complain of so little.

Emily peered around the dim room as she shifted to the edge of the bed. There was little enough to see: unidentifiable shapes barely visible through the gloom. It appeared to be night still, or again. She wasn't at all sure how long she'd suffered the brutal storm. For that matter, Emily had no idea how long she may have slept afterward.

Her gaze settled on a large black rectangle that might be a door, and she slid off the bed to move cautiously toward it, inching forward with care lest there be something in her path. But when Emily reached what she'd hoped was a door and stretched out her hand, her fingers encountered only heavy cloth. Drapes.

Gripping the material with both hands, she yanked them open. Midday sunlight exploded into the room, searing her eyes and sending her staggering back. Blinking rapidly, Emily turned away from the blinding light and got her first glimpse of the room she occupied. The sunlight lit it admirably. Too well. She almost wanted to slam the curtains closed again. The room she occupied was a gloomy prospect. No amount of sunlight could brighten the decor of gray and blood red with its coating of dust and detritus.

Grimacing, she rubbed her arms and shifted to place one foot on top of the other on the cold stone floor, then glanced at the loose cloth covering her arms. Her dress was gone. She wore a long, flowing white nightgown in its place. Embarrassment tried to claim her at the thought of someone— the sad-eyed man?—undressing and dressing her, but she shrugged it away. Surely it had been a maid and not her rescuer who had changed her? Emily hoped so, but another glance at the room was hardly reassuring. It did not reflect the efforts of a maid.

Her ruminations on the matter were interrupted when a click drew her gaze to the door she had been seeking. The large wooden panel swung inward and a head sporting gray hair in a neat bun poked in, swiveling until two bright eyes found her.

"Oh! Yer up."

"Yes. I—" Emily paused. The head had slipped back out of sight through the door. In the next moment, the wooden panel burst wide open and the head reappeared, this time atop the rather large, comforting body of an older woman carrying a tray.

"Well! I was beginning to think ye'd be sleeping the day away." The woman sailed cheerfully across the room to set the tray on a small table next to Emily. "Not that I'd be blaming ye if ye did. But I've been ever so curious since the master brought ye home." She fussed over the tray briefly, then pulled out a chair and smiled at Emily. "Here ye are, then. I've brought you some good, nourishing food to restore ye after yer trials. Have a seat, lass, and—och!"

Emily had moved automatically toward the chair, but paused abruptly at that alarmed sound. The woman sounded like a chicken about to lay an egg and looked about as ruffled, her matronly body bristling and jerking back as if to flap wings that didn't exist.

"Ye can't be standin' about barefoot on the castle's cold floors, lass. Ye'll be catching yer death, ye will. And ye've naught but the lady's gown on." Pausing, she slammed her palm into her forehead. "Oh, saints alive! I didn't think to leave ye any slippers or a robe. I'll fetch ye one right quick, ne'er fear. Ye just get off the stone floor and settle yerself at the table. I'll return directly."

The woman fled as quickly as she'd entered, leaving Emily feeling quite lost. She hadn't had the opportunity to ask a single question, and there were quite a few she would have liked answers to. After a moment, the scent wafting off the food drew her to the table. Emily's stomach growled as she surveyed the offering. There was quite an assortment: bread so fresh it was still warm, a steaming bowl of oatmeal, eggs, bacon, fresh fruit, cheese, and pastries that looked divine.

Overcome with hunger, Emily briefly forgot herself and fell on the food like a ravenous wolf. She had made great headway into the meal when a loud dragging sound, as if some huge piece of furniture were being tugged across a floor, reached her ears and made her pause and glance to the open door where the sound was emanating from. When her benefactor's ample behind came into view, Emily stood and moved curiously to the door. Huffing and puffing and bent almost double, the older woman dragged what turned out to be a chest to the doorway.

"Oh! Let me help." Emily rushed forward, concerned by the older woman's flushed face.

The woman waved her away. "Ye'll just be getting in the way. Back to the table, lass. I've got this."

Ignoring that order, Emily took up position on the far end of the chest to help maneuver it the rest of the way into the room and to the foot of the bed. She wasn't surprised to find the older woman out of breath when they both straightened, but the fact that she was as well was a tad alarming. Emily was usually much more stalwart than this and could only think that the storm had really taken her strength out of her.

"There now." The woman popped open the lid of the chest and began to rifle through the neatly folded clothes inside. "These were the master's mother's things. Or sister's. I think," she added with a small frown as she lifted out an old-fashioned gown and took in its almost medieval look. "Well, they were some relative's."

An ancient relative, Emily thought with amusement as she peered over the gown the woman was refolding and returning to the chest.

"Anyway, this is where he had me get the nightgown ye're wearing, and he said ye could make use of whatever ye needed." She grunted with satisfaction as she came up with a slipper, handed it over, then bent to hunt its partner.

Emily examined the soft cloth, then slipped the shoe onto one foot, happy to find it fit snugly and was comfortable. She donned the other slipper when it was found, then a robe as well.

"There we be." Beaming with satisfaction, the older woman steered her back toward the table. Her eyebrows rose in surprise when she saw the dent Emily had already put in the provided fare. "Well now, I like a lass with a healthy appetite."

Emily flushed at that approving comment. She had gobbled down a good portion of the food in the short time the woman had been gone. She'd felt near to starving the moment she'd spotted the food, which reminded her of her first question. While they'd breakfasted before setting out for the docks, the storm had hit before they could manage lunch aboard ship. Emily had no idea how long it had been since she'd eaten. It felt like days. "How long have I slept?"

"Well, now." Her hostess settled comfortably in a chair across from her and paused to reach for one of the pastries before answering her question. "It was near dawn yesterday when ye were brought here. A drowned rat ye were, I can tell ye. Barely alive, I think. I changed yer clothes and settled ye in bed and figured ye'd sleep the day away, but ye slept through the night too. I started to worry when ye didn't wake up first thing this morning. So I decided to fix ye a tray and see did the food not draw ye back to wakefulness."

"Dawn," Emily murmured thoughtfully. "The storm started just before midday. That means I was strapped to that mast for—"

The woman nodded solemnly at Emily's dismay. "It took a lot out of ye. Ye needed yer rest. Eat up," she added. "It's rare enough I get the chance to cook fer someone and ye could use fattening up."

"You're the cook here, then?" Emily asked.

The woman blinked, then again slapped a hand to her forehead. "Och! I've not even introduced myself, have I? I'm Mrs. MacBain, dear. Cook, housekeeper, and . . ." She shrugged, then glanced around the room. Embarrassment immediately covered her face as she took in its state.

"It must be difficult to keep so large a home clean if you're on your own," Emily said sympathetically, and the woman sighed.

"Aye. I don't generally bother with any but the main floor. Most of the rest of the castle is kept closed. We don't usually have guests." She turned her gaze back to Emily and took another pastry before moving the plate a little closer to her in silent invitation. "And now that ye know my name, who would ye be?"

"Emily." She took one of the offered pastries. Her mouth watered as she broke the soft bun and the fresh-baked, yeasty scent wafted to her nose. "Emily Wentworth Collins."

"Emily Wentworth Collins, is it?" Mrs. MacBain smiled as Emily bit into the pastry with a moan of pure pleasure, then added, "That's an important-sounding name. For an important lady?"

"Nay. I have no title, I'm afraid," Emily admitted, then cleared her throat and said, "My memory is rather vague, but I am sure I recall a man untying me from the mast."

"Aye." The woman heaved out a breath that sent little bits of powdery sugar flying. "The MacKay."

"The MacKay?" Emily echoed with interest. "Is he a handsome man? Pale? With sad eyes?"

"Aye. Keeran MacKay's a handsome devil and that's no lie. 'Tis a shame about him, really."

"A shame?" Emily queried softly.

"Hmm." The housekeeper's wrinkled face went solemn, then she seemed to shake off the mood and she turned a thoughtful gaze Emily's way. "I noticed ye wear no rings. Ye aren't married, are ye, dear?"

"No," Emily admitted, bewildered by the seeming change in subject. Being a naturally honest girl, she felt compelled to add, "Not yet."

"Not yet?" Mrs. MacBain asked, a question on her face.

"I was to marry an earl today," Emily explained, then corrected, "Well, I guess it would have been yesterday we were to wed. 'Tis why my uncle and I were traveling north. We were to arrive at the ancestral estate in the afternoon, spend the night, then the wedding was to take place the next day. I suppose I slept through the portion of time during which I was supposed to be married."

"Marrying an earl? And you not even a lady?"

Emily bit back a smile at Mrs. MacBain's shock over this idea, though she wasn't surprised by it. There was a time when such a thing would have been unheard of. However, times were changing, and commoners were no longer peons bound to their lords, but were free to perform commerce and amass great wealth. And with that change, impoverished but titled lords had begun to marry untitled but wealthy commoners to secure their place in society. Mrs. MacBain was obviously of an old-fashioned mind and didn't approve of such arrangements.

"Well, while not titled, I *have* had all the proper schooling. And I am told I'm quite wealthy. Then too, the earl wanted a healthy, young bride to beget an heir, and my uncle wanted the title and connections the earl holds for business purposes." She frowned now and glanced up at the kind woman. "Uncle John was washed overboard at the start of the storm. I don't suppose—?" She stopped her question when Mrs. MacBain sadly shook her head.

"The master said ye were the last soul left alive, dear. I am sorry."

Emily nodded. She felt as much grief at the loss of the captain and sailors who had been strangers to her until the morning they had boarded the ship as she did at the loss of her uncle. In truth, he had been as much of a stranger to her as those other lost souls. She sighed unhappily at that knowledge.

"Ye've said yer uncle and this earl wanted the wedding. What did *ye* want?" Mrs. MacBain asked, watching her closely.

"Me?" Emily blinked at the very idea. What she wanted didn't really come into it, and she had never been foolish enough to think it did. The woman's wants were never important. Her duty was to do as she was bid with as much cheer and obedience as could be mustered. Men made the decisions in this world. She had been trained in that from birth. It was the way of things.

"Aye, ye," Mrs. MacBain said, drawing her thoughts again. "Did ye wish to marry the earl?"

Emily shuddered at the very thought of the ancient, leering earl of Sinclair. The one time they had met, he had eyed her hungrily and announced to one and all that she would bear him "fine fruit." Hardly an impressive first meeting. "No. But my uncle wished it."

"I see. Well," Mrs. MacBain said reluctantly. "I suppose we should send a message to the earl."

"No!" Emily herself was startled by the shout that ripped from her throat. Forcing herself to take a calming breath, she tried for reason. She had been numb with a sort of horror ever since learning she was to marry the aged and repulsive earl of Sinclair, but had known there was no way to avoid it. As her guardian, her uncle had every right to arrange her life as he saw fit.

Now, however, he was dead. Did she still have to carry out his wishes and place herself in the earl's hands? In effect, handing over the reins of her life to that—from all accounts—lascivious man? Or was her life now, finally, her own? It seemed to be her own, as far as she could gather. No doubt a barrister would be placed in charge of her finances until she reached the age of twenty-five—as stated in her father's will—but the barrister could not order her to marry anyone. No one could now. She was free. The thought was a new and precious one.

Free. That horrid, torturous storm had freed her. But freed her to do what? She wasn't sure what she could or wanted to do, and would appreciate the chance to figure it out without the earl haranguing her or the family lawyers hovering about her with disapproval. And this was probably her only opportunity to ponder what she wished to do, she realized. At least it was as long as no notice was sent informing everybody that she still lived.

Emily glanced at Mrs. MacBain. Encouraged by her kindly expression, she admitted, "I do not wish to marry the earl. I never have."

"Then surely ye don't have to now?"

"No, but—" She hesitated, then admitted, "I fear if you

contact the earl and I am returned to him, I shall be pressured to honor the agreement and—"

When she hesitated again, Mrs. MacBain patted her hand with understanding. "Time is what ye need, deary. Time and space to sort the matter and decide how to handle it. And there is plenty of time and space here. It would be nice to have another woman's company for a bit."

Emily felt relief pour over her, then tensed again and asked, "But what of your employer?"

Mrs. MacBain shrugged that concern away. "It's doubtful his Lairdship would notice, let alone mind, if ye stayed on a bit."

"His Lairdship? Your employer is a lord?" Emily asked with surprise.

"Well, no. Not any more." Her gaze skittered away from the curiosity in Emily's face and she said, "Anyway, don't worry about the master. He's never about during the day and is often out at night, feeding. It's most likely you'll be sleeping while he's prowling about."

Feeding? Prowling? Emily was confused by the woman's odd choice of words and would have asked about them, but Mrs. MacBain distracted her by giving her hand a reassuring squeeze. Then the older woman stood and moved to the chest at the foot of the bed.

"Yer dress was quite ruined by the storm, but there is surely something suitable here for ye to wear." She began sorting through the contents of the chest as she spoke. The housekeeper fished out, examined, and discarded several gowns as apparently unsuitable before settling on a pale blue one with a matching girdle and long draping sleeves.

"Take yer time about eating, dear," Mrs. MacBain said as she set the gown across the foot of the bed. "Once ye've finished and changed, come below to the kitchens and I shall show ye to the library. The master is an avid reader, so there's quite a selection to entertain ye."

"About your master," Emily said as the woman moved toward the door. "I should like to speak to him, to thank him for rescuing me."

A cloud seemed to pass over the woman's face, then she forced a smile and waved a hand in an attempt at airy dismissal. "Oh, la. He willna be around until dar . . . dinnertime, but ye can speak to him then."

"Dinnertime?" Emily smiled. "No doubt it's your cooking that brings him home."

Another shadow crossed the woman's face at Emily's attempted compliment, but all she said was, "He prefers to dine out. Still, he'll be here then."

Leaving Emily to wonder why anyone with such a marvelous cook would prefer to seek his meals elsewhere, the housekeeper slid out into the hall and softly closed the door.

Emily peered around the room she had slept in, hardly aware of how gloomy it was anymore. She was free. That thought kept running through her mind, and yet Emily had been resigned to her fate for so long that she could hardly believe it had changed. She didn't have to marry the earl of Sinclair.

Smiling, she pushed away from the table and stood. She was quite full and finished with her meal, but there were things to do here. Emily was grateful to Mrs. MacBain for allowing her the time to sort out her situation, but wouldn't add to the woman's work. She was young and strong and would earn her keep by helping about the castle. And she would start by taking the breakfast tray below to the kitchen.

Keeran woke the moment the last rays of sunlight disappeared beyond the horizon. For a moment he lay quiet and still, listening to the activity in his home. There was a hum of energy on the fringes of his consciousness that he'd been aware of through his sleep, a stirring in the air that told him something was different. He usually awoke to the soothing awareness of the MacBains' calm presence somewhere in the keep, but this night was different. While he was aware of the older couple, their energy was less calm than usual, less soothing. There was an underlying excitement to their life force. There was also a third presence in his home. He knew it was the girl from the boat. She had been asleep when last he'd awoken, her presence quiet and undisturbing. Tonight, he could feel the energy pouring off of her in waves that permeated almost every corner of his castle. She was awake—that was obvious—and would now have to be dealt with.

Keeran tried to concentrate on her energy and sense exactly where she was in the castle, but found himself unable to. Her vibration seemed to fill his home. That realization made him scowl. He was usually able to sense where individual souls were, but this woman seemed somehow different.

He pushed the loose lid of his coffin aside and sat up, regretting that he had brought her here. Keeran hadn't intended to, but then he hadn't planned on rescuing damsels in distress in the first place.

He'd been returning to the castle after the hunt, eager to get in out of the rain and wind, when Keeran had heard her screams. They'd seemed distant at first. Recognizing that they were coming from the coast, he'd turned in that direction. Her cries had become louder the closer he'd got, until by the time he reached the shore it was as if she were screaming in his ear. She hadn't, of course, and he hadn't even been hearing her with his ears, but she had a strong mind and her distress had reached him clearly. Keeran had quickly taken in the situation. A ship was in trouble on the water. He'd known at once that she was the only one left alive and had sensed that the ship was about to shatter on the coral reef that had taken so many other ships over the years.

Before he'd even known what he intended to do, Keeran was on the ship freeing her. He had removed her to shore, planning to lay her beneath a tree on the beach for someone to find in the dawn. The villagers would have realized that she was from the ship, but would have assumed that she had somehow managed to make it ashore. As for the girl, she had been a drowned rat, already half-dazed when he'd reached her, but the blow she'd taken to the head as he'd untied her from the mast had knocked her unconscious. Keeran had felt sure she wouldn't recall his presence on the ship, or—if she did— would believe she'd imagined him.

However, Keeran's plan to leave her there on the beach had died when his drowned rat had stirred as he knelt to lay her in the sand. She had opened pain-filled eyes and peered straight at him with a sort of wonder that had made him pause.

"You saved me. Thank you." It was all she'd said before drifting back into unconsciousness, but he'd found himself staring at her, unable to abandon her. Then he'd peered down to see that her hand clasped his, holding him like a child clinging to her mother. Trusting that she would be safe.

Strangely reluctant to leave her alone and defenseless, he had straightened with her still in his arms and carried her home in the predawn hours to be left in his housekeeper's care.

When he had awoken last night, Keeran's first thought had been of her. He'd been concerned when Mrs. MacBain informed him that the girl had slept through the day and had yet to awake. Then he had thought she might perhaps awaken during the night and not know where she was. To prevent her suffering any unnecessary alarm, he had foregone his usual nightly hunt and watched over her through the night, disappointed when the approaching dawn had forced him from her side.

He now told himself that his disappointment had only been because he was eager to learn what he needed to know to see her back to her people and out of his home. Keeran preferred his life to move along in an orderly and routine fashion and knew instinctively that this woman's presence would disrupt that. And as he had feared, she already had. That realization filled him with irritation as he left the hidden room where he rested during the day. The energy pouring off of his guest was stronger than any he had felt in a long while. He found himself drawn to it and annoyed by it at the same time.

Keeran made his way to the stairs leading to the first floor at a quick clip. He had every intention of speaking to his unwanted houseguest, finding out who she was and where she belonged, and making the necessary arrangements to return her there as quickly as possible.

Chapter Two

Emily finished scrubbing the last little bit of the dining room floor, then sat back on her haunches and wiped her forehead with a sigh. She was hot and weary from hard work, but she was also deeply satisfied. She had gotten a lot done this afternoon.

It had taken a good deal of talking and cajoling, but Emily had finally convinced Mrs. MacBain to allow her to help about the castle. She had then taken a quick tour of the first floor of the castle before deciding on starting in the dining room. Mrs. MacBain had told her earlier that she only bothered with the kitchens, library, hallways, and the office, but still Emily had been dismayed at the state of the dining room, which obviously hadn't been cleaned in years, perhaps decades. It had taken little thought to decide that this room was where she should start her efforts, and she had set to it with a vengeance. In the one afternoon, she had swept and washed the stained and cobwebbed walls, cleaned the paintings, polished the oak table and chairs, and scrubbed the stone floor.

Her gaze slid around the now-pristine room, and Emily

smiled faintly. A new coat of paint would have been nice, but the room was much improved. So much so that she felt sure that Mrs. MacBain's employer might see his way clear to joining her in dining there this evening. At least, she certainly hoped so. She would be pleased to have a word or two with the man.

Emily grimaced at that thought. Earlier in the day she would have liked to dine with him so that she might thank him for rescuing her. But after her tour of the castle, she wanted to discuss an entirely different matter altogether. Specifically, his lack of consideration for his staff. Emily could not believe the amount of work that the elderly housekeeper tended to on her own. Most castles boasted a chef concerned only with the daily task of cooking, their time taken up with baking bread and making the full-course meals the lords, ladies, and other wealthy employers demanded. Mrs. MacBain did this daily, plus all the other chores a full staff would be expected to do: dusting, sweeping, scrubbing. This castle was huge and old and even with only part of the ground floor to tend to, the task was herculean. The ground floor alone consisted of the kitchens, an office, two separate salons, a sitting room, a dining room, a long book-filled library, a ballroom, and various other miscellaneous chambers. Some of the rooms were obviously kept closed, the dining room among them, but the others were spotless, obviously dusted and scrubbed daily.

Then there was *Mr.* MacBain. While collecting the paraphernalia she would need to clean the dining room, Emily and Mrs. MacBain had chatted. Along with learning that Mrs. MacBain's employer was "Laird Keeran MacKay—who was no longer a lord" for reasons that the older woman had somehow avoided explaining, Emily had learned that while Mrs. MacBain had the duties inside the house, Mr. MacBain tended the stables, yard, and everything else without help as well.

Emily had hidden her dismay from Mrs. MacBain, but inside she was seething over the situation and could not believe that Laird Keeran MacKay—who was no longer a lord—could be so cruel. She could understand that financial setbacks might make the man thrifty, but this was ridiculous. The couple were too old to be working this hard, and she intended to tell the man so when he returned to the castle this evening. The only question in her mind was whether she should do so before or after thanking him for saving her life.

"What the devil are you doing?"

Emily's heart leapt into her throat and she jerked around on her knees at that sharp question from the doorway. She hadn't heard anyone approaching and was taken completely by surprise to find herself staring at the handsome, dark-haired man with the sad eyes. However, his eyes weren't sad at the moment, rather they were cold with what might have been fury. And while he was handsome, the planes of his face were sharp and harsh as if chiseled from marble, definitely not the softer face from her memory. He looked more like an avenging angel than the angel of mercy who had saved her. Still, there was no mistaking this man as anyone but Keeran MacKay, the man who was no longer a lord.

"Well?"

The sharp question startled Emily out of her temporary paralysis and she blurted the first thing to come to mind. "Cleaning."

This answer only seemed to infuriate the man further. "I have servants for that. You are not expected to sing for your supper, nor clean for it. Get off my floor."

Flushing with embarrassment, Emily struggled to her feet, nearly losing her balance and falling when her legs cramped in protest at being on her knees for so long. Only the quick reaction of her host as he stepped forward to take her elbow in a hard grip kept her on her feet until she had regained her legs. This only increased Emily's humiliation. Where moments ago she had felt pride in her accomplishment, she now felt shame at her weakness and her rumpled condition. Her first meeting with her savior and host wasn't going at all as she'd planned. For one thing, she'd intended to clean up and make herself presentable before meeting him. For another, she had never imagined finding herself feeling at such a disadvantage. But then, she had never expected the man to be offended at her efforts to help Mrs. MacBain.

Reminded of the older woman and the unrealistic expectations of the man now glaring at her, some of Emily's embarrassment faded, being quickly replaced with righteous anger.

"Yes. You have servants," she agreed grimly. "*Two* servants expected to tend to this *entire* castle and its grounds. Surely you must realize that one poor elderly couple cannot tend to all this work on their own? They need help, and since you haven't seen fit to hire them assistance, I took it upon myself to do so to show my gratitude for how kind they have been."

She paused and huffed out a little breath, then sucked more air deep into her lungs, holding it there briefly in an effort to regain her temper. Emily had the mildest of temperaments. It was very hard to stir her anger, but she could not stand injustice of any sort and the situation the MacBains suffered here was ridiculously cruel in her mind. This man was working them into the grave. Though, she admitted to herself, he might not be wholly aware of the fact. Men seemed to be ever oblivious to domestic matters, and she realized his cruelty might merely be a matter of thoughtlessness. That possibility calmed her enough that she tried for a conciliatory tone as she said, "If it is a matter of financial distress—"

"I assure you I suffer no such distress," he snapped, obviously insulted at the suggestion, and Emily felt her temper shoot up again.

"Then it must be that you are simply a skinflint, my lord. Saving money on the backs of the MacBains."

A gasp from the doorway drew her attention to the elderly woman now standing there. The alarm on Mrs. MacBain's face and the direction of her gaze made Emily aware that—in her upset—she had been poking her host in the chest. Flushing, she withdrew her finger, cleared her throat, and stepped back, suddenly finding herself unable to look at the man she had just been berating.

Keeran turned away from Mrs. MacBain's alarmed expression and back to the woman before him. He had walked the earth for well over two hundred years and had never before met a woman like this one. Unless they were in his thrall, most females quailed before him, acting as skittish as spooked colts. But, while she was pale and stiff, this woman showed no signs of quailing any time soon. He was scowling his displeasure at this when it suddenly occurred to him why she was different from all other women. The girl was daft, of course. She'd been left strapped to that mast out in the wind and rain too long. Obviously all the banging about had shaken her senses. The waves had probably washed the brains right out of her head.

Satisfied with this explanation, Keeran felt himself relax until he peered back to his housekeeper and noted that she was still looking alarmed, as if she feared he might take a bite out of the woman right there in front of her. He hadn't seen that expression on her face in a good thirty years—not since she had gotten used to him and concluded that he would not harm her. To see it there now upset him almost as much as his guest's lack of fear discombobulated him.

"I—" Mrs. MacBain glanced from him to the tray she held, then to the woman who had been berating him just moments ago. "I was just . . . I thought—"

Irritated, Keeran waved her explanations away and moved past her out of the room. He was upset by both his housekeeper's anxiety and all these changes in his home. Keeran disliked being upset. He enjoyed peace and quiet. He preferred routine, the same routine day after day. That being the case, it was not surprising that at that moment he wished for nothing more than to send his unwanted houseguest home and—

Dear Lord, he had forgotten to find out where she belonged, he realized, and came to a halt. The woman had so overset him that he hadn't asked the questions he'd intended to. He turned to peer back up the hall and could hear the hushed conversation taking place in the dining room. Mrs. MacBain was asking rather nervously what had taken place. She also addressed the girl by name. *Emily.* A pretty name for a pretty girl who was now admitting that she had taken him to task for his lack of consideration in regard to his staff.

Shaking his head in wonder that she had dared to do so, Keeran turned away and continued up the hall. He would talk to the girl later, after he had fed. Every time she had blushed or flushed, a wave of hunger had rolled over him, making him almost faint. He would feed, calm down, then sit her down and talk to her. Hopefully by that time she would be calmer, and possibly would have those smudges washed off her nose and cheeks. She had been annoying, but she had also looked rather adorable with the smudges. It had been a long while since Keeran had found anyone adorable.

"Oh, child."

Emily felt her heart sink at Mrs. MacBain's expression. If she had looked alarmed, Emily wouldn't have worried, but Mrs. MacBain was shaking her head with sadness.

"It isna because he willna pay that we have no help. His Lairdship would be happy to pay. But none of the villagers will work in the castle. He even hired a couple from the south once to help, but the villagers scared them off. The couple didn't last a week."

"Scared them off?" Emily asked, dismayed to think that she may have been unfair in her attack on her host. "How? And why will the villagers not work here?"

"Fear mostly," the housekeeper admitted, then frowned and moved past her to set the tray on the table before glancing around. "Ye've done a fine job in here. Thank ye fer yer help."

"Why are the villagers afraid to work in the castle?" Emily asked, unwilling to allow her to change the subject.

Mrs. MacBain turned back to the tray. Emily suspected it was to avoid looking at her as she muttered, "Oh, there have been stories about the master and this castle being cursed for years. Tales of . . ." She hesitated again, then firmed her mouth and shook her head. "I'll not betray m'laird by repeating them. 'Tis enough to say that the villagers are afraid and so won't work here. Now, ye should eat before the food gets cold."

"You aren't afraid," Emily pointed out, unwilling to let the matter drop.

"Nay. But I was at first," she admitted reluctantly. "Until I had been here for a bit."

"What made you come to work here if you were afraid?" Emily asked.

"I felt I owed His Lairdship. He saved my boy."

"Saved him?"

"Aye. My Billy got himself lost in the woods. I don't know how many times I told him never to stray into the woods, but he and a couple other boys were having an adventure, wandered into the woods, and got lost. His Lairdship found them. They would surely have died of exposure ere someone found them had he not taken up the search. I came up to the castle the next morning to tell him I was grateful and he asked if Mr. MacBain and I would work here." She shrugged. "I couldn't say no. He had brought my boy back to me."

"And the parents of the other boys? Did he ask them too?"

She shook her head. "They never came to thank him that I know of. Neither did any of the parents of the other children His Lairdship has saved over the years, and there have been many," she assured her with a firm nod. "Children who were swimming when and where they shouldn't have, playing when and where they shouldn't have, and so on. His Lairdship always finds them and brings them home safe."

"I see," Emily murmured, and she thought she did. The laird of the MacBains saved the lives of local children, yet was reviled and feared because of some silly supposed curse from decades ago. It seemed terribly unfair to her. Terribly unfair.

Worse yet, she herself was one of those he had saved and then had reviled him for first being too unthinking and then being too cheap to hire help for the MacBains, when the truth was that he had the money and was willing, but no one would work for him. She bit her lip as shame overcame her. "And I chased him away from his own table with my accusations when he was obviously planning to dine in for a change. He will go hungry because of my assumptions."

"Oh, well, don't ye worry none. He'll scare up something to eat somewhere," Mrs. MacBain said vaguely. "Come, sit down to your own meal."

Suddenly indescribably weary, Emily did as the woman suggested and moved to sit at the table, before asking, "Where is your son now?"

"Oh, he passed on some time ago. He was still just a lad, but was killed while in the king's army. He worked here before he was a soldier though." She smiled and patted Emily's shoulder soothingly. "You should eat. Ye've worked hard today, harder than ye've any right to have worked, and while I appreciate it . . ." She shook her head and left the room. She had tried arguing Emily out of helping her all day. It seemed she saw little sense in trying to talk her out of it again.

Emily ate her food alone in the fine dining room she had almost managed to return to its former glory. The wooden table shone from her scrubbing and buffing and there wasn't an inch of the room that was not better for her efforts. She, on the other hand, could now use a good soak. Her efforts—while satisfying—had been exhausting. If she'd had the energy, she would have taken herself off to clean up before eating, but Emily feared that should she do that, she might not find the energy to return below to eat. So, she forced herself to finish a portion of the food Mrs. MacBain had worked so hard on, unable to eat all of it only because her muscles didn't seem to have the strength to lift the fork over and over.

It made her doubly grateful that the lord of this neglected castle had gone out for his meal. Emily didn't understand why he would want to when he had such a wonderful cook, but supposed it was for the best, at least for tonight. She would have been embarrassed to have had to eat with the man after the way she had treated him. It was something of a relief to her that she was going to manage to avoid him. But this was only a temporary reprieve, she knew. Emily still had to thank him for saving her life. And on top of that, she now owed the man an apology for maligning him unfairly.

Sighing wearily, Emily pushed herself away from the table and left the room. She would have to make a quick washup, change, then return below to the library to wait for Keeran MacKay's return. She owed him an apology and wouldn't rest until she had given it.

Keeran stood at the foot of the bed and watched his guest sleep. Emily. She slept like an angel, her expression serene in repose. One arm bent, a lightly curled hand by her cheek, the other lying open on the bed. He watched her for a moment, then turned to peer around the darkened room, able to see it clearly in the moonlight with his nocturnal predator's eyes.

The room was coated in dust and filth. Her cleaning efforts obviously hadn't reached up here. He wondered briefly on that, then let it go with a shrug. He had returned home from the hunt, hoping to find her still awake. When he had found no sign of either the girl or the MacBains on the main floor, he'd made his way here to the room they had settled her in that first night. He'd intended to wake her and force her to tell him where she belonged so that he might return her there, but the sight of her sprawled across the foot of the bed, still wearing the rumpled gown from earlier and still bearing the smudges on her cheek and nose, had made him pause. It was obvious she had sat down for a moment to rest and then simply drifted off to sleep, exhausted by her efforts that day.

Emily made a small murmur, and Keeran turned his gaze back to her as she sighed and shifted in her sleep. She was beautiful in moonlight, a pleasure to look upon. Perhaps it wouldn't be so bad that he hadn't found out where she belonged and wasn't sending her home on the morrow. She hardly seemed unsettling in her sleep. Aye, he wouldn't disturb her and insist she tell him where she belonged. Tomorrow was soon enough, he decided as he pulled the bed coverings down from the top of the bed to cover her.

She was just one woman. How much trouble could she cause in a day?

"I shall expect you at the castle within the hour." Emily nodded at the small crowd around her, then turned to smile at Mrs. MacBain. The older woman's returning smile was a little uncertain, but she ignored that as she joined her to start back to the castle.

Emily had awoken that morning, upset to find herself curled at the bottom of the bed. She truly had wished to make her apologies to Keeran MacKay for her behavior the night before and had been determined to thank him for saving her. It seemed, however, that she had fallen asleep before she could manage the task.

Determined to speak to him first thing, Emily had thrown the covers aside and hurried out of bed and about her ablutions. She had then rushed below, only to learn that the master of the castle had already left for the day. Emily had no idea where he had gone and hadn't been rude enough to inquire, but Mrs. MacBain had claimed that she didn't expect him back until dark, so Emily supposed he had traveled to a nearby city on business or some such thing.

It was while she had sat over another lovely breakfast that Emily had decided to visit the village on her host's behalf. The man was in dire need of household staff, and it was obvious that he'd had little success in the matter. She decided to use her own powers of persuasion for him. The man had saved her life, and she had treated him abominably in return for it. Emily felt she owed him. It was as simple as that.

Armed with all the information she could gather, and with a protesting Mrs. MacBain trailing her every step, Emily had taken the short walk down into the village. She had been determined not to return until she had succeeded in employing several servants for the castle.

It hadn't gone quite as she'd expected. She'd started out approaching those who were unemployed, which seemed to be the better part of the village. The response was less than enthusiastic. But she hadn't changed her tactics until an elderly woman had actually dared to spit on the ground at her feet, splattering the lovely slippers Mrs. MacBain had given her to wear. Then Emily had been forced to regroup. She had taken Mrs. MacBain aside and asked her to point out those who'd had children or relatives saved by the master of Castle MacKay. She had hoped that, like Mrs. MacBain, they would feel they owed it to the man. However, the others didn't appear to suffer the same conscience as the housekeeper did.

Emily had then asked Mrs. MacBain for the names of those who were both unemployed and whose child or relative had been rescued by The MacKay. Armed with this further knowledge, she had set to work. Resorting to pestering, bullying, and shaming when necessary, she had managed to convince more than half a dozen people to agree to work up at the castle. It wasn't as grand a success as she'd hoped for. The castle was in a sorry state and in need of a lot of work. She would have been happier with twice that number, but Emily would take what she could get. On top of that, the few she had managed to cajole into the duty had steadfastly insisted that they would not even set out for the castle until after sunrise and that they were to be allowed to be away well before sunset.

Emily could only shake her head over the superstition this revealed. Obviously this demand was a result of the mysterious curse supposedly plaguing the castle and its owner. It made her curious about the curse again, but Mrs. MacBain was remaining steadfastly closemouthed on the subject, and Emily would not betray the woman who had been so kind to her by asking any of the villagers to explain this curse.

Letting the mystery of the curse drop from her mind, Emily began to plan what she would have the workers do first. All the rooms needed cleaning. They could also all use a coat of paint, but—

She stopped suddenly as an idea occurred to her. "Mrs. MacBain?"

"Yes, dear?" The elderly woman paused as well.

"You go on back to the castle. I need to return to the village."

"Oh, but—"

"Go on," Emily interrupted her protest with a smile. "I can find my way. The path is clear."

After a hesitation, the woman conceded and continued along her way, leaving Emily to return to the village alone. Her steps were quick and excited as she walked. She was feeling quite pleased with herself. She had no doubt at all that Keeran MacKay would be pleased with what she had accomplished so far, but what she hoped to do now would surely please him even more.

* * *

Dear God, she had to go! That was Keeran's first thought on arising. His sleep had been disturbed by the presence of strangers in his home all afternoon. They hadn't been threatening, but their very presence had poked and prodded at his awareness as he'd attempted to rest. Now, he stormed up the stairs out of the dungeon, prepared for battle. Were he a dragon, he would be breathing fire.

He stormed up the hall toward the dining room, aware of the subtle changes made here and there. The floor shining clean, the hall tables polished to a fine sheen, a vase of flowers in the entry. Dear God! She was bringing his home to life and he couldn't stand it. It had taken decades to get used to the filth and neglect of a nearly servantless castle. Was he now expected to get used to it being clean again, only to have to relearn life with it the other way all over again when she left and the new servants refused to return?

"Oh, my laird." Mrs. MacBain rushed up as he neared the dining room. It seemed the likely place to find his guest; it was nearing dinner and that was where he'd found her yesterday. But the room was empty. He turned to his housekeeper, a forbidding expression on his face. "Where is she?"

"Ah . . ." She hesitated, her suddenly wary expression making Keeran curse inwardly. He detested the frightened way people reacted to him, but he hated it most of all from the MacBains, who should know better by now.

"She was only trying to help, my laird," Mrs. MacBain excused the girl. "She hoped to please ye to thank ye fer rescuing her. She—"

"Mrs. MacBain," Keeran interrupted patiently. "I realize she didn't mean to upset me. But I like routine. I only wish to ask who her family are so I can arrange to return her home." Much to his amazement, the woman's face now went through several changes, starting with alarm and ending in a calculating look he had never before seen on her face.

"Ah . . . well, my laird—"

"I am no longer Laird, Mrs. MacBain," he reminded her.

"Of course, my lair . . . ah, sir." She smiled brightly. "Miss Emily's abovestairs preparing for the evening meal."

Keeran nodded and turned toward the room. "I shall wait for her in the dining room."

"Ye're joining her?" She seemed alarmed at the prospect.

"No. I shall wait for her and speak to her before she eats."

"She'll be a while," the woman warned, then added, " I'm guessing a long while. I told her the meal wouldna be ready for two hours."

"Two hours?" He turned on her with dismay.

The housekeeper's head began bobbing like a heavy flower on a slim stem in a breeze. "Well, she just quit working and went upstairs but a moment ago. She worked ever so hard today, my lair . . . sir," she interrupted herself to add, then continued, "I knew she could benefit from a nice soak. Then she shall have to dry her hair by the fire, and dress, and I knew she would rush through it all and weary herself unnecessarily did I not be sure she had the time she needed. And she was ever so weary already from all the work she was doing around here trying to make ye happy, so I told her dinner wouldn't be for—"

"Very well," Keeran interrupted her diatribe. When she fell silent, he eyed her hopeful expression with suspicion, then sighed and decided, "I shall speak to her when I return, then. I shan't be late. Please ask her to wait for me."

"Aye, my lair . . . sir." Her head was bobbing in that odd way again, but she was smiling widely, obviously relieved. Keeran considered her suspiciously for one more moment, then turned away and continued out of the castle.

As he had the night before, Keeran would have to find his meal closer to home than he liked. He preferred to travel far and wide, varying where he struck to prevent alarming anyone near to his home. Not that he ever killed anyone while feeding. Keeran fed a bit here and a bit there to prevent harming anyone unduly. Of course, this method of sustaining himself was a bit riskier than feeding off one person, but left his victims healthy and well, if a little weak. To him, the risk was worth it. The beast—Carlotta, he had since learned, was her name—may have stolen his life and damned his soul to hell that night over two hundred years ago, but she could not take his humanity.

A bitter laugh slipped from his lips as he moved into the night. Many would argue that he was anything but human now. Yet still he clung to what bits of integrity he had learned as a human. He had no idea *what* he was now, or rather, he knew but preferred not to think about it. A vampire, a soul-less nightwalker, feeding off the lifeblood of those around him. And a coward. He had suffered this existence for two centuries and still he had not the courage to let the sun claim him.

Forcing these unpleasant thoughts away, Keeran set about his business. He wished to be back before his houseguest should retire again. Mrs. MacBain was acting oddly and he didn't trust her to tell the girl that he wished to speak with her.

As it happened, Keeran had underestimated his house-keeper's obedience. It seemed she had indeed passed along his message to Emily, for he found her in the library on his return. Unfortunately, while the girl had remained below to await him, she had been unable to remain awake. He found her curled up in his chair before the fireplace, sound asleep.

Pausing before her, Keeran found himself unable to disturb her slumber. She looked achingly innocent, and innocence was something he had known little of in the last two hundred years. Keeran found interaction with humans painful, knowing they had loved ones to go home to; that they lived, laughed, and loved as he never would again. So, other than the occasional servant he managed to convince to work for him, he had little interaction with the rest of society. What little contact the necessity to feed did force on him was usually with its less sterling members of society, ne'er-do-wells and drunkards he came across during his nightly hunts. Keeran preferred to avoid feeding on the innocent. Despite the fact that he left them mostly unharmed, he didn't care for the guilt that sullying them caused on the rare occasion when necessity had found him feeding on one.

Now, he found himself fascinated by the woman who, in rest, seemed innocence incarnate. Emily. Her hair shone golden in the firelight.

"An angel," he whispered. His hand moved of its own accord to caress one soft, golden tress. It felt as warm as he recalled sunlight to be and, had he a heart, he was sure it would have pained him at that moment. She was achingly beautiful. Keeran wouldn't have been at all surprised had she sprouted wings and begun to glow with heavenly light there before him.

"She couldn't stay awake. She worked herself to the point of exhaustion today."

Those soft words drew his gaze to his housekeeper, who had suddenly appeared to hover anxiously nearby. Keeran felt irritation sting him at her protective attitude. Did the woman yet not trust him not to harm the chit? If after knowing him for thirty years she did not, what hope was there for him in this world? To live eons without love or true friendship, to watch those around him age and die, one after another, endlessly. . . . Perhaps there *was* no hope for him.

Suddenly aware that his fingers still curled in the girl's fair hair, Keeran withdrew his hand and straightened. "We should put her to bed," he growled in a soft voice. "She cannot sleep here all night."

"I'll wake her and—"

"No," he said sharply when she started forward. "There is no need to wake her. I shall carry her abovestairs."

"But—"

"You will have to light the way," Keeran interrupted. He really didn't need her to light the path for him. As with all nocturnal beasts, Keeran's eyesight was exceptional in the dark. But, as he had hoped, his suggestion had soothed the old woman, assuring her that he expected her to accompany him, as was proper.

After a brief hesitation, Mrs. MacBain nodded reluctantly and picked up a candle from the table beside the door.

Satisfied that he would get his way, Keeran bent and gently scooped Emily into his arms. She was a soft and light bundle, her breath a warm caress against his neck as she sighed sleepily and cuddled against him. Keeran inhaled as he straightened, his chest squeezing at the scent of her. She smelt of sunlight and flowers, she smelt of life, and he felt a yearning stir within him. He wanted to drink of that life, to bathe in it and perhaps redeem the soul he was sure he'd lost.

Mrs. MacBain cleared her throat. Reminded of her presence, he turned toward where she waited by the door and carried Emily forward.

"I asked her if she was married," Mrs. MacBain said as she led him out of the library and along the hall toward the stairs to the bedrooms.

To Keeran, that comment came out of the blue. The question had never occurred to him. Now that she had brought it up, however, he suddenly felt himself tense in anticipation of the answer. A murmur of protest from the girl in his arms made Keeran realize that his hold had tightened possessively around her. He forced his muscles to ease as he asked, "Is she?"

"Nay."

This news was something of a relief to Keeran, though he couldn't say why. What matter was it to him whether Emily was married or not? He had just convinced himself of this when Mrs. MacBain added, "Not yet."

"Not yet?" he echoed, this time unable to deny the fact that this news had an effect on him. He didn't at all like the possibility that she might belong to another.

"Aye," Mrs. MacBain answered. "She was on her way to

marry the earl of Sinclair when the ship ran into the storm. It was her uncle's wish."

Keeran glanced down at the woman in his arms. The earl of Sinclair? His very skin crawled at the idea of that elderly degenerate touching this fresh young woman. He knew the man, had known him since the fellow's birth. The Sinclair had been a cruel, heartless child and had grown into no better of a man. The old bastard had already beaten several wives to death, yet persisted in finding new victims. Keeran didn't at all like the idea of the fragile young woman he carried being the next victim on The Sinclair's list.

"She doesn't wish to," Mrs. MacBain went on as she gripped a handful of the plain cloth of her long skirt and lifted it out of the way so that she could lead the way up the stairs. "And now that her uncle is gone, there is no one to make her. But she fears she may be forced into it does the earl learn she still lives. She needs somewhere to stay for a bit and sort the matter out."

Keeran was struggling with this news when she added, "I hope ye don't mind, my laird, but I told her she might rest here a bit till she sorted the matter out."

Keeran heard the trepidation in her words and knew she was concerned that he would be upset by her invitation for Emily to stay. Several hours earlier he might have been. He certainly hadn't been pleased with the chit in his arms when his rest had been disturbed by the work she had set into motion in his home. Now, however, holding her warm body close in his arms, he began to wonder why he had been so upset. So, the castle would be a pleasant home for a bit. He should enjoy it while he could, rather than bemoan that it would end soon enough. Besides, he didn't wish to see the girl married to The Sinclair. He would rather kill the man first.

"Ye did say some time ago that we were to think of the castle as our home, my laird," Mrs. MacBain hurried on.

"And . . . well . . . if this were my home, I would allow her to stay, so I—"

"I am no longer Laird, " Keeran reminded her grimly as he carried Emily up the stairs behind the housekeeper's swaying skirts. It was the only comment he intended to make on the woman's action.

Emily was dreaming of being encased in strong, hard arms that made her feel as safe as a babe. It was one of those rare dreams when you actually knew you weren't awake. In her dream, she was reading in the library when her host returned. She set the book aside and smiled a polite greeting. Keeran MacKay smiled back, a soft smile, his eyes warm as they took in the white gown she wore. Before she could speak, he had crossed the room and scooped her into his arms to hold her close against his strong chest.

"My lord! I mean, sir," she corrected herself on a gasp. "This isn't proper."

"Do not berate me, my little beauty. I cannot help myself. Your loveliness, your wit, the way you have set my home to rights. All of it has set my heart aflame. You are the perfect woman for me, my little dove. I want to marry you, cherish you, and keep you safe from the arms of the lascivious earl of Sinclair."

"Oh, my lord," Emily breathed, her heart full to bursting at his passionate proclamation.

"I am no longer Laird."

Emily blinked her eyes open and stared at the face mere inches from her own. Keeran MacKay. He was holding her in his arms. Only the warm expression was missing. His face was cold and hard. He could have been a marble bust. At least, he could have been were he presently as pale as he had been the first two times she had met him. At the moment, he was flush with color. Very flush, really. She hoped it wasn't from carrying her. Carrying her?

Emily realized they weren't in the library. Keeran was carrying her, not just holding her in his arms, but actually carrying her abovestairs. This wasn't part of her dream. Alarm suddenly coursing through her, she glanced a little wildly about to see that they were trailing Mrs. MacBain up the stairs. She wasn't dreaming anymore.

Chapter Three

"No."

Emily's gaze shot to Keeran's face. His expression was
stern and his arms tightened around her as he shook his
head. He must have guessed by the way she had tensed that
she was about to struggle and request to be set down.

Realizing the peril she would put them both in by struggling now, Emily forced herself to remain quiescent in his
arms. Still, she was terribly uncomfortable there. It was one
thing to dream that he had swept her into his arms and quite
another to actually be in them. The reality was that after
years of having proper behavior drummed into her head,
Emily was terribly uncomfortable allowing a virtual stranger
to carry her about. In truth, she was even embarrassed by her
dream now that she was awake. Why on earth would her sleeping mind think she would welcome the attentions of her host?
The answer to that was simple enough. Emily knew herself
well. She was aware that she'd been terribly lonely every moment since the death of her parents. She had yearned and
yearned for years for someone to love her.

At first, Emily had worked very hard to gain that love from her uncle. She had behaved herself at all times and worked hard at her studies, knowing that her nanny and tutor would inform him. She had hoped that he would be pleased, but if he was, he had never let her know. He had never even let her know that he realized she was alive. John Collins, her father's brother, had dumped her at her deceased parents' country estate, never to bother with her again until her twentieth birthday. That's when he had sent for her to be brought to London to attend her engagement party. To say that the news of her engagement had come as something of a surprise was an understatement. And it hadn't been a pleasant one. The earl of Sinclair didn't exactly live up to Emily's childhood dreams of the perfect husband. In truth, he was worse than her wildest nightmares. She could only be grateful that the negotiations had apparently taken two years, from her eighteenth birthday till her twentieth. It was the earl of Sinclair who had told her that. Licking his lips as he tried to peer down the neckline of her gown, he'd said her uncle was a greedy man who had dragged the marriage negotiations out over two years in an effort to keep as much of her inheritance as he could. The Sinclair had said the words in such a way that his admiration was obvious.

"Here we are, sir."

Mrs. MacBain's voice intruded on Emily's thoughts, and she glanced to that kindly older lady to see that they had reached the top of the stairs and traversed the hall while she had been lost in thought. They now stood outside the door to the guest room she'd been using and Mrs. MacBain was holding the door open. The older woman's eyebrows rose as they landed on Emily. "Oh. Ye're awake."

"Yes." Emily flushed, once again embarrassed to be in her host's arms. But when she began to shift in his arms, he merely tightened his hold a tad and strode forward, carrying her into her room and directly to the table where Mrs. MacBain had served her breakfast that first morning. He bent to deposit her in a chair at the table, then straightened and turned to his housekeeper.

"Hot cocoa."

Mrs. MacBain blinked in confusion. "Hot cocoa?"

"I would imagine a cup of warmed cocoa would help our guest get back to sleep," he pointed out. "Make it two cups please, Mrs. MacBain."

"Two cups?"

Emily couldn't help but notice the suspicion that crossed the older woman's face and the way she hesitated. She seemed torn between obeying her employer and remaining in the room where she no doubt felt she was needed to maintain the propriety of the situation. Men simply weren't supposed to be alone in a lady's room. It wasn't done. Still, Emily would be glad of the chance to speak to her host and finally thank him for saving her life and offering her shelter. Also, she had no wish to see the woman annoy her employer in an effort to protect Emily, an effort that surely wasn't needed. Keeran MacKay didn't appear the sort to attack her at the first opportunity, else he would have done so already. She had been in his home for two nights now without coming to harm.

Offering a reassuring smile to the housekeeper, she patted her hand and said, "We shall leave the door open, Mrs. MacBain."

The housekeeper glanced toward Emily uncertainly, then nodded and left the room. The moment her footsteps faded down the hall, Keeran MacKay finally took a seat and turned his attention to her.

His gaze seemed almost a physical touch as it slid over her features. Emily found herself unable to meet it, and glanced around the room before recalling that she wished to thank him. "I am sorry I fell asleep. I did try to stay awake. I wanted to speak to you, to thank you for saving me."

"You are most welcome." He looked terribly uncomfortable with her gratitude, so Emily let that subject drop and moved on.

"I also wished to apologize for what I said yesterday. Mrs. MacBain explained that it isn't your fault that—"

"Apology accepted," he interrupted, apparently equally uncomfortable with her regret.

With that, Emily didn't really know what else to say. Silence descended upon them, enclosing them in an oddly intimate quiet that the lack of light in the room only seemed to increase.

Emily glanced toward the candle Mrs. MacBain had set on the table by the door. It and the light spilling in from the hall were the only illumination to be had, leaving most of the room in darkness. Standing abruptly, she moved to collect the candle and started lighting several of the other candles spread around the room as she tried to think of something to talk about. In the end, however, it was he who broke the silence.

"Mrs. MacBain informs me you were to marry The Sinclair," Keeran said abruptly.

Emily's steps slowed, a grimace crossing her face. "Yes. My uncle arranged it."

"But your uncle is dead."

"Yes," she agreed.

"Will you be able to bow out of the wedding without fear of scandal?"

A little sigh slid from Emily's lips as she lit the last candle. Then she retraced her steps to the table and sank back into the seat he had set her in earlier, letting her shoulders drop dejectedly. "I have pondered the matter and fear I may not."

That realization was an unpleasant one that she had been trying to ignore. Emily had been taught well. A young woman alone in the world could not hope to avoid scandal if she broke off an engagement that had been arranged for her and agreed to. It seemed her choices were between marriage to the earl of Sinclair or ruin. Neither event seemed acceptable to her. But she could see no other option open to her.

Emily glanced toward her host, surprised to see displeasure on his face. She had to wonder if he too disagreed with marriage between the classes. That seemed the only reason to her that he might be dismayed at her possible nuptials. Not wishing to think about the future she was struggling desperately to find an alternative to, Emily shifted the subject to the changes she had in mind for his castle. Her host seemed rather annoyed and reticent on the subject at first, but soon ventured his opinions and desires on what should be done. When that conversation expired, they moved on to another and another.

Keeran MacKay had a keen mind and a sharp wit. Emily enjoyed talking to him So much so that once or twice the thought crossed her mind that she wished it were *him* she was supposed to marry, rather than the earl of Sinclair. Were she to marry a young, handsome, and kindly man like Keeran MacKay, rather than the unpleasant earl, she would have gone to her betrothed willingly and without reservation. And her future wouldn't have seemed so bleak.

Emily wasn't sure what made her glance toward the door. A sound perhaps, or simply movement spotted out of the corner of her eye? Turning her head, she spotted Mrs. MacBain standing in the doorway and she smiled at her in greeting, then tilted her head to peer at her curiously. The housekeeper appeared to be frozen to the spot, her expression stunned as she stared at her employer. Emily turned to glance at Keeran, bewildered to find that he was merely smiling softly. There should be nothing surprising in that. He had been laughing at a jest Emily had told him, when Mrs. MacBain had drawn her attention. It had taken a good deal of effort to get that laugh out of the man, but Emily had been determined to bring a smile to his lips. The sadness she had sensed in him from

the first made her own heart ache somewhat and she had
wanted to lessen it for him, if only for a moment or two.

"Well." Mrs. MacBain seemed to snap out of her amazement and continued forward with the tray bearing two cups
of hot cocoa. She glanced around the chamber as she walked
and scowled at the mess it remained. The woman had wanted
to have some of the workers clean this room as well today,
but Emily had argued against it. She would rather see the
main floor set to rights first. She'd started this project in an
effort to make things nice for her host as a thank you, not to
make herself more comfortable. Besides, she only slept here;
most of her waking time was spent below, so she also bene-
fitted more from concentrating on that part first. The guest room
could be seen to afterward, though she might not be here to
witness it by then.

"'Tis fine," she said now to the housekeeper and received
an affectionate, if exasperated, look for her efforts.

"'Tis not fine, but ye're a stubborn lass, so I'll let it go,"
the woman said.

Emily saw the curiosity cross Keeran's face, but he didn't
comment or ask what they were speaking of; he simply sat
quietly as his housekeeper set the cups of hot cocoa down.
The woman hesitated then and Emily knew she was considering what she should do next. Propriety required that she
stay, but it was obvious from Keeran's expression that he
would order her to go if she tried. Besides, Mrs. MacBain
had worked just as hard as Emily today. The woman must be
as tired as she was.

Reaching out, Emily patted the hand holding the empty
tray and smiled at her reassuringly. "The door is open, and
we know you are nearby. We will be fine."

What she really meant was that *she* would be fine.
Mrs. MacBain nodded solemnly. "Aye. O' course ye will.
And no doubt ye're so tired that ye'll drop right off to sleep
once yer done with yer cocoa." The last was said with a
speaking glance toward her employer.

Emily bit her lip to keep back her amusement at his disgruntled reaction to it. It was obvious he was unused to his employee speaking to him in such a way.

"She is only concerned about propriety," Emily said soothingly once the woman had left the room.

Keeran made a face, but didn't comment. Instead, he stood and moved toward the door.

Afraid he was about to close it after she had promised the older woman that it would remain open, Emily was on her feet at once and hurrying after him.

"Oh, but I said we would leave it open," she protested, catching at his hand to stop him.

"I was only going to be sure she wasn't lurking in the hallway outside the room," he assured her and continued forward, drawing her along with him.

"She was tired. I think she has probably gone to bed," Emily commented as they both peered out to find the hall empty. When Keeran didn't comment, she turned to glance at him and found him staring down at their still-entwined hands. She flushed deeply and would have released him, but he closed his fingers over her own, holding her.

"So warm."

Those almost reverent words raised curiosity in Emily, but she pushed it aside as she realized that, indeed, compared to him she was a raging furnace. The hand holding her own was cool in comparison. Not unpleasantly so, rather like a nice breeze on sun-baked skin, but it was surely a sign that the man had just returned from outdoors and had caught a chill on his journey back from wherever he had dined this night.

"And *you* are chill," she exclaimed. "Come. We should build a fire to warm you."

Tugging her hand free, she hurried away toward the fireplace and Keeran stared after her. Had she bothered to look, he knew she would have found amazement on his face, for that's what he was feeling at the moment—amazement at her concern and kindness in wishing to see to his well-being. Of course, Keeran was not feeling chilled and the fire would do him no good, but he was touched and even surprised by her concern for him.

She had given him one surprise after another tonight. Earlier, when Mrs. MacBain had been here, he had noted the affectionate way Emily touched and patted the hand of the older woman as she spoke to her and had actually felt jealous of those touches and the women's easy affection. But then she had touched him while they spoke as well, and he had realized it was in her nature. Still, he drank in every smile and touch like a flower soaking up sunshine, and he had felt himself bloom beneath it just as a flower might, his defenses unfolding and opening to allow her near. Dangerously near, he feared. It had been decades since he had found anything to smile about. As for laughter, he couldn't recall doing so since the night Carlotta had killed his father and changed Keeran forever. Yet tonight he had smiled several times and even laughed once or twice. He had also simply enjoyed talking to her.

Emily was an intelligent woman, with surprising wisdom for someone who had lived so few years. He found he liked her, and this was a sad thing to Keeran. Her life span would be just a blink of time in his life. Soon her beauty would fade, her body would begin to wear out, and then she would leave this life and pass on to her just reward. Keeran would most likely be alive long after she had turned to dust. It was heartbreaking for him to even consider this, which was why he usually avoided allowing people into his life.

Realizing that he was being most unchivalrous, Keeran roused himself and moved to join her in kneeling on the cold stone before the hearth. He took over the task of building the fire, loading several more logs into the fireplace, then using the candle she fetched to set the kindling alight. Within moments a cheery fire was burning, giving off a good amount of heat.

"There." Keeran glanced to Emily to see that she had sat back on her haunches to survey the results of their efforts. She smiled at him now with satisfaction. "That should soon warm you."

Keeran found a rusty return smile and offered it to her, then stiffened when dismay suddenly crossed her face.

"Oh. You have hurt yourself."

"No, I haven't," was his surprised response.

"Yes, you did." Leaning forward, she brushed one finger gently over his lower lip. Keeran was so startled by the action that he didn't move. Then he was so startled by his own reaction to that one brief touch that he simply stared at her as she examined her finger, turning it for him to see. "You must have bit your lip without realizing it."

Keeran stared at the drop of blood on the finger a bare inch from his face. The faint scent of it mingled with her own to make a heady perfume. Without even thinking, he found himself leaning forward that last inch and slipping his tongue out to lick the pearl of liquid off her soft flesh. Realizing what he was doing, he froze, then glanced to Emily's face. Her eyes were wide, but with surprise, not alarm, and even as he watched, he could sense the changes taking place within her as she curled her fingers closed as if to hold on to the sensation of his touch, letting her hand drop to rest in her lap. He could almost hear the blood suddenly rushing through her body as excitement stirred within her, and certainly could smell that intoxicating elixir as it rose to the surface of her skin to make her blush prettily. Her beauty in the flickering firelight combined with that mixed scent to make him almost dizzy.

"Keeran."

It was the first time Emily had spoken his name. It slid from her lips on a soft sigh, tinged with a heartfelt pleading that was echoed in the luminous depths of her eyes, and he knew instinctively that while she had not lived as long as he, she was certainly as lonely as he. Here was a kindred soul, yearning for love as he was, yet fearful it would never be given. Without considering what he was doing, Keeran gave in to his wants for a change and closed the last bit of distance between them, this time to press his lips softly over her own.

It was like kissing a sun-baked apple, warm and sweet, with a hint of tang. As a human, Keeran had always had a weakness for apples, and now he was like a starving man presented with a whole apple pie still warm from the oven. He devoured her lips. He licked them, slid his tongue out to urge them apart, then slid his tongue between them to taste her inner sweetness.

Emily moaned as his tongue invaded her mouth. She had never been kissed like this. In truth, she had never been kissed. But she liked it. She only wished he would hold her as he had in both her dream and when he had carried her up here. She longed to feel his arms around her, making her feel safe again, for at that moment, she felt rather as if she might be falling off a precipice.

As if reading her thoughts, Keeran slid his arms around her, tilting his head to the side as he drew her deeper into the kiss. Emily moaned again and allowed her own arms to creep around his shoulders, tightening the embrace they shared until her breasts were pressed nearly flat between them. That aroused a whole new series of sensations within her, ones that were overwhelming and frightening, yet exhilarating at the same time. Gasping a breath of protest when Keeran broke the kiss, Emily let her head drop and pressed her mouth to his neck. In her excitement, she nipped at the roughened flesh there. The sudden short, breathless laugh Keeran gave then confused her almost as much as his words when he teased, "That's *my* job."

Emily would have asked what he meant by that comment, but a startled look had come over his face as if he were stunned by his own teasing, and he started to withdraw. Desperate not to see this interlude end, Emily tightened her hold on his neck and pressed her lips to his again. When he stilled in surprise, but did not kiss her back, she moved her mouth across his, then shyly slid her own tongue out to brush it across his lips as he had done to her.

The response she got to this ploy was startling. Apparently she had done it correctly, she decided with pleasure, as he began to kiss her again with a sudden urgency. This time his arms did not remain still around her, merely holding her close. His hands began to roam over her back, then slid around to smooth up over the cool cloth of her gown to cup her breasts. Emily gasped, her back straightening in a jerk that lifted the generous mounds upward out of his touch. Fortunately, his lovely hands followed, and Emily shuddered and quivered as excitement began shooting through her, little bolts of lightning that centered at her nipples but ran down to her stomach and lower still, causing an ache between her legs.

"My lord," Emily moaned as he broke the kiss and his mouth began to travel down her neck.

"Yes," he groaned back, not bothering to correct her reference to his title as he had on the stairs. He continued to palm and knead at the tightening flesh of one breast, but his other hand slid away, encircling her to urge her lower body closer as he pressed her upper body away with his caress. Both of them were still on their knees, and Emily gasped as his knee nudged between both of hers. But she couldn't seem to draw breath at all when his hand dropped to catch her beneath her bottom and urge her upward until she rode his thigh. Their bodies came together like two pieces of a puzzle.

"Keeran." She breathed his name and let her head drop back, offering his nibbling lips better access to her throat as his thigh rubbed against her, building her excitement.

Keeran gave a low groan as she offered her throat to him and his hunger became confused. The sweetness she unknowingly offered was tempting and, had he not just fed, he wasn't sure he would have been able to resist a taste of her sweet-smelling blood. But he had just eaten and another hunger consumed him now, one he had not really suffered for many a year. Just the same, he withdrew his mouth from the area of her neck and the temptation it offered, allowing it to drop toward her breast. He could feel the hard, excited pebble her nipple had become and tongued it through the cloth of her gown, but soon became frustrated with the hindrance.

With a growl, he tore at the cloth, rending it downward to expose the flesh he hungered for. Emily gasped out what might have been an "oh" or a "no"—Keeran wasn't sure which. It was enough to make him hesitate, panting with effort as he struggled to regain control of himself. He could have wept with relief when she then slid her hands into his hair and drew his mouth hungrily back to her own. It had been a surprised "oh," not a request for him to stop.

Keeran wanted to roar with triumph as he reclaimed her lips. He thrust his tongue deep and found one naked breast with his hand. The heat of her seemed to encompass him as he touched and kissed her. She felt like a living flame in his arms, and she seemed to grow warmer with every passing moment, with every new caress. She was searing his cooler skin with her heat. Keeran wanted to feel that heat everywhere. He wanted to feel her skin burn against every portion of his flesh. She made him feel alive.

Keeran knew she was innocent, that he had nothing to offer her. All he could do was take, but he couldn't help himself. Breaking their kiss yet again, he ducked his head down and caught the warm flesh of her breast in his mouth to suckle eagerly. Her skin was salty and sweet all at once, a pleasure to his palate.

"Ohhh." Emily tightened her grip on Keeran's hair and pressed herself into him as he suckled. The ruined gown was drifting off her shoulders, leaving half her back bare to be heated by the fire. Keeran's cool caress of her flesh had been an exciting counterpoint as he had palmed her breast and teased her nipples. Now he was driving her wild with his mouth, showing her pleasure as she had never known, while at the same time causing a yearning she didn't understand. She wanted more, but what more could there be? How much excitement could she stand? And what would happen when she could stand it no more?

Cool fingers slid under her gown and brushed along the flesh of her inner leg. Emily instinctively clenched her legs around his thigh, trapping his hand there. She was suddenly aware that she had been riding his leg for several moments, unconsciously grinding herself against him, but she had no chance to feel embarrassed at this boldness. His hand did not remain trapped for long and was already creeping upward again. Emily found herself clutching at his hair reflexively, then tearing his head away from her bosom so that she might find his lips again. She seemed suddenly to need his mouth on hers more than she needed breath.

Keeran obliged her, claiming her lips, then urging them open so that he could thrust his tongue deep even as his fingers finally reached the center of her, the spot where all of her excitement and yearning were pooling. His touch was ice to fire and she felt the moisture created between her legs, then all she was aware of was that she was burning up as he caressed her.

Emily arched against him, her hands now slipping from his hair to clutch the cloth of his shirt. She was hardly aware that she had done so and that she was tugging at the expensive material until it rent apart, baring his chest. Though she had ruined the item of clothing, she felt no regret since the action allowed their flesh to meet. Emily groaned her pleasure into his mouth as her burning nipples rubbed across his chest. And she reveled in an answering groan from Keeran, pleased to know that he enjoyed it as much as she. *His* pleasure hadn't occurred to her until then. Emily had been too swept away by the sensations overwhelming her to even consider his enjoyment, but now her mind was turned in that direction and she wished to please him as he was pleasing her. The problem was, she was unsure how to do so and it was most difficult to think with him touching her the way he was.

Emily never got the chance to come up with an idea—if her poor woolly mind could have at that point—for it was at that moment that a shriek came from the hallway.

"Oh! Get away, ye silly cat, or ye'll be tripping me up and sending me to an early grave." More was said, but in an incomprehensible mutter that Emily couldn't make out. Not that she was paying much attention by that point. She and Keeran both froze at the first sound of the housekeeper's voice, then jerked apart to stare in horror at the open door leading into the hall. Emily had forgotten herself so much that the fact that the door was open had quite fled her mind. Not only had she behaved shamelessly, she had done so with the door wide open for anyone to see. Not that there was anyone to see but Mrs. MacBain and her husband. Still, Emily could not believe she could behave so badly. Where had all her propriety gone? She was settling into a nice round of self-recrimination when Keeran reminded her of the more important matter at hand by releasing her from his embrace and attempting to draw the torn edges of her gown together to cover her nakedness.

Flushing wildly, Emily glanced down to avoid his eyes and noted the damage she had done to his shirt as well. Reaching out, she tried to repair that damage at the same time, but she simply got in the way of Keeran's efforts.

"Never mind," he said, suddenly turning her away and urging her toward the bed. "I shall stop Mrs. MacBain in the hall and tell her that you are tired and taking yourself off to bed. I'll order her not to disturb you."

Emily nodded, then just as quickly shook her head. "But what of your shirt?"

Keeran drew the two sides to overlap, then tucked the shirt more firmly into the top of his black breeches. "It will be fine," he assured her when she looked doubtful. He started to turn away, then paused and turned back, pulling her close for another kiss. She suspected he had intended it to merely be a quick goodnight peck, but their passions were close to the surface yet and rekindled swiftly. The peck became a passionate melding of mouths that had Emily moaning in a heartbeat.

"Silly kitty. Get along with ye now. I've no time to be standing here petting the likes of ye."

Keeran pulled away with a curse as Mrs. MacBain's voice intruded again. It sounded terribly loud to Emily, as if she stood just outside the door or was speaking in an unusually loud tone.

"I had better go before she comes in here."

"Yes." Emily offered him a tremulous smile. "Thank goodness for the cat or she might already have come in."

Keeran paused, blinked, then nodded slowly and turned away. He pulled the door closed behind him. The moment it clicked into place, Emily hurried forward and pressed her ear to the wood to listen to what took place in the hall.

Mrs. MacBain's voice was loud and clear as she said, "Oh, sir. I was just coming to see if ye would care for more cocoa."

Keeran's voice was less loud and Emily couldn't quite make out what he said, then Mrs. MacBain spoke more quietly so that she couldn't be heard, either. Presuming they had moved off down the hall, Emily heaved a sigh and turned back to her room. It was aglow with candlelight and appeared terribly romantic. The dirt and dust were hardly noticeable in this soft light. Smiling, she drifted around the room, blowing out candles. Then she removed the torn gown, donned a fresh one, and climbed beneath the bedclothes. It was only once she was there, warm under the blankets and wrapped in the safe darkness of night, that she allowed herself to think about what had just taken place.

Keeran MacKay was an exceptional man who had done exceptional things to her. She couldn't wait for morning to come so that she could see him again.

He would have to avoid her from now on. Keeran told himself that sternly as he stared into the fireplace in the library. He was sitting in the same chair he had found Emily sleeping in when he had returned earlier, and he fancied he could still feel a trace of her heat there. He could definitely smell the sweet soap she had used in her bath. It seemed to cling to the fabric of the chair, a gentle reminder of her presence.

Keeran would have to content himself with that reminder. He had learned tonight that he didn't have the control he had always prided himself on. For over two hundred years, control had been an issue of utmost importance to him. The hunger, when it struck, was almost crippling in its strength, and the urge to drink and drink until his victim was dry, rather than stop and find another to feed from, could be strong, but he had fought these urges for what seemed like forever. Yet tonight another hunger had overwhelmed his supposed control, and it had taken only a matter of minutes. Seconds, perhaps. The scent of her, the taste of her mingled with that drop of blood he had unthinkingly licked from her finger, the look of yearning in her eyes . . . All of these things had combined to leave him helpless before desires he hadn't felt since his turning, in ways he hadn't even realized he still *could* feel.

Keeran wanted to tell himself that it had been so long since he had even felt these desires that he was simply taken by surprise, that the next time he would be more in control. But he knew it wasn't so. While it was true he hadn't felt desire for several decades, he knew that the next time he would not be more in control. Even now his body still ached for her, and he was fighting the insane urge to return to her room, climb into bed with her, and take all the sweetness and innocence she had to offer. The problem was that he had nothing to offer her in return. Eternal damnation and a waking death hardly seemed a fair trade for the passion, companionship, and love he was sure he could have with Emily. No. He would rather see her married to the earl of Sinclair than make her his partner in death. He definitely had to stay away from her. It would be hard to resist her, and he doubted she would aid in the endeavor, but for her own sake he had to.

Chapter Four

Emily finished applying the last bit of paint to the wall of the dining room, then stood back to survey her efforts. This was the special chore she had returned to the village for, earlier in the week. She had gone to purchase paint for the castle. Of course, it'd had to be ordered from the south and carted up to the village, but she had convinced the store owner—with the promise of a generous bribe—to leave his store in his wife's care and travel down to collect the paint himself to get it here quicker. Emily had been sure to order colors as close as possible to those that had already been peeling off the walls of the castle. She hadn't wished to upset Keeran unduly with too much change.

Her mouth turned into a sad moue at the thought of her host. He had given her a glimpse at the heights of passion, then withdrawn from her, leaving her to sink slowly on her own. And he *had* withdrawn from her. Much to Emily's disappointment, Keeran had already been gone for the day when she had gone below the morning after their interlude in front of the fire. She had been even more disappointed when not only did he not seek her out that evening, but there was no sign of him at all. But Emily had convinced herself that he must just be busy. However, when he was absent all the next day and evening, she'd been forced to admit that he was deliberately avoiding her. Emily had blamed herself. She had been too forward and allowed too many liberties, and now he no doubt had a disgust of her.

It was three nights before Emily saw Keeran again, and when she finally did see him, she was sure it was an accident, that he hadn't intended to run into her. That night, she had worked later than usual and was making her way toward the stairs when he had entered the hall from the other end. He'd paused, seemingly startled by her presence, then had moved slowly forward to meet her as if drawn by an invisible string. Pausing before her, Keeran had simply stared down at her for the longest time, a smile growing on his face that had confused her until he had reached out to run a finger lightly over her nose and announced, "You are the only woman I have ever met who looks adorable with dirt on her face."

Emily had blushed at the compliment, then caught his fingers as he would have drawn them away. Pressing them to her cheek, she'd said, "I'm sorry. I know I behaved badly. Truly, I have never behaved so with another man. I know that may be hard to believe, considering how I acted, but it's true. I—"

"Nay." Shock had covered his face at her words and he had moved his fingers to cover her lips, silencing her. "Nay. You have nothing to apologize for, Emily. I—"

"Then why have you avoided me these past days?" She'd been unable to keep the pain and bewilderment out of her voice.

Keeran had stared at her helplessly, then groaned and pressed his mouth to hers. Passion had exploded between them, and Emily had found herself pressed up against the wall as his mouth devoured her lips and his hands traveled her body. Then his mouth had dropped to her neck, and

Emily had given a surprised cry at the sharp pain that had claimed her as he nipped her throat.

Keeran had pulled away at once, horror on his face, then turned and rushed from the house. Emily had stared after him in shock, one hand pressed to the side of her throat. He had pulled away from her so swiftly that she had seen the long, sharp canine teeth protruding out over his lower lip. She'd stood there staring at the door he'd disappeared through, her thoughts in a whirl. He was never around in daylight. He'd somehow rescued her from that ship in a storm too violent for a rowboat to traverse it safely. He never ate at the castle, but "fed" elsewhere, as Mrs. MacBain had put it. The rumors in the village, the fact that the servants would not work before dawn or after dusk. . . . Keeran MacKay was a vampire.

Emily had still been leaning weakly against the wall when Mrs. MacBain had found her. The older woman had taken one look at her pale face and had begun to defend her employer. She had sat Emily down and told her what she knew of the tale of The MacKay; how he had been turned, and how he had lived his life since that day. Despite the villagers' fear of him, by all accounts he was a decent man, if man he could be called.

Emily had listened to the woman's words a little vaguely. In truth, this revelation didn't frighten her so much as shock her. Keeran MacKay hadn't hurt her in all the time she had been there. Besides, she had seen the horror on his face when he realized what he had done. He hadn't meant to nip her, perhaps hadn't bitten her at all, but nicked her by accident with one of his sharp teeth. Still, she had let the woman talk, taking each story of his kindness and courage to heart. It meant something that, despite the poor treatment he received from the villagers, Keeran still went out of his way to search out missing children and such. It meant that he was a good man, a decent man, and that he loathed himself as much as the villagers did—else he wouldn't allow them to treat him as they did. Now she understood the sadness and torment in the depth of his eyes. He saw himself as a monster and, as such, denied himself any semblance of a normal life, neither allowing friendships nor love to blossom, even balking at having a comfortable home. Her heart had ached for him in that moment, and Emily had determined that she would be his friend if he would allow nothing else.

She had taken to spending her evenings in the library, dozing until she heard him return home, then seeking him out and insisting he join her in tea by the fire. He did join her, though he never drank the tea, but merely warmed his hands on the steaming cups she poured him. They had never once spoken of what had happened or the fact that she knew what he was. They had spent many an enjoyable night talking by the fire, but had not had a repeat of the passion they had previously enjoyed. Keeran was now holding himself at a distance. Emily suspected he was afraid to let her in. She had done everything she could think of to try to break through the barrier he had erected, but nothing had worked. She was beginning to lose heart.

Emily felt time weighing on her and knew she must make a decision about her life soon. No matter how much she enjoyed his company and the peace of his home, she could not remain here forever. At least not without an invitation.

"My."

Emily turned at that long drawn out word and forced a smile for Mrs. MacBain as the woman peered around the newly painted room.

"It looks lovely."

"Yes, but I fear I have completely ruined this gown," Emily said ruefully as she glanced down at the stains and paint spatters covering her borrowed blue dress. She had worn it for most of the hard work, saving the few other gowns from the chest for the evenings when she relaxed in the library.

"'Tis a fair trade, I should say," Mrs. MacBain informed her grimly, and Emily managed not to grimace at those words with their gentle reprimand. The housekeeper had wanted Emily to allow the servants to do the painting, but she hadn't wished to pull them away from their efforts cleaning the rest of the keep just yet. They were making such good headway, she hesitated to distract them.

"I hope your employer feels the same way."

Mrs. MacBain glanced at her sharply at those stiff words, then reached out to pat her arm. "Never mind, dear. He'll come around."

Emily wasn't sure what the older woman meant by that, so didn't comment. She merely began collecting the paintbrush and paint together, intending to clean up.

"Leave those. I'll tend to them," the housekeeper insisted. "Mr. MacBain has already carried the water up for yer bath. It'll grow cold if ye don't use it soon. It's why I came to find ye. Why dinnae ye go bathe and change into yer night things? I'll bring yer dinner up to ye. Ye've circles under yer eyes from exhaustion, and should rest this evening."

Emily hesitated, but allowed herself to be convinced in the end and murmured her thanks as she left the room. She had been working at a frenzied pace these last days, trying to avoid thinking about leaving and how to handle the earl of Sinclair if he should try to pressure her into marrying him as she feared. It was beginning to catch up to her. That wasn't the reason the housekeeper was trying to convince her to remain in her room tonight, however. At least, Emily didn't think it was. She suspected the woman feared her employer's reaction to her painting the dining room.

A glance out the windows as she walked into the entry to start abovestairs showed her that the sun was sinking into the horizon. Emily supposed that was why Mrs. MacBain had fetched her to send her to her room: to get her out of the way before Keeran awoke and saw that she had painted his dining room. It was the one plan she had not mentioned to him, wanting to keep it as a special surprise. Mrs. MacBain was dubious about whether it would be a pleasant one.

Emily entered her room to find that the MacBains had indeed already prepared her bath. The tub sat before a roaring fire and several candles lit the room. Emily slid out of her dress and sank into the steaming water with a sigh.

She would have to leave all this soon. She would have liked to stay. It was why she had delayed her decision so long, but Emily had come to the conclusion as she painted today that, though she wasn't looking forward to the prospect, she couldn't continue to delay leaving indefinitely.

Pushing the thought from her mind, she concentrated on scrubbing the paint from her skin and washing her hair, then stepped out of the tub, dried herself, and donned the nightgown and robe that had been laid out on the chair near the fire. Finally, she sat in that chair to brush her long hair. The golden tresses had nearly dried when the door to her room suddenly burst open and Keeran stormed in.

Startled at his sudden appearance, Emily stood slowly and faced him, alarm on her face. He hadn't been in her room since the night he'd carried her up from the library. He didn't look pleased to be here now. A scowl made him appear rather ferocious as he moved to her at a quick clip.

"You have to stop. Just stop!" he snapped.

Emily's eyebrows flew up on her forehead. "Stop what?"

"Stop everything. You cannot simply show up one day and begin cleaning and painting and disrupting my life like this."

He looked more pained than angry, she decided, and felt herself relax as understanding reached her. Her voice was gentle when she asked, "Why? Because you do not feel you deserve it?"

He reacted as if she had slapped him, his head jerking back in reaction to her words. He spoke through gritted teeth when he said, "I do *not* deserve it. I am a monster. A beast. I—"

She gave a derisive snort that silenced him and left him staring at her blankly. Taking advantage of his silence, Emily said, "You are hardly a beast, Keeran. I have been here over a week and come to no harm."

"I nearly bit you," he reminded her grimly.

"Yes," she agreed. "But you didn't. Nor do you feed off your own people, from what I can tell, and those you do feed on suffer no lasting effects when they very easily could."

"You don't understand."

"But I do," she assured him. "I do understand. Beasts do not trouble themselves to hunt for lost children."

He stared at her silently for a moment, then said, "You shall depart and the servants shall follow and I shall be left to watch my home decay and fall into ruin again. It would be easier if you just leave it as is rather than give me this taste of life."

"Oh, Keeran," Emily breathed. Pained by what these words revealed of his life, she reached out and touched his cheek.

They stood frozen like that for a moment and she could see him struggle with himself, then he gave in with a groan and turned his mouth into her palm, placing a kiss there. Before her brain could quite register the gentle kiss, he turned back to her and pulled her into his arms. Emily went willingly, raising her mouth to be plundered even as she stepped into his embrace. He was hard and cool, handsome and tragic, exciting and passionate.

Emily opened to him like a bud, the petals of her mouth spreading to allow him in to taste her nectar. Keeran drank deeply of that nectar, his hands sliding over the soft, thin robe she wore and molding her to his body. But soon that wasn't enough and he knew he must have more. This, of course, was what he had feared, why he had tried to avoid her this last week. Not that he had succeeded. His much-vaunted control had deserted him with her entrance into his life, and, after those first two nights, Keeran had found himself seeking her out every evening, spending hours simply watching the glow of firelight on her golden hair and enjoying the way her lips moved as she spoke. But he had managed to maintain some restraint. He had not allowed himself to kiss or even touch her, keeping at least that distance between them. Now his sensation-starved hands were eager to feel more than the cloth of her robe. Tugging the sash loose, he dropped it to the floor, then slid his hands beneath the robe to spread over the warm flesh of her stomach. He encountered material again here, but it was the even thinner cloth of a nightgown, a gossamer web over her nakedness.

Keeran slid his fingers up over the material and groaned in his throat with pleasure as he caught her breasts in his hand. When Emily gasped, he caught the sound with his mouth as she pressed into his touch. As pleasurable as this was, he still yearned to touch her naked flesh. Reaching down, he caught at the long skirt of the gown and tugged it upward, gathering it until he could slip his hand beneath and across her warm skin. She felt as good as he recalled, her leg smooth and warm. Keeran let his hand drift around to her bottom, cupping the globe with one palm and urging her against his hardness, then let his hand drop and slid it around in front until he could trail his fingers up one inner thigh.

Emily cried out into his mouth and began to lean heavily into him as he reached what he sought. Keeran immediately eased them both to kneel on the fur that had been set before the fire. He had noticed when he first entered that this room had finally been seen to. It was now as clean as most of the rest of the castle and had several added comforts since his last visit. Keeran was grateful for this one as they came to rest on the soft fur.

Breaking their kiss, he trailed his lips over her throat, then quickly away as a new hunger tweaked at him. He had come directly here after awaking and seeing the newly painted dining room. He should have learned from the experience earlier in the week and fed first. He could still hardly believe that he had nearly bitten her then. But that hunger was threatening to make itself known and was held at bay only by his desire. Once away from the temptation of the pulsing vein in her throat, Keeran felt that hunger ease a bit and managed to push it out of his mind as he urged Emily further back over his arm and made his way toward the mound of one breast. That first night, desperate desire had made him mouth her through the cloth of her gown. Tonight that would not do. Tugging the scooped neckline to the side, he managed to force it far enough down her arm that one breast was revealed. Keeran immediately lowered his face and sucked one engorged nipple into his mouth, teasing it until Emily was shifting and making exciting little mewls of sound.

"Keeran . . . please . . . I want . . . " Her words ended on a gasp as he slid one finger inside of her, stretching and pleasuring her at the same time. His body tightened in anticipation as her wet heat closed around the digit. He could already imagine what it would feel like to be inside of her. He wanted to be there right then, but knew she wasn't ready. He would have to be patient. The fact that he could made him wonder if some bit of control didn't remain to him after all.

Emily was coming apart. Keeran's delicious touch was making her mindless. She wanted it to go on forever, but this time she wanted to touch him in return. Forcing his mouth away from the breast he had bared, she urged him back enough that she could reach between them and begin to tug at his shirt. She managed to free the cloth from his breeches, but then needed his cooperation to remove it completely. Much to her combined regret and relief, Keeran gave up caressing her long enough to tug the shirt up over his head. He didn't immediately return to caressing her again, but kissed her instead as she let her hands travel over his chest and shoulders, enjoying the feel of him.

She was aware that he was urging her backward as he kissed her. They were both still kneeling, so she was being forced back onto her haunches. She ended lying in an odd and even slightly uncomfortable position. But Emily forgot that discomfort when he suddenly straightened and pushed her gown up her thighs, stomach, then up further until her breasts were revealed as well. Shock took the place of confusion for a second, as she realized she was now splayed out before him like a buffet, her knees spread wide, her buttocks resting on her heels and raising the center of her as if in offering.

Uncertainty and shyness filled Emily then and she tried to rise back up, but Keeran held her in place by lowering his head to her breast again. The shock of sensation that shot through her as he suckled her was enough to make her hesitate, and when his hand slid between her open thighs once more, it was enough to keep her still.

If there was any discomfort now, Emily no longer felt it. She was aware only of the pleasure he brought her with his mouth and caresses. Disappointment drifted through her when he left her breast, but then the stretched muscles of her stomach quivered and jerked as he trailed kisses down over it. She had a moment's shock and embarrassment when he continued downward until his face disappeared between her legs. Then the sensations he awakened within her pushed those aside and she cried out with unbearable pleasure instead.

When his hands drifted up to catch both her breasts as he continued to caress her with his mouth, Emily caught at and covered them with her own, squeezing them tightly in place.

Keeran immediately pinched at her pebbled nipples, tweaking them and adding to her excitement until she thought she could stand no more. It was then that something burst within her, convulsing her muscles and making her cry out his name in mindless delight.

Keeran murmured soothing words and held her as she rode the crest of the ecstasy he had given her. Then he straightened and scooped her into his arms. Emily wrapped her own arms around his shoulders and pressed her face into his neck so that she could kiss him there with joy and gratitude. She felt as if she had taken an elixir and was now in some sort of drugged state, her mind floating loosely. She was glad he was carrying her, for the muscles in her legs—in her whole body, really—were trembling so that she didn't think she could walk.

Halfway to the bed he whispered her name and Emily lifted her head to peer at him. The moment she did, he bent to claim her lips in a kiss. Much to her amazement, the passion she'd thought had burnt itself out immediately burst back to life within her and she eagerly kissed him back.

He continued to kiss her as he crossed the room. When they reached the bed, rather than set her down, he settled on the soft surface with her still in his arms. Emily found herself seated in his lap, her arms clinging around his shoulders as he kissed and held her. Her gown had fallen to cover her breasts, but caught at her waist when he had picked her up. Now she felt him tugging it upward. They were forced to break the kiss so that he could lift it off over her head. He tossed it carelessly aside, then began to kiss her again as his hands slid unhampered over her body.

Emily allowed her hands to move over his chest and arms, then let them drop down over his stomach until they reached the top of his knee breeches. Keeran immediately groaned into her mouth and she felt the muscles in his stomach ripple. Feeling encouraged, she let her hand drop lower, but didn't get far before Keeran caught her hand and drew it away.

"But I want to touch you too," Emily whispered in protest when he broke their kiss to trail his lips over her cheek to one ear.

"Later," he assured her. "I am having enough trouble controlling myself."

Emily hadn't a clue what he was talking about when he spoke of control, but wasn't in the mood to question him. Contenting herself with running her hands over his shoulders, chest, and back, she sighed and arched and shifted into his caresses as his fingers slid between her legs and danced busily over her flesh, driving her to a fevered pitch. She was mindless with desire when he finally lifted her off of his lap to lay her back on the bed, and she shifted restlessly as he quickly removed the rest of his clothes.

Emily opened her arms in welcome when he rejoined her in bed, then dragged his head down to kiss him. She thought he would return to caressing her again and mentally prepared herself for the first shock of his touch. She wasn't quite prepared, however, when he suddenly slid into her. She cried out, more with surprise than pain, and stiffened beneath him at the unexpected intrusion, then realized that he, too, had stilled.

Emily opened her eyes to see his tense face, then shifted beneath him experimentally, wondering why there hadn't been more pain. Her nanny had said there would be horrendous pain the first time when she had spoken to her about the wedding night to come. But the small twinge Emily had experienced was far from horrendous.

A low groan from Keeran made her still her experimentation. She glanced at his face to see his agonized expression and wondered if she had misunderstood her nanny. Perhaps it wasn't the woman who suffered the first time. She was worrying over that when Keeran opened his eyes and speared her with a glance.

"Are you all right?" he asked gruffly.

Emily swallowed, then nodded solemnly.

"Thank God," he growled and immediately began to move. Emily almost protested when he withdrew from her, but the breath she had inhaled to speak with was expelled on a sigh as he immediately slid back into her again. Unsure what else to do, Emily slid her arms and then her legs around Keeran and simply held on, allowing her body to move, arch, and clench as it saw fit. Her body seemed to have a better idea of what to do than her mind did, which was perhaps a good thing, since her mind appeared to have decided to bow out of this undertaking. Emily was simply a mass of sensation now, her body singing to the tune he played.

Keeran drove into her over and over again, his body screaming with pleasure as her moist heat welcomed him. He had known it would be like this. Her body was a warm welcome on his return from battle, a flaming fireside after a cold ride through a blizzard. She heated him and made him feel as though his lifeless heart beat again.

Emily cried his name breathlessly, her nails biting into his back as she urged him on, and Keeran growled with the excitement that was building to an unbearable level. Bending his head, he caught her mouth in a passionate kiss, then made a trail of kisses to her neck, where the scent of her excited blood was intoxicating. He inhaled the sweet scent, his growl growing in his throat, then felt his body buck and instinctively sunk his teeth into her tender flesh as pleasure engulfed him.

Emily's eyes flew open with shock as she felt his teeth slice into her throat. There was one moment of searing pain, then ecstasy replaced it and slid through her body. She felt that explosion of pleasure she had experienced earlier, only far more intense, and allowed it to overwhelm her as darkness closed in.

Emily opened her eyes and found herself peering through the open drapes at the predawn sky. She stared at the lightening sky for a minute, then a sound made her turn her head to find Keeran dressed and seated in a chair beside the bed. He sat in shadow, his expression obscured. It was then she recalled what they had done, and his biting her. Had he *turned* her?

"Am I—?"

"No," he assured her quickly and leaned forward to clasp

her hands. "I stopped as soon as I realized what I was doing. I am sorry, Emily. So sorry. I never meant to . . . I shouldn't have . . ."

"It's all right," Emily said quietly, and meant it. She didn't mind that he had bitten her. She was only sorry that he had stopped before—

"Don't think that way!" he snapped harshly.

Emily blinked in surprise that he had been able to read her thoughts. It seemed they had a connection now, and if that was the case, he knew she loved him. There was now nothing to be gained by not speaking of her love and the fact that she wished to stay with him, that she, in fact, would do whatever was necessary to be allowed to stay with him.

His hand squeezed hers almost painfully, drawing her gaze again. "Never think that way. You do *not* want to be like me."

"Perhaps not, but I *would* like to be *with* you, and if I must become like you to do so—"

"No." He covered her mouth to silence her blasphemy. But he was looking tortured now, almost desperate. "You don't know what you're saying. You don't understand."

"You are the one who doesn't understand," Emily interrupted, knocking his hand away from her mouth with sharp impatience. "Do you think I just let every man I meet make love to me? Nay. I love you, Keeran."

"No."

"Yes."

"No!" he roared, suddenly on his feet and pacing away from the bed, then back. "You cannot love me."

"I can and I do," she insisted.

"Emily." He bent to take her hands beseechingly. "I have nothing to offer you."

"You have yourself. That is more than enough."

"You can't mean that."

"I do."

"No. You don't, you *can't* know what you're saying."

Keeran turned away, pacing several feet before stopping. He was tempted by her offer. To keep her with him for eternity, to have her to hunt with, to curl up by the fire in the library and read with on cold nights. . . . Keeran was tempted. Terribly tempted. He had never before wanted anything so much in this imitation of a life he lived. But he couldn't do it. Emily had crawled inside his heart. He didn't know how; he had thought that organ long dead, yet there it was. Not only had she cleaned and brightened his home, she had brightened his night and filled his heart as well. She was his sun and he wanted desperately to keep her with him. But the love that made him desperate to keep her by his side was the same love that wouldn't allow him to do it. Keeran had taken her innocence; he would not take her life. He could never condemn her to this eternal death, and damn her soul to eternal hell.

Emily watched Keeran's stiff back and waited breathlessly. She knew he was considering her words and making his decision. Her happiness depended on that decision. When he finally turned back to her, his expression held his answer, and Emily felt something begin to die within her. Her heart perhaps, or hope? He did not speak right away, but simply stood staring at her hard as if memorizing what she looked like. When he finally spoke, his voice was polite, as empty and polite as the words he mouthed.

"The dawn comes. I must leave you. I will arrange a carriage and outriders to take you home when I rise tomorrow night. With any luck you shall be able to leave first thing the morning after. You should sleep now." He didn't stay to wait for Emily's response, but strode from the room once the words had left his mouth.

Emily stared at the door he closed behind him and felt her heart breaking. She had lost. Her hopes of happiness had just walked out of the room.

Chapter Five

Emily did not sleep. For one moment, she considered bursting into weak tears and sobbing her broken heart out, but then she decided that would be a horrible waste of time, and time was something she now had very little of. The moment the sun set on this day, Keeran would make the necessary arrangements to see her out of his life. She had to think of a way to convince him to let her stay, to let her love him.

Tossing the bedclothes aside, she slipped out of bed and began to dress as she sought the answer to this problem. Several ideas occurred to her, but Emily discarded each of them for one reason or another. It was when she went down to join the MacBains in the kitchen that the perfect idea came to her. And it was prompted by Mrs. MacBain asking which room she planned to paint that day and if she wouldn't allow some of the new servants to help her this time.

Until that point, Emily had not even considered painting today. She had a more important matter to consider, but the housekeeper's question had made her decide that while she would not take the time, there was no reason she could not take a couple of the new servants off cleaning detail and put them to work painting. Then she had pondered which room to start with and the paint available. There was a sky blue to replace the faded blue in one salon, sunny yellow for the other . . .

Her thoughts had slowed as an idea began to niggle at her.

"Emily, dear?" Mrs. MacBain had said, rousing her from her thoughts. "Is something wrong?"

Emily had blinked and turned to glance at her. "No," she'd said slowly. "No. Nothing's wrong. In fact, you've given me a brilliant idea."

"I have?" the older woman asked with surprise.

"Yes." Emily's mouth widened in a glorious smile. "And if it works, you will have made me the happiest woman in the world."

"Oh . . . well . . . that's nice," she said uncertainly.

"Yes, it is," Emily agreed, and pushing away her untouched food, she stood excitedly. "I shall need your help. And all the servants. We shall need the paint too." She began pacing as she ticked off her list, then whirled and rushed forward to hug the housekeeper. "Oh, Mrs. MacBain, I think this might work."

Keeran woke to complete silence. He had become so accustomed to the activity and presence of others in his home that this silence seemed unusual and even ominous. Then he recalled what had happened last night and understood. Emily had probably told Mrs. MacBain that she was to leave tomorrow, and the new servants had already decided they were through with his home. This seemed the likely answer.

It was for the best, he told himself as depression settled over him. Now he could return to his routine. Endless days and nights of misery and gloom.

Impatient with his own morbid thoughts, Keeran sat up and slipped from his resting spot, telling himself that this had been his choice. Emily had offered to spend eternity with him. It was he who had turned her away, refusing to sully her any further than he already had.

Thoughts of Emily made him realize that her presence seemed somehow subdued this night. While he could feel her in his home, it was not the strong, vibrant presence he had become used to. It was quiet and tense, almost waiting. But waiting for what? he wondered as he mounted the stairs to the first level of his home.

There were no torches to light the way, and the MacBains were nowhere to be seen when he entered the kitchen. It was only then that he paused and closed his eyes, seeking them with his mind. He quickly realized that they were not there and felt concern grip him. Mrs. MacBain was terribly fond of Emily. Surely she wasn't so upset about his taking her innocence that she had quit his employ?

Nay, Keeran thought. The housekeeper couldn't know about that. Emily certainly wouldn't have told her. However, she might have told her that he was arranging tonight to send her away, he realized, and hoped that the older woman wasn't so upset with this news that she had quit. His next thought was that it didn't really matter. Once Emily was gone, he would hardly care if anyone else were there or not.

Leaving the kitchen, he moved silently along the dark hall, his steps slowing as he saw that candlelight was spilling from the open ballroom door ahead. Suspecting that he would find Emily there, Keeran hesitated, unsure he had the strength to resist her should he find himself in her presence. But in the end, he didn't have the willpower not to see her. Approaching the door cautiously, he peered into the room, then froze, his eyes widening at the display he found there.

His first thought was that Emily must have purchased every candle for sale in Scotland. And perhaps all those in England too. Hundreds of them littered the room. Some were in candleholders of varying sizes—seemingly every candleholder in his castle had been put to use—but most had simply been affixed to the floor by their own wax. None more than a foot apart, they littered the ballroom like a field of flaming flowers. And in the center stood Emily, a lone rose in her pink gown.

Keeran had never seen such a beautiful spectacle. Leaving his place by the door, he walked the wide path that had been left through the candles and joined her in the circle of light. Without a word, he took her in his arms and there in the field of flames he kissed her with the passion of centuries, then slowly stripped off her clothes and his own and lay her down on them. Her skin glowed opalescent in the candlelight as he made love to her, the small drops of perspiration that formed on her brow catching the light like diamonds.

Keeran's dead heart swelled and squeezed by turn, glory and pain battering him at once. This was a moment he knew he would remember into eternity and every time he recalled it, he would suffer both agony and exultation. This was a gift like no other.

"I love you," Emily whispered in the last moment of their passion, and Keeran squeezed his eyes closed, trying to memorize the sound and inflection of the words so that he could replay it in his head in the centuries to come. He was determined that memories were all he would allow himself to hold on to from this night.

When it was over, he rolled onto his back and pulled her to rest against him, cushioning her head on his shoulder and hushing her when she would have spoken. He just wanted to hold her for a moment and pretend that it could be for longer than that, that he needn't get up, re-don his clothes, and make his way to the village to hire someone to see her home to England.

They remained like that until Keeran felt Emily shiver against him, and he became aware of the gentle breeze wafting around them. Opening his eyes, he glanced around and realized that every door leading out onto the terrace beyond was open. No doubt this was to allow the smell of fresh paint to escape, for Keeran could see that the walls had been painted the sky blue of a sunny day as he recalled it to look. Unfortunately, it was also allowing a cool evening breeze in.

He started to sit up, intending to help her dress lest she catch a chill, but she stopped him with a hand on his chest. "Please. Just a little longer."

Keeran hesitated, then pulled her closer in his arms and remained reclining, no more eager than she was for this interlude to end and reality to intrude. He slid one hand along her arm and stared up at the ceiling, his mind tortured with the fact that he would soon lose her . . . until he noticed that the ceiling was freshly painted as well.

Emily held her breath. She had been waiting for him to notice the ceiling; it was her true gift to him, *and* her message. It was the idea that Mrs. MacBain's question had given her that morning.

"It's the sun," Keeran said suddenly, and she felt her throat constrict at his thick voice. He was obviously moved by the painting she and the servants had worked on for most of the day. While they had painted the walls the blue of a sunny day, the ceiling of the ballroom now sported a large, bright sun and fluffy white clouds on a paler blue sky.

"Yes," she managed to say past the lump in her throat. "The sun. Daylight. A sunny day, painted so that you can see it every night when you wake up, Keeran."

Easing her off his shoulder, he stood slowly and turned in a circle, his gaze drinking in this, his first sight of sunlight in more than two hundred years. "It looks so real."

He reached up as if to catch at a cloud, then let his hand drop slowly.

"Yes." Emily stood up beside him and touched his arm. "I can have the sun and you too, Keeran. This is enough for me."

He stared at her sadly, then shook his head. "But it isn't real."

"No," she admitted, then straightened her shoulders and prepared to argue for her happiness. While painting that day, she had considered very carefully what she should say, and now she took a deep breath and made her case. "No, it isn't real. But 'tis as real as my life will be if you send me away, Keeran, for I will always, until my death, only be pretending at living without you. I will be a pale portrait of the woman I could be, just as this is only a painting of daylight. There will be no passion, no husband, no family, no love, because none can replace you in my heart. I love you, Keeran. Do not send me away and damn me to a half-life without you."

"Ah, Emily." His voice was filled with regret, and she knew what was coming even before he said, "You will forget me. You will—"

"Learn to love another?" Emily interrupted with a sharpness that silenced him. "Do you see me as so fickle? Is my heart so weak and untrue to you? Then allow me to correct this mistaken impression of yours. *I will love no other.* I shall for the rest of my days sit and recall my time with you. I shall become a lonely old spinster, yearning for a lonely man who hides in his crumbling castle from the love of a woman who would explore the night world at his side and hold him in her heart forever, if only given the chance."

Dear God. Keeran closed his eyes. She was there, so close he could touch her if he had the courage. She was a flame of vibrant life that had brought laughter and joy to his empty home and light to his eternal night. She had stirred the dead ashes of his heart back to painful life so successfully that it now ached with his love of her. He wanted so badly to keep her with him, but—

"I am not a man," he argued desperately, having to fight himself and his own wants now, as well as fight her. "Carlotta took my soul and damned me to—"

"Perhaps she didn't," Emily interrupted.

"What are you saying? Of course she did. She turned me."

"Aye, she turned you, Keeran. But perhaps she couldn't take your soul with that act. Surely only you can give it away and damn yourself." Seeing the hope budding on his face, she took his hand. "Keeran, you told me that you wanted to stay on that bed and allow the sun to end your existence after she turned you. If that had happened, do you think you would have gone to hell or heaven?"

"Heaven. It was probably my only way to get there."

A smile blossomed on Emily's face. "Because you would have then been choosing your own death over others."

"Yes." His expression was tormented. "But don't you see? I didn't have the courage to do so. I damned myself with my own cowardice."

"By choosing life?" she asked, then shook her head. "Nay, Keeran. According to the Church, it is a sin to take your own life."

"Murder is a sin, too."

"But you have never killed anyone to continue your existence," she pointed out, then asked worriedly, "Have you?"

"No." He shook his head slowly.

She beamed her relief at him. "Then you are not the monster you think yourself to be. Keeran, I think whether we go to heaven or hell depends entirely on our own decisions, not on those made for us or things done to us. The woman who is violated does not carry the stain of that sin on her soul; her rapist does. Carlotta took your life and turned you into a vampire. But you chose not to take life to sustain your own, and *never* to use your strength and powers to harm others. In fact, you have taken the time and trouble to save many a life, despite how poorly you were treated for it in return. Surely, you cannot be damned."

He was silent for several moments, digesting what she said, then a smile spread his lips. "When put that way . . ." His eyes found hers, then he reached for her hand. "Emily."

"Yes." She answered his unspoken question. "I still want to be with you. I will give up the life I have known for an eternity with you."

"It can be hard at times," he warned.

"Life is hard at times," she said simply.

"You will miss the sun, and have to watch those you care for go to the grave before you."

"So long as it isn't you I must watch go to the grave, Keeran. I can bear anything else but that."

"Oh, my love." He pulled her into his arms and held her close, hugging her as if he would never let her go. "You have given me so much in the short time since you entered my life. Love, laughter, sunlight, hope. And I have so little to offer you in return."

"Aye." Emily sighed, then leaned back to peer up at him and say, "Saving my life, saving me from marrying The Sinclair, a home, love, eternal life. Really, you have so little to offer, I should ask for a dower."

A burst of laughter slipped from his lips. It was followed by a surprised expression that made Emily smile. He was always so surprised to find himself amused. His existence must have been terribly gloomy and lonely all these centuries. She would see to it that it never was again.

Reaching up, she slid one hand into the hair at the back of his head and drew him down for a kiss that soon turned passionate, but after a moment, Keeran caught her hands and broke the kiss. "We should go to your room."

"Nay." She pressed a kiss to the side of his mouth, then the column of his throat, before leaning back to smile at him. "Here. In the sunlight."

Keeran glanced around at the candles and fireplace, then finally to the sunrise she had painted. "Yes. Here in the sunlight."

Please turn the page for an exciting sneak peek of
Hannah Howell's newest historical romance,
HIGHLAND SINNER!

Chapter One

Scotland, early summer 1478

What was that smell?

Tormand Murray struggled to wake up at least enough to
move away from the odor assaulting his nose. He groaned as
he started to turn on his side and the ache in his head became
a piercing agony. Flopping onto his side, he cautiously ran
his hand over his head and found the source of that pain.
There was a very tender swelling at the back of his head. The
damp matted hair around the swelling told him that it had
bled but he could feel no continued blood flow. That indicated that he had been unconscious for more than a few minutes, possibly for even more than a few hours.

As he lay there trying to will away the pain in his head,
Tormand tried to open his eyes. A sharp pinch halted his attempt and he cursed. He had definitely been unconscious for
quite a while and something beside a knock on the head had
been done to him for his eyes were crusted shut. He had a
fleeting, hazy memory of something being thrown into his
eyes before all went black, but it was not enough to give him

any firm idea of what had happened to him. Although he ruefully admitted to himself that it was as much vanity as a reluctance to cause himself pain that caused him to fear he would tear out his eyelashes if he just forced his eyes open, Tormand proceeded very carefully. He gently brushed aside the crust on his eyes until he could open them, even if only enough to see if there was any water close at hand to wash his eyes with.

And, he hoped, enough water to wash himself if he proved to be the source of the stench. To his shame there had been a few times he had woken to find himself stinking, drunk, and a few stumbles into some foul muck upon the street being the cause. He had never been this foul before, he mused, as the smell began to turn his stomach.

Then his whole body tensed as he suddenly recognized the odor. It was death. Beneath the rank odor of an unclean garderobe was the scent of blood—a lot of blood. Far too much to have come from his own head wound.

The very next thing Tormand became aware of was that he was naked. For one brief moment panic seized him. Had he been thrown into some open grave with other bodies? He quickly shook aside that fear. It was not dirt or cold flesh he felt beneath him but the cool linen of a soft bed. Rousing from unconsciousness to that odor had obviously disordered his mind, he thought, disgusted with himself.

Easing his eyes open at last, he grunted in pain as the light stung his eyes and made his head throb even more. Everything was a little blurry, but he could make out enough to see that he was in a rather opulent bedchamber, one that looked vaguely familiar. His blood ran cold and he was suddenly even more reluctant to seek out the source of that smell. It certainly could not be from some battle if only because the part of the bedchamber he was looking at showed no signs of one.

If there is a dead body in this room, laddie, best ye learn about it quick. Ye might be needing to run, said a voice in his head that sounded remarkably like his squire, Walter, and Tormand had to agree with it. He forced down all the reluctance he felt and, since he could see no sign of the dead in the part of the room he studied, turned over to look in the other direction. The sight that greeted his watering eyes had him making a sound that all too closely resembled the one his niece Anna made whenever she saw a spider. Death shared his bed.

He scrambled away from the corpse so quickly he nearly fell out of the bed. Struggling for calm, he eased his way off the bed and then sought out some water to cleanse his eyes so that he could see more clearly. It took several awkward bathings of his eyes before the sting in them eased and the blurring faded. One of the first things he saw after he dried his face was his clothing folded neatly on a chair, as if he had come to this bedchamber as a guest, willingly. Tormand wasted no time in putting on his clothes and searching the room for any other signs of his presence, collecting up his weapons and his cloak.

Knowing he could not avoid looking at the body in the bed any longer, he stiffened his spine and walked back to the bed. Tormand felt the sting of bile in the back of his throat as he looked upon what had once been a beautiful woman. So mutilated was the body that it took him several moments to realize that he was looking at what was left of Lady Clara Sinclair. The ragged clumps of golden blond hair left upon her head and the wide, staring blue eyes told him that, as did the heart-shaped birthmark above the open wound where her left breast had been. The rest of the woman's face was so badly cut up it would have been difficult for her own mother to recognize her without those few clues.

The cold calm he had sought now filling his body and mind, Tormand was able to look more closely. Despite the mutilation there was an expression visible upon poor Clara's face, one that hinted she had been alive during at least some of the horrors inflicted upon her. A quick glance at her wrists and ankles revealed that she had once been bound and had fought those bindings, adding weight to Tormand's dark suspicion. Either poor Clara had had some information someone had tried to torture out of her or she had met up with someone who hated her with a cold, murderous fury.

And someone who hated him as well, he suddenly thought, and tensed. Tormand knew he would not have come to Clara's bedchamber for a night of sweaty bed play. Clara had once been his lover, but their affair had ended and he never returned to a woman once he had parted from her. He especially did not return to a woman who was now married and to a man as powerful and jealous as Sir Ranald Sinclair. That meant that someone had brought him here, someone who wanted him to see what had been done to a woman he had once bedded, and, mayhap, take the blame for this butchery.

That thought shook him free of the shock and sorrow he felt. "Poor, foolish Clara," he murmured. "I pray ye didnae suffer this because of me. Ye may have been vain, a wee bit mean of spirit, witless, and lacking morals, but ye still didnae deserve this."

He crossed himself and said a prayer over her. A glance at the windows told him that dawn was fast approaching and he knew he had to leave quickly. "I wish I could tend to ye now, lass, but I believe I am meant to take the blame for your death and I cannae; I willnae. But, I vow, I *will* find out who did this to ye and they will pay dearly for it."

After one last careful check to be certain no sign of his presence remained in the bedchamber, Tormand slipped away. He had to be grateful that whoever had committed this heinous crime had done so in this house for he knew all the secretive ways in and out of it. His affair with Clara might have been short but it had been lively and he had slipped in and out of this house many, many times. Tormand doubted even Sir Ranald, who had claimed the fine house when he had married Clara, knew all of the stealthy approaches to his bride's bedchamber.

Once outside, Tormand swiftly moved into the lingering shadows of early dawn. He leaned against the outside of the rough stonewall surrounding Clara's house and wondered where he should go. A small part of him wanted to just go home and forget about it all, but he knew he would never heed it. Even if he had no real affection for Clara, one reason their lively affair had so quickly died, he could not simply forget that the woman had been brutally murdered. If he was right in suspecting that someone had wanted him to be found next to the body and be accused of Clara's body, then he definitely could not simply forget the whole thing.

Despite that, Tormand decided the first place he would go was his house. He could still smell the stench of death on his clothing. It might be just his imagination, but he knew he needed a bath and clean clothes to help him forget that smell. As he began his stealthy way home Tormand thought it was a real shame that a bath could not also wash away the images of poor Clara's butchered body.

"Are ye certain ye ought to say anything to anybody?"

Tormand nibbled on a thick piece of cheese as he studied his aging companion. Walter Burns had been his squire for twelve years and had no inclination to be anything more than a squire. His utter lack of ambition was why he had been handed over to Tormand by the man who had knighted him at the tender age of eighteen. It had been a glorious battle and Walter had proven his worth. The man had simply refused to be knighted. Fed up with his squire's lack of interest in the glory, the honors, and the responsibility that went with knighthood Sir MacBain had sent the man to Tormand. Walter had continued to prove his worth, his courage, and his contentment in remaining a lowly squire. At the moment, however, the man was openly upset and his courage was a little weak-kneed.

"I need to find out who did this," Tormand said and then sipped at his ale, hungry and thirsty but partaking of both food and drink cautiously for his stomach was still unsteady.

"Why?" Walter sat down at Tormand's right and poured himself some ale. "Ye got away from it. 'Tis near the middle of the day and no one has come here crying for vengeance so I be thinking ye got away clean, aye? Why let anyone e'en ken ye were near the woman? Are ye trying to put a rope about your neck? And, if I recall rightly, ye didnae find much to like about the woman once your lust dimmed so why fret o'er justice for her?"

"'Tis sadly true that I didnae like her, but she didnae deserve to be butchered like that."

Walter grimaced and idly scratched the ragged scar on his pockmarked left cheek. "True, but I still say if ye let anyone ken ye were there ye are just asking for trouble."

"I would like to think that verra few people would e'er believe I could do that to a woman e'en if I was found lying in her blood, dagger in hand."

"Of course ye wouldnae do such as that, and most folk ken it, but that doesnae always save a mon, does it? Ye dinnae ken everyone who has the power to cry ye a murderer and hang ye and they dinnae ken ye. Then there are the ones who are jealous of ye or your kinsmen and would like naught better than to strike out at one of ye. Aye, look at your brother James. Any fool who kenned the mon would have kenned he couldnae have killed his wife, but he still had to suffer years marked as an outlaw and a woman-killer, aye?"

"I kenned I kept ye about for a reason. Aye, 'twas to raise my spirits when they are low and to embolden me with hope and courage just when I need it the most."

"Wheesht, nay need to slap me with the sharp edge of your tongue. I but speak the truth and one ye would be wise to nay ignore."

Tormand nodded carefully, wary of moving his still-aching head too much. "I dinnae intend to ignore it. 'Tis why I have decided to speak only to Simon."

Walter cursed softly and took a deep drink of ale. "Aye, a king's mon nay less."

"Aye, and my friend. *And* a mon who worked hard to help James. He is a mon who has a true skill at solving such puzzles and hunting down the guilty. This isnae simply about justice for Clara. Someone wanted me to be blamed for her murder, Walter. I was put beside her body to be found and accused of the crime. And for such a crime I would be hanged so that means that someone wants me dead."

"Aye, true enough. Nay just dead, either, but your good name weel blackened."

"Exactly. So I have sent word to Simon asking him to come here, stressing an urgent need to speak with him."

Tormand was pleased that he sounded far more confident of his decision than he felt. It had taken him several hours to actually write and send the request for a meeting to Simon. The voice in his head that told him to just turn his back on the whole matter, the same opinion that Walter offered, had grown almost too loud to ignore. Only the certainty that this had far more to do with him than with Clara had given him the strength to silence that cowardly voice.

He had the feeling that part of his stomach's unsteadiness was due to a growing fear that he was about to suffer as James had. It had taken his foster brother three long years to prove his innocence and wash away the stain to his honor. Three long, lonely years of running and hiding. Tormand dreaded the thought that he might be pulled into the same ugly quagmire. If nothing else, he was deeply concerned about how it would affect his mother who had already suffered too much grief and worry over her children. First his sister Sorcha had been beaten and raped, then his sister Gillyanne had been kidnapped—twice—the second time leading to a forced marriage, and then there had been the trouble that had sent James running for the shelter of the hills. His mother did not need to suffer through yet another one of her children mired in danger.

"If ye could find something the killer touched we could solve this puzzle right quick," said Walter.

Pulling free of his dark thoughts about the possibility that his family was cursed, Tormand frowned at his squire. "What are ye talking about?"

"Weel, if ye had something the killer touched we could take it to the Ross witch."

Tormand had heard of the Ross witch. The woman lived in a tiny cottage several miles outside of town. Although the townspeople had driven the woman away ten years ago, many still journeyed to her cottage for help, mostly for the herbal concoctions the woman made. Some claimed the woman had visions that had aided them in solving some problem. Despite having grown up surrounded by people who had special gifts like that, he doubted the woman was the miracle worker some claimed her to be. Most of the time such *witches* were simply aging women skilled with herbs and an ability to convince people that they had some great mysterious power.

"And why do ye think she could help if I brought her something touched by the killer?" he asked.

"Because she gets a vision of the truth when she touches something." Walter absently crossed himself as if he feared he risked his soul by even speaking of the woman. "Old George, the steward for the Gillespie house, told me that Lady Gillespie had some of her jewelry stolen. He said her ladyship took the box the jewels had been taken from to the Ross witch and the moment the woman held the box she had a vision about what had happened."

When Walter said no more, Tormand asked, "What did the vision tell the woman?"

"That Lady Gillespie's eldest son had taken the jewels. Crept into her ladyship's bedchamber whilst she was at court and helped himself to all the best pieces."

"It doesnae take a witch to ken that. Lady Gillespie's eldest son is weel kenned to spend too much coin on fine clothes, women, and the toss of the dice. Near everyone—mon, woman, and bairn—in town kens that." Tormand took a drink of ale to help him resist the urge to grin at the look of annoyance on Walter's homely face. "Now I ken why the fool was banished to his grandfather's keep far from all the temptation here near the court."

"Weel, it wouldnae hurt to try. Seems a lad like ye ought to have more faith in such things."

"Oh, I have ample faith in such things, enough to wish that ye wouldnae call the woman a witch. That is a word that can give some woman blessed with a gift from God a lot of trouble, deadly trouble."

"Ah, aye, aye, true enough. A gift from God, is it?"

"Do ye really think the devil would give a woman the gift to heal or to see the truth or any other gift or skill that can be used to help people?"

"Nay, of course he wouldnae. So why do ye doubt the Ross woman?"

"Because there are too many women who are, at best, a wee bit skilled with herbs yet claim such things as visions or the healing touch in order to empty some fool's purse. They are frauds and oftimes what they do makes life far more difficult for those women who have a true gift."

Walter frowned for a moment, obviously thinking that over, and then grunted his agreement. "So ye willnae be trying to get any help from Mistress Ross?"

"Nay, I am nay so desperate for such as that."

"Oh, I am nay sure I would refuse any help just now," came a cool, hard voice from the doorway of Tormand's hall.

Tormand looked toward the door and started to smile at Simon. The expression died a swift death. Sir Simon Innes looked every inch the king's man at the moment. His face was pale and cold fury tightened its predatory lines. Tormand got the sinking feeling that Simon already knew why he had sent for him. Worse, he feared his friend had some suspicions about his guilt. That stung, but Tormand decided to smother his sense of insult until he and Simon had at least talked. The man was his friend and a strong believer in justice. He would listen before he acted.

Nevertheless, Tormand tensed with a growing alarm when Simon strode up to him. Every line of the man's tall, lean body was tense with fury. Out of the corner of his eye, Tormand saw Walter tense and place his hand on his sword, revealing that Tormand was not the only one who sensed danger. It was as he looked back at Simon that Tormand realized the man clutched something in his hand.

A heartbeat later, Simon tossed what he held onto the table in front of Tormand. Tormand stared down at a heavy gold ring embellished with blood-red garnets. Unable to believe what he was seeing, he looked at his hands, his unadorned hands, and then looked back at the ring. His first thought was to wonder how he could have left that room of death and not realized that he was no longer wearing his ring. His second thought was that the point of Simon's sword was dangerously sharp as it rested against his jugular.

"Nay! Dinnae kill him! He is innocent!"

Morainn Ross blinked in surprise as she looked around her. She was at home sitting up in her own bed, not in a great hall watching a man press a sword point against the throat of another man. Ignoring the grumbling of her cats that had been disturbed from their comfortable slumber by her outburst, she flopped back down and stared up at the ceiling. It had only been a dream.

"Nay, no dream," she said after a moment of thought. "A vision."

Thinking about that a little longer she then nodded her head. It had definitely been a vision. The man who had sat there with a sword at his throat was no stranger to her. She had been seeing him in dreams and visions for months now. He had smelled of death, was surrounded by it, yet there had never been any blood upon his hands.

"Morainn? Are ye weel?"

Morainn looked toward the door to her small bedchamber and smiled at the young boy standing there. Walin was only six but he was rapidly becoming very helpful. He also worried about her a lot, but she supposed that was to be expected. Since she had found him upon her threshold when he was the tender of age of two she was really the only parent he had ever known, had given him the only home he had ever known. She just wished it were a better one. He was also old enough now to understand that she was often called a witch as well as the danger that appellation brought with it. Unfortunately, with his black hair and blue eyes, he looked enough like her to have many believe he was her bastard child and that caused its own problems for both of them.

"I am fine, Walin," she said and began to ease her way out of bed around all the sleeping cats. "It must be verra late in the day."

"'Tis the middle of the day, but ye needed to sleep. Ye were verra late returning from helping at that birthing."

"Weel, set something out on the table for us to eat then, I will join ye in a few minutes."

Dressed and just finishing the braiding of her hair, Morainn joined Walin at the small table set out in the main room of the cottage. Seeing the bread, cheese, and apples upon the table, she smiled at Walin, acknowledging a job well done. She poured them each a tankard of cider and then sat down on the little bench facing his across the scarred wooden table.

"Did ye have a bad dream?" Walin asked as he handed Morainn an apple to cut up for him.

"At first I thought it was a dream but now I am certain it was a vision, another one about that mon with the mismatched eyes." She carefully set the apple on a wooden plate and sliced it for Walin.

"Ye have a lot about him, dinnae ye."

"It seems so. 'Tis verra odd. I dinnae ken who he is and have ne'er seen such a mon. And, if this vision is true, I dinnae think I e'er will."

"Why?" Walin accepted the plate of sliced apple and immediately began to eat it.

"Because this time I saw a verra angry gray-eyed mon holding a sword to his throat."

"But didnae ye say that your visions are of things to come? Mayhap he isnae dead yet. Mayhap ye are supposed to find him and warn him."

Morainn considered that possibility for a moment and then shook her head. "Nay, I think not. Neither heart nor mind urges me to do that. If that were what I was meant to do, I would feel the urge to go out right now and hunt him down. And, I would have been given some clue as to where he is."

"Oh. So we will soon see the mon whose eyes dinnae match?"

"Aye, I do believe we will."

"Weel that will be interesting."

She smiled and turned her attention to the need to fill her very empty stomach. If the man with the mismatched eyes showed up at her door, it would indeed be interesting. It could also be dangerous. She could not allow herself to forget that death stalked him. Her visions told her he was innocent of those deaths but there was some connection between him and them. It was as if each thing he touched died in bleeding agony. She certainly did not wish to become a part of that swirling mass of blood she always saw around his feet. Unfortunately she did not believe that fate would give her any chance to avoid meeting the man. All she could do was pray that when he rapped upon her door he did not still have death seated upon his shoulder.

Please turn the page for an exciting sneak peek at
Jackie Kessler's next book in the *Hell on Earth* series:
the incubus Daunuan's story,
HOTTER THAN HELL!

Chapter One

Coitus Interruptus

Anyone in my position would've thought the buzzing in my head was anticipation. Five minutes to go, then the client would be eating from my hand. Literally. I had the grapes ready and waiting in the ice bucket, chilling. She liked it when I let the cluster dangle over her lips—she'd poke her tongue out, sinewy and slick against the ripe fruit, darting pink flesh over purple. Sweetness on sweetness, both begging to be sucked. Plucked. My blood pounded through me, boom boom, boom boom, sending happy signals to my brain and my balls, getting my body primed. T minus five minutes, and counting. Small talk until then—light touches here, knowing smiles there, lying about her job and mine. Thinking about sex. Killing time.

So it sort of wasn't my fault that I didn't sense the demon approaching.

The client had moved some things around in the bedroom since my last visit. Now her wedding photo was missing ("Getting it reframed") and the threadbare pink comforter had been replaced with one that was red and advertised sin. We sprawled on the bed, clothing still on, intentions thick in the air. She was decked out in a white silk sheath and pearls and lacy thigh-highs. I was a study of blacks. A bit cliché, but Tall, Dark, and Handsome was all the rage. She liked it, and I aimed to please.

"I got a new perfume," my client said. "Envy Me."

"I'd prefer to ravish you."

Her smile pulled into a grin—white teeth flashing in a lipstick sea of red. "The perfume, I mean. It's Gucci." She leaned forward, offering me her neck as she pressed her breasts against my chest and rubbed. Looking for a quick feel through the silk. My kind of woman. She purred, "Like it, baby?"

Inhaling deeply, I took in the peony and jasmine and other scents blending together with her eager sweat, her underlying smell of female in heat. "Nice," I lied. Me, I preferred the musk of her sex alone, without the cloying flowery scent over it. "You smell good enough to eat." No lie there.

"Yeah?" She was playful, almost kittenish. "You going to . . . eat me?"

Heh. Sex kittenish. "Oh yeah, doll. Eat you alive." Among other things.

"My big bad wolf."

That made me chuckle. Brushing her hair away from her face, I said, "You my little red riding hood?"

"Depends, baby. You want me to ride you?"

I smiled, wistful. "Like you would not believe."

My head buzzed, hummed as she oozed sex, her body practically begging me to climb on top of her. Soon, doll. Soon. She jiggled against me once more, reached her hand out toward my thigh—stroked once, lushly, then pulled back. She knew the dance by now: only teasing at first, quick-fingered taunts. Nothing overt. Not yet.

Seduction, after all, had its rules. Date Number One had

been all about getting her to kiss me. Number Two had been pleasing her like no other man or woman ever had before. Three had been making her want me more than anything else. (One thing about us Seducers: we always put our clients' desires ahead of our own. If not for the rules, I would've fucked her silly after I introduced myself.)

Here we were at Date Number Four: D-Day, the Big One. My Turn. Otherwise known as The Payoff. It set my blood to boil just thinking about it.

But first things first: I had to get her revving, ready, steady go on the first real touch. Thus a five-minute warmup of sexual tension. Seduction 101. Child's play. And never mind how that single stroke of hers on my leg had rippled up my back, settled into my stomach. I shifted; the front of my pants was too damn tight.

Sometimes the rules really sucked.

"Don," she said, her voice a low purr that went straight to my crotch. That's all she said: my name, or her version of my name. That's all she needed to say. Her hand again, now on my stomach. I wagged a no-no-no with my finger as I grinned, thinking about how she'd taste like candy. Thinking about how she'd call my name.

Mmm. Shivers.

"I've been waiting for this all week," she whispered.

"Me too."

"I couldn't stop thinking about you." She dropped her gaze to my fly, where she saw just how much I was thinking about her. Her desire filled the air, thick and pungent, as she begged me to come on, baby, let's get started already.

But damn, how I wanted to. Oh, the things I wanted to do. Would do. Four minutes—no, less now. Three and counting. I said her name, put just the right amount of foreplay into my voice.

She looked up at me through her makeup-crusted lashes, slowly ran her tongue over her fuck-me lips. Bedroom eyes; blowjob mouth. Intoxicating. Boom *boom,* boom *boom.*

"Now, baby," she said, her voice a throaty growl. The woman was giving way to the animal, to the instinct that tingled deep inside her. Giving way to lust. And all with no nudging from me. *Sweet.* She said again: "Now." Insistent. Demanding.

A hum again, this time strong enough to make me sit up. Frowning, I felt the buzz resonate through me, pitched high in warning. No this wasn't just anticipation. This was—

—her mouth on mine, her tongue jabbing through my lips and running against my teeth. My momentary caution faded into bemused surprise. She usually wasn't so direct, but who gave a damn? Screw the countdown to bliss. She was ready. Steady.

Go.

Heat rolled over me, bathed me in fire from head to toe. I opened my mouth to hers, pushed that heat into her. She said "Mmmmmm," melted into the kiss like chocolate over flame. I washed my hands over the silk of her body, and the buzzing in my head sputtered, died.

Oh, doll, how I'm going to make you scream. . . .

She groaned against me, and my tongue lapped up the sound. I left her mouth to kiss up the length of her jaw, now playing by the lobe of her ear. She squirmed against me, all soft and delicious, delectable, making contented sounds that told me I hit one of her sweet spots. Her hand clenched on my shoulder, then pushed. With a hungry "Rrrr," she rolled me onto my back, straddled my hips. The hem of her dress rode up, exposing the fullness of her upper thighs, the flash of white satin panties.

Boom *boom.*

"This is different," I murmured, my hands on her waist.

"You're always so good to me, baby." Her voice was thick with need, her eyes dark and brimming. Leaning down, she poured herself over me to whisper in my ear, "I want to ride you. Now."

Maybe I ditched the countdown, but other rules had to stay in place. Clients first, even on D-Day. That was ever the rule. So I ignored the ache in my groin and said, "Ladies first, doll."

"Don . . ."

"Maybe I'll take the grapes, run them over your naked body. Nibble them off your skin."

"I don't want grapes. I want you."

"You got me."

"No I don't. You never let me do you, bring you there." She gyrated over my crotch, a slow dry hump that did maddening things to me. "It's always been about me."

"I'm a giving sort of guy," I said, my voice husky.

"Your turn, baby," she said, punctuating her promise with wet kisses down my neck. Her fingers played by my crotch, and over the buzzing in my head and the pounding of my heart, I heard her unzip my fly. "I'm going to love you so fine," she said, "you're going to sing my name. I'm going to make you explode."

Down she kissed, down my chest, my stomach, my—

Wa-*hoo*.

Okay, maybe the customer was always right . . .

In the midst of mind-blowing pleasure, a deafening crash, followed by a man's shout: "What the fuck're you doing with my wife?"

Uh oh.

Louder than the man's words, the buzzing screamed its warning in my head.

Shit.

Getting interrupted in the middle of sex is bad enough. Worse is when the cause of *coitus interruptus* is a demon.

A glance told me all I needed to know: he was obscenely muscled, and his eyes glowed with malefic presence. Definitely not a Seducer; I would've felt the psychic connection. Sloth was out of the question. Pride, maybe, or Envy . . .

Between my legs, the client was still going to town. Side

effect of entrancing the clientele over the course of four dates: they wound up being a bit one-track minded. Usually it was anything but a problem; at the moment, though, the pleasure was a tad . . . distracting. Not that I was complaining.

Because my client didn't seem to be one to talk with her mouth full, I put on my charming face and said to her husband, "Your wife's told me so much about you."

He roared, a wordless cry of pure rage. Terrific—one of the Berserkers was riding his body. They weren't exactly known for their reasoning skills. How was I supposed to convince a demon of Wrath that the client was mine? Hell knew I had all the paperwork to prove it . . .

The husband cocked back a fist. The flesh burned red, and energy sizzled off his skin.

Whoops. I grabbed my client by her shoulders and pulled her off of me, then rolled with her to the floor. She landed on top of me, her mouth working like a landed fish. Sandwiched between the wall and the bed, we were trapped. Last Stand at the Sealy Corral.

From the other side of the bed: "I'll kill the both of you!"

The haze of passion began to clear from my client's eyes. Before the fear took hold, I ran a finger over her brow, pushing a command into her mind. She crumpled on my chest, dead asleep. I nudged her to the ground. Back in a second, doll.

Far over my head, a bolt of magic slammed into the wall. Smoking plaster fluttered down, singeing my face with tiny kisses. Maybe the man was possessed, but he was also a lousy shot.

He bellowed, "Think you can sleep with my wife?"

"Actually," I called back, "sleeping wasn't what I had in mind."

He screamed his fury, then the wall behind me exploded. I threw myself over the unconscious woman, shielding her from the smoking debris. I'd be blessed if I let another demon claim her. I'd been on her case for a month; she didn't die until I said so.

Sometimes, I was as possessive as a Coveter.

Pieces of the ruined wall crashed on me and around me, covered me in filth and soot. Dust made me sneeze, and sneezing during a fight was both dangerous and rather lame, so I stopped breathing. The stench of smoke lingered in my nostrils. Nice. Reminded me of home. Not including the part about getting buried by a falling wall. The wreckage hadn't killed me—when I was on a collection, the only thing human about me was my appearance—but getting slammed with it hurt like a bastard. My own fault; I should have known better than to taunt a Berserker.

Over the sound of the settling rubble, he shouted, "You dead yet, asshole?"

"Hate to break it to you, chuckles, but you missed."

Couldn't help it. For demons, Berserkers were just so fucking stupid.

"Seducer!" The man's voice deepened to that of a constipated buffalo's bellow. "I'm going to rip you apart!"

"Some nefarious ones just talk, talk, talk." I shot my arm out and leveled a blast overhead. The light fixture shattered and crashed down to the ground. I heard the man jump clear and land heavily in the far end of the room. Recharging my power as the man regained his footing, I reviewed the possibilities. It came down to three options.

One: I could kill the possessed human.

No, the paperwork involved in the accidental slaying of a mortal would kill my sex drive for the better part of a decade.

Two: I could run.

Hah, as if.

Three: I could banish the demon, leave the human alive.

Ding ding ding, we have a winner. Banishing, *sans* killing. That meant attacking him directly with my magic was right out. And *that* meant I had to figure out what his weakness was and kick-start the exorcism.

It occurred to me that priests had other uses besides between meal snacks. Live and learn.

The sound of clumping footfalls, along with labored breathing. Some mortals just couldn't take a hint. I scrambled to the foot of the bed and yanked on the baseboard until I pried the wood free. Shouting to do the Banshees proud, I leapt up and hurled the makeshift weapon at the human.

And . . . bull's-eye! The wood splintered against his torso with a satisfying crack. He staggered back three steps, blinked stupidly at the slivers embedded in his flesh. Then he snarled something about my parentage and aimed another blast my way. I hit the carpet two seconds before it rained plaster again.

Wood was a big no. What else? I didn't have any iron on hand . . .

He shouted, "Come out and fight like a man!"

"I'm not a man." I reached out blindly, found the ice bucket, heavy with grapes and melted ice. The rim and handle on the black lacquered wood gleamed with a silver sheen. Yes, maybe silver would do the trick. Come a little closer, chuckles. Give me a hug.

"Fight me!" Two voices spoke the same command—the mortal's ire blending with the demon's innate Wrath.

I gripped the bucket, getting ready for the windup. "Don't you think two on one is a bit unfair?"

"Fight me!"

"Come here and make me."

He shrieked his unholy rage, and then I heard him stomp toward me. Charge of the Dark Brigade. I popped up and pitched the ice bucket at the ballistic human, catching him full in the face. The silver handle bonked him about a second before the melted ice and chilled fruit splattered on his skin . . . skin that immediately bubbled and smoked. He roared in either fury or agony, and then he swatted madly at his face.

Gotcha.

I took a moment to zip up my fly. Then I stepped around

the wreckage strewn almost artfully through the ruins of the bedroom to approach the wounded demon. Under my feet, a collage of shattered glass sparkled amid the chunks of smoking plaster and plywood. Love really was a battlefield.

The man had fallen to the floor, clutching at his steaming face and gibbering in pain. Interesting. The silver handle was nowhere near him, yet he was still reacting so strongly . . . Ah. Smiling, I scooped up a handful of stray ice cubes. Allergic to water, my my. If I had any feelings, I would have felt sorry for the creature; having such an Elemental sensitivity would crimp any demon's style. But I've never been accused of being compassionate.

Water pooling in my hand, I squatted over the squirming form. "Need a towel?"

Beneath his clawed fingers, the flesh of the man's face looked rather spongy. Hmm. Hope that's not permanent. I didn't think the human would be long on the mortal coil with his face slipping off his skull. The thought of all the red tape associated with accidental slaughter made my stomach roil. Damned bureaucracy would be the death of me.

He snarled, "Bless yourself, asshole!"

"Don't suppose it'll help to tell you there's been a mix-up," I said, juggling the ice from hand to hand.

Lowering his fingers, the Berserker glared up at me through the human's red-rimmed eyes. "No mix-up, whoremaster."

"That's 'Mister Whoremaster' to you."

He spat at me, but the thick glob sizzled and vanished before it touched my skin. Company perk: adjustable heat aura.

"Bastard!"

"Now, now," I said, dangling a sweating cube over his face. "Play nice, kitty, or you get a bath. What do you mean, no mix-up?"

For a long moment, he stared his hatred at me, charged the air with fury so brutally raw that my flesh should have been flayed from my bones. Finally he said, "I was sent on purpose."

"A snafu, then. I've got all the paperwork. She's mine, chuckles."

"No snafu."

Oh really? "Explain yourself."

"Killers, the man and woman both."

I'd known about the woman; there was a reason she was a client, after all. The man, though, was a surprise. Then again, I hadn't bothered to research him. He wasn't the one I was supposed to fuck to death. "What, they get off on murder?"

"Thrill of the bloodshed." His eyes gleamed, and a smile unfurled on his softening face. "The gospel of butchery. The ecstasy of violence."

"Uh huh." I'd heard the Wrath party line before. "That's lovely. But she's still mine."

"No, whoremonger." He bared his teeth in a parody of a grin. "The flesh puppets, they were to kill you."

Jaw clenched, I said, "Kill *me*?" Humans, attacking a demon? Outside of some wildly popular television shows, that was unheard of. There had to have been a mistake.

"They were to bathe in your blood," he said with a sigh of pleasure. "Then I was to slit their throats, claim them both for Wrath."

Blinking, I repeated, "For *Wrath*?"

"Want I should speak in smaller words, rake?"

I didn't know which was more insulting—that the humans wanted to kill me, or that a Berserker was insinuating I was stupid. A snarl on my lips, I crushed the ice in one of my hands and wiped it over the remains of his forehead. His squeal of pain was almost worth the mess of melted flesh on my fingers.

After his screeching faded, I said, "Why me?"

Arms wrapped over his head, I almost didn't hear his muffled reply. "Would be telling."

I still couldn't grasp that the mortals had wanted to slice and dice me. *Me*. That wasn't in the Demon Playbook. Not that we had a playbook, but still . . . "She was *my* target," I insisted.

"Murder is murder. The more, the better." Panting, he peered out from his barricade of arms. "Kill two humans, kill one Seducer. All the same to Wrath. But destroying you, that would have given me pleasure." He chuckled wetly. "You understand pleasure, no?"

I sat heavily on my haunches. Well, this just sucked angel feathers. Where did humans get off, thinking they could actually take down a demon? Next thing you knew, they'd be shooting me with silver bullets and flinging Holy Water on me. Idiots.

No, my client couldn't have known I was a demon. To her and her husband—before he'd been possessed—I'd been just another flesh puppet, one whom they could play with and prey on. No more.

The man's breathing took on a burbling sound. I said, "You dying on me, chuckles?"

"You Seducers . . . all the same," the demon whispered. "Clap-carrying . . . sluts . . . suck the fight . . . out of a body."

Could I help it if I was a lover, not a fighter?

"Paperwork . . . keep you bound . . . for eons."

"Ah, go to Hell." I dropped the rest of the melting ice on him.

"Open your eyes, doll."

My client's eyelids fluttered, then opened. The confusion I saw staring back at me was like a shot of whisky burning the back of my throat. Mmmm. Straddling her hips, I rubbed against her, just once, just enough to send her body signals her brain was still too fuzzy to interpret. Beneath us, the ruined bed protested but still held. I was planning on breaking it within ten minutes. Anticipation . . .

She blinked, tried to open her mouth. Then she tried to

move her body. No dice; she was frozen on her back, her arms by her sides, her virginal white silk dress covering her from knockers to knees. Confusion sparked into fear. I inhaled deeply, took in the scent of her growing terror.

Boom *boom*.

"You're wondering why you can't move." I smiled, picturing all the things I was about to do to her. "You're wondering what happened. I'll recap."

I stretched over her, ran my hand from her cheek down to her chin, her neck, her breast, her belly. "You were going down on me when your loving husband came tearing into the room." I reached behind me until my hand found her crotch. Sliding between her legs, I ran two fingers over the whisper softness of her satin panties, felt the lips of her vulva quiver. "He was going to kill me, with help from you."

She stiffened beneath me.

Grinning, I said, "That's him on the floor. Had the audacity to die and not remove himself after. I'm afraid he's going to stink up the place in another day or so."

Her eyes slipped closed, and tears leaked through her lids. How touching. I pushed her underwear to the side and stroked my fingers over her clitoral hood, then pressed gently. Stroke, press.

"No worries, doll," I said. "You won't miss him for long."

Stroke. I heard her breath catch in her throat, and I grinned as I pressed, lingering. Now her inner muscles tensed with my touch, seemed to reach for my fingers as I moved them away. Passion in the depths of despair. Sin at its sweetest. The smell of her fear was now spiced with desire. Demonic aromatherapy.

"I have a question for you. I'll go easier on you if you tell me the truth. And believe me, I can smell the truth on you." I rubbed her sex harder. "You do believe me, don't you? Go ahead, doll. Speak."

"Yes," she said thickly.

"Good. Now then, tell me why you and Loving Husband didn't try to kill me on our first Date."

Shuddering from my touch, she said, "You were a surprise. We always pick our takes together. But you, you came on to me. He was out of town, and you picked me up . . ." Her voice turned into a moan as I reached inside her, nudging her toward bliss.

"So your man was away, and you decided to play?"

"You kissed me," she breathed, "and nothing else mattered . . ."

Have to love the demon gigolo mojo. Gigolojo at its best.

"Actually, doll, you kissed me." I slid my fingers out of her, then moved my hand up and down her inner thigh, tickling her flesh with her own wetness. She reeked of passion and panic. Mmmm. Soon, soon, soon. "That's how it works. You kiss me willingly, and then boom. Magic. But the fun starts when you call my name."

She opened her eyes, looked at me as those fat tears kept winding down her cheeks. "Please," she said. "I wasn't going to hurt you, not you . . ."

"Uh, uh, uh. That's a lie. Shame. Here you were doing so well until now." I pressed the nails of my fingers harder against her plump thigh. "You and hubby, you were going to kill me good and dead, then do whatever it is serial killers do to celebrate. Champagne, maybe? A blood bath? Tell me true."

"Sex," she whispered. "We have sex. We're already sticky with your blood, and we kiss, tasting you on us . . ."

"Why, doll, that's positively perverted. How impressive!" With my other hand, I cupped her full breast, feeling the hardness of her nipple poking through the silk of her dress. "How many have you killed? I'm just curious."

"Seven . . ."

"A powerful number. So they say." Now I had her other breast in hand, rolling the mound in my fingers, teasing her until the nipple was fully erect, begging me to have a taste.

"Please . . . why can't I move?"

I leaned down to whisper in her ear. "That would be because I commanded you not to move. Boom. Magic."

She bit her lip—a nervous tic that reminded me of someone else. "You a magician?"

A quick suck on her earlobe, then a sharp nip. "I eat magicians for breakfast."

She squeaked: a tiny, terrified sound. I nearly exploded in my pants.

"I'm an incubus," I said, stretching the last *S*. "And do you know what an incubus does to fragile human dolls like you?"

Stinking of terror, she whispered, "No . . ."

I leaned over her until my mouth was bare inches away from hers. "An incubus sucks the life from you. An incubus fucks you and kills you, then takes your soul to Hell."

"*No* . . ."

A quick kiss on her dry lips, wetting her mouth with mine. "So here's where we are, doll. Your man is dead. Your life was already forfeit. Now it's going to happen a bit sooner than I'd planned."

"Please . . ."

I loved it when they begged. "Tell you what, my little murderess. I'll give you a chance. All you have to do is not call my full name when I make you climax. If you can do that, I won't fuck you to death." I'd break her neck. But what was the point of telling her that? "What do you think? Tell me true."

"I . . ." She swallowed, said, "I don't know your full name."

"But you do." I licked the hollow of her throat, kissed the sensitive flesh. "In their souls, all humans know the nefarious ones. What do you say, doll? I'll screw you so hard you'll see stars." Between her legs, my fingers danced over her slit. She groaned, tried to move, groaned harder when I pressed down. "Think you can keep from calling my name when you come?"

Gasping, she said, "Yes."

"Wonderful." I kissed her neck, worked my way down to her breast. Debating whether I should let her move beneath me, I gave her fifty-fifty on being able not to call my name. She was evil down to the core. I had to admire that in a human.

She was mine three minutes and forty-nine seconds later.

Eugenie Markham is the most powerful shaman around, a mercenary who spends all her time banishing spirits and fey who cross into this world. When a teenage girl's abduction takes Eugenie into the Otherworld, she learns about a startling prophecy—a prophecy that threatens her world and reveals secrets about her own past. Determined to stop the prophecy *and* rescue the girl, Eugenie assembles an odd assortment of allies: a bored fairy King who's into bondage, a cursed spirit who fantasizes about killing her, and a hot shapeshifter who is both literally and figuratively a fox. As the danger increases and time starts running out, Eugenie realizes her greatest threat may actually be her own nature and the dark powers awakening within her.

Please turn the page for an exciting sneak peek of Richelle Mead's newest urban fantasy novel STORM BORN!

Chapter One

I'd seen weirder things than a haunted shoe but not many.
The Nike Pegasus sat on the office desk, inoffensive, colored
in shades of gray, white, and orange. The laces were loosened, and a bit of dirt clung to the soles. It was the left shoe.

As for me, well . . . underneath my knee-length coat, I
had a Glock 22 loaded with bullets carrying a higher-than-
legal steel content. A cartridge of silver ones rested in my
coat pocket. Two athames lay sheathed on my other hip, one
silver-bladed and one iron. Stuck into my belt near them was
my wand, hand-carved oak and loaded with enough charmed
gems to blow up the desk in the corner if I'd wanted to.

To say I felt overdressed was something of an understatement.

"So," I said, keeping my voice as neutral as possible,
"what makes you think your shoe is . . . uh, possessed?"

Brian Montgomery, late thirties, with a receding hairline
in serious denial, eyed the shoe nervously and moistened his
lips. "It always trips me up when I'm out running. Every
time. And it's always moving around. I mean, I never actually
see it, but . . . like, I'll take them off near the door, then I

come back and find this one under the bed or something. And sometimes . . . sometimes I touch it, and it feels cold . . . really cold . . . like . . ." He groped for similes and finally picked the tritest one. "Like ice."

I nodded and glanced back at the shoe, not saying anything.

"Look, Miss . . . Odile . . . or whatever. I'm not crazy. That shoe is haunted. It's evil. You've gotta do something, okay? I've got a marathon coming up, and until this started happening, these were my lucky shoes. And they're not cheap, you know. They're an investment."

It sounded crazy to me—which was saying something— but there was no harm in checking, seeing as I was already out here. I reached into my coat pocket, the one without ammunition, and pulled out my pendulum. It was a simple one, a thin silver chain with a small quartz crystal hanging from it. New Age stores that sold more elaborate ones were ripping you off.

I laced the end of the chain through my fingers and held my flattened hand over the shoe, clearing my mind and letting the crystal hang freely. A moment later, it began to slowly rotate of its own accord.

"Well, I'll be damned," I muttered, stuffing the pendulum back in my pocket. There was something there. I turned to Montgomery, attempting some sort of badass face because that was what customers always expected. "It might be best if you stepped out of the room, sir. For your own safety."

That was only half true. Mostly I just found lingering clients annoying. They asked stupid questions and could do stupider things, which actually put me at more risk than them.

He had no qualms about getting out of there. As soon as the door closed, I found a jar of salt in my satchel and poured a large ring on the floor. I tossed the shoe into the middle of it and invoked the four cardinal directions with the silver athame. Ostensibly the circle didn't change, but I felt a slight flaring of power indicating it had sealed us in.

Trying not to yawn, I pulled out my wand and kept holding the silver athame. It had taken four hours to drive to Las Cruces, and doing that on so little sleep had made the distance seem twice as long. Sending some of my will into the wand, I tapped it against the shoe and spoke in a singsong voice.

"Come out, come out, whoever you are."

There was a moment's silence, then a high-pitched male voice snapped, "Go away, bitch."

Great. A shoe with attitude. "Why? You got something better to do?"

"Better things to do than waste my time with a mortal."

I smiled. "Better things to do in a shoe? Come on. I mean, I've heard of slumming it, but don't you think you're kind of pushing it here? This shoe isn't even new. You could have done so much better."

The voice kept its annoyed tone, not threatening but simply irritated at the interruption. "*I'm* slumming it? Do you think I don't know who you are, Eugenie Markham? Dark-Swan-Called-Odile. A blood traitor. A mongrel. An assassin. A murderer." He practically spit out the last word. "You are alone among your kind and mine. A bloodthirsty shadow. You do anything for anyone who can pay you enough for it. That makes you more than a mercenary. That makes you a whore."

I affected a bored stance. I'd been called most of those names before. Well, except for my own name. That was new—and a little disconcerting. Not that I'd let him know that.

"Are you done whining? Because I don't have time to listen while you stall."

"Aren't you being paid by the hour?" he asked nastily.

"I charge a flat fee."

"Oh."

I rolled my eyes and touched the wand to the shoe again. This time, I thrust the full force of my will into it, drawing upon my own body's physical stamina as well as some of the power of the world around me. "No more games. If you leave on your own, I won't have to hurt you. *Come out.*"

He couldn't stand against that command and the power within it. The shoe trembled, and smoke poured out of it. Oh, Jesus. I hoped the shoe didn't get incinerated in the process. Montgomery wouldn't be able to handle that.

The smoke billowed out, coalescing into a large, dark form about two feet taller than me. With all his wisecracks, I'd sort of expected a saucy version of one of Santa's elves. Instead, the being before me had the upper body of a well-muscled man while his lower portion resembled a small cyclone. The smoke solidified into leathery gray-black skin, and I had only a moment to act as I assessed this new development. I swapped the wand for the gun, ejecting the clip as I pulled it out. By then, he was lunging for me, and I had to roll out of his way, confined by the circle's boundaries.

A keres. A male keres—most unusual. I'd anticipated something fey, which required silver bullets; or a spectre, which required no bullets. Keres were ancient death spirits originally confined to canopic jars. When the jars wore down over time, keres tended to seek out new homes. There weren't too many of them left in this world, and soon, there'd be one less.

He bore down on me, and I took a nice chunk out of him with the silver blade. I used my right hand, the one I wore an onyx and obsidian bracelet on. Those stones alone would take a toll on a death spirit like him without the blade's help. Sure enough, he hissed in pain and hesitated a moment. I used that delay, scrambling to load the silver cartridge.

I didn't quite make it because soon he was on me again. He hit me with one of those massive arms, slamming me against the walls of the circle. They might be invisible, but they felt as solid as bricks. One of the downsides of trapping a spirit in a circle was that I got trapped too. My head and left shoulder took the brunt of that impact, and pain shot through me in small starbursts. He seemed pretty pleased with himself, as overconfident villains so often are.

"You're as strong as they say, but you were a fool to try to cast me out. You should have left me in peace." His voice was deeper now, almost gravelly.

I shook my head, both to disagree and get rid of the dizziness. "It isn't your shoe."

I still couldn't swap that goddamned cartridge. Not with him ready to attack again, not with both hands full. Yet I couldn't risk dropping either weapon.

He reached for me, and I cut him again. The wounds were small, but the athame was like poison. It would wear him down over time—if I could stay alive long enough. I moved to strike at him once more, but he anticipated me and seized hold of my wrist. He squeezed it, bending it in an unnatural position and forcing me to drop the athame and cry out in pain. I hoped he hadn't broken any bones. Smug, he grabbed me by the shoulders with both hands and lifted me up so that I hung face-to-face with him. His eyes were yellow with slits for pupils, much like some sort of snake's. His breath was hot and reeked of decay as he spoke.

"You are small, Eugenie Markham, but you are lovely and your flesh is warm. Perhaps I should beat the rush and take you myself. I'd enjoy hearing you scream beneath me."

Ew. Had that thing just propositioned me? And there was my name again. How in the world did he know that? None of them knew that. I was only Odile to them, named after the dark swan in *Swan Lake,* a name coined by my stepfather because of the form my spirit preferred to travel in while visiting the Otherworld. The name—though not particularly terrifying—had stuck, though I doubted any of the creatures I fought knew the reference. They didn't really get out to the ballet much.

The keres had my upper arms pinned—I would have bruises tomorrow—but my hands and forearms were free. He was so sure of himself, so arrogant and confident, that he paid no attention to my struggling hands. He probably just perceived the motion as a futile effort to free myself. In seconds, I had the clip out and in the gun. I managed one clumsy shot and he dropped me—not gently. I stumbled to regain my balance again. Bullets probably couldn't kill him, but a silver one in the center of his chest would certainly hurt.

He stumbled back, surprised, and I wondered if he'd ever even encountered a gun before. It fired again, then again and again and again. The reports were loud; hopefully Montgomery wouldn't foolishly come running in. The keres roared in outrage and pain, each shot making him stagger backward until he was against the circle's boundary. I advanced on him, retrieved athame flashing in my hands. In a few quick motions, I carved the death symbol on the part of his chest that wasn't bloodied from bullets. An electric charge immediately ran through the air. Hairs stood up on the back of my neck, and I could smell ozone, like just before a storm.

He screamed and leapt forward, renewed by rage or adrenaline or whatever else these creatures ran on. But it was too late for him. He was marked and wounded. I was ready. In another mood, I might have simply banished him to the Otherworld; I tried not to kill if I didn't have to. But that sexual suggestion had just been out of line. I was pissed off now. He'd go to the world of death, straight to Persephone's gate.

I fired again to slow him, my aim a bit off with the left hand but still good enough to hit him. I had already traded the athame for the wand. This time, I didn't draw on the power from this plane. With well-practiced ease, I let part of my consciousness slip this world. In moments, I reached the crossroads to the Otherworld. That was an easy transition; I did it all the time. The next crossover was a little harder, especially with me being weakened from the fight, but still nothing I couldn't do automatically. I kept my own spirit well outside of the land of death, but I touched it and sent that connection through the wand. It sucked him in, and his face twisted with fear.

"This is not your world," I said in a low voice, feeling the power burn through me and around me. "This is not your world, and I cast you out from it. I send you to the black gate, to the lands of death where you can either be reborn or fade to oblivion or burn in the flames of hell. I really don't give a shit. *Go*."

He screamed, but the magic caught him. There was a trembling in the air, a buildup of pressure, and then it ended abruptly, like a deflating balloon. The keres was gone too, leaving only a shower of gray sparkles that soon faded to nothing.

Silence. I sank to my knees, exhaling deeply. My eyes closed a moment, as my body relaxed and my consciousness returned to this world. I was exhausted, but exultant too. Killing him had felt good. Heady, even. He'd gotten what he deserved, and I had been the one to deal it out.

Minutes later, some of my strength returned. I stood and opened the circle, suddenly feeling stifled by it. I put my tools and weapons away and went to find Montgomery.

"Your shoe's been exorcised," I told him flatly. "I killed the ghost." No point in explaining the difference between a keres and a true ghost; he wouldn't understand.

He entered the room with slow steps, picking up the shoe gingerly. "I heard gunshots. How do you use bullets on a ghost?"

I shrugged. It hurt from where the keres had slammed my shoulder to the wall. "It was a strong ghost."

He cradled the shoe like one might a child and then glanced down with disapproval. "There's blood on the carpet."

"Read the paperwork you signed. I assume no responsibility for damage incurred to personal property."

With a few grumbles, he paid up—in cash—and I left. Really, though, he was so stoked about the shoe, I probably could have decimated the office.

In my car, I dug out a Milky Way from the stash in my glove box. Battles like that required immediate sugar and calories. As I practically shoved the candy bar in my mouth, I turned on my cell phone. I had a missed call from Lara.

Once I'd consumed a second candy bar and was on I-10 back to Tucson, I called her back.

"Yo," I said.

"Hey. Did you finish the Montgomery job?"

"Yup."

"Was the shoe really possessed?"

"Yup."

"Huh. Who knew? That's kind of funny too. Like, you know, lost souls and soles in shoes . . ."

"Bad, very bad," I chastised her. Lara might be a damned good secretary, but there was only so much I could be expected to put up with. "So what's up? Or were you just checking in?"

"No. I just got a weird job offer. Some guy—well, honestly, I thought he sounded kind of schizo. But he claims his sister was abducted by fairies, er, gentry. He wants you to go get her."

I fell silent at that, staring at the highway and clear blue sky ahead without consciously seeing either one. Some rational part of me attempted to process what she had just said. I didn't get that kind of request very often. Okay, never. A retrieval like that required me to cross over physically into the Otherworld. "I don't really do that."

"That's what I told him." But there was uncertainty in Lara's voice.

"Okay. What aren't you telling me?"

"Nothing, I guess. I don't know. It's just . . . he said she's been gone almost a year and a half now. She was fourteen when she disappeared."

My stomach sank a little at that. God. What an awful fate for someone so young. It made the keres's lewd comments to me downright trivial.

"He sounded pretty frantic."

"Does he have proof she was actually taken?"

"I don't know. He wouldn't get into it. He was kind of paranoid. Seemed to think his phone was being tapped."

I laughed at that. "By who? The gentry?" "Gentry" was what I called the beings that most of western culture referred to as fairies or sidhe. They looked just like humans but embraced magic instead of technology. They found "fairy" a derogatory term, so I respected that—sort of—by using the term old English peasants used to use. *Gentry.* Good folk. Good neighbors. A questionable designation, at best. The gentry actually preferred the term "shining ones," but that was just silly. I wouldn't give them that much credit.

"I don't know," Lara told me. "Like I said, he seemed a little schizo."

Silence fell as I held on to the phone and passed a car doing forty-five in the left lane.

"Eugenie! You aren't really thinking of doing this."

"Fourteen, huh?"

"You always said that was dangerous."

"Adolescence?"

"Stop it. You know what I mean. Crossing over."

"Yeah. I know what you mean."

It was dangerous—super dangerous. Traveling in spirit form could still get you killed, but your odds of fleeing back to your earthbound body were better. Take your own body over, and all the rules changed.

"This is crazy."

"Set it up," I told her. "It can't hurt to talk to him."

I could practically see her biting her lip to hold back protests. But at the end of the day, I was the one who signed her paychecks, and she respected that. After a few moments, she filled the silence with info about a few other jobs and then drifted on to more casual topics: a sale at Macy's, a mysterious scratch on her car . . .

Something about Lara's cheery gossip always made me smile, but it also disturbed me that most of my social contact came via someone I never actually saw. The majority of my face-to-face interactions came from spirits and gentry lately.

It was after dinnertime when I arrived home, and my

housemate Tim appeared to be out for the night, probably at a poetry reading. Despite a Polish background, genes had inexplicably given him a strong Native American appearance. In fact, he looked more Indian than some of the locals. Deciding this was his claim to fame, Tim had grown his hair out and taken on the name "Timothy Red Horse." He made his living reading faux-Native poetry at local dives and wooing naïve tourist women by using expressions like, "my people" and "the Great Spirit" a lot. It was despicable to say the least, but it got him laid pretty often. What it did not do was bring in a lot of money, so I let him live with me in exchange for housework and cleaning. It was a pretty good deal as far as I was concerned. After battling the undead all day, scrubbing the bathtub just seemed like a bit much.

Scrubbing my athames, unfortunately, was a task I had to do myself. Keres blood could stain.

I ate dinner afterwards, then stripped and sat in my sauna for a long time. I liked a lot of things about my little house out in the foothills, but the sauna was one of my favorites. It might seem kind of pointless in the desert, but Arizona had mostly dry heat, and I liked the feel of the moisture on my skin. I leaned back against the wooden wall, enjoying the sensation of sweating out the stress. My body ached—some parts more fiercely than others—and the heat let some of the muscles loosen up.

The solitude also soothed me. Pathetic as it was, I probably had no one to blame for my lack of a social life except myself. I spent a lot of time alone and didn't mind. When my stepfather Roland had first trained me as a shaman, he'd told me that in a lot of cultures, shamans lived outside of normal society. The idea had seemed crazy to me at the time, being in junior high, but it made more sense now that I was older.

I wasn't a complete misanthrope, but I found I often had a hard time interacting with other people. Talking in front of groups was murder. Even talking one-on-one was uncomfortable. I had no pets or children to ramble on about, and I couldn't exactly talk about things like the incident in Las Cruces. *Yeah, I had kind of a long day. Drove four hours, fought an ancient minion of evil. After a few bullets and knife wounds, I obliterated him and sent him on to the world of death. God, I swear I'm not getting paid enough for this crap, you know?* Cue polite laughter.

When I left the sauna, I had another message from Lara, telling me the appointment with the distraught brother had been arranged for tomorrow. I made a note in my day planner, took a shower, and retired to my room where I threw on black silk pajamas. For whatever reason, nice pajamas were the one indulgence I allowed myself in an otherwise dirty and bloody lifestyle. Tonight's selection had a cami top that showed serious cleavage, had anyone been there to see it. I always wore a ratty robe around Tim.

Sitting at my desk, I emptied out a new jigsaw puzzle I'd just bought. It depicted a kitten on its back clutching a ball of yarn. My love of puzzles ranked up there with the pajama thing for weirdness, but they eased my mind. Maybe it was the fact that they were so tangible. You could hold the pieces in your hand and make them fit together, as opposed to the insubstantial stuff I usually worked with.

While my hands moved the pieces around, I kept turning over the knowledge that the keres had known my name. What did that mean? I'd made a lot of enemies in the Otherworld. I didn't like the thought of them being able to track me personally. I preferred to stay Odile. Anonymous. Safe. Probably not much point worrying about it, I supposed. The keres was dead. He wouldn't be telling any tales.

Two hours later, I finished the puzzle and admired it. The kitten had brown tabby fur, its eyes an almost azure blue. The yarn was red. I took out my digital camera, snapped a picture, and then broke up the puzzle, dumping it back into its box. Easy come, easy go.

Yawning, I slipped into bed. Tim had done laundry today; the sheets felt crisp and clean. Nothing like that new sheets smell. Despite my exhaustion, however, I couldn't fall asleep. It was one of life's ironies. While awake, I could slide into a trance with the snap of a finger. My spirit could leave my body and travel to other worlds. Yet for whatever reason, sleep was elusive. Doctors had recommended a number of sedatives, but I hated to use them. Drugs and alcohol bound the spirit to this world, and while I did indulge occasionally, I generally liked being ready to slip over on a moment's notice.

Tonight I suspected my insomnia had something to do with a teenage girl . . . But no. I couldn't think about that. Not yet. Not until I spoke with the brother.

Sighing, needing something else to ponder, I rolled over and stared at my ceiling, at the plastic glow-in-the-dark stars. I started counting them, as I had so many other restless nights. There were exactly thirty-three of them, just like last time. Still, it never hurt to check.

**Please turn the page for an
exciting sneak peek of
SUCCUBUS DREAMS!**

Chapter One

I wished the guy on top of me would hurry up because I was getting bored.

Unfortunately, it didn't seem like he was going to finish anytime soon. Brad or Brian or whatever his name was thrust away, eyes squeezed shut with such concentration that you would have thought having sex was on par with brain surgery or lifting steel beams.

"Brett," I panted. It was time to pull out the big guns.

He opened one eye. "Bryce."

"Bryce." I put on my most passionate, orgasmic face. "Please . . . please . . . don't stop."

His other eye opened. Both went wide.

A minute later, it was all over.

"Sorry," he gasped, rolling off me. He looked mortified. "I don't know . . . didn't mean . . ."

"It's all right, baby." I felt only a little bad about using the *don't stop* trick on him. It didn't always work, but for some guys, planting that seed completely undid them. "It was amazing."

And really, that wasn't entirely a lie. The sex itself had

been mediocre, but the rush afterward . . . the feel of his life and his soul pouring into me . . . yeah. That was pretty amazing. It was what a succubus like me literally lived for.

He gave me a wary smile. The energy that flowed through me was no longer in him. Its loss had exhausted him, burned him out. He'd sleep soon and would probably continue sleeping a great deal over the next few days. His soul had been a good one, and I'd taken a lot of it—as well as his life itself. He'd now live a few years less, thanks to me.

I tried not to think about that as I hurriedly put on my clothes. He seemed surprised at my abrupt departure but was too worn out to fight it. I promised to call him—having no intention of doing so—and slipped out of the room as he lapsed into unconsciousness.

I'd barely cleared his front door before shape-shifting. I'd come to him as a tall, sable-haired woman but now once again wore my preferred shape, petite with hazel-green eyes and light brown hair that flirted with gold. Like most of my life, my features danced between states, never entirely set-tling on one.

I put Bryce out of my mind, just like I did with most men I slept with, and drove across town to what was rapidly be-coming my second home. It was a tan, stucco condo, set into a community of other condos that tried desperately to be as hip as new construction in Seattle could manage. I parked my Passat out front, fished my key out of my purse, and let myself inside.

The condo was still and quiet, wrapped in darkness. A nearby clock informed me it was three in the morning. Walk-ing toward the bedroom, I shape-shifted again, swapping my clothes for a red nightgown.

I froze in the bedroom doorway, surprised to feel my breath catch in my throat. You'd think after all this time, I would have gotten used to him, that he wouldn't affect me like this. But he did. Every time.

Seth lay sprawled in the bed, one arm tossed over his

head. His breathing was deep and fitful, and the sheets lay in a tangle around his long, lean body. Moonlight muted the color of his hair, but in the sun, its light brown would pick up a russet glow. Seeing him, studying him, I felt my heart swell in my chest. I'd never expected to feel this way about anyone again, not after centuries of feeling so . . . empty. Bryce had meant nothing to me, but this man before me meant everything.

I slid into bed beside him, and his arms instantly went around me. I think it was instinctual. The connection between us was so deep that even while unconscious we couldn't stay away from each other.

I pressed my cheek to Seth's chest, and his skin warmed mine as I fell asleep. The guilt from Bryce faded, and soon, there was only Seth and my love for him.

I slipped almost immediately into a dream. Except, well, I wasn't actually *in* it, at least not in the active sense. I was watching myself, seeing the events unfold as though at a movie. Only, unlike a movie, I could *feel* every detail. The sights, the sounds . . . it was almost more vivid than real life.

The other Georgina was in a kitchen, one I didn't recognize. It was bright and modern, far larger than anything I could imagine a noncook like me needing. My dream-self stood at the sink, elbow deep in sudsy water that smelled like oranges. She was hand-washing dishes, which surprised my real self—but was doing a shoddy job, which did not surprise me. On the floor, an actual dishwasher lay in pieces, thus explaining the need for manual labor.

From another room, the sounds of "Sweet Home Alabama" carried to my ears. My dream-self hummed along as she washed, and in that surreal, dreamlike way, I could feel her happiness. She was content, filled with a joy so utterly perfect, I could barely comprehend it. Even with Seth, I'd rarely ever felt so happy—and I was pretty damned happy with him. I couldn't imagine what could make my dream-self feel this way, particularly while doing something as mundane as washing dishes.

I woke up.

To my surprise, it was full morning, bright and sunny. I'd had no sense of time passing. The dream had seemed to last only a minute, yet the nearby alarm clock told me six hours had passed. The loss of the happiness my dream-self had experienced made me ache.

Weirder than that, I felt . . . not right. It took me a moment to peg the problem: I was drained. The life energy a succubus needed to survive, the energy I'd stolen from Bryce, was almost gone. In fact, I had less now than I'd had before going to bed with him. It made no sense. A burst of life like that should have lasted a couple of weeks at least, yet I was nearly as wiped out as he'd been. I wasn't low enough to start losing my shape-shifting, but I'd need a new fix within a couple of days.

"What's wrong?"

Seth's sleepy voice came from beside me. I rolled over and found him propped on one elbow, watching me with a small, sweet smile.

I didn't want to explain what had happened. Doing so would mean elaborating on what I'd done with Bryce, and while Seth theoretically knew what I did to survive, ignorance really was bliss.

"Nothing," I lied. I was a good liar.

He touched my cheek. "I missed you last night."

"No, you didn't. You were busy with Cady and O'Neill."

His smile turned wry, but even as it did, I could see his eyes start to take on the dreamy, inward look he got when he thought about the characters in his novels. I'd made kings and generals beg for my love in my long life, yet some days, even my charms couldn't compete with the people who lived in Seth's head.

Fortunately, today wasn't one of those days, and his attention focused back on me.

"Nah. They don't look as good in a nightgown. That's very Anne Sexton, by the way. Like 'candy story cinnamon hearts.'"

Only Seth would use bipolar poets as compliments. I glanced down and ran an absentminded hand over the red silk. "This does look pretty good," I admitted. "I might look better in this than I do naked."

He scoffed. "No, Thetis. You do not."

And then, in what was an astonishingly aggressive move for him, he flipped me onto my back and began kissing my neck.

"Hey," I said, putting up a halfhearted struggle. "We don't have time for this. I have stuff to do. And I want breakfast."

"Noted," he mumbled, moving on to my mouth. I stopped my complaining. Seth was a wonderful kisser. He gave the kind of kisses that melted into your mouth and filled you with sweetness. They were like cotton candy.

But there was no real melting to be had, not for us. With a well-practiced sense of timing that you could probably set a watch to, he pulled away from the kiss and sat up, removing his hands as well. Still smiling, he looked down at me and my undignified sprawl.

I smiled back, squelching the small pang of regret that always came at these moments of retreat.

But that was the way it was with us, and honestly, we had a pretty good system going when one considered all the complications in our relationship. My friend Hugh once joked that all women steal men's souls if they're together long enough. In my case, it didn't taken years of bickering. A too-long kiss would suffice. Such was the life of a succubus. I didn't make the rules, and I had no way to stop the involuntary energy theft that came from intimate physical contact. I could, however, control whether that physical contact happened in the first place, and I made sure it didn't. I ached for Seth, but I wouldn't steal his life as I had Bryce's.

I sat as well, ready to get up, but Seth must have been feeling bold this morning. He wrapped his arms around my waist and shifted me onto his lap, pressing himself against my back so that his lightly stubbled face was buried in my neck and hair. I felt his body tremble with the intake of a heavy, deep breath. He exhaled it just as slowly, like he sought control of himself, and then strengthened his grip on me.

"Georgina," he breathed against my skin.

I closed my eyes, and the playfulness was gone. A dark intensity wrapped around us, one that burned with both desire and a fear of what might come.

"Georgina," he repeated. His voice was low, husky. I felt like melting again. "Do you know why they say succubi visit men in their sleep?"

"Why?" My own voice was small.

"Because I dream about you every night." In most circumstances, that would have sounded trite, but from him, it was powerful and hungry.

I squeezed my eyes more tightly shut as a swirl of emotions danced within me. I wanted to cry. I wanted to make love to him. I wanted to scream. It was all too much sometimes. Too much emotion. Too much danger. Our increased flirtation and sexual taunting fed a complication that didn't need any more stoking.

Opening my eyes, I shifted so that I could see his face. We held each other's gazes, both of us wanting so much and unable to give or take it. Breaking the look first, I slipped regretfully from his embrace. "Come on. Let's go eat."

Seth lived in easy walking distance to the assorted shops and restaurants adjacent to the University of Washington's campus. We got breakfast at a small café, and omelets and conversation soon replaced the earlier awkwardness. Afterward, we wandered idly up University Way, holding hands. I had errands to run, and he had writing to do, yet we were reluctant to part.

Seth suddenly stopped walking. "Georgina."

"Hmm?"

His eyebrows rose as he stared off at something across the street. "John Cusack is standing over there."

I followed his incredulous gaze to where a man very like Mr. Cusack did indeed stand, smoking a cigarette as he leaned against a building. I sighed.

"That's not John Cusack. That's Jerome."

"Seriously?"

"Yup. I told you he looked like John Cusack."

"Keyword: *looked*. That guy doesn't look like him. That guy is him."

"Believe me, he's not." Seeing Jerome's impatient expression, I let go of Seth's hand. "Be right back."

I crossed the street, and as the distance closed between my boss and me, Jerome's aura washed over my body. All immortals have a unique signature, and a demon like him had an especially strong one. He felt like waves and waves of roiling heat, like when you open an oven and don't stand far enough back.

"Make it fast," I told him. "You're ruining my romantic interlude."

Jerome dropped the cigarette and put it out with his black Kenneth Cole oxford. He glanced disdainfully around. "This place? Come on, Georgie. This isn't romantic. This place isn't even a pit stop on the road to romance."

I put an angry hand on one hip. "What do you want?"

"You."

I blinked. "What?"

"We've got a meeting tonight. An all-staff meeting."

"When you say all-staff, do you mean like *all*-staff?"

The last time Seattle's supervising archdemon had gathered everyone in the area together, it had been to inform us that our local imp wasn't "meeting expectations." Jerome had let us all tell the imp good-bye and then banished the poor guy off to the fiery depths of hell. It was kind of sad, but then my friend Hugh had replaced him, so I'd gotten over it. I hoped this meeting wouldn't have a similar purpose.

Jerome gave me an annoyed look, one that said I was clearly wasting his time.

"When is it?"

"Seven. At Peter and Cody's. Don't be late. Your presence is essential."

Shit. I hoped this wasn't actually *my* going-away party. I'd been on pretty good behavior lately. "What's this about?"

"Find out when you get there. Don't be late," he repeated.

Stepping off the main thoroughfare and into the shadow of a building, the demon vanished.

A feeling of dread spread through me. Demons were never to be trusted, particularly when they looked like quirky movie stars and issued enigmatic invitations.

"Everything okay?" Seth asked me when I rejoined him.

I considered. "As much as it ever is."

He wisely chose not to pursue the subject, and we eventually separated to take care of our respective tasks. I was dying to know what this meeting could be about, but not nearly as much as I wanted to know what had made me lose my energy overnight. And as I ran my errands, I also found the strange dream replaying in my head. How could it have been so vivid? And why couldn't I stop thinking about it?

The puzzle distracted me so much that seven rolled around without me knowing it. Groaning, I headed off for my friend Peter's place, speeding the whole way. Great. I was going to be late. Even if this meeting didn't concern me and my impending "unemployment," I might end up getting a taste of Jerome's wrath after all.

About six feet from the apartment door, I felt the hum of immortal signatures. A lot of them. The greater Puget Sound area had a host of hellish employees I rarely interacted with, and they'd apparently all turned out.

I started to knock, decided an all-staff meeting deserved more than jeans and a T-shirt, and shape-shifted my outfit into a brown dress with a low-cut, surplice top. My hair settled into a neat bun. I raised my hand to the door.

An annoyed vampire I barely remembered let me in. She inclined her chin to me by way of greeting and then continued her conversation with an imp I'd only ever met once. I think they worked out of Tacoma, which as far as I was concerned might as well be annexed to hell itself.

Others walked around—vampires, lesser demons, etc.— and I nodded politely as I made my way through the guests. It could have been an ordinary cocktail party, almost a celebration. I hoped that meant no smiting tonight, since that would really put a damper on the atmosphere. No one had noticed my arrival except for Jerome.

"Ten minutes late," he growled.

"Hey, it's a fashionable—"

My words were cut off as a tall, Amazonian blonde nearly barreled into me.

"Oh! You must be Georgina! I've been dying to meet you."

I raised my eyes past spandex-clad double-D breasts and up into big blue eyes with impossibly long lashes. A huge set of beauty pageant teeth smiled down at me.

My moments of speechlessness were few, but they did sometimes occur. This walking Barbie doll was a succubus. A really new one. So shiny and new, in fact, it was a wonder she didn't squeak. I recognized her age both from her signature and her appearance. No succubus with any sense would have shape-shifted into that. She was trying too hard, haphazardly piling together an assortment of male-fantasy body parts. It left her with a Frankensteinian creation that was both jaw-dropping and probably anatomically impossible.

Unaware of my astonishment and disdain, she took my hand and nearly broke it with a mammoth handshake.

"I can't wait to work with you," she continued. "I am *so* ready to make men everywhere suffer."

I finally found my voice. "Who . . . who are you?"

"She's your new best friend," a voice nearby said. "My, my look at you. Tawny's going to have a tough standard to keep up with."

A man elbowed his way toward us, and whatever curiosity I'd felt in the other succubus's presence disappeared like ashes in the wind. I forgot she was even there. My stomach twisted into knots as I ID'd the mystery signature. Cold sweat broke out along the back of my neck and seeped into the delicate fabric of my dress.

The guy approaching was about as tall as me—which wasn't tall—and had a dark, olive-toned complexion. There was more pomade on his head than black hair. His suit was nice, expensive and tailored. A thin-lipped smile spread over his face at my dumbstruck discomfiture.

"Little Letha, all grown up and out to play with the adults, eh?" He spoke low, voice pitched for my ears alone.

Now, in the grand scheme of things, immortals had little to fear in this world. There were, however, three people I feared intently. One of them was Lilith the Succubus Queen, a being of such formidable power and beauty that I would have sold my soul—again—for one kiss. Someone else who scared me was a nephilim named Roman. He was Jerome's half-human son and had good reason to want to hunt me down and destroy me some day. The third person who filled me with fear was this man standing before me.

His name was Niphon, and he was an imp, just like my friend Hugh. And, like all imps, Niphon really only had two jobs. One was to run administrative errands for demons. The other, his primary one, was to make contracts with mortals, brokering and buying souls for hell.

And he was the imp who had bought mine.